KT-394-364

Acknowledgments

The future holds many interesting scientific advances. One of the most challenging and fascinating is the DNA – or molecular – computer. We are very grateful for all the generous help of Kathleen Foltz, Ph.D., who shared her cutting-edge understanding of the field. Dr. Foltz is an associate professor in the Department of Molecular, Cellular, and Developmental Biology at the University of California, Santa Barbara. Recently the National Science Foundation names her a Presidential Faculty Fellow. She is also a member of the Marine Science Insitute.

Robert Ludlum's
THE
PARIS OPTION

The Covert-One Novels

The Hades Factor (with Gayle Lynds)
The Cassandra Compact (with Philip Shelby)
The Paris Option (with Gayle Lynds)

Also by Robert Ludlum

The Scarlatti Inheritance
The Osterman Weekend
The Matlock Paper
The Rhinemann Exchange
The Gemini Contenders
The Chancellor Manuscript
The Holcroft Covenant
The Bourne Identity
The Matarese Circle
The Road to Gandolfo
The Parsifal Mosaic
The Aquitaine Progression
The Bourne Supremacy
The Icarus Agenda
Trevayne
The Bourne Ultimatum
The Road to Omaha
The Scorpio Illusion
The Apocalypse Watch
The Cry of the Halidon
The Matarese Countdown
The Prometheus Deception
The Sigma Protocol

Also by Gayle Lynds

Mosaic
Masquerade
Mesmerized

Robert Ludlum's
THE
PARIS OPTION

A Covert-One Novel

Robert Ludlum and
Gayle Lynds

HarperCollins*Publishers*

GALWAY COUNTY LIBRARIES

HarperCollins*Publishers*
77–85 Fulham Palace Road,
Hammersmith, London W6 8JB

www.fireandwater.com

Published by HarperCollins*Publishers* 2002
1 3 5 7 9 8 6 4 2

First published in the USA by
St Martin's Griffin 2002

Copyright © Myn Pyn LLC 2002

Robert Ludlum and Gayle Lynds assert the moral right to
be identified as the authors of this work

A catalogue record for this book
is available from the British Library

ISBN 0 00 710172 4

Set in Transitional 521

Printed and bound in Great Britain by
Clays Ltd, St Ives plc

All rights reserved. No part of this publication may be
reproduced, stored in a retrieval system, or transmitted,
in any form or by any means, electronic, mechanical,
photocopying, recording or otherwise, without the prior
permission of the publishers.

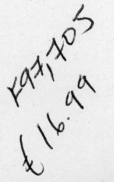

Prologue

Paris, France
Sunday, May 4
The first warm winds of spring gusted along Paris's narrow back streets and broad boulevards, calling winter-weary residents out into the night. They thronged the sidewalks, strolling, linking arms, filling the chairs around outdoor café tables, everywhere smiling and chatting. Even the tourists stopped complaining—this was the enchanting Paris promised in their travel guides.

Occupied with their glasses of *vin ordinaire* under the stars, the spring celebrators on the bustling rue de Vaugirard did not notice the large black Renault van with darkened windows that left the busy street for the boulevard Pasteur. The van circled around the block, down the rue du Docteur Roux, and at last entered the quiet rue des Volontaires, where the only action was of a young couple kissing in a recessed doorway.

The black van rolled to a stop outside L'Institut Pasteur, cut its engine, and turned off its headlights. It remained there, silent, until the young couple, oblivious in their bliss, disappeared inside a building across the street.

The van's doors clicked open, and four figures emerged clothed completely in black, their faces hidden behind balaclavas. Carrying compact

Uzi submachine guns and wearing backpacks, they slipped through the night, almost invisible. A figure materialized from the shadows of the Pasteur Institute and guided them onto the grounds, while the street behind them remained quiet, deserted.

•

Out on the rue de Vaugirard, a saxophonist had begun to play, his music throaty and mellow. The night breeze carried the music, the laughter, and the scent of spring flowers in through the open windows of the multitude of buildings at the Pasteur. The famed research center was home to more than twenty-five hundred scientists, technicians, students, and administrators, and many still labored into the night.

The intruders had not expected so much activity. On high alert, they avoided the paths, listening, watching the windows and grounds, staying close to trees and structures as the sounds of the springtime gaiety from the rue de Vaugirard increased.

But in his laboratory, all outside activity was lost on Dr. Émile Chambord, who sat working alone at his computer keyboard on the otherwise unoccupied second floor of his building. His lab was large, as befitted one of the institute's most distinguished researchers. It boasted several prize pieces of equipment, including a robotic gene-chip reader and a scanning-tunneling microscope, which measured and moved individual atoms. But more personal and far more critical to him tonight were the files near his left elbow and, on his other side, a spiral-bound notebook, which was open to the page on which he was meticulously recording data.

His fingers paused impatiently on the keyboard, which was connected to an odd-looking apparatus that appeared to have more in common with an octopus than with IBM or Compaq. Its nerve center was contained in a temperature-controlled glass tray, and through its sides, one could see silver-blue gel packs immersed like translucent eggs in a jellied, foamlike substance. Ultrathin tubing connected the gel packs to one another, while atop them sat a lid. Where it interfaced with the gel packs was a coated metallic plate. Above it all stood an iMac-sized machine with a complicated control panel on which lights blinked like impulsive little eyes. From this machine, more tubing sprouted, feeding into the pack array, while wires and cables connected both the tray and the machine to the keyboard, a monitor, a printer, and assorted other electronic devices.

Dr. Chambord keyboarded in commands, watched the monitor, read the dials on the iMac-sized machine, and continually checked the temperature of the gel packs in the tray. He recorded data in his notebook as he worked, until he suddenly sat back and studied the entire array. Finally he gave an abrupt nod and typed a paragraph of what appeared to be gibberish—letters, numbers, and symbols—and activated a timer.

His foot tapped nervously, and his fingers drummed the lab bench. But in precisely twelve seconds, the printer came to life and spit out a sheet of paper. Controlling his excitement, he stopped the timer and made a note. At last he allowed himself to snatch up the printout.

As he read, he smiled. *"Mais oui."*

Dr. Chambord took a deep breath and typed small clusters of commands. Sequences appeared on his screen so fast that his fingers could not keep up. He muttered inaudibly as he worked. Moments later, he tensed, leaned closer to the monitor, and whispered in French, "... one more ... one ... more ... there!"

He laughed aloud, triumphant, and turned to look at the clock on the wall. It read 9:55 P.M. He recorded the time and stood up.

His pale face glowing, he stuffed his files and notebook into a battered briefcase and took his coat from the old-fashioned Empire wardrobe near the door. As he put on his hat, he glanced again at the clock and returned to his contraption. Still standing, he keyboarded another short series of commands, watched the screen for a time, and finally shut everything down. He walked briskly to the door, opened it onto the corridor, and observed that it was dim and deserted. For a moment, he had a sense of foreboding.

Then he shook it off. *Non,* he reminded himself: This was a moment to be savored, a great achievement. Smiling broadly, he stepped into the shadowy hall. Before he could close the door, four black-clothed figures surrounded him.

•

Thirty minutes later, the wiry leader of the intruders stood watch as his three companions finished loading the black van on the rue des Volontaires. As soon as the side door closed, he appraised the quiet street once more and hopped into the passenger seat. He nodded to the driver, and the van glided away toward the crowded rue de Vaugirard, where it disappeared in traffic.

The lighthearted revelry on the sidewalks and in the cafés and *tabacs* continued. More street musicians arrived, and the *vin ordinaire* flowed like the Seine. Then, without warning, the building that housed Dr. Chambord's laboratory on the legendary Pasteur campus exploded in a rolling sheet of fire. The earth shook as flames seemed to burst from every window and combust up toward the black night sky in a red-and-yellow eruption of terrible heat visible for miles around. As bricks, sparks, glass, and ash rained down, the throngs on the surrounding streets screamed in terror and ran for shelter.

PART ONE

Chapter One

Diego Garcia Island, Indian Ocean

At 0654 hours at the vital U.S. Army, Air Force, and Naval installation on Diego Garcia, the officer commanding the shift at the control tower was gazing out the windows as the morning sun illuminated the warm blue waters of Emerald Bay on the lagoon side of the U-shaped atoll and wishing he were off duty. His eyes blinked slowly, and his mind wandered.

The U.S. Navy Support Facility, the host command for this strategically located, operationally invaluable base, kept all of them busy with its support of sea, air, and surface flight operations. The payback was the island itself, a remote place of sweeping beauty, where the easy rhythms of routine duty lulled ambition.

He was seriously contemplating a long swim the instant he was off duty when, one minute later, at 0655 hours, the control tower lost contact with the base's entire airborne fleet of B-1B, B-52, AWACS, P-3 Orion, and U-2 aircraft, on a variety of missions that included hot-button reconnaissance and antisubmarine and surveillance support.

The tropical lagoon vanished from his mind. He bawled orders, pushed a technician from one of the consoles, and started diagnostics. Everyone's attention was riveted on the dials, readouts, and screens as they battled to regain contact.

Nothing helped. At 0658, in a controlled panic, he alerted the base's commanding officer.

At 0659, the commanding officer informed the Pentagon.

Then, oddly, inexplicably, at 0700, five minutes after they had mysteriously disappeared, all communications with the aircraft returned at the precise same second.

Fort Collins, Colorado
Monday, May 5

As the sun rose over the vast prairie to the east, the rustic Foothills Campus of Colorado State University glowed with golden light. Here in a state-of-the-art laboratory in a nondescript building, Jonathan ("Jon") Smith, M.D., peered into a binocular microscope and gently moved a finely drawn glass needle into position. He placed an imperceptible drop of fluid onto a flat disk so small that it was no larger than the head of a pin. Under the high-resolution microscope, the plate bore a striking—and seemingly impossible—resemblance to a circuit board.

Smith made an adjustment, bringing the image more clearly into focus. "Good," he muttered, and smiled. "There's hope."

An expert in virology and molecular biology, Smith was also an army medical officer—in fact, a lieutenant colonel—temporarily stationed here amid the towering pines and rolling foothills of Colorado at this Centers for Disease Control (CDC) facility. On unofficial loan from the U.S. Army Medical Research Institute of Infectious Diseases (USAMRIID), he was assigned basic research into evolving viruses.

Except that viruses had nothing to do with the delicate work he was watching through the microscope this dawn. USAMRIID was the army's foremost military medical research facility, while the CDC was its highly touted civilian counterpart. Usually they were vigorous rivals. But not here, not now, and the work being done in this laboratory had only a peripheral connection to medicine.

Smith was part of a little-known CDC-USAMRIID research team in a worldwide race to create the world's first molecular—or DNA—computer, therefore forging an unprecedented bond between life science and computational science. The concept intrigued the scientist in Smith and challenged his expertise in the field of microbiology. In fact, what had brought him into his lab at this ungodly early hour was what he hoped would turn out to be a breakthrough in the molecular circuits based on special organic polymers that he and the other researchers had been working night and day to create.

If successful, their brand-new DNA circuits could be reconfigured many times, taking the joint team one step closer to rendering silicon, the key ingredient in the wiring of current computer circuit boards, obsolete. Which was just as well. The computer industry was near the limits of silicon technology anyway, while biological compounds offered a logical—although difficult—next step. When DNA computers could be made workable, they would be vastly more powerful than the general public could conceive, which was where the army's, and USAMRIID's, interests came in.

Smith was fascinated by the research, and as soon as he had heard rumors of the secret joint CDC-USAMRIID project, he had arranged to be invited aboard, eagerly throwing himself into this technological competition where the future might be only an atom away.

"Hey, Jon." Larry Schulenberg, another of the project's top cell biologists, rolled into the empty laboratory in his wheelchair. "Did you hear about the Pasteur?"

Smith looked up from his microscope. "Hell, I didn't even hear you open the door." Then he noticed Larry's somber face. "The Pasteur," he repeated. "Why? What's happened?" Like USAMRIID and the CDC, the Pasteur Institute was a world-class research complex.

In his fifties, Schulenberg was a tan, energetic man with a shaved head, one small diamond earring, and shoulders that were thickly muscled from years of using crutches. His voice was grim. "Some kind of explosion. It's bad. People were killed." He peeled a sheet from the stack of printouts on his lap.

Jon grabbed the paper. "My God. How did it happen? A lab accident?"

"The French police don't think so. Maybe a bomb. They're checking out former employees." Larry wheeled his chair around and headed back to the door. "Figured you'd want to know. Jim Thrane at Porton Down e-mailed me, so I downloaded the story. I've got to go see who else is here. Everyone will want to know."

"Thanks." As the door closed, Smith read quickly. Then, his stomach sinking, he reread . . .

Labs at Pasteur Institute Destroyed

Paris—A massive explosion killed at least 12 people and shattered a three-story building housing offices and laboratories at the venerable Pasteur Institute at 10:52 P.M. here last night. Four survivors in critical condition were found. The search continues in the rubble for other victims.

Fire investigators say they have found evidence of explosives. No person or group has claimed responsibility. The probe is continuing, including checking into recently released employees.

The identified survivors include Martin Zellerbach, Ph.D., a computer scientist from the United States, who suffered head injuries. . . .

Smith's heart seemed to stop. *Martin Zellerbach, Ph.D., a computer scientist from the United States, who suffered head injuries.* Marty? His old friend's face flashed into Jon's mind as he gripped the printout. The crooked smile, the intense green eyes that could twinkle one moment and skitter off, lost in thought or perhaps outer space, the next. A small, rotund man who walked awkwardly, as if he had never really learned how to move his legs, Marty had Asperger's Syndrome, a rare disorder at the less severe end of the autism spectrum. His symptoms included consuming obsessions, high intelligence, crippling lack of social and communications skills, and an outstanding talent in one particular area—mathematics and electronics. He was, in fact, a computer genius.

A worried ache settled in Smith's throat. *Head injuries.* How badly was Marty hurt? The news story did not say. Smith pulled out his cell phone, which had special scrambler capabilities, and dialed Washington.

He and Marty had grown up together in Iowa, where he had protected Marty from the taunts of fellow students and even a few teachers who had a hard time believing anyone so smart was not being intentionally rude and a troublemaker. Marty's Asperger's was diagnosed when he was older and at last he was given the medication that helped him function with both feet firmly attached to the planet. Still, Marty hated taking meds and had designed his life so he could avoid them as often as possible. He did not leave his cozy Washington, D.C., bungalow for years at a time. There he was safe with the cutting-edge computers and the software he was always designing, and his mind and creativity could soar, unfettered. Businessmen, academicians, and scientists from around the globe went there to consult him, but never in person, only electronically.

So what was the shy computer wizard doing in Paris?

The last time Marty consented to leave was eighteen months ago, and it was far from gentle persuasion that convinced him. It was a hail of bullets and the beginning of the near catastrophe of the Hades virus that had caused the death of Smith's fiancée, Sophia Russell.

The phone at Smith's ear began to ring in distant Washington, D.C., and at the same time he heard what sounded like a cell phone ringing just outside his laboratory door. He had an eerie sense . . .

"Hello?" It was the voice of Nathaniel Frederick ("Fred") Klein.

Smith turned abruptly and stared at his door. "Come in, Fred."

The chief of the extremely secret Covert-One intelligence and counterintelligence troubleshooting organization stepped into the laboratory, quiet as a ghost, still holding his cell phone. "I should've guessed you would've heard and called me." He turned off his phone.

"About Mart? Yes, I just read about the Pasteur. What do you know, and what are you doing here?"

Without answering, Klein marched past the gleaming test tubes and equipment that crowded the line of lab benches, which soon would be occupied by other CDC-USAMRIID researchers and assistants. He stopped at Smith's bench, lifted his left hip, and sat on the edge of the stone top, arms crossed, face grim. Around six feet tall, he was dressed as usual in one of his rumpled suits, this one brown. His skin was pale; it rarely saw the sun for any length of time. The great outdoors was not where Fred Klein operated. With his receding hairline, wire-rimmed glasses, and high, intelligent forehead, he could be anything from book publisher to counterfeiter.

He contemplated Smith, and his voice was compassionate as he said,

"Your friend's alive, but he's in a coma. I won't lie to you, Colonel. The doctors are worried."

For Smith, the dark pain of Sophia's death could still weigh heavily on him, and Marty's injury was bringing it all back. But Sophia was gone, and what mattered now was Marty.

"What the hell was he doing at the Pasteur?"

Klein took his pipe from his pocket and brought out his tobacco pouch. "Yes, we wondered about that, too."

Smith started to speak again . . . then hesitated. Invisible to the public and to any part of the government except the White House, Covert-One worked totally outside the official military-intelligence bureaucracy and far from the scrutiny of Congress. Its shadowy chief never appeared unless something earthshaking had happened or might happen. Covert-One had no formal organization or bureaucracy, no real headquarters, and no official operatives. Instead, it was loosely composed of professional experts in many fields, all with clandestine experience, most with military backgrounds, and all essentially unencumbered—without family, home ties, or obligations, either temporary or permanent.

When called upon, Smith was one of those elite operatives.

"You're not here because of Marty," Smith decided. "It's the Pasteur. Something's going on. What?"

"Let's take a walk outside." Klein pushed his glasses up onto his forehead and tamped tobacco into his pipe.

"You can't light that here," Smith told him. "DNA can be contaminated by airborne particles."

Klein sighed. "Just one more reason to go outdoors."

Fred Klein—and Covert-One—trusted no one and nothing, took nothing for granted. Even a laboratory that officially did not exist could be bugged, which, Smith knew, was the real reason Klein wanted to leave. He followed the intelligence master out into the hall and locked his door. Side by side, they made their way downstairs, past dark labs and offices that showed only occasional light. The building was silent except for the breathy hum of the giant ventilation system.

Outside, the dawn sunlight slanted low against the fir trees, illuminating them on the east with shimmering light while on the west they remained tarry black, in shadows. High above the campus to the west towered the Rocky Mountains, their rough peaks glowing. The valleys that creased the slopes were purple with night's lingering darkness. The aromatic scent of pine filled the air.

Klein walked a dozen steps from the building and stopped to fire up his pipe. He puffed and tamped until clouds of smoke half-hid his face. He waved some of the smoke away.

"Let's walk." As they headed toward the road, Klein said, "Talk to me about your work here. How's it going? Are you close to creating a molecular computer?"

"I wish. The research is going well, but it's slow. Complex."

Governments around the world wanted to be the first to have a working DNA computer, because it would be able to break any code or encryption in a matter of seconds. A terrifying prospect, especially where defense was concerned. All of America's missiles, secret systems at NSA, the NRO's spy satellites, the entire ability of the navy to operate, all defense plans—anything and everything that relied on electronics would be at the mercy of the first molecular computer. Even the largest silicon supercomputer would not be able to stop it.

"How soon before the planet sees an operational one?" Klein wanted to know.

"Several years," Smith said without hesitation, "maybe more."

"Who's the closest?"

"Practical and operational? No one I've heard of."

Klein smoked, tamped down his burning tobacco again. "If I said someone had already done it, who'd you guess?"

Precursor prototypes had been built, coming closer to practicality each year, but an actual, complete success? That was at least five years away. Unless . . . Takeda? Chambord?

Then Smith knew. Since Klein was here, the clue was the Pasteur. "Émile Chambord. Are you saying Chambord is years ahead of the rest of us? Even ahead of Takeda in Tokyo?"

"Chambord probably died in the explosion." Klein puffed on his pipe, his expression worried. "His lab was completely destroyed. Nothing left but shattered bricks, singed wood, and broken glass. They've checked his home, his daughter. Looked everywhere. His car was in the Pasteur parking lot, but they can't find him. There's talk."

"Talk? There's always talk."

"This is different. It comes from top French military circles, from colleagues, from his superiors."

"If Chambord were that near, there'd be more than talk. Someone *knew*."

"Not necessarily. The military checked in with him regularly, but he claimed he was no farther along than anyone else. As for the Pasteur itself, a senior researcher of Chambord's stature and tenure doesn't have to report to anyone."

Smith nodded. This anachronism was true at the renowned institute. "What about his notes? Records? Reports?"

"Nothing from the last year. Zero."

"No records?" Smith's voice rose. "There have to be. They're probably in the Pasteur's data bank. Don't tell me the entire computer system was destroyed."

"No, the mainframe's fine. It's located in a bomb-proof room, but he hadn't entered any data in it for more than a year."

Smith scowled. "He was keeping longhand records?"

"If he kept any at all."

"He *had* to keep records. You can't do basic research without complete data. Lab notes, progress sheets. Your records have to be scrupulous, or your work can't be verified or reproduced. Every blind alley, every mistake, every backtrack has to be chronicled. Dammit, if he wasn't saving his data in the computer, he had to be keeping it longhand. That's certain."

"Maybe it is, Jon, but so far neither the Pasteur nor the French authorities have found any records at all, and believe me, they've been looking. Hard."

Smith thought. Longhand? Why? Could Chambord have gotten protective once he realized he was close to success? "You figure he knew or suspected he was being watched by someone inside the institute?"

"The French, and everyone else, don't know what to think," Klein said.

"He was working alone?"

"He had a low-level lab assistant who's on vacation. The French police are searching for him." Klein stared toward the east, where the sun was higher now, a giant disk above the prairie. "And we think Dr. Zellerbach was working with him, too."

"You *think*?"

"Whatever Dr. Zellerbach was doing appears to have been completely unofficial, almost secret. He's listed only as a 'general observer' with Pasteur security. After the bombing, the police immediately went to his hotel room but found nothing useful. He lived out of one suitcase, and he made no friends either there or at the Pasteur. The police were surprised by how few people actually recalled him."

Smith nodded. "That's Marty." His reclusive old friend would have insisted on remaining as anonymous as possible. At the same time, a molecular computer that was near fruition was one of the few projects that might have seduced him from his determined isolation in Washington. "When he regains consciousness, he'll tell you what Chambord's progress was."

"If he wakes up. Even then it could be too late."

Jon felt a sudden anger. "He *will* come out of the coma."

"All right, Colonel. But when?" Klein took the pipe from his mouth and glared. "We've just had a nasty wake-up call that you need to know about. At 7:55 Washington time last night, Diego Garcia Island lost all communications with its aircraft. Every effort to revive them, or trace the source of the shutdown, failed. Then precisely five minutes later, communications were restored. There were no system malfunctions, no weather problems, no human error. Conclusion was it had to be the work of a computer hacker, but no footprints were found, and every expert short of heaven says no existing computer could've pulled it off without leaving a trace."

"Was there damage?"

"To the systems, no. To our worry quotient, one hell of a lot."

"How does the timing compare to when the Pasteur was bombed?"

Klein smiled grimly. "A couple of hours later."

"Could be a test of Chambord's prototype, if he had one. If someone stole it."

"No kidding. The way it stands, Chambord's lab is gone. He's dead or missing. And his work is destroyed . . . or missing."

Jon nodded. "You're thinking the bomb was planted to hide his murder and the theft of his records and prototype."

"An operational DNA computer in the wrong hands is not a pretty picture."

"I was already planning to go to Paris, because of Marty."

"I thought so. It's a good cover. Besides, you'll have a better chance of recognizing a molecular computer than anyone else in Covert-One." Klein raised his anxious gaze to stare out across the enormous prairie sky as if he could see ICBMs raining down. "You've got to find out whether Chambord's notes, reports, and data were destroyed, or whether they were stolen. Whether there really is a functional prototype out there somewhere. We'll work the usual way. I'll be your only contact. Night or day. Whatever you need from any part of the government or military on both sides of the pond, ask. But you must keep a lid on it, understand? We don't want any panic. Worse, we don't want an eager Second or Third World country cutting a unilateral deal with the bombers."

"Right." Half the nonadvanced nations had little love for the United States. Neither did the various terrorists who increasingly targeted America and Americans. "When do I leave?"

"Now," Klein said. "I'll have other Covert-One experts on it, of course. They'll be following other leads, but you'll be the main thrust. The CIA and FBI have sent people out, too. And as for Zellerbach, remember I'm as concerned as you. We all hope he regains consciousness quickly. But there may be damn little time, and many, many other lives are at stake."

Chapter
Two

Paris, France

It was the end of his shift and nearly six P.M. when Farouk al Hamid finally peeled off his uniform and left L'Hôpital Européen Georges Pompidou through an employees' entrance. He had no reason to notice he was being followed as he walked along the busy boulevard Victor to the Massoud Café tucked away on a side street.

Worn out and depressed from his long day of mopping floors, carrying great hampers of soiled linen, and performing the myriad other backbreaking jobs of a hospital orderly, he took a seat at a table neither outside nor inside, but exactly where the series of front glass doors had been folded back and the fresh outside spring air mingled with the aromatic cooking odors of the kitchen.

He glanced around once, then ignored his fellow Algerians, as well as the Moroccans and Saharans, who frequented the café. Soon he was drinking his second glass of strong coffee and shooting disapproving glances at those who were indulging in wine. All alcohol was forbidden, which was a tenet of Islam ignored by too many of his fellow North Africans, who, once they were far from their homelands, felt they could leave Allah behind, too.

As Farouk began to seethe, a stranger joined him at the table.

The man was not *Arabe,* not with those pale blue eyes. Still, he spoke in Arabic. *"Salaam alake koom, Farouk.* You're a hardworking man. I've been watching you, and I think you deserve better. So I have a proposition to make. Are you interested?"

"Wahs-tah-hahb?" he grumbled suspiciously. "Nothing is for free."

The stranger nodded agreeably. "True. Still, how would you and your family enjoy a holiday?"

"Ehs-mah-lee. A holiday?" Farouk asked bitterly. "You suggest the impossible."

The man spoke a higher-class Arabic than Farouk did, if with some odd accent, perhaps Iraqi or Saudi. But he was not Iraqi, Saudi, or Algerian. He was a white European, older than Farouk, wiry and darkly tanned. As the stranger waved for the waiter to bring more coffee, Farouk al Hamid noted that he was well dressed, too, but again from no particular nation he could identify, and he could identify most. It was a game he played to keep his mind from his weary muscles, the long hours of mindless labor, the impossibility of rising in this new world.

"For you, yes," the old stranger agreed. "For me, no. I am a man who can make the impossible possible."

"La. No, I will not kill."

"I haven't asked you to. Nor will you be asked to steal or sabotage."

Farouk paused, his interest growing. "Then how will I pay for this grand holiday?"

"Merely by writing a note to the hospital in your own hand. A note in French saying you're ill and you've sent your cousin Mansour to take your place for a few days. In exchange, I'll give you cash."

"I do not have a cousin."

"All Algerians have cousins. Haven't you heard?"

"That is true. But I have none in Paris."

The stranger smiled knowingly. "He has only now arrived from Algiers."

Farouk felt a leap inside him. A holiday for his wife, for the children. For *him.* The man was right, no one in Paris would know or care who came into work at the mammoth Pompidou Hospital, only that the work was done and for small money. But what this fellow, or someone else, wanted would not be good. Stealing drugs, perhaps. On the other hand, they were all heathens anyway, and it was none of his affair. Instead, he concentrated on the joy of going home to his family to tell them they would be holidaying . . . where?

"I would like to see the Mediterranean again," Farouk said tentatively, watching the man closely for a sign that he was asking too much. "Capri, perhaps. I have heard Capri's beaches are covered by silver sand. It will be very expensive."

"Then Capri it is. Or Porto-Vecchio. Or, for that matter, Cannes or Monaco."

As the place names rolled off the stranger's tongue, magical, full of promises, Farouk al Hamid smiled deep into his tired, hungry soul and said, "Tell me what you wish me to write."

Bordeaux, France

A few hours later, the telephone rang in a shabby rooming house tucked among the wine warehouses on the banks of the Garonne River outside the southern city of Bordeaux. The only occupant of the room was a small, pasty-faced man in his mid-twenties who sat on the edge of his cot, staring at the ringing phone. His eyes were wide with fear, his body trembling. From the river, shouts and the deep braying of barge horns penetrated the dismal room, and the youth, whose name was Jean-Luc Massenet, jerked like a plastic puppet on a string as each loud noise sounded. He did not pick up the telephone.

When the ringing finally stopped, he took a notepad from the brief-case at his feet and began to write shakily, his speed accelerating as he rushed to record what he remembered. But after a few minutes, he thought better of it. He swore to himself, tore off the sheet of paper, crumpled it into a wad, and hurled it into the wastebasket. Disgusted and afraid, he slapped the notepad down onto the little table and decided there was no other solution than to leave, to run away again.

Sweating, he grabbed the briefcase and hurried toward the door.

But before he could touch the knob, a knock sounded. He froze. He watched the door handle turn slowly right and left, the way a mouse watches the swaying head of a cobra.

"Is that you in there, Jean-Luc?" The voice was low, the French a

GALWAY COUNTY LIBRARIES

native's. Surely whoever spoke was no more than an inch from the door. "Captain Bonnard here. Why don't you answer your phone? Let me in."

Jean-Luc shuddered with relief. He tried to swallow, but his throat was as dry as a desert. Fingers fumbling, he unlocked the door and flung it open onto the dreary hallway.

"*Bonjour, mon Capitaine.* How did you—?" Jean-Luc began.

But with a gesture from the brisk, compact officer who strode into the room, he fell silent, respectful of the power of the man who wore the uniform of an elite French paratroop regiment. Captain Bonnard's troubled gaze took in every detail of the cheap room before he turned to Jean-Luc, who was still standing motionless in the open doorway.

"You appear frightened, Jean-Luc. If you think you're in such great danger," he said dryly, "I suggest you close the door." The captain had a square face, reassuring in its strong, clear gaze. His blond hair was clipped short around his ears in the military way, and he exuded a confidence to which Jean-Luc gratefully clung.

Jean-Luc's ashen face flushed a hot pink. "I . . . I'm sorry, Captain." He shut the door.

"You should be. Now, what's this all about? You say you're on vacation. In Arcachon, right? So why are you here now?"

"H-hiding, sir. Some men came looking for me there at my hotel. Not just any men. They knew my name, where I lived in Paris, everything." He paused, swallowed hard. "One of them pulled out a gun and threatened the front desk man. . . . I overheard it all! How did they know I was there? What did they want? They looked as if they'd come to kill me, and I didn't even know why. So I sneaked out and got to my car and drove away. I was sitting in a hidden cove I'd found, just listening to the radio and trying to decide whether I could go back to get the rest of my luggage, when I heard the news about the horrible tragedy at the Pasteur. That . . . that Dr. Chambord's presumed dead. Do you have any news? Is he okay?"

Captain Bonnard shook his head sorrowfully. "They know he was working late that night in his lab, and no one's seen him since. It's pretty clear to the investigators that it's going to take at least another week to search through the rubble. They found two more bodies this afternoon."

"It's too terrible. Poor Dr. Chambord! He was so good to me. Always saying I was working too hard. I hadn't had a vacation, and he's the one who insisted I go."

The captain sighed and nodded. "But go on with your story. Tell me why you think the men wanted you."

The research assistant wiped his eyes with the heels of his hands. "Of course, once I knew about the Pasteur and Dr. Chambord . . . it all made sense, why they were after me. So I ran away again, and I didn't stop running until I found this boardinghouse. No one knows me here, and it's not on the usual routes."

"*Je comprends.* And that's when you called me?"

"*Oui.* I didn't know what else to do."

But now the captain seemed confused. "They came after you because Émile Chambord was caught in the explosion? Why? That makes no sense, unless you're saying the bombing was no simple matter."

Jean-Luc nodded emphatically. "There's nothing important about me except that I'm—I was—the laboratory assistant to the great Émile Chambord. I think the bomb was intended to murder him."

"But why, for God's sake? Who would want to kill him?"

"I don't know who, Captain, but I think it was because of his molecular computer. When I left, he was ninety-nine percent certain he'd made an operational one. But you know how he could be, such a perfectionist. He didn't want word to get out, not even a hint, until he was one hundred percent sure it worked. You understand how significant a machine like that would be? A lot of people would kill him, me, and anyone else to get their hands on a real DNA computer."

Captain Bonnard scowled. "We found no evidence of such a success. But then, there's a mountain of debris as high as the Alps. Are you sure of what you say?"

He nodded. "*Bien sûr.* I was with him every step of the way. I mean, I didn't understand a lot of what he did, but . . ." He hesitated as a new fear made him rigid. "His computer was destroyed? You didn't find his notes? The proof?"

"The lab is rubble, and there was nothing on the Pasteur's mainframe."

"There wouldn't be. He was worried it could be accessed too easily,

F97,705

perhaps even hacked into by spies. So he kept his data in a notebook, locked into his lab safe. *The whole project was in the notes in his safe!"*

Bonnard groaned. "That means we can never reproduce his work."

Jean-Luc said cautiously, "Maybe we can."

"What?" The captain frowned. "What are you telling me, Jean-Luc?"

"That perhaps we can reproduce his work. We can build a DNA computer without him." Jean-Luc hesitated as he fought back a shudder of fear. "I think that's why those armed men came to Arcachon, looking for me."

Bonnard stared. "You have a copy of his notes?"

"No, I have my own notes. They're not as full as his, I admit. I didn't understand everything he did, and he'd forbidden either me or the strange American helping him to make notes. But I secretly copied down nearly everything from memory up to the end of last week. That's when I left for vacation. I'm sure my record isn't as complete or as detailed as his, but I think it'd be enough for another expert in the field to follow and maybe even improve on."

"Your notes?" Bonnard appeared excited. "You took them with you on vacation? You have them *now?*"

"Yessir." Jean-Luc patted the briefcase at his feet. "I never let them out of my sight."

"Then we'd better move, and fast. They could be tracking you from the village and be only minutes away." He strode to the window and looked down on the nighttime street. "Come here, Jean-Luc. Does anyone look like them? Anyone suspicious? We need to be certain, so we'll know whether to use the inn's front or back door."

Jean-Luc approached Captain Bonnard at the open window. He studied the activity below, illuminated in the glow of street lamps. Three men were entering a waterfront bar, and two were leaving. A half dozen others rolled barrels from a warehouse, one barrel after another in a parade, and hoisted them into the open bed of a truck. A homeless man sat with his feet in the street, his head nodding forward as if he were dozing off.

Jean-Luc scrutinized each person. "No, sir, I don't see them."

Captain Bonnard made a sound of satisfaction in his throat. "*Bon.* We must move swiftly, before the thugs can find you. Grab your briefcase. My Jeep is around the corner. Let's go."

"*Merci!*" Jean-Luc hurried back to his briefcase, grabbed it, and rushed onward to the door.

But as soon as the young man had faced away, Bonnard grabbed a thick pillow from the cot with one hand while, with the other, he reached for the holster at the small of his back and slid out a 7.65mm Le Française Militaire pistol with a specially crafted silencer. It was an old weapon, the manufacture of the line ending in the late 1950s. The serial number, which had been stamped into the right rear chamber area of the barrel, was now filed off. There was no safety device, so anyone who carried the Militaire had to be very careful. Bonnard liked the feeling of that small danger, and so for him, such a gun was merely a challenge.

As he followed Massenet, he called out softly, "Jean-Luc!"

His youthful face full of eagerness and relief, Jean-Luc turned. Instantly he saw the weapon and the pillow. Surprised, still not quite understanding, he reached out a protesting hand. "Captain?"

"Sorry, son. But I need those notes." Before the research assistant could speak again, could even move, Captain Darius Bonnard clamped the pillow around the back of his head, pushed the silenced muzzle against his temple, and pulled the trigger. There was a popping sound. Blood, tissue, and pieces of skull exploded into the pillow. The bullet burned itself through and lodged in the plaster wall.

Still using the pillow to protect the room from blood, Captain Bonnard supported the corpse to the bed. He laid the body out, the pillow beneath the head, and removed the silencer from the gun. He dropped the silencer into his pocket and pressed the gun into Jean-Luc's left hand. As soon as he arranged the pillow just so, he put his hand over Jean-Luc's and squeezed the trigger once more. The noise was thunderous, shocking in the tiny room, even to Captain Bonnard, who was expecting it.

This was a rough waterfront area, but still the sound of a gunshot would attract attention. He had little time. First he checked the pillow. The second shot had been perfect, going through so closely to the first hole that it looked like one large perforation. And now there would be powder burns on Jean-Luc's hand to satisfy the medical examiner that he, distraught over the loss of his beloved Dr. Chambord, had committed suicide.

Moving quickly, the captain found a notepad with indentations that indicated writing on the previous sheet. From the wastebasket he seized the single crumpled paper and pushed it and the notepad into his uniform pocket without taking the time to decipher either. He checked under the bed and under every other piece of old furniture. There was no closet. He dug the first bullet out of the wall and moved a battered bureau six inches to the left to hide the hole.

As he snatched up Jean-Luc's briefcase, the rise-and-fall scream of a police siren began in the distance. His heart palpitating with the rush of adrenaline, he analyzed the sound. *Oui*, it was heading here. With his usual control, he forced his careful gaze to survey the room once more. At last, satisfied that he had missed nothing, he opened the door. As Captain Bonnard vanished into the gloom of the upstairs hall, the police car screeched to a stop in front of the rooming house.

Chapter Three

Paris, France
Tuesday, May 6
The C-17 cargo jet that had left Buckley Air Force Base near Denver on Monday for a previously scheduled pole route to Munich carried a single passenger whose name appeared nowhere on its personnel roster or manifest. The big jet made an unscheduled stop in Paris in the dark at 0600 hours Tuesday, ostensibly to pick up a package that was needed in Munich. A U.S. Air Force staff car met the cargo jet, and a man in the uniform of a U.S. Army lieutenant colonel carried a sealed metal box, which was empty, onboard. He stayed there. But when the aircraft flew off some fifteen minutes later, the nonexistent passenger was no longer aboard.

Not long afterward, the same staff car stopped a second time, now at the side entrance to a detached building at Charles de Gaulle International Airport just north of Paris. The vehicle's back door opened, and a tall man, also wearing the uniform of a U.S. Army lieutenant colonel, emerged. It was Jon Smith. Trim, athletic, somewhere in his early forties, he looked military through and through. He had a high-planed face, and his dark hair, a little longer than usual, was worn neatly smooth under his army cap. As he stood up, his navy blue eyes surveyed all around.

There was nothing particularly unusual about him as he finally walked to the building in the quiet hours before dawn, just another army officer, carrying an overnight bag and an IBM Thinkpad in a heavy-duty aluminum case. A half hour later, Smith emerged again, out of uniform. This time he was wearing the casual clothes he favored—a tweed jacket, blue cotton shirt, tan cotton trousers, and a trench coat. He also wore a hidden canvas holster under his sports jacket, and in it was his 9mm Sig Sauer.

He walked briskly across the tarmac and moved with other passengers through de Gaulle customs, where, because of his U.S. Army identification, he was waved through without a search. A private limousine was waiting, back door open. Smith climbed in, refusing to let his limo driver handle either his suitcase or his laptop.

The city of Paris was known for its joie de vivre in all things, including driving. For instance, a horn was for communication: A long blast meant disgust—get out of my way. A tap was a friendly warning. Several taps were a jaunty greeting, especially if they were rhythmic. And speed, deftness, and a devil-may-care attitude were necessary, particularly among the world atlas of drivers who manned the city's numerous taxi and limo fleets. Smith's driver was an American with a heavy foot, which was just fine with Smith. He wanted to get to the hospital to see Marty.

As the limo hurtled south on the boulevard Périphérique around the crowded city, Smith was tense. In Colorado he had successfully handed off his research into molecular circuits. He regretted having had to do it, but it was necessary. On the long flight to France, he had called ahead to check again on Marty's condition. There had been no improvement, but at least there had been no decline either. He had also made other phone calls, this time to colleagues in Tokyo, Berlin, Sydney, Brussels, and London, tactfully sounding them out about their progress in developing molecular computers. But all were cagey, hoping to be first.

After filtering for that, he had gotten the sense that none was close to success. All commented on the sad death of Émile Chambord but without mentioning his project. It seemed to Smith that they were as uninformed as he had been.

The driver turned the limo off onto the avenue de la Porte de Sèvres and soon arrived at the eight-hundred-bed European Hospital Georges Pompidou. A glistening monument to modern architecture with curved walls and a glassy facade, it rose like a giant layered Luden's cough drop, directly across the street from the Parc André Citroën. Carrying his luggage, Smith paid the driver and entered the hospital's glass-topped, marble-lined galleria. He took off his sunglasses, slid them into his pocket, and gazed around.

The galleria was so cavernous—more than two football fields in length—that palm trees swayed in the internal breeze. The hospital was nearly brand-new, having opened just a couple of years ago amid official fanfare that it was the hospital of the future. As Smith headed toward an information desk, he noted department-store-style escalators that led up to patients' rooms on the floors above, bright arrows pointing to the operating theaters, and, infusing the air, a light scent reminiscent of Johnson's Lemon Wax.

Speaking perfect French, he asked for directions to the intensive care unit where Marty was being treated, and he took the escalator up. There was a subdued bustle as shifts changed and nurses, technicians, clerical help, and orderlies came and left. It was all done smoothly, quietly, and only the most experienced eye would have noticed the exchanges that signaled the handing off of responsibilities.

One of the theories that made this model hospital different was that services were clustered in groups, so that the specialist went to the patient, rather than the reverse. Entering patients arrived at any one of twenty-two different reception points, where they were met by personal hostesses, who guided them to their private rooms. There a computer was positioned at the foot of each bed, case notes existed in cyberspace, and, if surgery were necessary, robots often conducted parts of it. The enormous hospital even boasted swimming pools, health clubs, and cafés.

Beyond the desk that fronted the ICU, two gendarmes stood outside the door into the unit itself. Smith identified himself formally in French to the nurse as the American medical representative of Dr. Martin Zellerbach's family. "I'll need to talk to Dr. Zellerbach's lead physician."

"You wish to see Dr. Dubost, then. He's arrived for rounds and has already seen your friend this morning. I'll page him."

"*Merci.* Will you take me to Dr. Zellerbach? I'll wait there."

"*Bien sûr. S'il vous plaît?*" She offered him a distracted smile and, after one gendarme had examined his army medical identification, took him inside the heavy swinging doors.

Instantly, the hospital noises and the vigorous ambience vanished, and he was moving in a hushed world of soft footsteps, whispering doctors and nurses, and the muted lights, bells, and winking LEDs of machines that seemed to breathe loudly in the silence. In an ICU, machines owned the universe, and patients belonged to them.

Smith anxiously approached Marty, who was in the third cubicle on the left, lying motionless inside the raised side rails of a narrow, machine-operated bed, as helpless among the tubes and wires and monitors as a toddler held by each hand between towering adults. Smith looked down, his chest tight. Frozen in a coma, Marty's round face was waxen, but his breathing was even.

Smith touched the computer screen at the end of the bed and read Marty's chart. Marty was still in a coma. His other injuries were minor, mostly scrapes and bruises. It was the coma that was worrisome, with its potential for brain damage, sudden death, and even worse—a permanent suspended state neither dead nor alive. But there were a few good signs, too, according to the cyberchart. All his autonomic responses were working—he was breathing unaided, occasionally coughed, yawned, blinked, and showed roving eye movements—which indicated that the lower brain stem, the vital part that controlled these activities, was still functioning.

"Dr. Smith?" A small man with gray hair and an olive complexion walked toward him. "I understand you've come from the United States." He introduced himself, and Smith saw the embroidery on the front of his long white physician's coat—Edouard Dubost. He was Marty's doctor.

"Thank you for seeing me so quickly," Smith told him. "Tell me about Dr. Zellerbach's condition."

Dr. Dubost nodded. "I have good news. Our friend here seems to be doing better."

Immediately Smith felt a smile grow across his face. "What's happened? I didn't see anything on his chart from this morning."

"Yes, yes. But you see, I wasn't finished. I had to go around the corner for a moment. Now we'll talk, and I'll type at the same time." The doctor leaned over the computer. "We're fortunate with Dr. Zellerbach. He's still in a coma, as you can see, but this morning he spoke a few words and moved his arm. He was responding to stimulation."

Smith inhaled with relief. "So it's less severe than you originally thought. It's possible he'll awake and be fine."

He nodded as he typed. "Yes, yes."

Smith said, "It's been more than twenty-four hours since the explosion. Of course, anything past that makes it more worrisome that he'll regain complete consciousness."

"Very true. It's natural to be concerned. I am, too."

"You'll put in an order to have the nurses work with him? Ask him questions? Try to get him to move more?"

"I'm doing that right now." He typed a dozen more words and straightened up. He studied Smith. "Don't worry, Doctor. We know what we're doing here. Your friend is in excellent hands. A week from now, with luck he'll be complaining loudly about his aches and pains, the coma completely forgotten." He cocked his head. "He's your dear friend, I can see that. Stay as long as you like, but I must continue rounds."

Warmed by the hope that Marty would not only emerge from the coma but with all his brain functions intact, Smith sat beside the bed, among the flashing dials and gauges of the monitors, and watched him, thinking all the way back to Council Bluffs and high school, where he and Marty had met and Jon's uncle had first diagnosed Marty's Asperger's Syndrome . . . to Sophia's murder and the Hades virus pandemic, when he had needed Marty's genius with all things electronic.

He took Marty's hand and squeezed it. "Did you hear your doctor? He thinks you're going to be all right. Mart, can you hear me?" He waited, watching the still face. "What in God's name happened at the Pasteur, Mart? Were you helping Chambord develop his molecular computer?"

Marty stirred, and his lips trembled as if he was trying to speak.

Excited, Jon continued, "What is it? Tell me, Mart. Please! We both know you're never at a loss for words." He paused, hoping, but when Marty made no other sign, he put an encouraging warmth in his voice and continued, "This is a hell of a way for us to meet again, Mart. But you know how it is, I need you. So here I am, asking you to lend me that extraordinary mind of yours once more. . . ."

Talking and reminiscing, he stayed with Marty an hour. He squeezed Marty's hand, rubbed his arms, massaged his feet. But it was only when he mentioned the Pasteur that Marty tried to rouse himself. Smith had just leaned back in the chair and stretched, deciding he had better get on with the investigation into Dr. Chambord's molecular computer, when a tall man in a hospital orderly's uniform appeared in the opening to Marty's cubicle.

The man was dark, swarthy, with a huge black mustache. He was staring at Smith, his brown eyes hard and cold. Intelligent and deadly. And, in the split second when Smith's gaze and his connected, he seemed startled. The shock was in the bold eyes only briefly, and then, just before the man turned and hurried away, there seemed a hint of mischief or amusement or perhaps malice . . . somehow familiar.

That flitting sense of familiarity stopped Smith for a heartbeat, and then he was up and rushing after the orderly, snatching his Sig Sauer from its holster inside his jacket. It was not only the man's eyes and expression that had been wrong, but the way he had carried the folded linens, draped over his right arm. He could be hiding a weapon beneath. Was he there to kill Marty?

Outside the ICU, all eyes were on Smith as he furiously burst through the large swinging doors, his trench coat flapping. Ahead, the orderly knocked people out of the way as he put on a burst of speed and tore off down the corridor, escaping.

Pounding in pursuit, Smith shouted in French, "Stop that man! He's got a gun!"

With that, all pretense was gone, and the orderly flourished a mini-submachine gun not much bigger than Smith's Sig Sauer. He turned, expertly trotting backward, and raised the terrorist weapon without panic or haste. He swung it back and forth as if to sweep the corridor clean. The fellow was a professional of some kind, letting the threat of his gun do the work without having to fire a shot.

Screams erupted as nurses, doctors, and visitors dove to the floor, into doorways, and around corners.

Smith hurled breakfast carts out of the way and thundered on. Ahead, the man rushed through a doorway and slammed the door. Smith kicked it in and raced past a terrified technician, through another door, and past a hot-therapy tank in which a naked man sat, the nurse hurriedly covering him with a towel.

"Where is he?" Smith demanded. "Where did the orderly go!"

The nurse pointed at one of three rooms, her face pasty with fear, and he heard a door bang shut in that direction. He tore onward, punched open the only door in that room, and skidded into another corridor. He looked left and right along the hallway, chrome bright in its newness. Terrified people had pressed themselves against the walls as they gazed right, as if a deadly tornado had just swept past, barely leaving them alive.

Smith ran in the direction they stared, accelerating, while far down the corridor the orderly hurled an empty gurney lengthwise to block his path. Smith swore. He took a deep breath, demanding his lungs respond. If he had to stop to move the gurney, the man would surely get away. Without breaking stride, Smith summoned his energy. Telling himself he could do it, he leaped over the gurney. His knees felt weak as he landed, but he caught his balance and sprinted onward, leaving behind another trail of frightened people. Sweat poured off him, but at last he was gaining on the orderly, who had been slowed by throwing the gurney into position. Smith accelerated again, hopeful.

Without a backward glance, the man slammed through yet another door. It had an exit sign above it. The fire stairs. Smith hurtled in after him. But from the corners of his eyes, he caught a glimpse of someone hiding to the left of the door, behind it as he swung it in.

He had time only to lower a protective shoulder. In the shadowy stairwell, the orderly sprang out and crashed into him. The impact shook him, but he managed to remain on his feet. He smashed his shoulder into the orderly, sending him reeling back toward the stairs.

The orderly staggered. He hit the back of his head against the steel balustrade. But he had given way with Smith's thrust and quickly regained his balance, while Smith, meeting less resistance than he had expected, dropped his Sig Sauer and lost his footing. He stumbled and crashed to the cement floor, taking a hard blow to his back where it struck the wall. Ignoring the pain, he stumbled back up to his feet and grabbed for his pistol, just in time to see the man's shadow loom. Smith lashed out, too late. A searing pain exploded in his skull, and blackness and silence descended.

Chapter Four

When the morning express train from Bordeaux pulled in that Tuesday at the Gare d'Austerlitz, Captain Darius Bonnard was the third passenger off, striding through the throngs of arriving and departing Parisians, provincials, and tourists as if he did not know they existed. The truth was, he was watching for the slightest sign of interest directed toward him. There were too many who would try to stop his work if they discovered it, enemies and friends alike.

He stayed focused, his scrutiny covert, as he headed toward the exit, a compact, vigorous man with blond hair, impeccably attired in his French officer's uniform. He had spent his entire adult life in the service of France, and his current assignment might be the most important in all the nation's illustrious history. Certainly it was the most important to him. And the most dangerous.

He pulled his cell phone from his pocket, dialed a number, and when the voice answered, he announced, "I'm here." As soon as he hung up, he dialed a second number and repeated the message.

Outdoors, he bypassed the ranks of taxis, plus four official and unofficial drivers eager for his business, and climbed into the rogue cab that had just pulled up.

"*Salaam alake koom*," the gravelly voice greeted him from the backseat.

As he settled in beside the robed man, Captain Bonnard replied with the customary response: "*La bahs hamdililah.*" He slammed and locked the door.

In the street, other drivers shouted curses at this breach of taxicab etiquette.

As the vehicle pulled away, driving southwest into narrow side streets, Captain Bonnard turned to the man who had spoken. In the shadowed interior, shafts of sunlight played intermittently across the hooded, green-brown eyes. Most of the man's face was cloaked in the voluminous white robes and gold-trimmed kaffiyeh of a desert bedouin, but from what little Bonnard could see, the man had satin-black skin. Bonnard knew his name was Abu Auda and that he was a member of the Fulani tribe from the Sahel region at the southern edge of the Sahara, where the dry, forbidding desert met lush forest and grasslands. The green-brown eyes revealed that a blue-eyed Berber or ancient Vandal was somewhere in his family line.

"You've brought them?" the Fulani asked in Arabic.

"*Naam.*" The French captain nodded. He unbuttoned his tunic, opened his uniform shirt, and took out a letter-sized, zippered leather portfolio. Abu Auda's gaze followed each of the movements as Bonnard handed over the portfolio and reported, "Chambord's assistant is dead. What of the American, Zellerbach?"

"We found no notes, as was expected, although we searched thoroughly," Abu Auda told him.

The man's strange eyes bored into Bonnard as if they could reach the Frenchman's soul. Eyes that trusted no one and nothing, not even the god to whom he prayed five times daily without fail. He would worship Allah, but he would trust no one. As Captain Bonnard's face held steadfastly impassive under the heat of the bedouin's examination, the hard eyes finally turned their attention to the portfolio.

Abu Auda felt it all over with long, scarred fingers, then pushed it inside his robes. His voice was strong and measured as he said, "He'll be in touch."

"No need. I'll see him soon." Bonnard gave a curt nod. "Stop the taxi."

The desert bedouin gave the command, the vehicle pulled to the curb, and the Frenchman stepped out. As soon as the door clicked closed behind him, the taxi peeled away.

Captain Bonnard walked to the nearest corner, speaking into his cell phone again. "You followed?"

"*Oui*. No problems."

Seconds later, a large Citroën with darkened windows slowed as it neared the corner. Its rear door opened, and the captain stepped inside. The expensive car made a U-turn, taking him to his office where he had phone calls to make before he met with Abu Auda's boss.

■

As Jon Smith regained consciousness in the stairwell at the huge Pompidou Hospital, an image lingered in his mind. It was a face, leering at him. Swarthy, a thick black mustache, brown eyes, and a triumphant smile that faded away like the grin of the Cheshire Cat. But the eyes . . . He concentrated on the eyes that accompanied the smile down the stairs, fading, fading . . . *Voices speaking, what? French? Yes, French. Where the devil was he . . . ?*

". . . are you all right? Monsieur?"

"How do you feel?"

"Who was the man who attacked you? Why was he—?"

"Stand back, you idiots. Can't you see he's still unconscious? Give me room so I can examine—"

Smith's eyes snapped open. He was lying on his back on hard concrete, a gray cement ceiling overhead. A ring of concerned faces peered down—female and male nurses, a doctor kneeling over him, a gendarme and uniformed security people above and behind.

Smith sat up and his head swam with pain. "Damn."

"You must lie back, monsieur. You've had a nasty blow to the skull. Tell me how you feel."

Smith did not lie down again, but he allowed the white-coated doctor to aim his penlight into his eyes. He endured the examination with little patience. "Great. I feel absolutely great." Which was a lie. His head pounded as if someone were in there with a sledgehammer. Abruptly, he remembered. He grabbed the doctor's hand in a vise grip, pushed away the light, and gazed all around. "Where is he?" he demanded. "That Arab orderly. *Where is he!* He had a submachine gun. He—"

"He wasn't the only one with a gun." The gendarme held up Smith's

Sig Sauer. His expression was severe, distrustful, and Smith sensed he was very close to being arrested. The gendarme continued, "Did you buy this here in Paris? Or did you, perhaps, find some way to sneak it into the country?"

Smith patted his suit jacket pocket. It was empty, which meant his identification was gone. "You've got my ID?" When the gendarme nodded, Smith continued, "Then you know I'm a U.S. Army colonel. Pull the ID out of its case. Under it is a special permit to bring my gun in and carry it."

The policeman did as asked, while around Smith the hospital crew watched suspiciously. At last the gendarme gave a slow nod and returned the identification case.

"My Sig Sauer, too. *S'il vous plaît.*" A security guard handed it down, and Smith said, "Now tell me about the 'orderly' with the submachine gun. Who was he?"

The doctor looked up at the security man. "The other man was an orderly?"

"Must've been Farouk al Hamid," the guard said. "This is his section."

Another guard disagreed. "That wasn't Farouk. I saw him running, and it wasn't Farouk."

"Had to be. It's his section."

A nurse chimed in, "I know Farouk. That man was too tall to be Farouk."

"While they try to sort through the mystery, I'm going to finish my examination," the doctor announced to Smith. "This will take only a moment." He shone the light in one of Smith's eyes, then the other.

Smith struggled to contain his frustration. "I'm okay," he said again and this time meant it. His head was clearing, the pain subsiding.

The doctor removed the light and sat back on his heels. "Are you dizzy?"

"Not a bit." Which was the truth.

The doctor shrugged and got up. "I understand you're a physician, so you know the dangers of head injuries. But you seem like something of a hothead." He frowned and peered worriedly at Smith. "You're obviously eager to be out of here, and I can't stop you. But at least your eyes are clear and tracking, your skin color's good, and you may actually be thinking rationally, so I'll just warn you to take care of yourself and avoid further injuries. And if you start feeling worse or lose consciousness again, come back straightaway. You know the dangers of a concussion. You may have one."

"Yes, Doctor." Jon struggled to his feet. "Thanks. I appreciate your concern." He decided to ignore the comment about his being a hothead. "Where's the hospital's chief of security?"

"I'll take you," one of the guards told him.

He led Smith down the emergency stairs to a tucked-away office of several rooms, all equipped with the latest in electronic surveillance and computers. The security chief's office looked out over a parking area, and on the wall were several framed photographs that were personal. One was a black-and-white photo of five exhausted, hollow-eyed men with defiant faces in field uniforms. They were sitting on wooden crates with thick jungle all around. Smith studied the photo for a moment, then recognized Dien Bien Phu, where in 1954 the French were defeated in a brutal, humiliating siege that proved the end of France's longtime control of the region.

The guard explained, "Chief, this is the gentleman who tried to stop the armed orderly."

Smith held out his hand. "Lieutenant Colonel Jon Smith, U.S. Army."

"Pierre Girard. Have a seat, Colonel."

Girard did not get up from behind the clean lines of his modern desk or shake Smith's hand, but nodded to one of the straight chairs. A thick, burly man of medium height, the security chief wore a stained gray suit and loosened tie. He looked more like a longtime Sûreté CID detective than a private security man.

Smith sat. "The orderly, or whoever he was, and there appears to be some doubt, came to the ICU to kill Martin Zellerbach, I think."

Girard glanced toward the guard. "The man wasn't an orderly as reported?"

"It's Farouk al Hamid's station," the guard explained, "but some witnesses say it wasn't him."

The chief reached for his telephone. "Get me personnel." He waited, his face neutral. A former detective, no doubt of it, accustomed to bureaucracy. "You have an orderly named Farouk al Hamid who works the . . . yes, ICU. He did? I see. Thank you." Girard hung up and told

Smith, "He wrote a note saying he was sick, his cousin would do his job, and he sent the note with the cousin, who, it seems, was our tall orderly with the gun."

"And who," Smith said, "was no orderly, and maybe not even Algerian."

"A disguise." Girard nodded to himself. "Possibly. May I ask why someone would want to assassinate Mr. Zellerbach?" The security chief made the usual hash of the French trying to pronounce a German name.

"It's *Dr.* Zellerbach. He's a computer scientist. He was working with Dr. Émile Chambord at the Pasteur the night of the bombing."

"A great pity to lose Chambord." Girard paused. "Then it's possible your Dr. Zellerbach saw or heard something incriminating there. Perhaps now the bombers are trying to stop Dr. Zellerbach from awakening and giving us the information."

It was a policeman's answer, and Smith saw no reason to elaborate further. "I'd say that it was more than possible."

"I'll alert the police."

"I'd appreciate you or the police doubling the guard on him in the ICU and, if he's moved, posted wherever he's sent."

"I will contact the Sûreté."

"Good." Smith stood. "Thank you. I've got an appointment, so I'm going to have to leave." That was not exactly the truth, but close.

"Of course. The police will need to speak to you, though, eventually, I expect."

Smith gave Girard the name and number of his hotel and left. At the ICU, there was no change in Marty. He sat beside Marty's bed again, studying the round, sleeping face, worrying. Marty looked so vulnerable, and Smith found his throat tight with emotion.

At last he stood up, pressed Marty's hand once more, and told him he would be back. He left the ICU but stayed on the same floor, returning to the fire stairs. On the landing, he searched for anything the gunman might have dropped, for any clue at all. He found nothing but a trace of blood on the post of the balustrade, evidence he really had wounded the gunman, which could be useful information if the man ever reappeared.

Still on the deserted stair landing, he activated his cell phone with its special scrambler capacity and dialed. "Someone tried to kill Marty in the hospital," he reported.

The head of Covert-One, Fred Klein, answered from across the Atlantic Ocean in his usual growl. "Do we know who?"

"Looks like a pro. It was a good setup. The guy was disguised as an orderly, and if I hadn't been there, he could've gotten away with it."

"The French guards didn't pick up on him?"

"No, but maybe the Sûreté will do better now," Smith said.

"Better yet, I'll talk to the French myself, ask them to send special forces soldiers to guard Zellerbach."

"I like that. There's something else you need to know. The guy had a mini-submachine gun. He was carrying it hidden under bed linen."

There was an abrupt silence at the other end of the connection. Klein knew as well as Smith that the submachine gun changed the picture. It turned what had appeared a straightforward assassination attempt into something far more complex. When Klein spoke again, he asked the question, "Meaning what exactly, Colonel?"

Smith was sure Klein knew perfectly well what he was thinking, but he said it anyway: "He had the firepower to kill Marty from where he was standing. My being there would've been no deterrent, if he'd been willing to shoot me and maybe everyone else in the ICU, too. His initial plan was probably to go in with a knife, something quiet, so he wouldn't attract attention. The submachine gun was only for last-ditch protection."

"And?"

"And that suggests he realized that if he opened fire and killed a handful of us, his escape from the hospital would've been far more difficult, and that means he didn't want to take any chances that he might be captured, alive or dead. Which, in turn, suggests again that the bombing was no random act or the crazed vindictiveness of some fired employee, but part of a careful plan by people with a specific goal who will go to great lengths to not be discovered."

Klein was silent again. "You think it's clearer now that Dr. Chambord was the target. And therefore Marty, too, because he was working with Chambord."

"Has there been any group or individual claiming credit for the bombing?"

"Not yet."

"There won't," Smith decided.

Klein gave a cold chuckle. "I always thought you were wasted in medicine and research, Jon. Very well, we think the same, but so far everyone else is whistling in the dark in hopes Chambord's death was collateral to the bombing, an accident." There was a deep sigh at the far end. "But that part's my job. Yours is to dig deeper and turn up those notes and any type of prototype computer he developed." His voice grew hard. "And if you can't grab them, you've got to destroy them. Those are your orders. We can't run the risk of that kind of power staying in the wrong hands."

"I understand."

"How's Zellerbach doing? Any change in his condition?"

Smith reported the improvement. "It's good, but there's still no guarantee it means a full recovery."

"Then we'll hope."

"If he knows anything, or took notes, he could've stored the data on his mainframe back in D.C. You'd better send a Covert-One computer expert."

"Already did, Colonel. Had a hell of a time getting in, and when he did, he found nothing. If Zellerbach kept notes, he followed Chambord's lead and didn't put them into his computer."

"It was an idea."

"Appreciated. What do you plan next?"

"I'm going to the Pasteur. There's an American biochemist I've worked with there. I'll see what he can tell me about Chambord."

"Be careful. Remember, you have no official position in this. Covert-One has to remain hidden."

"It's just friend going to friend, nothing more," Smith reassured him.

"All right. Another thing . . . I want you to meet General Carlos Henze, the American who commands NATO forces in Europe. He's the only person over there who knows you're assigned to investigate, but he thinks you're working for army intelligence. The president called him personally to set this up. Henze's got his contacts at work, and he'll fill you in on what he's found out over there. He doesn't know anything about me or Covert-One, of course. Memorize this: Pension Cézanne, two P.M. sharp. Ask for M. Werner. The password is *Loki*."

Chapter Five

Washington, D.C.

It was early morning, and a spring breeze blew the scent of cherry blossoms across the Tidal Basin and in through the open French doors of the Oval Office, but President Samuel Adams Castilla was too distracted to notice or care. He stood up behind the heavy pine table he used as a desk and glared at the three people who sat waiting for him to continue. He was just a year into his second term, and the last thing Castilla needed was a military crisis. Now was the time to solidify his accomplishments, get the rest of his programs through a fractious Congress, and build his historical image.

"So this is the situation," he rumbled. "We haven't got enough evidence yet to determine whether a molecular computer actually exists, and if it does, who has it. What we do know is that it's not in our hands, dammit." He was a big man with thick shoulders and a waist that had spread as wide as Albuquerque. Usually genial, he glared through his titanium glasses and worked at controlling his frustration. "The air force and my computer experts tell me they have no other explanation for what happened on Diego Garcia. My science adviser says he's consulted top people in the field, and they claim there could be many reasons for the blip in communications out there, starting with some rare atmospheric anomaly. I hope the science folks are right."

"So do I," Admiral Stevens Brose agreed promptly.

"So do all of us," added National Security Adviser Emily Powell-Hill.

"Amen," said Chief of Staff Charles Ouray from where he leaned against the wall near the fireplace.

Admiral Brose and National Security Adviser Powell-Hill were sitting in leather chairs facing the president's desk, which he had brought with him from Santa Fe. Like all presidents, he had chosen his own decor. The current furnishings reflected his rural Southwestern taste, now modified by five years of the cosmopolitan sophistication he had unexpectedly found he enjoyed in this loftiest seat of federal government, plus all the official trips to capitals, museums, and banquets around the planet. The ranch furniture from the New Mexico governor's residence had been thinned and joined with elegant French side tables and a comfortable British club chair before the fireplace. The red-and-yellow Navajo drapes and the Amerindian vases, baskets, and headdresses now blended with Senegalese masks, Nigerian mud prints, and Zulu shields.

Restless, the president walked around the desk. He leaned back against it, crossed his arms, and continued, "We all know terrorist attacks tend to be by people whose main goal is to get attention for their cause and expose what they consider evil. But this situation has at least two kinks so far: This bomb wasn't against the usual symbolic target—an embassy, a government building, a military installation, a famous landmark—and it wasn't some lone suicide bomber taking out a crowded bus or busy nightclub. Instead, the target was a research and teaching facility. A place that helps humanity. But specifically, the building where a molecular computer was being built."

Emily Powell-Hill, a former U.S. Army brigadier general, raised her perfect eyebrows. In her fifties, she was slender, long-legged, and highly intelligent. "With all due respect, Mr. President, the information you have about a DNA computer's being completed appears to be largely speculation, projection from insufficient data, and plain old guesswork. It's all based on a rumor about what might easily have been a random bombing with random victims. Is it possible your source's disaster scenario comes from paranoia?" She paused. "In an attempt to put it delicately . . . everyone knows the counterintelligence mentality tends to jump at the smallest shadow. This sounds like one of their knee-jerk ideas."

The president sighed. "I suspect you've got something else you'd like to say on the subject."

"As a matter of fact, Mr. President, I do. My science people assure me DNA computer technology is stuck in the early developmental stages and treading water. A functional unit isn't expected for at least a decade. Maybe two decades. Which is just one more reason to cast a very suspicious eye on what may be an overreaction."

"You could be right," the president said. "But I suspect you'll find your scientists also agree that if anyone could make such a leap, Chambord would be at the top of the list."

Charles Ouray, the president's chief of staff, was frowning. "Can anyone explain in words an old political warhorse like me can understand exactly what makes a DNA machine so special and such a big threat?"

The president nodded at Emily Powell-Hill, and she focused on Ouray. "It's all about switching from silicon, the foundation of computers, to carbon, the foundation of life," she told him. "Machines are slavishly fast and precise, while life's ever-changing and subtle. DNA computers will integrate the most powerful lessons from both worlds in a technology that's far superior to anything most people can imagine today. And in large part, it'll be because we've figured out how to use DNA molecules in place of microchips."

Ouray grimaced. "Integrating life and machinery? Sounds like something you'd read in a comic book."

"At one time, you probably did," the president agreed. "A lot of technologies we take for granted now appeared early on in science fiction and comic books. The truth is, researchers have been working for years to figure out how to take advantage of DNA's natural ability to reorganize and recombine quickly in complex, predictable patterns."

"You've lost me, Mr. President," Ouray said.

The president nodded. "Sorry, Chuck. Say you want to mow a lawn like out there on the Mall." He waved his big hand vaguely in that direction. "The electronic solution would be to use a few giant lawn mowers, and each would cut thousands of blades of grass every second. That's the way supercomputers operate. Now, the DNA solution's just the opposite. It'd use billions of tiny mowers that'd each cut just one blade. The trick is that all those little DNA mowers would cut their blades *at the same time*. That's the key—nature's massive parallelism. Take it from me, a molecular computer's going to dwarf the power of today's biggest supercomputer."

"Plus, it'll use almost no energy and be a lot cheaper to operate," Emily Powell-Hill added. "When one's created. *If* one's created."

"Swell," growled Admiral Stevens Brose, chairman of the Joint Chiefs, from the second leather chair, where he had been listening quietly. He was sitting awkwardly, his ankles crossed, his big chin jutting forward. Confidence and worry battled on his square face. "If that DNA thing really exists, and it's controlled by someone who doesn't like us, or maybe they want something we're not going to give, and that's the case with probably half the world right now . . . I don't even want to think about the future. Our military moves, fights, lives, and breathes on electronics, command codes, and communications codes. Hell, computers run everything now, including ordering liquor supplies for the Joint Chiefs' cocktail parties. The way I see it, railroads were the key to the Civil War, aircraft to World War Two, and encrypted and protected electronics are going to be the big decider in future wars, God help us."

"Defense implications are your responsibility, Stevens," the president told him. "So of course that's what you think of first. Me, I've got to take into account other problems, too. Civilian situations."

"Like what?" Chuck Ouray asked.

"I'm told a DNA computer can shut down oil and gas pipelines, and there goes our fuel supply. It can cut off air traffic control operations at hubs across the continent, everywhere from New York City to Chicago and Los Angeles. The number of deaths we could expect from that is catastrophic. Of course, it can access funds-transfer networks at the Federal Reserve, which means our treasury could be emptied in a heartbeat. It can also open the gates to the Hoover Dam. With that, we can expect the drowning deaths of hundreds of thousands of people."

Chuck Ouray's complexion paled. "You're not serious. Tell me you're not serious. Even the Hoover Dam's floodgates are accessible?"

The president said simply, "Yes. They're computerized, and the computer's connected to the Western utilities power grid."

There was an appalled silence in the room.

The president adjusted his weight. His solemn gaze swept over his three advisers. "Of course, as Emily said earlier, we still aren't certain there *is* a fully functioning DNA computer. We'll take it one step at a time. Chuck, see what the CIA and NSA can tell us. Contact the Brits and find out what they know, too. Emily and Stevens, get the latest from your people. We'll meet again later today."

■

As soon as the door closed behind the NSA director, the head of the Joint Chiefs, and the chief of staff, the side door that led into the president's private study opened. Fred Klein stepped into the Oval Office, wearing a rumpled gray suit and chewing on his empty pipe.

Klein took the pipe from his mouth and pronounced dryly, "I thought that went well."

The president sighed and returned to his big leather desk chair. "It could've been worse. Sit down, Fred. Don't you know something more than your intuition and Diego Garcia about this mess?"

Klein took the seat that Admiral Brose had vacated. He ran a hand over his receding hairline. "Not much," he admitted. "But I will."

"Has Jon Smith found out anything yet?"

Klein told the president about the attack on Martin Zellerbach that Smith interrupted. "When we hung up, Smith was going to the Pasteur to interview a colleague. After that, he'll see General Henze."

The president pursed his lips. "Smith's obviously good, but a few more people over there might be better. You know I'll authorize whatever or whoever you need."

Klein shook his head. "A terrorist cell is small and moves fast. It'll spot a large effort, which means that if the CIA and MI6 kick up any of their usual dust, their usefulness is over. We designed Covert-One for surgical situations just like this. Let's give Smith a chance to be the fly on the wall, a piece of the scenery no one notices. Meanwhile, as you know, I've got other Covert-One operatives on special leads and tasks. If Smith needs help, I'll let you know, and we'll act accordingly."

"We need something from him . . . from someone . . . soon, dammit." The president's brows knit together with worry. "Before we get a taste worse than Diego Garcia."

Paris, France

Private and nonprofit, L'Institut Pasteur was one of the great scientific centers of the world, with some twenty branches located on five continents. It had been at least five years since Smith had been to its headquarters here in Paris for a WHO conference on molecular biology, one of the Pasteur's prime areas of research. He was thinking about that and what he would find now as he stopped his taxi at 28 rue du Docteur Roux, named for one of the institute's earliest researchers. He paid the driver and walked toward the annex's kiosk.

Located in the eastern part of the Fifteenth Arrondissement, the Pasteur Institute stretched into the distance on both sides of the heavily trafficked street. In one of life's ironies, the grounds on the east were called simply the institute or the old campus, while the grounds on the west, although significantly larger, were known as the annex. The whole leafy place gave off the feel of a gracious college, and Smith could see many of its buildings—everything from nineteenth-century ornate to twenty-first-century sleek—rising among the trees on either side of the street. He could also see French soldiers on patrol on the institute's streets and sidewalks, an unusual sight but no doubt in response to the horrific bombing.

Smith showed his identification to the Pasteur security guard at the annex's kiosk, where one of the soldiers stood sentry, a 5.6mm FAMAS assault rifle in his arms. Behind the man, gray tendrils of smoke rose above the rooftops.

As Smith put away his ID, he nodded at the smoke and asked the Pasteur guard in French, "Is that where Dr. Chambord's lab was?"

"*Oui.* Little's left. A few exterior walls and heartbreak." The man gave a sad, Gallic shrug.

Smith felt like walking. There was much to sort through, and Marty's condition preyed on his mind. He looked up. As if echoing his thoughts, the day had grown somber, the sun lost behind a thick cloud cover that cast a monochromatic pall. He waited for a car to drive into the annex, then he crossed the street to the sidewalk, heading toward the smoke, which was the first physical sign of the disastrous attack. Soon he saw the second sign—pewter-gray ash and soot that dusted vegetation and structures. An alkaline stink stung his nose. Finally there were the corpses of wild birds—sparrows, hawks, jays—which lay scattered on the lawns, broken dolls flung from the sky, killed by the blast or resulting fire.

The farther he went, the heavier the ash grew, a ghostly blanket over buildings, trees, bushes, signs . . . everything and anything. Nothing was spared, left unsullied. At last he turned a corner and the site itself appeared—large, haphazard mounds of blackened brick and debris, above which three exterior walls towered precariously, dismal skeletons against the gray sky. He shoved his hands deep into his trench-coat pockets and halted where he was to study the dispiriting scene.

The building must have been spacious, about the size of a warehouse. Dogs sniffed the ruins. Rescue workers and firemen dug grimly, and armed soldiers patrolled. The charred remains of two cars stood at the curb. Beside them, some kind of metal sign had been melted into a distorted fist of steel. Nearby, an ambulance waited, in case another survivor was found or one of the workers injured.

Heart heavy, Smith waited as a soldier with a careful face approached and demanded identification. As he handed it over, he asked, "Any sign of Dr. Chambord?"

"I can't talk about it, sir."

Smith nodded. He had other ways to find out, and now that he had seen the devastation, he knew there was nothing he could learn here. It was lucky anyone had survived. Lucky Marty had. As he left, he thought about the monsters who had done this. Anger built in his chest.

He returned to the rue du Docteur Roux and crossed the street to the old campus. Calming himself, he showed his identification at the kiosk there, where another Pasteur security guard and armed soldier controlled access. After a thorough check, they gave him directions to the office and lab of his old friend and colleague Michael Kerns.

As he headed off past the old building where Louis Pasteur had lived and worked and was now buried, he was struck by how good it was to be back in this cradle of pure science, despite the circumstances. After all, this was where Pasteur had conducted his brilliant nineteenth-century experiments in fermentation that had led not just to pioneering research in bacteriology but to the principle of sterilization, which had forever changed the world's understanding of bacteria and saved untold millions of lives.

After Dr. Pasteur, other researchers here had gone on to produce critical scientific breakthroughs that had led to the control of virulent diseases like diphtheria, influenza, the plague, polio, tetanus, TB, and even yellow fever. It was no wonder the institute boasted more Nobel Prize winners than most nations. With more than a hundred research units and labs, the complex housed some five hundred permanent scientists while another six hundred from all corners of the globe worked temporarily on special projects. Among those was Michael Kerns, Ph.D.

Mike's office was in the Jacques Monod Building, which housed the department of molecular biology. The door was open. When Smith stepped inside, Mike looked up from his desk, where a mass of papers covered with calculations were spread before him.

Kerns took one look at Smith and jumped up. "Jon! Good Lord, man. What are you doing here?" White lab coat flapping, Kerns came around the desk with the athletic grace of the Iowa Hawkeye running back he had once been. A few inches under six feet and sturdy, he pumped Smith's hand vigorously. "Damn, Jon, how long's it been?"

"Five years, at least," Smith reminded him with a smile. "How's the work going?"

"So near and yet so far." Kerns laughed. "As usual, right? What brings you to Paris? More viruses for USAMRIID to hunt down?"

Taking the opening, Smith shook his head. "It's my friend Marty Zellerbach. He was hurt in the bombing."

"The Dr. Zellerbach who they say was working with poor Chambord? I never met him. I'm so sorry, Jon. How is he?"

"In a coma."

"Damn. What's the prognosis?"

"We're hopeful. But he had a nasty cranial injury, and the coma's hanging on. Still he's showing signs he may come out of it." Smith shook his head again, his expression glum. "Is there any news about Chambord? Have they found him yet?"

"They're still looking. The blast really shattered the building. It's going to take days for them to dig through it all. They've found some body parts that they're trying to identify. Very sad."

"Did you know Marty was working with Chambord?"

"Actually, no. Not until I read it in the paper." Kerns returned behind his desk and waved Smith to an aged armchair in the cluttered office. "Just chuck those files onto the floor."

Smith nodded, moved the pile of folders, and sat.

Kerns continued, "I said I never met Zellerbach, right? But it'd be more accurate to say I never even heard he was here. He had no official appointment to the staff, and I never saw his name listed as being on loan or visiting. I'd have known about that. It must've been some private arrangement with Chambord." Kerns paused. "I probably shouldn't be telling you this, but I was concerned about Émile. This last year, he was acting strange."

Smith came alert. "Chambord was acting strange? In what way?"

"Well . . . " Kerns pondered, then leaned forward like a conspirator, his hands clasped in from of him, resting on his papers. "He used to be a happy guy, you know what I mean? Convivial, outgoing, one of the boys, if you like, for all his seniority and fame. A hard worker who didn't seem to take his work all that seriously, despite its importance. A very level head. Oh, eccentric enough, like most of us, but in a different way from last year. He had the right attitude—his ego was never oversized. In fact, once when a dozen or so of us got together for drinks, he said, 'The universe will go on fine without us. There's always someone else to do the work.' "

"Self-effacing, and in many ways true. And it was after that he changed?"

"Yes. It was almost as if he vanished. In the corridors, at meetings, in the cafés, at bull sessions, staff parties, all that. And it happened just like that." He snapped his fingers. "He seemed to cut us all off, sharp as a slice with a knife. He'd disappeared, as far as most of us were concerned."

"Was this a year ago, about the same time he quit entering his progress data into the computer?"

Kerns was astonished. "I hadn't heard that. Damn, does that mean we have no idea what he accomplished over the last twelve months?"

"That's what it means. You know what he was working on?"

"Of course, everyone knew. A molecular computer. I heard he was making big strides, too. That he might even get there first, in under ten years. It was no secret, so . . . "

"So?"

Kerns leaned back. "So why the secretiveness? That was what was so different about him. Secretive, withdrawn, distracted, avoiding his colleagues. Come to work, go home, return to work, nothing else. Sometimes he was here for days in a row. I heard he even had a good bed put in there. We just wrote it off to a hot line of research."

Smith did not want to appear too interested in Chambord, or his notes, or the DNA computer. He was in Paris for Marty, after all. Nothing more, as far as Kerns or anyone else was concerned. "He wouldn't be the first to be so wrapped up in his work. A scientist who doesn't feel that compelled doesn't belong in research." He paused and asked casually, "So what's your theory?"

Mike chuckled. "In my wildest moments, stolen research. Spies. Industrial espionage, maybe. Some kind of cloak-and-dagger."

"Did something happen to make you think that?"

"Well, there's always the issue of the Nobel Prize. Whoever creates the first molecular computer will be a shoo-in. Of course, that means not just money but prestige—the Mount Olympus of prestige. No one at the Pasteur would turn it down. Probably no one in the world. Under those conditions, any of us might get a little nervous and clandestine, protecting our work until we were ready to go public."

"Good point." But stealing was one thing, mass murder, which the bombing had caused, was quite another. "There must've been something else, though, to make you think Chambord was worried about his work being stolen. Something unusual, maybe even suspicious, that triggered the idea."

"Now that you mention it . . . I wondered sometimes about a few of the people I spotted Chambord with once or twice outside the Pasteur. Also about a car that picked him up here some nights."

Smith allowed only a fraction of his interest to show on his face. "What kind of people?"

"Oh, ordinary enough. French, well dressed. They were always in civvies, or I might've said they were military. But I guess if Chambord was making progress on his DNA computer, that'd make sense. The military would want to keep tabs on everything he was doing, if he'd let them."

"Natural enough. What about the car? Do you remember the year and make?"

"Citroën, recent. Don't know the exact year. It was big and black. I'd see it when I was working late. I'd be heading for mine, and a few times it'd drive up. The rear door would swing open, Chambord would duck and climb in—he was very tall, you know—and it'd drive off. It was odd, because he had his own little Renault. I mean, I'd spot the Renault parked in the lot after the big car drove off."

"You never saw who was with him in the Citroën?"

"Never. But at the time, I was tired and was thinking about getting home."

"Did the Citroën bring him back?"

"I wouldn't know."

Smith thought it over. "Thanks, Mike. I can see you're busy, and I don't want to take any more of your time. I'm just looking into Marty's activities here in Paris, to get an assessment of his health before the bombing. Sorry to get so far off track with Chambord. Marty's got Asperger's Syndrome, and he's usually fine, but since I haven't talked to him in a while, I just want to make sure. What can you tell me about Chambord's family? They might know more about Marty."

"Émile was a widower. Wife died about seven years ago. I wasn't here then, but I heard it hit him hard. He buried himself in work then, too, was aloof for a while, I'm told. He has one child, a grown-up daughter."

"You have her address?"

Kerns turned to his computer and soon provided it. He cocked his head at Smith. "Her name's Thérèse Chambord. I gather she's a successful actress, stage mostly, but a few French flicks. A stunner, from what I've heard."

"Thanks, Mike. I'll tell you how things go with Marty."

"You do that. And we've got to have a drink together at least, before you go home. With luck, Marty, too."

"Good idea. I'd like that." He stood up and left.

∎

Once outside, Smith gazed across the big campus toward the smoke, blowing thin against the clouds. He shook his head and turned away, heading back to the street, his mind on Marty. Using his cell phone, he called the Pompidou Hospital and talked to the ICU head nurse, who reported that Marty remained stable, fortunately still showing an occasional sign that he might wake up. It was not a lot, but Smith held close the hope that his longtime friend would pull through.

"How are *you* feeling?" she asked.

"Me?" He remembered the blow to his head when he fell. Now it all seemed a long time ago and, compared to the devastation at the Pasteur, unimportant. "I'm doing fine. Thanks for asking."

As he hung up, he reemerged onto the rue du Docteur Roux and considered what he had learned from Mike Kerns: For the past year, Émile Chambord had acted like a man in a hurry, like someone with a secret. And he had been seen with well-dressed men who could have been military types out of uniform.

Smith was mulling that when he had a feeling he was being watched. Call it what you will—training, experience, a sixth sense, a subliminal impression of an image, paranoia, or even parapsychology. . . . But there was that tingle on the back of his neck, the slight shrinking of the skin.

They were out there, the eyes observing him. It had begun the instant he had stepped out onto the sidewalk.

Chapter
Six

Captain Darius Bonnard could almost smell the camels, the dates rotting in the sun, the goat-fat stink of couscous, and even the rank but miraculous odor of stagnant water. He had changed out of his captain's uniform and was now wearing a civilian suit, lightweight but still too heavy for the apartment where he had just arrived. He was already sweating under his blue pin-striped shirt.

He gazed around. The place looked like the inside of every bedouin tent in which he had sat miserable and cross-legged from the Sahara to all the godforsaken desert outposts of the former empire where he had served in his time. Moroccan rugs covered every window and lay two deep in a cushion on the floor. Algerian, Moroccan, and Berber hangings and artifacts decorated the walls, and the leather and wood furniture was low and hard.

With a sigh, the captain lowered himself to a chair inches off the floor, grateful that at least he was not expected to sit cross-legged on the floor. For a moment of déjà vu, he half-expected hot sand to gust from under the tent's walls and burn around his ankles.

But Bonnard was not in the Sahara, nor in a tent, and he had more pressing matters on his mind than an illusion of camel dung and blowing sand. His expression was fierce as he warned in French, "Sending that man to kill Martin Zellerbach in the hospital was a stupid move, M. Mauritania. Idiocy! How did you think he'd pull it off and escape successfully? They'd have caught him and flayed the truth out of him. And with Zellerbach's doctor friend there, too. *Merde!* Now the Sûreté has doubled their alert, and it'll be ten times more difficult to eliminate Zellerbach."

As Captain Bonnard ranted, the second man in the room, whom the captain had called M. Mauritania, the only name by which he was known in the international underworld of spies and criminals, remained expressionless. He was a stocky figure, with a round face and soft, well-manicured hands below the cuffs of a white shirt impeccably shot from the sleeves of a pearl-gray English suit direct from some custom tailor on Savile Row. His small features and bright blue eyes contemplated Bonnard and his outrage with the long-suffering patience of someone forced to listen to the incessant barking of a dog.

When the captain finally finished his tirade, Mauritania, who wore a French beret, tucked a lock of brown hair behind his ear and answered in French, in a voice as hard as his hands were soft. "You underestimate us, Captain. We're not fools. We sent no one to assassinate Dr. Zellerbach at the hospital or anywhere else. It would've been stupid to do at any time, and more than stupid to do now, when it's quite possible he'll never regain consciousness anyway."

Bonnard was taken aback. "But we decided there was no way we could take the chance of letting him live. He might know too much."

"*You* decided. *We* decided to wait. That's our choice to make, not yours," Mauritania said in a tone that ended the matter. "In any case, you and I have more important matters to consider."

"Such as, if you didn't send that assassin, who did? And why?"

Mauritania inclined his small, neat head. "I wasn't thinking of that. But, yes, it's a concern, and we'll discover all we can in the matter. Meanwhile, we've studied the notes of the research assistant, which you gave us. We find they coincide precisely, if sketchily, with Chambord's own data and reports. Nothing appears to have been forgotten or lost. Now that we have them, there should be no trouble from that direction. They've already been destroyed."

"Which will keep our activities nicely secret, as I told you," Bonnard said, a touch of colonial condescension in his certainty. He heard it and did not care. "But I'm not at all sure about allowing Zellerbach to live. I'd suggest—"

"And I," Mauritania cut him off, "suggest you leave Zellerbach to us. You must pay attention to greater dangers, such as the police investigation into the 'suicide' of Chambord's assistant. Under the circumstances, more than the police will be asking questions. How is the official probe into the suicide proceeding?"

The Mauritanian had pulled Bonnard back, and for a moment the captain fought his disgust. But on the other hand, the reason he was doing business with the underworld leader was that he needed someone tough and savvy, as relentless as himself. So what else should he expect? Besides, he saw the logic of the question.

He forced himself to sound more accommodating. "I've heard nothing. But after the assistant ran away when he spotted your men, he stopped for petrol. The people at the station reported the assistant had heard about Émile Chambord's death and was distraught, actually in tears. Devastating grief. That should give the motivation. He couldn't go on without his mentor."

"You know nothing more? Not even from your French army headquarters?"

"Not a word."

Mauritania considered. "That doesn't worry you?"

"No news is good news." Bonnard gave a cold smile at the cliché.

Mauritania's nose wrinkled with disgust. "That's a Western proverb as dangerous as it's stupid. Silence in a matter such as this is far from golden. A suicide is difficult to fake well enough to fool police detectives with any brains or experience, to say nothing of the Deuxième Bureau. I suggest you or your people find out what the police and secret service actually know about the assistant's death, and find out quickly."

"I'll look into it," Bonnard agreed grudgingly. He adjusted his weight, preparing to stand.

But Mauritania raised his small hand, and, with a sigh, Bonnard sank back down onto the low, hard chair.

"One more thing, Captain Bonnard. This friend of Zellerbach's . . . What do you know about him?"

Bonnard would soon be missed from work and wanted to leave. He controlled his impatience and said, "The man's name is Lieutenant Colonel Jonathan Smith. He's an old friend of Zellerbach's, a medical doctor, and was sent here by Zellerbach's family. At least that's what Smith told the hospital, and from what I've been able to learn from my other sources, it's accurate. Zellerbach and Smith grew up together in some place called Iowa." He had trouble pronouncing it.

"But from what you've also told me about the assassination attempt on Zellerbach at the hospital, this Dr. Smith acted more like a man with combat or police experience. You say he came to the hospital armed?"

"He did, and I agree his actions were far from medical."

"Possibly an agent? Placed in the hospital by someone who's unconvinced by our charade?"

"If Smith is, he's not CIA or MI6. I'm familiar with all their people in Europe and on the European desks at Langley and London SIS. He's definitely American, so unlikely Mossad or a Russian. And he's not one of ours. That I'd definitely know. My sources within American intelligence say he's simply an army research scientist assigned to a U.S. military medical research facility."

"Absolutely American?"

"The clothes, the manner, the speech, the attitude. Plus the confirmation by my contacts. My reputation on it."

"Perhaps he could be a Company man whom you don't know? Langley lies about such things. Their business is to lie. They've grown rather good at it."

"*My* contacts don't lie. Plus, he's in none of our files at military intelligence."

"Could he be an agent from an organization you don't know, or don't have sources to?"

"Impossible. What do you take us for? If the Second Bureau doesn't know any such organization, it doesn't exist."

"Very well." Mauritania nodded. "Still, we'd better continue to watch him, your people and mine." He rose in a single fluid motion.

With relief, Captain Bonnard struggled to his feet from the low chair. His legs felt nearly paralyzed. He had never understood why these desert people were not all cripples. "Perhaps," he said, massaging behind his knee, "Smith is nothing more than what he appears. The United States thrives on a culture of guns, after all."

"But he'd hardly be allowed to carry one to Europe on a commercial flight without some predetermined reason, and a very important one at that," Mauritania pointed out. "Still, perhaps you're right. There are ways to acquire guns here, too, including for foreigners, yes? Since his friend was the victim of violence, Smith may have come for revenge. In any case, Americans always seem to feel less vulnerable when they have a weapon. Rather silly of them."

Which left Captain Bonnard with the distinct impression that the enigmatic and occasionally treacherous terrorist chief did not think Bonnard was right at all.

●

On high alert, Jon Smith strolled toward the boulevard Pasteur, all the while pretending to look for a taxi to hail. He kept turning his head left and right, apparently studying the traffic for a potential ride, but really probing for whoever was out there watching him.

Automotive exhaust filled the air. He looked back toward the institute's entrance, where the guards were checking identifications. Finally he decided on three potentials: A youngish woman, mid-thirties or so, dark-haired, no figure to speak of, lumpy face. Altogether unremarkable in a dull black skirt and cardigan. She had stopped to admire the gloomy brick-and-stone church of Saint-Jean Baptiste de la Salle.

The second potential was a middle-aged, equally colorless man, wearing a dark blue sports coat and corduroy jeans, despite the warm May weather. He stood before a street vendor's cart, poring over the items as if he were looking for a lost masterpiece. The third person was a tall old man, leaning on a black ebony cane. He was standing in the shadow of a tree near the curb, watching the smoke at the Pasteur drift upward.

Smith had close to two hours before the meeting President Castilla had arranged with General Henze, the NATO commander. It would probably not take that long to lose whoever was interested in him, which meant maybe he could get some information first.

All this time, he had continued to pretend to be looking for a taxi. With a dramatic shrug of disgust, he walked onward toward the boulevard

Pasteur. At the intersection, he turned right, sauntering toward the bustling Hôtel Arcade with its glass, steel, and stucco facade. He glanced into store windows, checked his watch, and finally stopped at a café, where he chose an outside table. He ordered a *demi*, and when the beer arrived, he sipped and watched the passing parade with the relaxed smile of a recently arrived tourist.

The first of the trio to appear was the tall old man who had been leaning on his cane in the shadow of a tree, watching the smoke from the bombed building, which could be suspicious in itself. Criminals were known to be drawn back to the scene of an attack, although this man looked too old and disabled to have taken on the duties of a sneak bombing. He limped along, using the cane expertly, and found a seat at a café directly across the street from Smith. There he took a copy of *Le Monde* from his pocket and, after the waiter brought coffee and pastry, unfurled it. He read as he sipped and ate, apparently with no interest in Smith. In fact, he never looked up from his newspaper again.

The second to arrive was the lumpy-faced young woman with the dark hair and nondescript appearance, who suddenly was walking past the café not five feet from where Smith sat. She glanced directly at him and continued on without showing the faintest interest, as if he were simply empty space. Once past, she paused as if considering stopping for a drink, too. She seemed to dismiss the thought and moved on, disappearing into the crowded Hôtel Arcade.

The third person, the man who had been shopping with such concentration at the street vendor's cart, did not appear.

As he finished his beer, Smith replayed his observations of the tall old man and the nondescript woman—their facial features, the rhythm of their movements, the way they held their heads and used their hands and feet. He did not leave until he was certain he had memorized them.

Then he paid and moved briskly back along the boulevard toward the Pasteur métro station at the intersection with the rue de Vaugirard. The old man with the cane soon appeared behind, moving well for his age and apparent infirmity. Smith had seen him instantly. He monitored the fellow with his peripheral vision and continued to watch for anyone else who appeared suspicious.

It was time to use an old tradecraft trick: He ducked into the métro, watching. The man with the cane did not follow. Smith waited until a train pulled into the station, and then he joined the stream of passengers that was exiting back to the street. A block away, under the leaden sky, the old fellow was still walking along. Smith hurried after, keeping just close enough to observe, until the man turned into a bookstore with a GONE TO LUNCH sign in French posted in the glass door. Key in hand, he unlocked the door. Once inside, he turned the sign around to OPEN, dropped his cane into a stand by the door, and shrugged out of his suit coat.

There was no point in pressing the situation, Smith decided. After all, the fellow did have a key. On the other hand, he wanted to make certain. So he stopped outside the big plate-glass window and watched as the man shoved his arms into a beige sweater-vest and methodically buttoned it from the top down. When the man finished, he took a seat on a high stool behind the counter, looked up, saw Smith, and smiled and gestured for him to come in. He obviously either owned or worked at the bookstore. Smith felt a stab of deep disappointment.

Still, someone had been surveilling him, and he had narrowed the potentials to the dark-haired woman or the man who had been checking out the street vendor's wares. In turn, whichever of the two it was, he or she had also recognized Smith's suspicions and exited the chase.

He gave the bookseller a friendly wave and hurried back to the métro station. But then, with a sinking feeling, he felt the hairs on the back of his neck rise again. Someone was still nearby, studying him. Frustrated, worried, he stood outside the station and gazed all around. He saw nothing. He had to lose his tail. He could not lead them to his meeting with the general. He turned and rushed down into the station.

■

In a doorway partially shielded by a bush, the dull-looking woman in the shopkeeper's black outfit scrutinized Smith as he carefully surveyed the area. Her hiding place was recessed and dark, which was perfect, since it allowed her dusky clothing to disappear into the gloom. She took care to keep her face far back in the shadow, because although she was tan, the paler color of her skin might reflect just enough light for the very observant Smith to notice.

He looked uneasy and suspicious. He was handsome, with almost American Indian features—high cheekbones, a planed face, and very dark blue eyes. Right now the eyes were hidden behind black sunglasses, but she remembered the color. She shivered.

At last he seemed to make a decision. He hurried into the métro. There was no further doubt in her mind: He had realized he was being followed, but he did not know it was specifically she, or he would have followed after she passed his table outside the café and stared straight at him.

She sighed, irritated by the situation. It was time to report in. She pulled her cell phone from a pocket beneath her heavy black skirt. "He figured out he was being tailed, but he didn't make me," she told her contact. "Otherwise, he appears to be here really because he's worried about his injured friend. Everything he's done since he arrived is consistent with that." She listened and said angrily, "That's your call. If you think it's worthwhile, send someone else to tail him. I've got my own assignment. . . . No, nothing definite so far, but I can smell something big. Mauritania wouldn't have come here unless it was imperative. . . . Yes, *if* he's got it."

She clicked off the cell phone, looked carefully around, and slipped out of the shadows. Jon Smith had not reappeared from the métro, so she hurried back to the café where he had sat. She searched the pavement beneath the chair he had used. She nodded to herself, satisfied. There was nothing.

■

Smith made four changes of trains, returned rapidly to the street, and plunged back down again at two of the stations. He watched everywhere until, finally, after an hour of this, he was confident he had lost his tail. Relieved but still wary, he caught a taxi to the address Fred Klein had given him.

It turned out to be a private *pension* in an ivy-covered, three-story brick building on a small courtyard off the rue des Renaudes, secluded from the street and the bustle of the city. At her post inside the elegant front door, the concierge was as discreet as the building itself. A matronly woman with steel-trap eyes and a face that revealed nothing, she showed no reaction when he asked for M. Werner, but she came from behind her counter to lead him up the stairs with decidedly unmatronly movements. He suspected that more metal than just her house keys was hidden under her cardigan and apron.

He did not have to guess about the bantamweight sitting on a chair in the second-floor corridor, reading a Michael Collins detective novel. The concierge vanished back down the stairs like a magician's rabbit, and the small ramrod on the chair studied Smith's ID without getting up. He wore a dark business suit, but there was a bulge under his armpit that, all things considered, looked to Smith to be an old regulation-issue 1911 Colt semiautomatic. The man's stiff and precise mannerisms hinted at an invisible uniform that was all but tattooed to his skin. Obviously, he was a career enlisted man; an officer would have stood. In fact, he was a privileged enlisted man, to still be carrying the old Colt .45— probably a master sergeant for the general.

He returned Smith's ID, gave a slight nod of his bullet head as a salute to rank, and said, "What's the word, Colonel?"

"Loki."

The bullet head pointed. "The general's waiting. Third door down."

Smith walked to it, knocked, and when a guttural "Come in" sounded, he opened the door and stepped into a sunny room with a large window and a view of tangled, blooming gardens that Monet would have liked to paint. Standing inside was another bantamweight, but ten years older and forty pounds lighter than the one in the hallway. He was rail thin, his back turned to Smith as he stared out at the watercolor-perfect gardens.

As Smith closed the door, the general demanded, "What's going to happen with this new technology that's supposed to be out there somewhere, Colonel? Are we looking for a result on the order of a nuclear bomb, or is it more like a peashooter? Or maybe nothing at all? What are they planning?" Small as he was, his voice was six feet tall and should have belonged to a heavyweight. It was as rough as redwood bark and hoarse, probably from a youth spent bellowing orders over gunfire.

"That's what I'm here to find out, sir."

"You have a gut hunch?"

"I've been in Paris just a few hours. A would-be assassin has threatened me and Dr. Martin Zellerbach, who worked with Dr. Chambord, with an automatic weapon."

"I heard about that," the general admitted.

"I've also been tailed by someone who knows their job. Plus, of course, there's the incident at Diego Garcia. I'd say it's definitely not nothing."

The general turned. "That's all? No theories? No educated guesses? You're the scientist. An M.D. to boot. What should I be worrying about? Armageddon in the hands of sweet damn all, or just a schoolboy's bloody nose and our vaunted American ego bruised?"

Smith gave a dry smile. "Science and medicine don't teach us to theorize or make wild guesses in front of generals, sir."

The general brayed a laugh. "No, I suppose not."

General Carlos Henze, U.S. Army, was the Supreme Allied Commander of Europe (SACEUR) for NATO's combined forces. As wiry as a coiled spring, Henze wore his graying hair short, which, of course, was expected in the military. But it was not the boot-camp buzz affected by marine generals and other stiff-necks to show they were plain, nononsense soldiers who slogged through the muck like any other hero. Instead, his hair grew down to an inch above the collar of his immaculately tailored, charcoal-brown, two-piece suit, which he wore with the easy familiarity of the CEO of a *Fortune* 500 corporation. He was the new breed of general, integrated and fully prepared for the twenty-first century.

The general gave a crisp nod. "All right, Colonel. What say I tell you what *I* know, okay? Have a seat. That couch will do."

Smith sat on the ornate velvet couch from the time of Napoleon III, while the general returned to his window and bucolic view, his back again to Smith, who found himself wondering if this was Henze's way of focusing a roomful of division and regimental commanders on the matter at hand. It was a good trick. Smith thought he might try using it in one of the meetings with his notoriously disorganized fellow research scientists.

The general said, "So we've maybe got some kind of new machine that can access and control all the world's electronic software and hardware, including any country's codes, encryptions, electronic keys for launching missiles, command structures, and instructions. That about sum up what the gizmo will be able to do, assuming it exists?"

"For military purposes, yes," Smith agreed.

"Which is all that concerns me and, right now, you. History can handle the rest." His back still facing Smith, the general raised his gaze to the steely clouds that hid the May sky, as if wondering whether the sun would ever shine again. "Every sign is that the man who built it is dead, and his records are ash. No one claims responsibility for the bomb that killed him, which is unusual among terrorists but not unheard of." This time Henze simply stopped speaking, an almost imperceptible stiffening of his back and shoulders indicating he expected a response, either yes or no.

Smith repressed a sigh. "Yes, sir, except that we can add the probable assassin, affiliation unknown, who attempted to kill Dr. Zellerbach in the hospital this morning."

"Right." Now Henze turned. He stalked to a brocade chair, dropped into it, and glared at Smith as only a general could. "Okay, I've got some information for you, too. The president said I was to extend all help, and keep mum about you, and I'm not in the habit of ignoring orders. So this is what my people and the CIA have found out: The night of the explosion, a black van was seen parked behind the Pasteur annex on the rue des Volontaires. Just minutes before the explosion, it left the area. You know Chambord had a research assistant?"

"Yes. Last I heard, the French authorities were looking for him. He's been found?"

"Dead. Suicide. He killed himself last night in a miserable little hotel outside Bordeaux. He'd been vacationing in a village on the coast, painting the fishermen, of all fool things. According to one of the kid's Paris friends, Chambord had told him he was working too hard, take a vacation, and that's his idea of fun. These French. So what was he doing in a fleabag on the wrong side of the Garonne?"

"They're sure it was suicide?"

"So they say. The CIA tells me the owner of the fleabag remembers the assistant was carrying a briefcase when he checked in. He noticed, because it's more luggage than most of his so-called guests have. You know what I mean—it's that kind of 'hotel.' The deal was that the assistant was alone, no girlfriend, no boyfriend. And if he did have a briefcase, it's missing now."

"You figure the bombers hit again, made the murder look like a suicide, and then took the briefcase and whatever was in it."

Henze jumped up, paced, and marched back to his favorite post at the window. "Thinking about it is, the president tells me, *your* job. But I will say the CIA is of the opinion the suicide has a rank odor, even though the Sûreté seems satisfied."

Smith pondered. "The research assistant would've known Chambord's progress, but that alone wouldn't necessarily have been enough reason to kill him. After Chambord's death, and the rumors of success, we'd have to act as if Chambord built a working molecular machine anyway. So I'd say there had to be more reason. Most likely, the briefcase, as you suspect. The assistant's notes . . . maybe Chambord's own notes . . . something inside that they considered dangerous or critical."

"Yeah," Henze growled, and turned to give Smith a baleful stare. "So, because Diego Garcia happened, it looks like the bombers have the data for whatever Chambord created, which you think's an honest-to-God working molecular supercomputer—"

"A *prototype*," Smith corrected.

"What does that mean?"

"It's probably bulky, not easily portable. Glass and tubes and connections. Not yet the sleek commercial models we'll see in the future."

The general frowned. "The important question is, will it do the job?"

"With a competent operator, it sure looks like it."

"Then what's the difference? They have this damn thing, and we have *bubkes*. Now, ain't that a kick in the eye."

"Yessir. In fact, I'd say that was a serious mule kick."

Henze nodded soberly. "So get it out of my eye, Colonel."

"I'll do my best, General."

"Do better. I'm going to have my Deputy Commander at NATO— that's General La Porte to you—get in touch. He's a Frenchman. Their military is naturally concerned. Since this is their country, the White House wants to keep them feeling happy, but not give them any more than we absolutely have to, understand? La Porte has already been sniffing around about you and Dr. Zellerbach. I get the impression he senses he's being left out of the loop everywhere—that's the French again. I told him you're here as a friend of Dr. Zellerbach, but I can see he's skeptical. He's heard about that little fracas at the Pompidou Hospital, so be prepared for a bunch of personal questions, but stick to your story." Henze crossed to the door, opened it, and held out his hand. "Keep in touch. Whatever you need, call. Sergeant Matthias over there will walk you out."

Smith shook the iron hand. Out in the corridor, the short, stocky sergeant was not happy to leave his post. He opened his mouth to argue with the general—a career master sergeant, for sure—but caught his boss's eye and thought better of it.

Without a word, he escorted Smith down the stairs and past the concierge, who was smoking a Gitane behind her counter. As Smith passed, he spotted the butt of a 9mm pistol in the waistband of her skirt. Someone was taking no chances with the security around General Carlos Henze, U.S.A.

The sergeant stopped at the door, watching until Smith walked safely across the courtyard, through the archway that led to the street, and on out to the sidewalk. Smith paused beside a tree and gazed all around at the thick traffic, the few pedestrians . . . and his heart seemed to stop. He whirled.

He had caught a glimpse of a face in the backseat of a taxi as it turned from the street to the courtyard. Chilled, Smith counted to five and slipped back around to where he could get a view of the *pension's* entrance through bushes.

Although the fellow wore a hat, Smith had recognized the dark features, the thick mustache, and now he recognized the lean figure as well. It was the fake orderly who had gone to the hospital to kill Marty. The same man who had knocked Smith unconscious. He had just reached the *pension's* door. The same door through which Smith had left. The sergeant was still standing there. He stepped politely aside to let the killer enter. An utter professional, the sergeant looked protectively around, stepped back, and closed the door.

Chapter Seven

A heavy spring twilight settled like a darkening blanket on Seine-St-Denis on the north side of Paris, beyond the boulevard Périphérique. Smith paid his taxi driver and got out, smelling the metallic odor of ozone. The warm air was close, almost stifling with humidity, threatening rain.

Pausing on the sidewalk, he jammed his hands into his trench-coat pockets and studied a narrow, three-story beige brick apartment building. This was the address Mike Kerns had given him for Thérèse Chambord. The place was quaint, picturesque, with a peaked roof and decorative stonework, and it stood in a row of similar structures that had probably been constructed in the late fifties or early sixties. Her building appeared to be divided into three apartments, one to a floor. There were lights on in windows in each story.

He turned and surveyed the street, where cars were parked with two wheels up on the curbs in the French way. A sporty Ford cruised past, its headlights shooting funnels of white light into the dusk. The block was short, porch lights and street lamps glowed, and at the end, near an elevated rail service, rose an ultramodern, eight-story hotel of poured concrete, also painted beige, perhaps to blend in with the lower apartment buildings.

Wary, Smith turned on his heel and walked to the hotel. He stood in the lobby a half hour, cautiously watching through the glass walls, but no one followed him onto the street or into the hotel. No one went into or left Thérèse Chambord's building either.

He searched through the hotel until he found a service entrance that opened onto a cross street. He slipped out and hurried to the corner. Peering around, he saw no sign of surveillance at the lobby entrance or anywhere else in the neighborhood near Thérèse Chambord's apartment. There were few, if any, places to hide, except for the cars parked on both sides. But all appeared empty. With a nod to himself, he moved briskly back to Mlle. Chambord's address, still surveying all around.

In the recessed entryway, there was a white calling card with her name engraved on it, slid into the address slot for the third floor. He rang her bell and announced his name and purpose.

He rode the elevator up, and when it opened, she was standing in her open doorway, dressed in a slim white evening suit, a high-necked, off-white silk blouse, and high-heeled, ivory pumps. It was as if she were an Andy Warhol painting, white on white, with a violent and focusing touch of blood red in a pair of long, dangling earrings and again at her full lips. Then there was the contrast of her hair, satin black, suspended in an ebony cloud above her shoulders, theatrical and appealing. She was an actress all right. Still, her dramatic flair could also be the simple reflex of talent and experience.

A large black handbag hung over her left shoulder as if she were about to go out. He walked toward her.

She spoke flawless English, no trace of an accent. "I don't know what I can tell you about my father, or that poor man in the hospital they say might've been in his lab with him when . . . when the bomb exploded, Mr. . . . . Smith, is it?"

"Dr. Jon Smith, yes. Can you give me ten minutes? Dr. Zellerbach is a very old and close friend. We grew up together."

She studied her watch, biting her lower lip with small, incredibly white teeth, as she calculated in her head. At last she nodded. "All right, ten minutes. Come in. I have a performance tonight, but I'll forgo a few minutes of yoga."

The apartment was not what he expected from the building's quaint facade. Two walls were composed entirely of glass, giving it a very modern feel. On a third wall, tall glass doors opened onto a wraparound balcony with a railing of stark, geometric wrought-iron patterns.

On the other hand, the rooms were large but not enormous, with elegant period furniture from Louis Quatorze to Second Empire, haphazardly mixed and heavily packed into the room in the Parisian fashion that never seemed cluttered and somehow ended up being totally, and improbably, harmonious. Smith glimpsed two bedrooms through half-open doors as well as a small but efficient kitchen. Regal, warm, comfortable, and contemporary.

"Please." Her swift glance looked him up and down, and she motioned to a sturdy Second Empire love seat.

He smiled. She had weighed him in that glance and seated him accordingly. She leaned back in a more delicate Louis Quinze armchair. At a distance, standing in the doorway, she had seemed tall, a large and imposing woman, but once she was up close and seated, he realized she was barely five foot six. It was her presence that was large. She filled a doorway and a room. He guessed that onstage she could appear any size she wanted, as well as coarse or delicate, young or old. She projected an image that was larger than she, a sense of self that could control a stage as it did a living room.

He thanked her and asked, "Did you know Marty—Dr. Zellerbach—was working with your father?"

"Not for sure, no. My father and I were close, but we lived such busy and separate lives that we didn't see each other as much as we would've liked. We talked often on the telephone, though, and I recall he mentioned once he'd gotten the oddest and most wonderful collaborator—an eccentric recluse from America who suffered from an obscure autistic disorder. But the fellow was also a computer genius. He implied that this Dr. Z, as he called him, had simply walked in one morning, fresh from the airport, and volunteered to be part of the research. When Dad realized who he was, and what he could do, he showed him everything. Dr. Z was soon advancing Dad's work with the most original innovations. But that's all I know about your friend." She added, "I'm sorry."

She *was* sorry. Smith could hear it in her voice. Sorry for Marty, for her father, for herself, and for Smith. It was in her eyes, too, the impact of her father's shocking disappearance, the conclusion that it must mean he had been killed. An impact that left her walking in a mental limbo neither in the present nor in the past, but suspended between.

He saw pain in her eyes. "It's a lot harder for you," he said. "At least Marty has a good chance."

"Yes." She gave a vague nod. "I suppose that's true."

"Did your father say anything that led you to think someone might've wanted to murder him? Someone whom he was afraid might try to steal his work?"

"No. As I said, Dr. Smith, we saw each other infrequently, but even less so these last twelve months. In fact, we talked on the telephone less often, too. He was deeply immersed in his lab."

"Did you know what he was working on?"

"Yes, the DNA computer. Everyone knew what the project was. He hated secrets in science. He always said there was no place for such ego-centered nonsense."

"From what I've heard, that was true up until last year. Any idea what happened to change him?"

"No." There was no hesitation.

"What about new friends? Women? Envious colleagues? A need for money?"

She almost smiled. "Women? No, I think not. Of course, a child, especially a daughter, never knows for certain, but my father barely had time for my mother when she was alive, even though he was devoted to her. She knew that, and it enabled her to put up with her giant rival— his laboratory. Dad was, as you Americans would say, a workaholic. He had no need for money and never even spent his large salary. He had few friends, only colleagues. None was new or particularly envious that I knew about. But then, they had no reason to be. All his associates had great reputations of their own."

Smith believed her. The profile was prevalent among world-class scientists, especially the workaholic part. Enormous envy was unusual—their egos were far too big to envy anyone. Compete, yes. Competition was fierce, and nothing delighted them more than the false starts, wrong lines of reasoning, and errors of their rivals. But if a competitor got ahead on the same project, they would be far more likely to applaud—and then go to work improving on the other person's success.

He asked, "When you did talk to him, was there a hint he was close to the goal? A working prototype?"

She shook her head, and the cloud of long black hair resettled on her shoulders. "No. I'd remember that."

"How about your intuition? You say you and he were close."

She thought about it long enough to glance nervously at her watch. "There was a sense about him . . . a feeling of elation the last time we had lunch. We were at a bistro near the Pasteur."

"When?"

"Oh, perhaps three weeks ago, probably less." She looked at the watch again and stood up. "I really must go." She smiled at him, a bold, direct smile. "Would you like to come to the theater tonight? See the performance and perhaps talk over dinner later?"

Smith smiled in return. "I'd like nothing better, but not tonight. Rain check, as we Americans say?"

She chuckled. "You'll have to tell me the derivation of that phrase sometime."

"It'll be my pleasure."

"Do you have a car?"

Smith admitted he did not.

"May I drive you? I'll take you wherever you want." She locked the apartment door behind them, and they rode down in the elevator together.

In the intimate space, she smelled of spring lilacs. At the apartment building's front door, Smith pushed it open and gallantly held it.

In appreciation, Thérèse Chambord gave him a dazzling smile of the perfect white teeth. *"Merci beaucoup."* She walked through.

Smith watched her step into the dark night, elegant and composed in her white evening suit. It was one of those moments of personal enjoyment that he would not have minded lasting. He repressed a sigh, smiled at himself, and started to follow. He felt the motion before it actually registered. The door slammed back into him. Hard. Caught completely off guard, he skidded back and landed awkwardly on the floor.

Outside in the night somewhere, Thérèse Chambord screamed.

He yanked out his Sig Sauer, jumped back up to his feet, and rammed into the door, knocking it aside as if it were not there at all.

He hit the dark sidewalk running, looking everywhere for Thérèse. Beneath his feet, glass crunched. His head jerked up. Above him, the entry lights were shattered, and out along the curb, the street lamps had also been shot out. Whoever they were, they were thorough. They must have used silencers, or he would have heard the noise.

Gathering rain clouds blocked all moonlight and starshine. The whole street was dark, full of impenetrable shadows.

As his heart thudded against his ribs, Smith spotted four figures. From ski masks to athletic shoes, they were clothed completely in black and therefore almost invisible. They were heaving and wrestling a violently resisting Thérèse Chambord into an equally black van. She was a streak of white, tape across her mouth, as she valiantly tried to fight them off.

He altered course and put on a burst of speed, heading for the van and Thérèse. *Faster*, he told himself. *Faster!*

But as he neared, a single, silenced gunshot made a loud *pop* in the quiet night. A bullet whined past so close that it singed his cheek. His ear rang, and a for a long moment he thought his head was going to crack open with pain. He blinked furiously as he dove to the street, made himself roll and then spring up, the Sig Sauer poised out in front of him, ready to fire. A wave of nausea wracked him. Had he reinjured his head?

He blinked harder, forced himself to concentrate, and saw they had forced Thérèse Chambord into the van. He ran again, his feet pounding, fury shaking him. He raised his Sig Sauer and fired a warning shot into the ground at the feet of one of the men who were trying to kidnap Thérèse.

"Stop!" Smith bellowed. "Stop, or I'll kill you all!" His head throbbed. He kept blinking his eyes.

Two of the attackers spun expertly, crouched, and squeezed off rounds, forcing Smith to hit the ground again.

As he raised up, aiming the Sig Sauer, the pair leaped into the van next to Thérèse, while the third jumped into the passenger seat. The man in the passenger seat struggled to close the door as the van ground gears and sped backward out of the driveway. The side door was still open.

Smith aimed for the tires, squeezing off careful rounds. But there was a fourth man. As he ran alongside the van, preparing to leap inside through the open sliding door, the man fired back at Smith.

Two of the kidnapper's shots bit into the pavement, sending chunks of concrete thudding into the back of Smith's head. He swore, rolled away, and fired. His bullet hit the fourth man in the back just as he had turned to jump inside the van. Blood sprayed out into the dark air, and the man's body arched in a bow. His hand slid off where he gripped the door handle, and he fell screaming as the rear wheel powered over him.

Tires screeching, the van sped on out into the street and away. Smith chased after it, panting. As his feet hammered, his muscles began to ache. He ran and ran until his heart thundered and the van turned the corner and disappeared, a pair of red taillights the only sign that it existed and had not been part of some twisted nightmare.

He stopped and leaned over, gasping for breath. He propped his empty hand and his gun hand on his thighs as he tried to fill his lungs. He hurt all over. And Thérèse Chambord was gone. At last he caught his breath. He filled his lungs and stood upright in a pool of yellow lamplight. His gun hand dangled at his side. He closed his eyes and inhaled, mentally testing his head. His mind. It did not hurt, and he was no longer dizzy.

He was beginning to think he did have a mild concussion from the gunman this morning at the hospital. He would have to be more careful, but he was not going to stop.

Cursing, he ran back to where the fourth attacker lay facedown and unmoving on the dark Seine-St-Denis driveway, blood oozing out beneath. Smith checked him. He was dead.

Sighing, he searched the man's pockets. He found French coins, a wicked-looking clasp knife, a package of Spanish cigarettes, and a wad of loose facial tissues. No wallet, no identification. The dead man's pistol lay on the pavement near the curb. It was a battered, old-model Glock, but well oiled and cared for. He examined it, focusing on the butt. A leather skin had been shrunk around the original grip, for comfort or silence, or maybe just as a mark of individuality. Smith looked closer. A design had been tooled faintly into the leather: It was a spreading tree with three points of flame rising over the base of the trunk, consuming it.

Smith was studying it when police klaxons began to wail in the distance. He lifted his head, listening. He must not be found here. Pocketing the dead man's Glock, he hurried away.

∎

The Hôtel Gilles was on the Left Bank, not far from the colorful shops and restaurants of the boulevard Saint-Germain. A discreet little hotel, it was where he had stayed many times when visiting Paris. He entered the tiny lobby and headed to the nineteenth-century registration desk, set in a hand-crafted, wrought-iron gilt cage. With every step, he worried more about Thérèse Chambord.

The manager greeted him with a Gallic cry of recognition, an emotional hug, and a stream of rapid English. "Colonel Smith! So much delight! I am without speech. You will be with us for long?"

"It's good to see you, too, Hector. I may be here for weeks, but I'll be in and out. Keep the room in my name whether I'm here or not until I officially check out. Okay?"

"It is done. I refrain from examining the reservations, they are as nothing for you."

"*Merci beaucoup*, Hector."

In the pleasant although far-from-modern hotel room, he slung his bag and laptop onto the bed. Using his cell phone with its built-in scrambler, he dialed Fred Klein, waiting as the call bounced off innumerable relays around the world to finally be picked up wherever Fred was.

"So?" Fred Klein said.

"They've kidnapped Thérèse Chambord."

"I just got the news. One of her neighbors saw quite a bit of it, including some crazy man who tried to stop the kidnapping. The French police relayed the information. Fortunately, the neighbor didn't get a good look at the man's face."

"Fortunately," Smith agreed dryly.

"The police have no clue who the kidnappers are, or why, and it's got them mighty unhappy. Why kill Chambord but only kidnap his daughter? If the bombers have full data for the molecular computer, why kidnap her at all? Was she taken by the same people who blew up the Pasteur and killed Chambord, or by other people entirely? Are there two groups involved—one that has the data and another that wants it, so they've snatched Mlle. Chambord in the hope she has something to tell them?"

"That's an unpleasant thought. A second group. Damn."

"Hope I'm wrong." Klein sounded frustrated.

"Yeah. Swell. But we've got to keep it in mind. What about the police report about me and Thérèse Chambord? Do I need to take a new cover?"

"So far you're clear. They've questioned a taxi driver who took a man fitting your description to the Champs Élysées, where he got out and went into a nightclub. Luckily for us, no one in the nightclub recalls exactly what you look like, and of course you didn't give your name. The police have no other leads. Nice work."

"Thanks," Smith said tiredly. "I need some help with the meaning of a symbol I found: It's a tree with a broad canopy, and there are three flames burning at its base as if fire is about to consume it." He explained how he had found the picture tooled lightly into the kidnapper's leather pistol grip.

"I'll check on the image. How did your meetings with Mike Kerns and General Henze go?"

Smith relayed what he had learned from both men, including the black Citroën that periodically was seen picking up Chambord. "And there's something else you need to know. I hope it's not what it could be." He told the head of Covert-One about the "hospital orderly" who had been welcomed by the master sergeant into the highly secure *pension* where General Henze was staying.

Klein swore under his breath. "What the devil's going on? It can't mean the general's mixed up in anything. Not with his record. If it's anything more than some bizarre coincidence, I'd be shocked. But it's got to be looked into. I'll handle it from my end."

"Could the sergeant be a security problem? A mole of some kind?"

Klein's voice hardened. "That's unthinkable, too. You stay away from it. We don't want anything to hurt your cover. I'll have Sergeant Matthias investigated from this end, too, and I'll find out about that tree symbol." Klein clicked off.

Smith sighed, exhausted. He hoped an explanation of the tree graphic would lead him to Thérèse. With luck, the terrorists would not be far away. He moved his suitcase from the bed and pushed down on the familiar mattress. The bed was springy but firm in the French way, and he looked forward to spending some quality time in it, sleeping.

In the bathroom, he stripped off his clothes and plunged into the shower. It had been installed in the ancient tub since he was here last. Once he had washed off the trip and the exertions of the day, he wrapped himself in a terry-cloth robe, sat at the window, and pushed open the shutters so he could gaze out across the steepled rooftops of Paris.

As he sat there, his mind wandering and weary, the black sky suddenly split open with a bright bolt of lightning. Thunder crashed, and rain poured down. The storm that had threatened all day had finally arrived. He lifted his face outside his window and let the cool raindrops splash him. It was difficult to believe that only yesterday he had been in his laboratory at Fort Collins, the dawn rising over the sweeping prairies of eastern Colorado.

Which made him think of Marty. He closed the shutters. As the rain made a rhythmic tattoo, he dialed the hospital. If anyone was listening in, they would hear the concerned friend they expected, using the phone innocently. No suspicions nor subterfuge.

The ICU nurse told him Marty's condition was basically unchanged, but he was still showing small signs of progress. Feeling grateful, he said *bonsoir*, hung up, and dialed the hospital's security office. The chief was gone for the day, but an assistant reported nothing alarming or suspicious had happened involving either Marty or the ICU since the attempt on his life this morning. Yes, the police had increased the security.

Smith was beginning to relax. He hung up, shaved, and was about to climb into bed when his cell phone gave off its low buzz. He answered it.

Without preamble, Fred Klein reported: "The tree and fire are the emblem of a defunct Basque separatist group called the Black Flame. They were supposedly broken up years ago in a shootout in Bilbao where all their leaders were killed or, later, imprisoned. All but one of those locked up committed 'suicide' in prison. They haven't been heard from for years, and Basque terrorists usually claim responsibility for their acts. However, the more violent groups don't always. They're more focused on real change, not just propaganda."

"So am I," Smith said, and he added, "And I've got one advantage."

"What would that be?"

"They didn't really try to kill me. Which means they don't know what I'm actually doing here. My cover's holding."

"Good point. Get some sleep. I'll see if I can come up with anything more on your Basques."

"One more favor? Dig deeper into Émile Chambord's past, will you? His whole history. I've got a hunch something's missing somewhere, and maybe it's there. Or maybe it's something vital that he could tell us, if he were alive. Thérèse might know it, too, without realizing it, and that could be why she's been taken. Anyway, it's worth a shot." He hung up.

Alone in the darkened room, he listened to the sound of the rain and of tires on the wet street below. He thought about an assassin, a general, and a band of Basque fanatics who might be back in action with a vengeance. Fanatics with a purpose. With a deep sense of disquiet, he wondered where they would strike next, and whether Thérèse Chambord was still alive.

Chapter Eight

The hypnotic rhythms of a classical Indian raga floated on the hot, heavy air, trapped by the thick carpets and wall hangings that lined Mauritania's apartment. Seated cross-legged in the exact center of the main room, he swayed like a sinuous Buddha to the gentle yet strident sound. His eyes were closed, and a beatific smile wreathed his face. He sensed rather than saw the disapproving look of his lieutenant, Abu Auda, who had just entered.

"*Salaam alake koom.*" Mauritania's eyes remained closed as he spoke in Arabic while continuing to weave back and forth. "Forgive me, Abu Auda, it's my only vice. The classical Indian raga was part of a rich culture long before the Europeans developed what *they* claim to be classical music. I enjoy that fact nearly as much as the raga itself. Do you think Allah will forgive me for such indulgence and hubris?"

"Better him than me. All it is to me is distracting noise." Large and powerful-looking, Abu Auda snorted contemptuously. He was still in the same white robes and gold-trimmed kaffiyeh he had worn in the taxi when Captain Bonnard turned over to him the research notes of the dead lab assistant. Now, alas, the robes were not only dirty from too many days in the grime of Paris, but wet from the rainstorm. None of his women was in Paris to take care of him, which was irritating but could not be helped. He pushed back his kaffiyeh to reveal his long black face, strong, bony chin, small, straight nose, and full mouth set in stone. "Do you wish my report, or are you going to continue to waste my time?"

Mauritania chuckled and opened his eyes. "Your report, by all means. Allah may forgive me, but you won't, yes?"

"Allah has more time than we," Abu Auda responded, his expression humorless.

"So he does, Abu Auda. So he does. Then we'll have this oh-so-vital report of yours, shall we not?" Mauritania's eyes were amused, but beneath the surface was a glint that turned his visitor from complaints to the business at hand.

Abu Auda told him, "My watcher at the Pasteur Institute reports your person, Smith, appeared there. Smith spoke to Dr. Michael Kerns, apparently an old comrade. My man was able to hear only part of the conversation, when they were speaking of Zellerbach. After that, Smith left the Pasteur, drank a small beer at a café, and then took the métro, where our miserable incompetent lost him."

Mauritania interrupted, "Did he lose Smith, or did Smith lose him?"

Abu Auda shrugged. "I wasn't there. He did report a curious fact. Smith appeared to wander aimlessly until he reached a bookshop, where he watched for a time, smiled at something, continued on to the métro, and went down into the station."

"Ah?" Mauritania's blue eyes grew brighter. "As if, perhaps, he noticed he was being watched when he left the Pasteur?"

The green-brown eyes snapped. "I'd know more if my idiot hadn't lost him at the métro station. He waited too long to follow him down. By Allah, he'll pay!"

Mauritania scowled. "What then, Abu?"

"We didn't find Smith again until tonight, when he arrived at the daughter's home. Our man there saw him, but we don't believe Smith knew. Smith was upstairs in her apartment nearly fifteen minutes, and then they rode down in the elevator together. As soon as she stepped outside, four assailants attacked. Ah, the fine quality of their work! Would to God they were ours. They eliminated Smith from the action first inside the door, separating him from the woman, and then they dragged the woman away. By the time Smith recovered and came after them, they had her inside the van, even though she fought them hard. He killed one, but the rest escaped. Smith inspected the dead man, took his pistol, and left before the police arrived. He found a taxi at a nearby hotel. Our man trailed him to the Champs Élysées, where he also lost him."

Mauritania nodded, almost with satisfaction. "This Smith doesn't want to become involved with the police, is suspicious of being followed, skilled at eluding a tail, is calm under attack, and can use a pistol well. I'd say our Dr. Smith is more than he seems, as we suspected."

"At the very least, he's got military training. But is Smith our main concern? What of the daughter? What of the five men, for there must've been a driver in the van? Weren't you concerned about the daughter before this happened? Now people we don't know, and who are experienced and well trained, have kidnapped her. It's disturbing. What do they want? Who are they? What danger are they to us?"

Mauritania smiled. "Allah has answered your wish. They're ours. I'm glad you approve of their skills. Obviously, it was wise of me to hire them."

Abu Auda frowned. His gaze narrowed. "You didn't tell me."

"Does the mountain tell the wind everything? You had no need to know."

"With time, even the mountain can be destroyed by the elements."

"Calm yourself, Abu Auda. This was no reflection on you. We have a long and honorable history together, and now, at last, we're in a position to show the world the truth of Islam. Who else would I want to share that with? But if you'd known about these men I hired, you would've only wanted to be with them. Not with me. I need you, as you well know."

Abu Auda's frown disappeared. "I suppose you're right," he said grudgingly.

"Good. Of course I am. Let's return to the American, Jon Smith. If Captain Bonnard is correct, then Smith belongs to no known secret service. For whom, precisely, does he work?"

"Could our new allies have sent him? Some plan of their own they haven't bothered to tell us? I don't trust them."

"You don't trust your dog, your wives, or your grandmother." Mauritania gave a small smile and contemplated his music. He closed his eyes a moment as the raga rhythm subtly altered. "But you're right to be careful. Treachery is always possible, often inevitable. Not only a wily desert Fulani can be devious."

"There's another thing," Abu Auda went on as if he had not heard. "The man I assigned to watch the Pasteur Institute says he can't be certain, but he thinks there was someone else watching not only Smith but *him*. A woman. Dark-haired, young, but unattractive and poorly dressed."

Mauritania's blue eyes snapped open. "Watching both Smith *and* our man? He has no idea who she was?"

"None."

Mauritania uncoiled and stood up. "It's time to leave Paris."

Abu Auda was surprised. "I don't like going away without knowing more about Smith and this unknown female who watches us."

"We expected attention, didn't we? We'll observe and be careful, but we must also move. Relocation is the best defense."

Abu Auda smiled, displaying a dazzling set of white teeth against his black skin. "You sound like a desert warrior yourself. Perhaps you learn after all these years."

"A compliment, Abu?" Mauritania laughed. "An honor indeed. Don't worry about Smith. We know enough, and if he's actually searching for us, we'll deal with him on our terms. Report to our friends that Paris has become too crowded, and we're moving early. It may be necessary to adjust our timetable forward. Beginning now."

The giant warrior nodded as he followed the small terrorist, who glided from the room, his feet seeming barely to touch the carpet, soundless.

Folsom, California

The attack began at six P.M. in the headquarters of the California Independent System Operator (Cal-ISO) in the small prison town of Folsom, east of Sacramento. Cal-ISO was an essential component of the state's power system and integral to the movement of electricity throughout California. Although it was May, Californians were already worrying that summer might bring the return of rolling blackouts.

One of the operators, Tom Milowicz, stared at the dials of the big grid. "Jesus Christ," he breathed.

"What is it?" Betsy Tedesco glanced his way.

"The numbers are spinning south. Into the toilet!"

"What are you saying?"

"It's too much, too fast. The grid's going to crash! Get Harry!"

Arlington, Virginia

In a secret installation across the Potomac River from the nation's capital, the elite computer specialists of the FBI cyber team quickly determined the catastrophe to be the work of a hacker, country of origin still undetermined. Now they battled to bring the California power grid back online and stop the hacker's progress. But as the team discovered, it was already too late.

The hacker had written—"compiled"—software that allowed him or her to shatter the tough firewalls that usually protected the most sensitive parts of the Cal-ISO power system. He had bypassed trip wires, which were intended to alert security personnel to unauthorized entry, had bypassed logs that pinpointed intruders while they were committing an illegal infiltration, and had opened closed ports.

Then the extraordinarily adept hacker had moved on, invading one power supplier after another, because Cal-ISO's computers were linked to a system that controlled the flow of electricity across the entire state. In turn, the California system was tied into the transmission grid for the whole Western United States. The invader hacked from system to system with phenomenal speed. Unbelievable, to anyone who did not witness it.

Lights, stoves, air conditioners, heaters, cash registers, computers, ATMs, breathing devices—all machines, from luxury to life-giving, as long as they required electricity—went dead as power to Seattle, San Francisco, Los Angeles, San Diego, and Denver suddenly ceased.

Outside Reno, Nevada

The battered old Chrysler Imperial of Ricky Hitomi rocked with the shrieks and laughter of his five best friends as it powered down the rural blacktop through the night. They had met at his girlfriend Janis Borotra's house and smoked a few joints in the barn before all piling into Ricky's heap. Now they were heading for more fun at Justin Harley's place. They were high-school seniors and would graduate in a week.

Occupied with their wild partying, their minds dulled with weed, none saw or heard the fast-moving freight train in the distance. Nor did they notice that the gate at the crossing was still up, the warning lights dark, and the alarm bells silent. When Janis finally heard the screaming train whistle and shrieking brakes, she shouted at Ricky. It was too late. Ricky was already driving onto the rail crossing.

The freight train blasted into them and carried the car and their battered bodies a mile before it could stop.

Arlington, Virginia

Panic spread in the secret FBI cyber installation across the Potomac River from the nation's capital. A decade ago, the nation's telephones, power grids, and emergency 911 number and fire dispatches had been separate systems, individual, unique. They could be hacked, but only with great difficulty, and certainly the hacker could not get from one system to another, except under very unusual circumstances.

But deregulation had changed all that. Today hundreds of new energy firms existed, as well as online power traders, and everything was linked through the multitude of telephone companies, whose interconnections also had resulted from deregulation. This vast number of electronically joined entities looked a lot like the Internet, which meant the best hackers could use one system as a door to another.

Defeated by the power and speed of the hacker, the FBI experts watched helplessly as switches flipped and the violent mischief continued. The velocity at which firewalls were breached and codes blown shocked them. But the worst aspect of the nightmare was how quickly the hacker could adjust his access code.

In fact, it seemed almost as if their counterattack caused his code to evolve. The more they fought him and his computer, the smarter his computer became. They had never seen anything like it. It was impossible . . . horrifying. A machine that could learn and evolve far faster than a human thought.

Denver, Colorado

In her penthouse atop the opulent twenty-story Aspen Towers apartment building, Carolyn Helms, founder and CEO of Saddle Leather Cosmetics for Western Men, was entertaining her business associates at an intimate birthday dinner—her forty-second. It was a joyous occasion. She had made them a lot of money, and they were a great team, anticipating an even more exciting and lucrative future.

Just as her longtime close friend and executive vice president George Harvey toasted her for the third time, she gasped, clutched her heart, and collapsed. George fell to his knees to check her vital signs. Her treasurer, Hetty Sykes, called 911. George began CPR.

The paramedic rescue team of the Denver Fire Department arrived within four minutes. But as they rushed into the building, the lights went off and the elevators froze. The building was in complete darkness. In fact, from what they could tell, the whole city was. They searched for the stairs. As soon as they found them, they began the long run up twenty stories to the penthouse.

By the time they arrived, Carolyn Helms was dead.

Arlington, Virginia

Phones rang in the secret Virginia headquarters of the cyber crime squad.

Los Angeles: "What in hell happened?"

Chicago: "Can you fix it? Are we *next?*"

Detroit: "Who's behind it? Find out pronto, you hear? You'd better not let this happen in our court!"

One of the FBI team shouted to the room: "The main attack came through a server in Santa Clara, California. I'm tracking back!"

Bitterroot Mountains on the Border Between Montana and Idaho

A Cessna carrying a party of hunters home with their meat and trophies landed neatly between the double row of blue lights that marked the rural strip. The Cessna turned and taxied toward a lighted Quonset hut, where hot coffee and bourbon were waiting. Inside the little plane, the hunters were cracking jokes and recounting the successes of their trip when suddenly the pilot swore.

"What in hell—?"

Everywhere they could see, all electric lights had disappeared—the runway, the little terminal, the Quonset hut, the shops and garages. Suddenly there was a noise, hard to distinguish over the sound of their own plane's engine. Then they saw it: A landing Piper Cub, owned by a bush pilot, had veered off course in the darkness. The Cessna pilot pulled hard on his stick, but the Piper was going so fast there was no escape.

At impact, the Piper burst into flames and ignited the Cessna. No one survived.

Arlington, Virginia

A dozen FBI computer forensics specialists were analyzing the initial attack against Cal-ISO, looking for signs of the hacker. The cyber sleuths scanned their screens as their state-of-the-art software analyzed for footprints and fingerprints—the trail of hits and misses all hackers left behind. There were none.

As they labored, power returned inexplicably, without warning. The FBI team watched their screens with disbelief as the Western states' massive complex of power plants and transmission lines throbbed back to life. Relief spread through the room.

Then the chief of the cyber team swore at the top of his lungs. "He's breaking into a telecommunications satellite system!"

Paris, France
Wednesday, May 7

A harsh buzzing shattered Smith's instantly forgotten dream. He grabbed his Sig Sauer from under his pillow and sat up, alert, in a pitch-black room filled with alien odors and misplaced shadows. There was a faint spattering of rain outside. Gray light showed around the drapes. Where was he? And then he realized the buzz came from his cell phone, which rested on his bedside table. Of course, he was in his hotel room, not far from the boulevard Saint-Germain.

"Damnation." He snatched up the phone. Only one person would call at this hour. "I thought you told me to get some sleep," he complained.

"Covert-One never sleeps, and we operate on D.C. time. It's barely the shank of the evening here," Fred Klein told him airily. As he continued, his tone grew grave: "I've got unfortunate news. It looks as if Diego Garcia wasn't an atmospheric glitch or any other malfunction. We've been hit again."

Smith forgot his rude awakening. "When?"

"It's still going on." He told Smith everything that had happened since Cal-ISO went offline. "Six kids are dead in Nevada. A train hit their car because the crossing signal was out. I've got a stack of notices here of civilians who were hurt and killed because of the blackout. There'll be more."

Smith thought. "Has the FBI traced the attack back?"

"Couldn't. The hacker's defenses were so swift it seemed as if his computer was learning and evolving."

Jon's chest tightened. "A molecular computer. Can't be anything else. And they've got someone who can operate it. Check whether any computer hackers are missing. Get the other agencies on it."

"Already have."

"What about Chambord and his daughter? Do you have anything for me?"

"In my hand. His bio, but it doesn't seem useful."

"Maybe you've missed something. Give me the highlights."

"Very well. He was born in Paris. His father was a French paratroop officer, killed during the siege at Dien Bien Phu. His mother was Algerian and raised him alone. He showed a genius for math and chemistry early, went through all the best French schools on scholarships, did his doctoral work at Cal Tech, postdoc at Stanford under their leading geneticist, and post–post doc at the Pasteur Institute. After that, he held professional positions in Tokyo, Prague, Morocco, and Cairo, and then returned about ten years ago to the Pasteur. As for his personal life, his mother raised him as a Muslim, but he showed little interest in religion as an adult. Hobbies were sailing, single-malt Scotch whiskies, hiking in the countryside, and gambling, mainly roulette and poker. Not much of Islam in there. That help?"

Smith paused, thinking. "So Chambord was a risk-taker, but not extreme. He liked his little relaxations, and he didn't mind change. In fact, it sounds as if he could be restless. Certainly he wasn't bogged down by a need for stability or continuity, unlike a lot of scientists. He trusted his own judgment, too, and could make big leaps. Just the characteristics one wants in fine theoretical and research scientists. We already knew he didn't especially follow rules and procedures. It all fits. So what about the daughter? Is she the same type?"

"An only child, close to her father, especially since her mother's death. Science scholarships exactly like her father, but not with his early brilliance. When she was about twenty, she was bitten by the acting bug. She studied in Paris, London, and New York, and then worked in provincial French towns until she finally made a splash in live theater in Paris. I'd say her personality's a lot like Chambord himself. Unmarried, apparently never even been engaged. She's been quoted as saying, 'I'm too single-minded about my work to settle down with anyone outside the business, and actors are wrapped up in themselves and unstable, just as I probably am.' That's Chambord all over again—modest, realistic. She's had plenty of admirers and boyfriends. You know the drill."

Smith smiled in the dark room at Klein's primness. It was one of the odd quirks about the lifelong clandestine operative. Klein had seen or done just about everything anyone could, was nonjudgmental, but drew the line at discussing anything remotely graphic about people's sexual behavior, despite being quite ready to send a Juliet agent to seduce a target, if that's what had to be done to get what was needed.

Smith told him, "That fits my assessment of her, too. What it doesn't fit is her kidnapping. I've been thinking about her being able to operate a prototype DNA computer. If she's been out of science for years and hasn't seen much of her father in months, then why did they want her?"

"I'm not cer—" Klein's voice abruptly vanished, cut off in mid-word.

The silence in Smith's ear was profound. A void that almost reverberated. "Chief?" Smith was puzzled. "Chief? Hello! Fred, can you hear me?"

But there was no dial tone, no buzz, no interruption signal. Smith took the cell phone from his ear and examined it. The battery was live. The charge was full. He turned it off, turned it on, and dialed Klein's private number at Covert-One in Washington, D.C.

Silence. Again, there was no dial tone. No static. Nothing. What had happened? Covert-One had innumerable backup systems for power fail-ures, enemy interference, satellite blackout, sunspot interference. For everything and anything. Plus, the connection was routed through the top-secret U.S. Army communications system run out of Fort Meade, Maryland. Still, there was nothing but silence.

When he tried other numbers and continued to be unable to get through, he powered up his laptop and composed an innocent-sounding e-mail: "*Weather abruptly changing. Thunder and lightning so loud you can't hear yourself speak. How are conditions there?*"

As soon as he sent it off, he pulled back the drapes and opened the shutters. Immediately, the fresh scent of the rain-washed city filled the room, while pale, predawn light formed a backdrop for the dramatic sky-line. He wanted to stay and enjoy the view, the sense of newness, but too much was preying on his mind. He pulled on his bathrobe, dropped the Sig Sauer into the pocket, and returned to the computer, where he sat again at the desk. An error message stared at him from his screen. The server was down.

Shaking his head, worried, he dialed his cell phone again. Silence. He sat back, his anxious gaze moving around the room and then back to his laptop's screen.

Diego Garcia's communications.

The Western power grid.

Now the U.S. military's ultrasecret, ultrasecure wireless communica-tions.

All had failed. Why? The first salvos from whoever had Chambord's DNA computer? Tests to make certain it worked, and that they, whoever "they" were, could control the machine? Or perhaps, if the world was lucky, this shutdown was caused by an exceptionally good hacker on an ordinary silicon computer.

Yeah. He really believed *that*.

If those who had the DNA computer were suspicious of him, then they might be able to track him here through his cell phone conversation with Fred Klein.

He jumped up, dressed, and threw clothes into his overnight bag. He repacked his laptop, holstered his Sig Sauer, and, grabbing his luggage, he left. As he trotted down the stairs, he watched and listened, but there was no sign anyone else in the hotel was awake so early. He sped past the deserted front desk and slipped out the door. Paris was beginning to awaken. He moved quickly along the narrow side street. He scanned every doorway, studied the dark windows that watched him like the hundred eyes of a Greek monster, and finally blended into the growing traffic and few pedestrians on the boulevard Saint-Germain.

Eventually he was able to hail a sleepy taxi driver who delivered him to the Gare du Nord rail station, where he checked his suitcase and laptop. Still watching all around, he took a different taxi to the Pompidou Hospital to visit Marty. As soon as the wireless communications were up and running again, he knew Fred Klein would be in touch.

Chapter
Nine

In her usual battered flat shoes and dowdy clothes, the dark-haired woman walked timidly along the exotic Paris street, redolent in the early morning with the odors of North Africa and the Middle East.

As she peered up, Mauritania stepped from his building's vestibule. The diminutive terrorist was dressed in a loose raincoat and light corduroy trousers, looking like any Parisian workman. He glanced at her, and in that glance was the eagle eye of two decades of on-the-run experience. It missed little. Since her clothes were properly faded and cared-for, the flat shoes patched by a cheap repair shop, and the battered handbag that of a woman three times her age, as would be expected in a young but frightened soul, Mauritania was reassured. In his usually cautious way, he rounded several corners and doubled back, but the woman never appeared again. Satisfied, he entered the métro.

The woman had followed Mauritania through the first few turns, until his maneuvers convinced her he would be gone long enough for her purposes. She hurried back to his building, where the windows remained unlighted and showed no sign of activity. She picked the front-door lock, climbed the stairs to the third-floor apartment where Mauritania was staying, and picked that lock as well.

She stepped into what first appeared to be a tent in the wilds of Arabia or the heart of the Sahara. The rugs seemed to shift under her feet as if resting on sand. Carpets on the walls and ceiling closed claustrophobically in on her, and the rugs over the windows explained the dark windows at all times of the day and night. Amazed, she remained unmoving for some time, taking it all in, until she finally shook her head and went to work. Listening to be certain she was alone, she methodically searched every square inch of the rooms.

∎

In the Pompidou Hospital, Smith sat beside the still-unconscious Marty, who lay small and frail in the muted light of the ICU. Outside the cubicle, a man in plainclothes had joined the pair of uniformed gendarmes. Marty's sheets and blankets were still smooth, as if he had not stirred in days. But that was far from true. Marty was occasionally moving on his own, and meanwhile therapists were coming in regularly to work with him.

Smith knew all this, because as soon as he had arrived, he checked Marty's computer chart. The chart also showed that his physical condition was continuing to improve. In fact, Marty would likely be moved from the ICU soon, even though he remained in a coma.

"Hi, Marty." Smith smiled at him, took his hand, which was warm and dry, and again reminisced, recalling their childhoods, the years growing up together, and college. He covered the same territory as before, but with more details, because as he recounted the past, it grew more vivid in his own mind. As he was chatting, filling the time while, more important, trying to stimulate Marty's brain, he had an idea.

"The last time we had a good long talk," Smith said, "you were still at home in Washington." He studied the sleeping features. "I heard you boarded an airplane and flew over here by yourself. Man, was I impressed. The only way I could convince you to even get near a plane was when we had trigger-happy gunmen on our tails. Remember? And now here you are, in Paris."

He waited, hoping the name of the city would elicit a response. But Marty's face remained listless.

Smith continued, "And you've been working at the Pasteur."

For the first time, he saw Marty rouse. It was almost as if a wave of energy passed through him when he heard the word *Pasteur*. His eyelids fluttered.

"I'll bet you wonder why I know all this," Smith continued, hope growing inside him. "The daughter of Émile Chambord—"

Marty's chin quivered at the mention of the scientist's name.

"—told me you arrived unannounced at her father's lab. Just walked right in and volunteered to help."

Marty's lips seemed to shape a word.

Excited, Smith leaned close. "What is it, Marty? I know you want to tell me something. It's about the Pasteur and Dr. Chambord, isn't it? Try, Marty. *Try*. Tell me what happened. Tell me about the DNA computer. *You can do it!*"

Marty's mouth opened and closed. His chubby face flushed. He was struggling to assemble thoughts and words, the effort straining his whole body. Smith had seen this in other coma victims. Sometimes they awoke quickly, all their faculties intact; other times it was a rebuilding process. For some, it was slow, for others, faster, much as if they were retraining a muscle that had been weakened by lack of use.

Just then, Marty gave Smith's hand a squeeze. But before Smith could squeeze back, Marty went limp, his face exhausted. It was all over in seconds, the struggle valiant but apparently too overwhelming for the injured man. Smith silently cursed the bomber, cursed whoever was behind all the violence. Then, as he sat there holding Marty's hand, he resumed talking again. The antiseptic quiet of the room was broken only by his low voice and the inhuman clicks and whirs of machines, the blinking and flashing of LEDs and gauges. He continued on, working the key words into his conversation: Émile Chambord. The Pasteur Institute.

A woman spoke behind him. "M. Smith?"

He turned. "*Oui?*"

It was the nurse from the ICU front desk, and she held out a plain but expensive white envelope. "This is for you. It arrived not long ago, but I've been so busy I forgot you were here. I'm sorry. If I'd remembered, you could've spoken to the messenger yourself. Apparently, whoever wrote you has no idea where you're staying."

Smith thanked her and took the envelope. As she returned to the front desk, he tore it open. The message was simple and to the point:

Lt. Col. Dr. Smith,

General the Count Roland la Porte will be at his Paris home this morning. He requests you report to him at your convenience. Please call me at the following telephone number to name the hour you will arrive. I will give you directions to the general's home.

Captain Darius Bonnard

Aide-de-Camp to the General

Smith remembered that General Henze had told him to expect an invitation to talk with the French general. This polite summons must be it. From what Henze had said, it sounded as if General La Porte was in the loop with the local police and the Deuxième Bureau about both the bombing and Émile Chambord. With luck, he might be able to throw more light on Dr. Chambord and the elusive DNA computer.

▪

A large part of the grandeur of Paris arose from its magnificent private residences, many of which were tucked on side streets under branching trees near the boulevard Haussmann. One of those fine houses, it turned out, belonged to General Roland la Porte. Built of gray stone, it was five stories tall, fronted by a baronial columned entrance, and surrounded by balustrades and fine decorative stonework. It looked as if it had been built in the 1800s, during the sweeping imperial reconstruction of Paris by Baron Georges-Eugène Haussmann. In those days, it would have been called a town mansion.

Jon Smith used the old-fashioned knocker. The door was heavy and carved, the brass fittings gleaming.

The man who answered the door wore a paratrooper's uniform with the rank of captain and the insignia of the French general staff. He decided in crisp English, "You must be Lieutenant Colonel Jonathan Smith. You've made good time. Please come in." Short, blond, and compact, he stood aside and gestured Smith to enter. "I'm Darius Bonnard." He was all business, definitely military style.

"Thank you, Captain Bonnard. I guessed as much." As instructed, he had called ahead, and Bonnard gave him directions.

"The general's taking his coffee now. He's asked that you join him."

The captain led him through a spacious entry foyer, where a graceful staircase curved upward to the second and third floors. They passed through a European-style doorway that had no frame and was wallpapered in the same French fleur-de-lis pattern as the grand entry. The room Smith entered was large, with a high ceiling on which were painted life-sized nymphs and cherubs on a pale blue background. There were gilded cornices, handsome moldings and wainscoting, and slender, delicate Louis Quatorze furniture. The place looked more like a ballroom than a coffee room.

A hulking man was sitting by the window, sunbeams dancing above his head. Nodding Smith to a simple straight chair with a brocaded seat, he said in good but accented English, "Sit over there, if you will, Colonel Smith. How do you take coffee?"

"Cream, no sugar, sir, thank you."

General the Count Roland la Porte wore an expensive business suit that would have been large on a defensive end in the NFL, but it fit him perfectly. Besides his great girth, he had a regal bearing, dark, thick hair worn as long and straight as that of a young Napoleon at the siege of Toulon, and a broad Breton face with piercing blue eyes. The eyes were remarkable, as immobile as a shark's. Altogether, his presence was formidable.

"My pleasure," he said, smoothly polite. His oversized hands dwarfed the sterling coffee service as he poured and handed a bone-china cup to Smith.

"Thank you, General." Smith took it and said shamelessly, "It's a privilege to meet one of the heroes of Desert Storm. Your flanking maneuver with the French Fourth Dragoons was bold. Without it, the allies never would've been able to secure the left flank." Smith silently thanked Fred Klein for the thorough briefing he had received before he flew out of Colorado, because while he was in Iraq patching up the wounded on all sides, he had never heard of La Porte, who had been a lieutenant colonel back in those days.

The general asked, "You were there, Colonel?"

"Yessir. With a surgical unit."

"Ah, of course." La Porte smiled at a memory. "Our tanks had not been camouflaged for the western Iraqi desert, so we French stood out like polar bears. But the Dragoons and I held our ground, ate the sand, as we say in the Legion, and turned out to be most lucky." He studied Smith. "But you understand all that, don't you? In fact, you have had combat experience, yes? Line command also, I think."

So La Porte had his people looking into him, as General Henze had warned. "Only briefly, yes. Why do you ask?"

The general's unblinking blue eyes fixed him like a butterfly on a pin and then retreated, still unblinking, but with a small smile. "Forgive me. It's an old soldier's vanity. I pride myself on my judgment of people. I guessed your training and experience from your carriage, your movements, your eyes, and your action at the Pompidou Hospital yesterday." La Porte's unmoving gaze peeled layers from his skin. "Few would have your unusual combination of medical and scientific expertise, and the skills and daring of a soldier."

"You're far too kind, General." Also too nosy, but then, as General Henze had said, La Porte was suspicious that something was up, and he had the interests of his country to protect.

"Now to something far more important. Has there been any change in your friend's condition at the hospital?"

"Not so far, General."

"And what is your honest prognosis?"

"As a friend or as a doctor?"

A tiny furrow of annoyance appeared between the general's hard eyes. He did not like fencing or hair-splitting. "As a friend *and* as a doctor."

"As a doctor, I'd say that his coma indicates his prognosis must be considered guarded. As a friend, I know he will recover soon."

"Your sentiments as a friend are, I'm sure, shared by all. But I fear it's your medical opinion we value most. And that doesn't give me confidence we can rely on Dr. Zellerbach to help us with information about Dr. Chambord."

"I think that's wise," Smith agreed regretfully. "Tell me, is there any news about Dr. Chambord? I checked the newspaper as I rode over in the taxi, but it said that as of last night, there were no new facts."

The general grimaced. "Unfortunately, they have found a part of his body, alas." He sighed. "I understand there was an arm with an attached hand. The hand wore a ring his colleagues sadly identified, and the fingerprints have been confirmed as a match with those on file at the Pasteur. That won't be in the newspapers for a few days. The officials are still investigating, and they're keeping as much to themselves as they can for now. They hope to find the perpetrators without giving away everything. I'd appreciate your keeping that information to yourself."

"Of course." Smith contemplated the sad confirmation that Émile Chambord was indeed dead. What a pity. Despite every sign to the contrary, he had held out hope that the great scientist had survived.

The general had been silent, as if considering the frailty of the human condition. "I had the honor of meeting your Dr. Zellerbach. Such a shame that he's injured. I'd be devastated if he doesn't recover. I'd appreciate your conveying that to his family in America, should the worst occur."

"I'd be happy to. May I ask how you met Dr. Zellerbach, General? I wasn't aware myself that Marty was even in France or at the Pasteur."

The general seemed surprised. "Didn't you think our military would be interested in Dr. Chambord's research? Of course they were. Intensely interested, in fact. Émile introduced Dr. Zellerbach to me during my last visit to his lab. Naturally, Émile would not allow any of us to just drop by. He was a dedicated and busy man, so an invitation was a grand event. That was two months ago or so, and your Dr. Zellerbach had just arrived. It's a pity about Émile's work being destroyed in that wretched bombing. Do you think any of it survived?"

"I have no personal knowledge, General. Sorry." Two could play the fishing game. "I suppose I'm surprised you'd involve yourself personally. After all, you've got a great many important responsibilities at NATO."

"I'm still French, no? Besides, I knew Émile personally for many years."

"And was he close to success?" Smith asked, careful to keep his voice neutral. "A practical, working DNA computer?"

La Porte tented his fingers. "That's the question, isn't it?"

"It could be the key to who planted the bomb and why. No matter what happens to Marty, I want to do what I can to help catch the bastard who injured him."

"A true friend." La Porte nodded. "Yes, I'd like the miscreant punished, too. But, alas, I can be of little help to you there. Émile was close-mouthed about his work. If he had made a—how do you Americans say it?—'breakout,' he didn't inform me. Nor did Dr. Zellerbach or poor Jean-Luc Massenet tell me or anyone else, as far as we know."

"The research assistant? That was terrible. Have the police formed an opinion of why he killed himself?"

"A tragedy, too, to have lost that young man. Apparently, he was devoted to Émile, and when Émile died, he was cast adrift. He could not face life alone. At least that's what I've been told. Knowing the charismatic power of Émile's personality, I can almost understand the lad's suicide."

"So what's your take on the bombing, General?"

La Porte gave the Gallic gesture of confusion—a shrug with hands spread and head tilted. "Who knows what raving lunatic would do such a thing? Or perhaps it was some perfectly sane man with some personal hatred of science, or of L'Institut Pasteur, or even of France, to whom the bombing of a crowded building seemed a thoroughly reasonable response." La Porte shook his large head, disgusted. "There are times, Colonel, when I think the patina of civilization and culture we all profess to share is cracking. We return to the barbarians."

"The French police and Secret Service know no more than that?"

La Porte repeated his mannerism of tenting his long fingers. His unblinking blue eyes regarded Smith as if they could dissect his thoughts. "The police and the Second Bureau do not confide everything to a mere general, especially one who is, as you pointed out, on duty at NATO. However, my aide, Captain Bonnard, heard rumors that our police have evidence that the attack on the Pasteur could've been the work of an obscure Basque separatist group thought wiped out years ago. As a rule, the Basques confine their 'events' to Spain, but I'm sure you know there are many Basque people who live in three small regions of Basse-Pyrenees on the Spanish border with France. It was probably inevitable something would spill over across the border, even to Paris, sooner or later."

"Which group, do you think?"

"I believe they were called the Black Flame." He picked up what appeared to be a TV remote control, pressed a button, and Captain Bonnard stepped into the grand room through a side door. "Darius, would you be so kind as to prepare a copy of the file the Sûreté sent over about the bombing for Colonel Smith?"

"It will be waiting for him whenever he leaves, *mon général.*"

"Thank you, Darius. What would I do without you, eh?"

Saluting, but smiling, the aide left the gilded room. General La Porte picked up the coffeepot. "Now, a second cup, Colonel, and tell me more about your friend. He is, I'm told, a genius, but with some sort of unfortunate affliction."

The general refilled their cups while Smith described Marty's history. "Asperger's Syndrome makes it difficult for him to function in our world. He tends to avoid people, is terrified of strangers, and lives alone in D.C. Still, he's an electronic genius. When he's off his medication and in his manic state, he has insights and leaps of creativity that are dazzling. But if he stays off the meds too long, he borders on incoherence, and eventually he simply starts raving. The medicine allows him to function with people in daily practicalities, but he tells me it feels to him as if he's underwater, and his thinking, while still brilliant, is slow and painful."

General La Porte seemed genuinely affected. "How long has he had this affliction?"

"All his life. It's not a well-known condition, often misdiagnosed and misunderstood. Marty's happiest when he's off his meds, but that's difficult for other people to be around. That's one reason he lives alone."

La Porte shook his head. "Still, he's also a great treasure, eh? But in the wrong hands, a potential danger."

"Not Marty. No one could get him to do what he didn't want to. Especially since they wouldn't know what he was actually doing."

La Porte chuckled. "Ah, I see. That's reassuring." He glanced at a clock in the shape of a temple that stood on a sideboard—green stone and gilded columns and cherubs. He stood up, towering over Smith. "You've been most illuminating, Colonel, but I have a meeting and must leave. Finish your coffee. Then Captain Bonnard will give you that copy of the Black Flame file and see you out."

As Smith watched the massive general leave, his gaze was drawn to all of the paintings, mostly of French landscapes, hung around the room. Many appeared to be of museum quality. He recognized two fine late Corots and a muscular Théodore Rousseau, but he had never seen the large painting of a massive castle built of dark red stone. The painter had rendered it in intense and brooding shades of red and purple, where bright afternoon sunshine illuminated the angles in the stone walls and towers. Smith could not place the painting, and he did not recognize the style of any nineteenth-century French landscapist. Something about it, though, was unforgettable.

He stood up, raising his shoulders to stretch, not bothering to finish his coffee. Instead, he was already thinking about the rest of his day. He had not heard from Fred Klein, so it was time to check whether his cell phone worked.

He started for the doorway through which he had entered, but before he had taken two steps, Captain Bonnard appeared in it, file folder in hand, as quiet and unobtrusive as a wraith. The captain's accurate anticipation that he was leaving gave Smith a chill. Had Captain Bonnard been eavesdropping on the entire conversation? If so, he was a much more trusted employee than Smith had realized, or he wanted to know himself what Smith had told the general.

∎

From the high, paned-glass window of the general's study, Darius Bonnard watched Smith climb into a taxi. He continued to watch until the vehicle blended into traffic and disappeared. Then he walked across the room, through the rectangles of morning sunlight that patchworked the parquet floor. He sat at his ornate desk, dialed his telephone, and tugged impatiently on his lower lip.

Finally a quiet voice answered. *"Naam?"*

"Smith's gone. He's got the file. And the general is off to one of his meetings."

"Good," Mauritania said. "Did you learn anything new from the general's interview with Smith? Do we have any indication of who Smith truly is and why he's in Paris?"

"He stuck to his story that he was here merely to take care of his friend."

"Is that what you believe?"

"I know Smith's not CIA or NSA."

There was a pause at the other end of the line, and the sounds of a large, echoing space full of hurrying people indicated that Mauritania was on a cell phone. "Perhaps. Still, he's been a bit busier than that, wouldn't you say?"

"He could simply be concerned about avenging his friend, as he told the general."

"Well, I suppose we'll know soon enough." There was a cold smile in the terrorist's voice as he continued, "By the time we've discovered the truth of Jon Smith, it'll no longer matter. He—everything—will be as irrelevant as a few more grains of sand upon the Sahara. Whoever he is—whatever he or any of them intend—will be too late."

■

The dark-haired woman had slowly and meticulously searched Mauritania's entire silent apartment and found nothing. The terrorist and the others she had seen come and go were careful. In fact, she found nothing of a personal nature. It was as if no one actually lived here.

As she turned toward the door to leave, a key turned in the lock. Her heart pounded, and she sprinted away. Across the living room, she slipped into the narrow space behind the rug that covered the far window and listened as the door opened and someone entered. The footsteps stopped abruptly just inside the doorway and remained unmoving for some seconds, as if the newcomer sensed something wrong.

To the woman, it seemed that the breathing of the unseen person was like the slow switch of a rattlesnake's tail. She drew a 9mm Beretta from under her skirt, careful not to touch the rug that hid her. She must not make it move.

She heard a careful footstep. And a second. Coming toward the windows. A man, and small. Mauritania himself? In her narrow space, she listened. Mauritania was good, she had known that all along, but not as good as he thought. A quick, normal walk would have been quieter and more deadly. Harder to react to. He had guessed the best places to hide, but he moved too slowly, giving her time to prepare.

Looking warily around, M. Mauritania studied the room, an old Russian-made Tokarev TT-33 7.62mm pistol in his hand. He heard nothing, saw nothing unusual, but he was sure someone either was here or had been here, because he had seen marks of tampering on the locks to the doors to the building and apartment.

He glided delicately to the first window and quickly drew back a corner of the heavy rug covering it. The space behind was empty. He repeated the maneuver on the second and last carpet, the Tokarev ready to fire. But that space was also empty.

The woman looked down and saw it was Mauritania. Her Beretta was in her hand, ready in case he gazed up. She was hanging in a compact ball from a single titanium hook she had carried under her skirt and, once she realized her danger, had silently implanted over the top frame of the high window. There was no way he could react fast enough to raise his pistol to shoot her before she killed him. She held her breath that he would not look up, as her muscles strained to keep herself in a tight knot. She did not want to kill him, it could be a setback for her investigation, but if she had to—

A suspended few seconds passed. One . . . two . . . and he stepped back and allowed the rug to drop into place.

She analyzed his retreating steps, quick now, into the other two rooms. Then there were a few moments of silence, and she heard something heavy being dragged. It sounded as if a floor rug was being pulled back. When a board creaked and clattered, she suspected he had decided whoever had broken into the apartment was gone, and it was safe to retrieve something from a secret hiding place in the floor she had missed.

There were two soft clicks as the apartment door opened and closed. She waited, listening for another sound. For a sense of movement. There was nothing.

She dropped down to the windowsill. Her body was cramped from hanging in the clenched ball, but as she straightened she glanced out the window—Mauritania stood alone across the street, watching the building, waiting.

Why was he still here? Why was he watching the building? She did not like that. If he really believed his "visitor" had left, he would be gone, too . . . unless he was particularly security-conscious right now because of whatever he was up to.

She had a sudden, chilling insight: He had retrieved nothing; he had left something behind.

Stiff as she was, she did not hesitate. She raced across the living room to the back room of the bizarre apartment, pulled a rug down to expose the rear window, hurled the window up, and climbed out on the fire escape.

She was almost to the bottom when the floor above exploded in a sheet of flame.

She slid down the rest of the way and ran left through another building to the front where she peered out into the street. Mauritania still stood across the street from the now-burning building. She smiled grimly. He thought he had eliminated a tail. Instead, he had made a mistake.

When he turned and walked away at the first sound of the fire engines, she was not far behind.

Chapter
Ten

The Café Deuxième Régiment Étranger was on the rue Afrique du Nord, one of the serpentine streets that circled below the great dome of Sacré-Coeur. Smith unbuttoned his trench coat and sat alone at a small table in the corner, taking a long drink of his *demi* and eating a roast beef sandwich as he studied the Second Bureau's dossier on the Black Flame. The café's owner was a former Legionnaire whose leg Smith had saved in the MASH unit during the Gulf War. Displaying his usual hospitality, he saw to it that no one bothered Smith while Smith read the file from first word to last. Then he sat back, ordered another *demi*, and mulled what he had learned:

The "small" evidence against the Black Flame was that the Deuxième Bureau, acting on the tip of an informant, had picked up a former member of the terrorist group in Paris just an hour after the Pasteur's bombing. Less than a year ago, the man had been released from a Spanish prison for his part in long-ago crimes attributed to the Black Flame. After he and his associates were arrested, the Black Flame dropped from sight, apparently no longer active.

When the Bureau grabbed him in France, he was armed but swore he was completely out of politics, working as a machinist in Toledo, Spain. He claimed he was in Paris simply to visit an uncle, knew nothing about the Pasteur's bombing, and had been with his uncle all day. There was a Xerox of a photo of him. According to the date, the photo was shot when he was taken into custody. He had heavy black brows, thin cheeks, and a prominent chin.

The uncle confirmed the man's story, and the police's subsequent investigation failed to turn up evidence that directly connected him to the bombing. Still, there were a few holes, since the man had several hours unaccounted for that day. The Bureau was holding him incommunicado and interrogating him around the clock.

Historically, the Black Flame's center of operations was always mobile, never settling in any single spot for longer than a week. The organization favored the Basque provinces of the western Pyrenees: Vizcaya, Guipúzcoa, and Álava in Spain, and, only occasionally, Basse-Pyrenees, France. The most frequent choices were in and around Bilbao and Guernica, where the majority of the Black Flame's sympathizers had lived.

As a movement, the Spanish Basque nationalists had only one goal— separation from Spain into a Basque Republic. Failing that, the more moderate groups had occasionally offered to settle for an autonomous region within Spain. The Basques' desire for independence was so strong that, despite their extremely devout Catholicism, they fought against the Church during the Spanish Civil War and supported the secular left-wing Republic, since it promised them at least autonomy, while the Catholic fascists would not.

Smith wondered how the bombing of the Pasteur Institute in Paris might figure into that long-standing goal. Perhaps it was to embarrass Spain. No, probably not. None of the Basque terrorist acts had yet shamed Spain.

It could be that the point was to incite friction between Spain and France, which might ultimately make possible convincing the French government to pressure Spain to accede to Basque demands. That made more sense, since it was a tactic that had been used by other revolutionaries, although with only varying degrees of success.

Or had the French Basques decided to unite with their brothers and sisters south of the border, spreading the terrorism into two countries, in the hope that by carving their new country from small areas of both, they would encourage the French, who would lose less, to force the Spanish to make a deal? Of course, there was the added incentive that the involvement of two nations could trigger the United Nations and maybe the European Union to lean on both Spain and France to find a solution.

Smith nodded to himself. Yes, that might work. And a DNA computer would be invaluable to terrorists, giving them a compelling weapon for many purposes, including convincing governments to capitulate to their goals.

But assuming the Black Flame had Chambord's molecular machine, why attack the United States? It made no sense unless the Basques wanted to force the United States to support their objective and increase the pressure on Spain. But if any of that was true, there should be contact and demands. There had been none.

As Smith continued to consider it all, he turned on his cell phone, hoping to hear a dial tone. There was one. He dialed Klein's secret, secure number in D.C.

"Klein here."

"Are all of the wireless systems back up?"

"Yes. What a mess. Discouraging."

"What exactly did he do?" Smith asked.

"After he took down the Western utilities grid, our phantom hacker got into the key code of one of our telecommunications satellites, and the next thing our people knew, he'd infiltrated the whole spectrum— dozens of satellites. The FBI's forensics team threw everything they had and knew at him, but he broke every code, figured out every password, acted as if firewalls and keylocks were jokes, and zeroed in on the army's wireless transmissions. The speed was blinding. Unbelievable. He cracked codes that were supposed to be uncrackable."

Smith swore. "What in God's name did he want?"

"Our people think he was just playing, building his confidence. The Western grid came back on after a half hour, and so did the wireless communications. Precisely, as if he timed it."

"He probably did. Which means you're right, it was all a test. Also a warning, and to make us sweat."

"He's succeeded. Right now, to say our technology's being outclassed is the understatement of the century. The best defense is to find him and that machine."

"Not just him. This isn't the work of a solitary hacker, not considering the attack on the Pasteur and the kidnapping of Thérèse Chambord. There's still been no contact?"

"None."

Smith looked at his beer. It was a very good beer, and until he had called Klein, he had been enjoying it. Now he pushed it away. "Maybe they don't want anything from us," he said grimly. "Maybe they're planning simply to *do* something, no matter what we say or do."

He could almost see Klein, wherever he was, staring into space, seeing a vision of apocalypse. "I've considered that, too. A straightforward, no-warning attack, after they've finished testing the prototype enough to get the bugs worked out. It's my nightmare."

"What does the Pentagon think?"

"It's best to serve the brass reality in small doses. But that's my job. What else have you got on your end?"

"Two things. First is news that the police have matched Émile Chambord's fingerprints with a hand that came out of the rubble. General La Porte told me about it this morning."

"Jesus," Klein breathed. "So he's dead. Chambord's really dead. Damnation! I'll have Justice phone over there to see what else they know." He hesitated. "Well, that just makes Zellerbach all the more important. How is he?"

Smith filled him in. "I think there's an excellent chance we're going to get Marty back whole," he concluded. "Anyway, that's the way I'm operating."

"I hope you're right. And I especially hope he recovers in a timely fashion. I don't mean to be crass, Colonel. I know how fond you are of Zellerbach, but what he knows could make all the difference. Is the protection on him secure enough?"

"About as tight as it can be. French special forces guarding, Sûreté watching. Anything tighter, and they'd be tripping over their own feet." He paused. "I need a reservation on the next flight to Madrid."

"Madrid? Why?"

"To rent a car and drive to Toledo. Toledo's where I pick up the trail of the Black Flame." He described the report Captain Bonnard had acquired from the Sûreté and copied for him. "Now that you've found out the symbol on the handgrip of the gun was for the Black Flame, Toledo's my best lead. If the Black Flame really is responsible for Thérèse Chambord's kidnapping, then I'm hoping to use them to find her and the DNA prototype." He paused. "I've been to Toledo several times, but I'd like some help on this. Can you get me the Basque's home address and a detailed map of the city? Somebody at the Sûreté must have it."

"I'll have information, a map, and a flight reservation in your name waiting at De Gaulle."

Washington, D.C., The White House

President Sam Castilla was leaning back in his executive chair, his eyes closed in the unseasonable spring warmth that had settled into the Oval Office already at this early hour, because he insisted on keeping the air-conditioning off and the French doors open. By his own reckoning (he had sneaked a few surreptitious glances at his watch), the National Security Adviser, the admiral, and the three generals had been talking, pointing at charts, and arguing for an hour and twenty-six minutes. Despite the gravity of the situation, he found himself thinking longingly of how the Apaches would stake their enemies spread-eagled in the fierce sun to die very, very slowly.

He finally opened his eyes. "Gentlemen, it's a well-known fact that only an egomaniacal idiot would run for this job that I happen to have, so is there anyone who can tell me in a few words, which I won't need *The New York Times* or my science advisers to interpret, what's happened now and what it means?"

"Of course, sir." National Security Adviser Emily Powell-Hill took the challenge. "After the break-in to the Western power grid and the shutdown of the army's wireless communications system, the hacker went on to steal all of our command and electronic-surveillance codes. Every one. Nothing is left for us to hide behind. Nothing is left to protect our hardware, software, or people. We can be paralyzed for God knows how long. Completely unable to defend against attack. Blind, deaf, dumb, and toothless."

Despite his earlier levity, the president was stunned by the enormity of the consequences. "I expect that's as bad as it sounds?"

"So far," she said, "what the hacker's done has been of relatively short duration. Hit and run, rather than a sustained attack. But by stealing the codes, he's proved he's capable of not only an attack, but of war. Until the codes are changed, we're no longer in a position to fight or defend. Even after we change the codes, he can steal them again."

President Castilla inhaled sharply. "Exactly what did we lose while he was in our systems?"

"All military wireless communications systems routed through Forts Meade and Detrick," Admiral Stevens Brose explained. "NSA's worldwide surveillance center at Menwith Hill in Britain, FBI communications, CIA's worldwide photographic and electronic surveillance. The NRO was literally blind. And of course, Echelon went down."

"None was out of commission for long, sir," Emily Powell-Hill said, rushing to give the president the only good news. "But—"

The silence in the Oval Office was thicker than a New Mexico brush patch. NSA's Powell-Hill, the four military leaders, and the president sat silently, contemplating their private arrays of dark thoughts. Anger, panic, determination, worry, and sober calculation played across their faces.

The president fixed each of them in turn with his quiet, too-sober gaze. "To use one of my famous, colorful homespun metaphors . . . so far all we've seen are smoke signals in the Diablos, but the Apache can cut the wires at any time."

Stevens Brose nodded. "I'd say that about sums it up, sir. If we assume they have the DNA computer, the questions are: Why are they doing this? What are they planning? It seems to me there's no reason to hope they're simply applying pressure to make someone do what they want, because they haven't asked for anything. Considering the military and communications targets they've invaded, it seems clear they wanted that molecular computer for some kind of strike on someone or something. Since we've been the major target so far, and we seem to be number one on just about everyone else's hit list, too, then I'd say the odds greatly favor that they're after us."

"We need to know who *they* are," NSA's Powell-Hill decided.

Admiral Brose shook his head. "At the moment, Emily, in all due respect, that's about the least important question. They could be anyone from the Iraqi government to a Montana militia, from any country or terrorist gang in between. What matters first is to stop them. Later we can exchange calling cards."

"This is all about the DNA computer," the president said, "and it started when the Pasteur lab was bombed. Now we think there's going to be an attack on us, but we don't know what, when, or where."

Admiral Brose said promptly, "Right, sir."

"Then we'd better find the DNA computer." That was Klein's idea. The president had fought him on it, but in the end had acquiesced. With so few options now, it made even more sense.

The military men exploded in talk, Army Lieutenant General Ivan Guerrero in the lead. He complained, "That's ridiculous, not to mention insulting. We're not helpless. We command the most powerful military force on earth."

Air Force General Kelly agreed, "And the most advanced weaponry."

"We can give you ten divisions to root those bastards out, for God's sake," Marine Lieutenant General Oda insisted.

"And none of your divisions, ships, tanks, or aircraft can protect your electronic codes and systems," the president said quietly. "Fact is, anyone with a working DNA computer *now*, before we've had a chance to even begin developing adequate defenses, makes us impotent."

Admiral Brose shook his head. "Not entirely. We haven't been idle, Mr. President. Each of us has developed backup systems for our services that operate outside the normal command structures and electronics networks. We planned it for an emergency, and this sure as hell is one. We'll deploy them separately and install the most advanced firewalls. We're already changing all the command and communication codes."

"With the help of our British friends, we've got similar backups in place at NSA," Powell-Hill added. "We can be operational within hours."

The president gave a grim smile. "From what I understand, at best that will simply slow this new enemy of ours down. All right, change your codes, military first. Make your tactical electronics systems as self-contained as you can. Also, contact the other NATO governments and coordinate defenses and data with them. Meanwhile, our intelligence community must concentrate on finding the computer. Finally, for God's sake, take our offensive missiles offline as fast as you can, before they start launching them!"

With everyone agreed, they filed out of the Oval Office.

President Castilla waited impatiently until everyone was gone. At last Fred Klein stepped out from behind the closed door that led into the study. Klein looked tired, large circles under his eyes. His suit was even more wrinkled than usual.

The president heaved a worried sigh. "Tell me the truth, Fred. Will any of what they're planning help?"

"Probably not. As you said, we might slow the attackers down. But once they know what they're doing with the DNA computer, there's little we can do. It's simply too powerful. For instance, if you've got a modem on a computer and you e-mail your grandkids once a month, that's enough for a molecular computer to break into your machine, steal every piece of data on it in seconds, and wipe the hard drive clean."

"Seconds? E-mail from grandchildren? Good Lord. No one's safe."

"No one," Klein echoed. "As you and Stevens Brose said, our best chance is to find it. Once we have it, we'll have them. But we've got to do it before they put into effect whatever their master plan is."

"This is like wrestling a grizzly with both arms tied behind your back. The odds stink." The president studied the Covert-One chief. "How are they planning to hit us? How and where?"

"I don't know, Sam."

"But you will, won't you?"

"Yes, sir. I will."

"And in time."

"I hope so."

Chapter Eleven

Toledo, Spain

Smith drove out of Madrid on the N401 express highway, heading south toward Toledo. As promised, the Basque's home address, a map, and directions had been waiting for Smith at De Gaulle airport. The little rented Renault ran smoothly as he drove among green, rolling fields, drenched in the long shadows of afternoon. Sheep grazed in the lacy shade of poplar trees.

Smith rolled down his window, rested his arm on the frame, and a warm wind blew through, rustling his hair. The La Mancha sky, where Miguel de Cervantes's melancholy knight had tilted at his windmills, was wide and blue. But Smith's mind soon turned from the pastoral scenery and the deluded Don Quixote. He had his own windmills to charge, and his were very real.

As he drove, he was constantly aware that a tail might have picked him up. But as time passed, and the few other cars on the road came and went as one would expect, he began to think not. He turned his mind to the newspaper stories of the electronic shutdowns, which he had studied on the flight from Paris. Compared to the details Fred Klein had related, the news articles were cursory and gave no hint that the massive problems appeared to be the result of a futuristic computer at work. So far, the U.S. government had been successful in keeping that under wraps.

Even without the whole story, the articles were shocking and depressing, particularly since Smith knew what they meant. As he thought about them and wondered what he would find in Toledo, the ancient city came into view, rising on the plain ahead, the towers of the Cathedral and the Alcázar standing majestically above the roof tiles of the rugged skyline. He had read that Toledo's origins were so old they were lost in the pre-Roman days of the Celts. When the Romans arrived in the second century B.C., they had made it their city for seven hundred imperial years, until the barbarian Visigoths moved in and took over for the next two hundred, ending in A.D. 712.

That was when, legend had it, King Rodrigo laid lascivious hands on Florinda, daughter of the Count Julian, whom he spotted bathing naked in the Río Tajo. Instead of taking the matter to the courts, the outraged father—idiot that he was—promptly rode to the Arabs for help. Since they were already planning to invade, the Arabs were only too happy to oblige. Thus Toledo changed hands once more and grew into a cosmopolitan and enlightened Moorish center. It finally returned to Spanish control in 1085, when the king of Castile conquered it.

Surrounded on three sides by the river, the city was perched high above it on a craggy outcrop. It was a natural fortress, needing only a pair of walls on its exposed north side to be all but impregnable in those long-ago days. More recent growth was beyond those walls and also south, on the other side of the river—recent being anything built in the last three or four centuries.

Smith continued through the slightly wider northern streets, nearing the northern walls. Watching all around, at last he drove into the old city through the Puerta de Bisagra, a stone entryway built in the ninth century, and plunged his car into the maze of narrow, twisting streets and alleys that haphazardly spiraled toward the city's great pride, its Gothic Cathedral, and its equally great sorrow, the Alcázar, all but destroyed during the Spanish Civil War, although now rebuilt.

Using the detailed map, he watched carefully for the markers that would lead him to the Basque's home address. He got lost in the twilight that was spreading across the city, reversed course, and discovered many of the streets were so narrow that iron upright posts blocked vehicles from entering. Most were wide enough for a car, but only just. As he plowed ahead in the Renault, people stepped into recessed doorways to give him room to pass. Buildings, monuments, plazas, churches, synagogues, mosques, stores, elegant restaurants, and houses—many of them medieval—filled every square inch of this rugged promontory. The scenery was breathtaking, but also dangerous. It provided too many opportunities for ambush.

The Basque's address was an apartment building near the Cuesta de Carlos V, in the shadow of the Alcázar itself, just below Toledo's summit. The directions that were included with the map warned that the address was on a particularly steep, sloping lane, where not even the smallest car could pass. He parked two blocks away and walked, keeping to the deepening shadows. A multitude of languages filled the air as sightseers moved through the beautiful old city, taking pictures.

As soon as he saw the house ahead, he slowed. It was a typical flat-front, brick structure of four stories with a shallow-pitched, red-tile roof. The windows and door were unadorned square holes in the brick, set deeply in, only two windows to a floor. As he passed, he saw the front door was open. The narrow foyer was lighted, showing an enclosed staircase. The Basque supposedly rented a room on the second floor.

Smith continued on to the end of the block, where there was a small plaza rimmed with shops and bars. Streets spilled into it from four directions. He stopped at an outdoor café where he took a table facing back along the street. The air was scented with spices—cardamom, ginger, and chiles. From here, he could keep the Basque's apartment building in view. He ordered a beer and tapas, and waited as a band began playing from one of the nearby clubs. It was saucy *merengue* music from the former Spanish outpost of the Dominican Republic. The vibrant music filled the night, and Smith ate, drank, and watched. No one seemed to show any interest in him.

At last he saw three men enter the open front door of the apartment building, where light spilled out. One of them looked very much like the photo of the Basque that had been in the Sûreté's file. The same heavy black brows, thin cheeks, and thick chin. Smith paid his bill and returned to the narrow street. Night had fallen, and shadows spilled black and nearly impenetrable down to the cobblestones. As he moved quietly toward the apartment building, he had the sense again that he was being observed. His nerves felt raw, and he paused in the deep shadow of a tree.

The gun seemed to come from nowhere, the cold muzzle pressed into the back of his neck. The voice was a hoarse whisper in Spanish. "We were warned you might show up."

There were a few pedestrians on the narrow street, but he and the gunman were almost invisible where they stood. Streetlights in the old city were few and far between.

"You expected me?" Smith said in Spanish. "Interesting. The Black Flame is back with a vengeance."

The muzzle jammed deeper. "We're going to walk across the street and in through the door you've been watching." He held up a small walkie-talkie that Smith could just make out with his peripheral vision and spoke into it: "Cut the lights. I'm bringing him in."

At that moment, the terrorist's attention was divided, thinking about Smith while relaying his information. As the man clicked off the walkie-talkie, Smith figured he had few options. He had to take a chance.

He slammed an elbow back hard into the man's stomach and ducked. There was a quiet *pop* as the fellow jerked his weapon's trigger. It was a silenced pistol, the noise lost in the sound of music and traffic out in the plaza. The bullet shot harmlessly over Smith's back and pinged into the cobblestones. Before the terrorist could recover, Smith continued his lunge forward and kicked back with his left foot. He connected with the man's chin. There was a grunt, and the man went down.

Smith checked the man's vital signs: He was alive but unconscious. He picked up the man's Walther, a good German pistol, and slung him over his shoulder. Because the terrorists in the apartment building had been alerted, it would not be long before they came out looking. Smith hurried along the street, carrying the dead weight back to his car. The terrorist shuddered and moaned as Smith dumped him into the front passenger seat.

Smith hurried around to the driver's side and got in, just in time to see a flash of light. It was the man again. He had awakened and was flourishing a knife. But he was weak, and Smith yanked it away and stared into the black eyes in the car's shadows.

"*Bastardo!*" the man groaned.

"Now we talk," Smith told him in Spanish.

"I don't think so." His face was unshaved, and there was a wild look in his gaze. He blinked rapidly, as if fighting to think.

Smith studied him. He was a little over six feet and muscled, almost hulking. His hair was thick, black, and curly, an inky mass in the shadowy car. He was young. The beard and large size hid his true age. Smith guessed he might be twenty. A young man in middle-class America, but in the world of terrorists, fully grown.

The eyes widened, then narrowed. He reached up unsteadily and rubbed his chin. "Are you going to murder me, too?"

Smith ignored the question. "What's your name?"

The youth thought about it, seemed to decide he could reveal that. "Bixente. My name's Bixente."

No last name, but Smith would tolerate that. While he held his pistol in one hand, he moved the knife up with the other until the blade touched Bixente's chin. He flinched and jerked his head back.

"A name's a good start," Smith told him. "Tell me about the Black Flame."

Silence. Bixente trembled, looking younger.

Smith pressed the flat of the blade along Bixente's cheek. He rolled it back and forth once, and Bixente recoiled.

Smith assured him, "I don't want to hurt you. Let's just have a friendly conversation."

Bixente's face twisted, and it seemed to Smith that he was fighting some internal battle. Smith took the blade away from the young man's skin. It was another gamble, but sometimes psychology was more potent than force. He held the knife up where Bixente could see it and said, "Look, I just want some information. You're too young to be involved in all this anyway. Tell me about yourself. How did you get mixed up with the Black Flame?" He lowered the knife.

Bixente's gaze followed it down. Then he looked up, his expression puzzled. He had not expected that. He admitted, "They killed my . . . my brother."

"Who killed your brother?"

"The Civil Guard . . . in prison."

"Your brother was a leader of the Black Flame?"

Bixente nodded.

"So you want to be like your brother. For a Basque homeland."

"He was a soldier, my brother." Pride in his face and voice.

"And you want to be one, too." Jon understood. "What are you—nineteen? Eighteen?"

"Seventeen."

Smith repressed a sigh. He was even younger than he had thought. An overgrown kid. "Someday you'll be old enough to make stupid decisions about important matters, but not yet. They're using you, Bixente. I'll bet you're not from Toledo, are you?"

Bixente named a remote village in the north of Spain, a Basque stronghold, known for its sheep, dogs, and high pastureland.

"Are you a shepherd?"

"I was raised for it, yes." He paused, and there was a moment of longing in his voice. "I liked it."

Smith studied him. He was strong and physical, but inexperienced. An attractive candidate for extremists. "All I want to do is talk to the men with you, nothing more. As soon as we're finished, you can head for home and be safe by tomorrow."

Bixente's trembling slackened, although he said nothing.

"When did the Black Flame start up again?" According to the file, they had fallen off the authorities' watch list after their leadership had been killed or imprisoned.

Bixente's gaze dropped, his face guilty. "When Elizondo got out of prison. He's the only one of the old leaders who wasn't killed or still in jail. He got everyone who'd been a member back together and collected a few new ones."

"Why did Elizondo think the bombing of the Pasteur Institute was going to help the cause of Basque independence?"

Bixente still did not look up. "They never told me much, especially not Elizondo. But I heard them talking about working for someone who would give them a lot of money to fight again."

"Someone paid them to bomb the Pasteur and kidnap Thérèse Chambord?"

"I think so. At least that's what I figured from what I heard." The youth heaved a sigh. "A lot didn't want to do it. If they were going to go into action again, they wanted it to be for Euskadi. But Elizondo said it took a lot of money to fight a war, and that's why we lost the first time. If we wanted to fight for Euskadi again, we had to have money. Besides, it'd be good for us to bomb a building in Paris, because many of our people live in France now. That would tell our brothers and sisters across the mountains that we wanted them with us, and we could win."

"Who hired Elizondo to bomb the Pasteur? Why?"

"I don't know. Elizondo said it didn't matter why the bomb was to be planted. It was better that way. It was all for money anyway, for Euskadi, and the less we understood of it, the better. It wasn't our problem. I don't know exactly who he's been doing business with, but I heard a name . . . the Crescent Shield or something like that. I don't know what it means."

"Did you hear anything about why they kidnapped the woman? Where they've taken her?"

"No, but I think she's somewhere around here. I'm not sure."

"Did any of them say anything about me?" Smith asked.

"I heard Zumaia say you'd killed Jorge in Paris, and they figured you might come to Spain because Jorge had made a mistake. Then Elizondo got word from somebody you might come to Toledo itself. We should be prepared."

"Jorge's gun had the hand-tooled grip?"

"Yes. If you hadn't killed him, Elizondo might've. He wasn't supposed to put our symbol on anything, especially a gun grip. Elizondo wouldn't have known, except that Zumaia told him afterward."

Which meant they had not been worried about him, or maybe even known about him, until he appeared at the scene of Thérèse Chambord's kidnapping. He frowned at Bixente, who still had not raised his gaze. His shoulders were slumped.

"How did you recognize me?" Smith asked.

"They sent your photo. I heard them talking. One of our people in Paris saw you or heard about you or followed you. I'm not sure. He's the one who sent the photo." His expression was stricken. "They're planning to kill you. You're too much trouble. I don't know anything more than that. You say you'll release me. Can I go now?"

"Soon. Do you have money?"

Bixente looked up, surprised. "No."

Smith took his wallet from his jacket and handed him one hundred American dollars. "This will get you back to your family."

Bixente took the money and shoved it into his pocket. More of his fear was gone, but his shoulders were still slumped, and guilt filled his face. That was a danger Smith did not want. He might decide to warn his friends.

Smith made his voice hard. "Remember, the bombing and kidnapping were for money only, not for a Basque homeland. And because you didn't take me into that house, you've got a lot more to fear from them than you do from me. If you try to go back to them, they'll suspect you. If they suspect you enough, they'll kill you. You've got to hide for a while."

He swallowed hard. "I'll go into the mountains above my village."

"Good." Smith took nylon rope and electrician's tape from his suitcase. "I'm going to tie you up, but I'll leave the knife behind so you can cut yourself free. This is just to give you some time to think. To see that my advice is good." And to give Smith time to get away, in case Bixente changed his mind and tried to return to the terrorists.

The youth was unhappy with the solution but nodded. Smith tied him up, taped his mouth, and buried the knife under the backseat. He figured it would take the teenager at least a half hour to work himself over the seat, dig out the knife, and cut himself free. Smith locked the car, stowed his suitcase, laptop, and trench coat in the trunk, pocketed the keys, and moved quickly off. If Thérèse Chambord was somewhere nearby, the DNA prototype might be, too.

Chapter Twelve

Night had turned the beautiful little city into an atmospheric scene from history, with black shadows and yellow lamplight and Spanish music floating on the summery air. Smith entered the small plaza where he had stopped before to watch the house, planning to swing around a side street that would give him a different approach. Now that the hour was later, and the crowds had dwindled, Toledo had become a different city. Quiet and serene, it resembled one of El Greco's moonlit paintings, strategic pieces of its rich architecture glowing in floodlights.

But as he left the plaza, he saw four men emerge from the chaos of streets and alleys. He recognized one, thick and pockmarked, from the night Thérèse Chambord was kidnapped. There was also the man who resembled the photo of the Basque who had been taken into custody in Paris. The Black Flame. They were looking for him.

As the four Basque killers circled Smith, he raised his voice just enough so that he knew they could hear. He said in Spanish, "Which of you is Elizondo? All I want is to talk. I'll make it worth your while. Let's talk, Elizondo!"

None responded. Their expressions deliberate, they continued to close in, guns low at their sides, ready to raise and fire in the blink of their dark eyes. Around them, the historic buildings loomed like evil spirits from another world.

"Stop where you are," Smith warned, and flashed his silenced 9mm.

But the gun was not enough to stop them. They tensed but never broke stride, their circle tightening like a garrote. They did, however, glance for orders to a wiry older man who wore the red Basque beret.

Smith studied the four a second longer, figuring the odds. As the *merengue* music pulsed in the shadowy night, he spun around and took off. As he ran, a fifth man, older, suddenly stepped out of another alley some ten yards ahead to block his path. Behind him, the terrorists' feet hammered closer over the cobblestones. Heart pounding, Smith skidded around the corner of the first alley he came to and raced headlong down it, away from his pursuers.

•

A tall, elderly Anglican priest was hiding in the recessed doorway of a closed *estanco*, a tobacco shop, from which the faint, sweet odors of its wares seeped. In the night, he was all but invisible in his black clerical suit, only the faint reflection of light from his white, turned collar hinting at his presence.

He had tailed the men from the house of the Basque who had been arrested in Paris. When they had ducked into hiding, any passersby near enough to hear would have been astonished, perhaps offended, by a most unclerical mutter: "Shit! What the hell are they up to now?"

The faux cleric had hoped to observe a meeting that would give him what he had come to Toledo to learn. But what he saw now was no meeting. The Basque militant he had recognized in Paris, Elizondo Ibar-güengoitia, had led him first to San Sebastian and then here to Toledo, but there was no sign of the kidnapped woman. Nor of any corroboration of the suspicions of the cleric's bosses.

He was growing irritated by so much nonsense. Dangerous nonsense, at that. Which was why he held an even more unclerical item—a silenced 9mm Glock.

This time his wait was brief. A rangy, athletic man appeared from the plaza.

"Bloody damn!" the faux cleric grumbled, surprised.

Shortly afterward, the five Basques also emerged onto the street, one by one. Each carried a pistol, held discreetly down at their sides, convenient for use but only barely visible to anyone else. The cleric left the shelter of the corner.

.

Halfway down the alley, Smith flattened back against the building, Sig Sauer steady in both hands. He focused on the mouth of the alley where he had just entered. A trio of tourists—a well-dressed man and two young women—danced past on the street, in rhythm with the throbbing music. They were having a good time, oblivious to the tense drama around them.

As they disappeared from sight, Smith continued to wait. And wait. It was only a few seconds, but it seemed like an hour. As a new tune began, the thickset Basque peered around the corner, weapon and face at the same time. Smith squeezed off a silenced round, aimed carefully high; he wanted to hit no innocent bystander. The noise was lost in the loud music, and the bullet bit just where he wanted—into the wall above the Basque's head.

With an explosion of smoke, sharp-edged pieces of brick hailed down on the killer. He made a guttural sound and fell back, as if yanked by a leash. Which made Smith smile grimly. Then he ran.

No gunshots followed him, and he swerved into an intersecting alley. Threw himself back against the wall again, flat. No head or gun followed around the corner. Relieved, he ran again, now steeply uphill, surveying everywhere as he dodged through a jungle of deserted passageways, and his path leveled. As the music faded in the background, the last few notes sounded foreboding, somehow menacing.

Sweating, he sprinted on, encountered a man who was walking along, kicking a stone ahead of him, weaving as if he'd had too much *vino*. The man looked up and stared at Smith's harried appearance as if he were looking at an apparition. He turned abruptly and scrambled away.

When Smith saw no more of the terrorists, he began to hope he had lost them. He would have to wait, then he would double back to their house. He looked behind once more, expecting the passageway to be empty. Then he heard the distinctive *pop-pop* of a silenced pistol, and simultaneously a bullet burned past his cheek. Chips burst out from the wall where the bullet struck. Another silenced gunshot followed, and a piercing whine echoed as the bullet ricocheted off walls, hit the cobblestones, and clattered into a corner, trapped.

By that time, Smith was flat on his belly, raised up on his elbows. He squeezed off two rounds at two indistinct shapes in the night.

There was a loud, bloodcurdling scream. And he was alone again. The street dark, claustrophobic. He must have hit one.

But he was not quite alone. A shadow as dark as the night, the walls, and the cobblestones lay on the empty street not a hundred feet away. He rose to his haunches and, staying low, approached cautiously. The thick figure of a man took shape—arms flung wide, blood spreading, making the cobblestones gleam liquidly with moonlight. Blank eyes stared up, sightless. Smith recognized him—the squat, pockmarked man he had seen first in Paris. Now he was dead.

He heard a faint crunch on the cobblestones and looked up from where he crouched. There were the remaining men. Moving toward him.

Smith leaped up and ran through another confusion of streets and alleys, up and down among the densely packed buildings, where even the narrowest streets seemed to have to fight their way through architecture for room. He crossed a broader street where tourists craned to look upward, admiring a row of unadorned houses built for ordinary townspeople in the Middle Ages. Near them were two of the terrorists, their gazes sweeping the area. Because they were not looking at the houses, too, they stood out like wolves against the snow.

Smith turned and ran again. Their shouts followed as he accelerated away along another street just as a car turned into it from the other end. A family group hopped into recessed doorways to let the sporty Fiat pass. The Basques were too close. Desperate, he raised his free hand over his eyes and dashed straight toward the car, its headlights almost blinding him.

Smith bellowed a warning. He heard brakes screech. The Fiat laid rubber in its effort to halt, the stink nasty in the air. The vehicle slammed to a stop less than ten feet before it would have hit him, and Smith never broke stride. He leaped up onto the hood. His athletic shoes struggled for traction, caught on the shiny paint, and he raced across the roof and over the trunk. He was drenched in sweat when he landed. He kept running.

Gunshots whined past as the terrorists tried to get a bead on him. He wove back and forth, panting, his whole body straining. Window glass shattered above him from a stray bullet. A woman shouted, and a baby cried. Smith heard the Basques yelling as they stormed up over the Fiat, too, slipping and scrambling. The last sound he heard from the alley was their thundering feet. And he was neither safe, nor had he found out a damn thing about Thérèse Chambord or the molecular computer.

Angry, he changed direction again, this time weaving through new slumbering streets. He watched frantically all around. Finally he saw an open area of bright light ahead and heard the sounds of people laughing and talking.

He slowed, trying to catch his breath. He approached the area cautiously and realized it was the Plaza del Conde. On the other side was the Casa y Museo del Greco. This was the old Jewish quarter, the Judería, in the southwest part of the city, just above the river. Although he saw no one immediately suspicious, he knew the terrorists could not be far away. Elizondo would not give up easily, and in the end, although Toledo was not small, it was compact. No place was all that far from another.

He needed to slip past the plaza. Hurrying would draw attention. In the end, exhaustion made him decide. He worked his way slowly, trying to be casual as he hugged shadows wherever he could. At last he reached a line of tourists who were staring appreciatively at the closed museum that housed some of El Greco's famous paintings. It was a reconstruction of a typical Toledan home of the period, and they murmured and pointed out interesting features while he moved past behind them.

He had caught his breath by the time he reached the Calle San Juan de Dios, where there were fewer tourists, but at the same time he knew he could not continue at this furious pace much longer. Running up and down the hills was brutal even for someone like himself, who kept in shape. He decided he had to risk staying on this larger street. He studied each intersection before he crossed it . . . and then he had an idea.

Ahead, a man with a camera slung around his neck and a flash in his hand seemed to be in search of local color. He ambled into one of the alleys, head craning from right to left, up and down, searching for just the right shot. They were about the same height and build.

It was an opportunity. The fellow headed down another street, this one not much wider than the alley. It was quiet, no one else in sight. At the last second, he seemed to hear Smith come up behind.

He half-turned. "Hey!" he protested in English. "Who are you? What the . . . ?"

Smith pressed the silencer into the man's spine. "*Quiet*. You're American?"

"You're damned—"

Smith jammed the pistol again. "Quiet."

The man's voice dropped to a whisper. But his anger did not decrease. ". . . right I am! You better remember that. You'll regret—"

Smith interrupted, "I need your clothes. Take them off."

"My *clothes?* You've got to be crazy. Who do . . ." He turned to face Smith. He stared at the Sig Sauer, and fear flashed across his face. "Jesus, what *are* you?"

Smith lifted the silencer to the man's head. "The clothes. Now."

Without another word, his eyes never leaving Smith, the tourist stripped to his underwear. Smith stepped back and took off his own shoes, shirt, and trousers, keeping the man covered with the Sig Sauer the whole time.

Smith advised him, "Put on only my pants. Your T-shirt will do for a shirt. That way, you won't look too much like me."

The man paled as he zipped up Smith's trousers. "You're scaring the hell out of me, mister."

Dressed in the man's running shoes, gray slacks, blue Hawaiian sport shirt, and Chicago Cubs baseball cap, Smith said, "When you walk back to your hotel, use routes where you can see other people. Take pictures. Act normal. You'll be fine." He loped off. When he looked back, the man was still standing in the shadows of the buildings, staring after him.

It was time for the hunted to become the hunter. Smith continued at a slow, even gait that covered territory but did not exhaust him, until again he heard noise. This time he found himself at the Monasterio de San Juan de los Reyes, built as a sacred burial spot for the kings and queens of Castile and Aragon. Visitors who had paid for a nighttime tour of the city stood outside the church, fascinated by the exterior, which was bizarrely decorated with chains worn by Christian prisoners held by the Moors until the Reconquista.

Smith angled around and entered a *taberna* that had a wide opening onto the street. He took a table just inside where he had a sweeping view, the church dominating part of it. Grabbing a handful of paper napkins, he blotted his sweaty face, ordered *café con leche*, and settled in to wait. The terrorists knew his general direction of movement, and they would have been guarding against his doubling back. Eventually they would find him.

He had barely finished his coffee when he saw the wiry older man who wore the red Basque beret walking past in the company of a second man. Their heads moved constantly, scanning for him. Their gazes passed over him. They did not even hesitate. It was the blue Hawaiian shirt, Smith decided with satisfaction.

He stood up, dropped euros onto the table for his coffee, and followed until he lost them on the other side of the church. Swearing under his breath, he padded onward warily. They could not be far.

Finally he stepped out onto a grassy slope high above the meandering Río Tajo. He hunched down, low and unobtrusive, allowing his eyes to adjust. Off to his left, back in the town, he could see the silhouettes of the Sinagoga del Transisto and the Sephardic Museum. Across the river, in the more modern part of the city, the lighted rooms of the elegant Parador hotel winked at him. Around him, bushes dotted the grassy bank, while the river, still swollen by winter rains, flowed below, its quiet rushing sound warning of its power.

His sense of urgency was growing. *Where were they?* Then to his left and slightly below, he heard a low conversation. Two men. A rattle of small stones beyond the voices, and then another, different, voice joined in. Three men now, and as Smith listened, trying to catch what was being said, he felt both a chill and a surge of excitement—they were speaking Basque. Even at this distance, he recognized his name. They were talking about him, searching for him now. They were a scant hundred feet away on an incline that was relatively open.

A fourth man scrambled up toward the three from the direction of the river below, and when he reached them, he said Smith's name again. And conversed in Spanish: "He's not down there, and I know I saw him leave the *taberna* and follow Zumaia and Iturbi. He's got to be here somewhere. Maybe closer to the bridge."

There was further discussion, this time in a mixture of Basque and Spanish. Smith was able to gather that the ones called Zumaia and Iturbi had searched through the edge of the city, which was where he had lost them. Their leader, Elizondo, joined them from farther upstream. They decided Smith could still be nearby.

As they spread out in a pattern to do a thorough search, Smith scrambled across grass and sand and slid under the low branches of a willow tree that curled down over the hill toward the river. His nerves edgy, he lay close to the trunk, barely breathing, holding his Sig Sauer, safe for the moment.

∎

After eating his dinner at La Venta del Alma, a charming inn across the Río Tajo from the old city, M. Mauritania walked out onto the terrace of Toledo's most luxurious hotel, the Parador Conde de Orgaz. He checked his watch. He still had time: The departure would not be for nearly an hour.

Mauritania indulged himself by raising his gaze to marvel at the night view. Old Toledo was perched above the moonlit river in a sparkling display of lights and shadows, so lovely that it might have come to life from a poetic *Arabian Nights* stanza or a magnificent Persian love poem. The crass Western culture with its narrow concept of God and insipid savior did not understand Toledo. But then, they would turn a woman into a man, corrupting both the truth of woman and the truth of man. Nowhere was this more visible than in the great city of the Prophet, where every monument, every glorious memory, was viewed as a bauble and lie for money.

He drank in the sight of Toledo, reveled in it. It was a divine place, a living reminder of that glorious era nearly a thousand years ago when Arabs ruled, creating a benevolent center of Muslim learning here in the midst of ignorance and savagery. Scholars had thrived, and Muslims, Christians, and Jews had lived in harmony and cooperation, learned each other's tongues, and studied each other's cultures and beliefs.

But now, he thought angrily, the Christians and the Jews called Islam barbaric and wanted to wipe all traces of it from the earth. They would fail, and Islam would rise again, rule again. He would show them that.

He turned the collar of his leather jacket up against the growing night chill and contemplated the riches of this city, now decadent. Everyone came to photograph it and buy cheap relics of its past because they had more money than soul. Few came to learn from it, to contemplate what Toledo had been, to understand what the light of Islam had brought here when Christian Europe was going through its intolerant Dark Ages. He thought bitterly of his own poor, starving country today, where the sands of the Sahara were slowly smothering the life out of the land and the people.

And the infidels wondered why he hated them, planned to destroy them, wanted to bring back the enlightenment of Islam. Bring back a culture where money and greed were nothing. Bring back the power that had ruled here for centuries. He was no fundamentalist. He was a prag-matist. First he would teach the Jews a lesson. Then the Americans. While the Americans waited, they would sweat.

Mauritania was aware he was an enigma to Westerners. He counted on it, with his delicate hands and face, his round body, apparently so weak and ineffectual. But inside, to himself, he knew the truth: He was heroic.

For some time he stood silent in the night on the terrace of the palatial hotel, studying the spire of the great Christian Cathedral and the hulking mass and stubby towers of the al-Qasr, built nearly fifteen hun-dred years ago by his own desert people. While his face remained im-passive, he raged inwardly. His fury burned and grew, banked by centuries of outrage. His people would rise again. But slowly, carefully, in small steps that would begin with the blow, he would strike soon against the Jews.

Chapter
Thirteen

On the slope above the moonlit Río Tajo, Smith lay hidden beneath the willow tree, listening. The terrorists had quit talking, and behind him, the city was growing quiet. Below, a waterbird shrieked, and something splashed in the river.

Smith swung the Sig Sauer toward the river as a swimmer emerged and scrambled up, a gray wraith in the moonlight. Another was patrolling past on the hill below Smith. The one from the river muttered something in Basque, joined his comrade, and the pair continued out of earshot.

Smith slowly let out his breath, rose to his haunches, and followed, staying low to the ground as the men continued to search the slope. There were a half dozen of them now, heading in the general direction of the Puente de San Martin bridge. When the man at the top of the slope neared the bridge road, the group exchanged a series of hand signals, and all turned abruptly and swept down toward the moving water. Smith rolled behind boulders, scraping his elbows, before they could spot him.

At the riverbank, they crouched, consulting. Smith heard the names Zumaia, Iturbi, and Elizondo. He could see none of their faces. They were speaking quietly in rapid Basque and Spanish, and Smith caught the gist: Elizondo decided that if Smith had been here, he had somehow evaded them and was now heading back into the city, where he might contact the local police. That would be bad for them. Although Smith was a foreigner, the police would be less friendly to a Basque group.

Zumaia was not convinced. All argued the point and eventually compromised. Because of the time factor, Zumaia, a man called Carlos, and the others would stake out various places around the city in hopes of spotting Smith. Elizondo would give up the chase, since he was supposed to be at some farmhouse across the river for a meeting that was vital.

It was two words about the appointment that riveted Smith—Crescent Shield. If he understood correctly, Elizondo was going to that farmhouse to meet the group's representatives. He would walk, since their cars were too distant now to fetch.

Smith's luck had improved. Lying motionless, he tried to control his impatience as the men made their final plans and moved up toward the city. If he tried to follow Elizondo across the bridge, which was well lighted by street lamps, he would likely be seen. He had to find another way. He could tail at a distance, but that risked losing the terrorist leader, and he was in no position to ask too many questions of the locals. The solution was to be on the other side of the river before Elizondo crossed.

As the terrorists moved off, Smith stripped off the shirt and trousers he had taken from the American tourist. He jumped up and ran down to the shore as he rolled the clothes into a tight bundle. Using his belt, he tied the roll to the back of his head and waded in, careful to avoid splashing. The water was cold, and it smelled of mud and rotting vegetation.

He slipped into the black river. Head held high, he struck out in a powerful breaststroke. His hands dug in, pushed back water, and he thought about Marty lying unconscious in the Pompidou Hospital. About the men and women who had died at the Pasteur. About Thérèse Chambord. Was she even still alive?

Angry and worried, he pulled the water in mighty strokes. When he looked up at the bridge, he could see Elizondo, illuminated by the street lamps, his red beret easy to spot. He and Elizondo were making about the same speed. Not good.

Smith was weary, but there was no getting around it. He needed to go faster. The molecular computer was out there somewhere. Adrenaline jolted him. He pulled and kicked harder, slicing through the murky river, battling a slow current. He glanced up. The terrorist was still there, walking steadily but not so rapidly as to call attention to himself.

Smith was ahead. He continued his sprint, working his muscles, until at last he stumbled up onto the shore, panting, his legs rubbery. But there was no time to rest. He shook off the worst of the water, yanked on his clothes, and combed his fingers through his hair as he ran up onto the street and across. He ducked between two parked cars.

He had made it just in time. Elizondo was striding off the bridge. Beneath his beret, his sun-darkened face held a somber, angry expression. He looked like a man with a problem. When he turned left, Smith slipped from between the cars and trailed behind, keeping him in sight. Elizondo led him past an area of gracious country houses, *cigarrales*, where rich professionals lived, on up a hill and beyond the Parador hotel and past tractlike modern housing. Eventually they were in the countryside, with only the stars, the moon, and the fields for company. Somewhere cattle lowed.

At last Elizondo turned left again, this time onto a dirt road. During the long hike, he had looked back several times, but Smith had been able to use trees, bushes, and vehicles to hide from the probing gaze. But this dirt road was too lonely and isolated, too little cover. Smith slipped into a woodland windbreak and wove through it parallel to the road.

Because his Hawaiian shirt had short sleeves, bushes scratched his exposed arms. He could smell the cloying odor of some night-blooming flower. At last he plowed to the end of the windbreak, where he stayed back in the woods, studying the large clearing that spread before him. There were barns, chicken coops, and a corral that formed an L with a farmhouse, all bathed eerily in moonlight. This was his lucky night—just one house to choose from.

He studied the vehicles. Three cars were parked at the edge of the open area near the L. One was an old Jeep Cherokee, but the two others were what held his attention—a sleek, late-model black Mercedes sedan and an equally large new black Volvo station wagon. The farm appeared modest, not wealthy enough to support two new, expensive cars. All of which made Smith think that Elizondo was meeting more than one member of the Crescent Shield.

When Elizondo reached the front door, it opened before he could knock. As Smith watched, the terrorist hesitated, took a quick breath, and disappeared inside. Low to the ground, Smith left the cover of the windbreak and moved toward a lighted window on the right side of the house. When he heard the brittle crunch of shoes on gravel, he slid into the cover of an old oak, his nerves taut. The sound came from his left.

A craggy black man emerged from around that corner of the house, silent and phantomlike, dressed in the white robes of a desert Arab. He stopped there, barely twenty feet from Smith, cradling a British-made L24A1 5.56mm assault rifle as he scanned the night. He looked like a man accustomed to weapons and distances. A desert warrior, but not an Arab, or even a Tuareg or Berber. Perhaps a Fulani from the tribe of fierce nomads who once ruled the southern edge of the Sahara.

Meanwhile, a second man materialized around the house's other corner, the right side, farther from Smith. He was carrying an old Kalashnikov assault weapon. He moved into the farmyard.

Huddled beneath the tree, Smith tightened his grip on his Sig Sauer as the guard with the Kalashnikov turned and advanced toward the corral. He would pass within ten feet of Smith. At the same time, the tall bedouin said something in Arabic. The one with the Kalashnikov responded and stopped, so close to Smith that he could smell the onions and cardamom on him. Smith lay motionless as the two men talked more.

Suddenly it was over. The Kalashnikov-armed guard turned and retraced his steps, passed the lighted window that had been Smith's goal, and disappeared, perhaps to a post at the back of the house. But the bedouin in the white robes remained a statue, his head rotating like a radar antenna, searching the night. Without realizing it, he was preventing Smith from approaching the house. Smith imagined this was how the deep-desert warriors of the Sahara had always stood night watch, but on a high sand dune waiting for the foreign troops that had made the mistake of marching into their desert.

At last the white-robed bedouin patrolled out into the yard and around the corral, chicken coops, and cars, still watching everywhere. Then he returned to the farmhouse, his head oscillating, until he reached the front door. He opened it and backed inside. It was a remarkable display—and warning—of two highly trained sentries at work. They would miss little.

On his belly, Smith crawled quickly back from the tree until he was in the cover of the windbreak again. He circled wide through the vege-tation and once more left its shelter, this time to hurry across the open space toward the rear of the farmhouse, where the light was less, the windows fewer—only three—and all were barred. Thirty feet away, he dropped onto his back, cradled his Sig Sauer against his chest, and slith-ered toward the left window. Above him, gray clouds scudded across the night sky, while beneath him, an occasional rock bit into his flesh. He gritted his teeth.

Near the house now, he raised up and peered around, checking for the guard with the old Kalashnikov. The man was nowhere to be seen. Smith searched wider in the night, heard voices, and saw the glow of a pair of cigarettes. They were in the field behind the house, two men, and beyond them the bulky shadows of three helicopters. The Crescent Shield was both well organized and well supplied.

Smith saw no other guards. He crawled closer and raised up to peer in through the first window. What he saw was an ordinary sight: a lighted room, and through an open door across from him, a second lighted room. In the more distant one, Elizondo was seated in a stiff armchair, his nervous gaze following a figure who paced, appearing and disappearing across the open doorway.

Short and thickset, the pacer wore an impeccable dark gray business suit of English cut. His face was soft, round, and somehow enigmatic. Not an English face despite the suit, but of no particular ethnicity Smith could identify. Too dark for a northern European, lighter than many Italians or Spanish, with neither Oriental nor Polynesian features. Nor did he appear to be Afghan, Central Asian, or Pakistani. Possibly Berber, Smith decided, recalling the bedouin robes on the statuelike sentry he had first seen.

Straining to hear, Smith realized he was listening to a polyglot from many countries—French, Spanish, English, others. He heard "Mauritania," "dead," "no more trouble," "excellent," "in the river," "count it," and, finally, "I trust you." The last phrase was spoken by Elizondo in Spanish as he rose to his feet.

The small, round-faced man stopped pacing and extended his hand. Elizondo shook it. It appeared that some kind of transaction had been completed amicably. As Elizondo disappeared, and Smith heard the front door open and close, he wondered about the word *Mauritania*. Had they been talking about someone from Mauritania? Smith thought that might be it. He also thought Elizondo had been the one who had spoken the name, and his tone indicated that whatever it meant, it was good news for him.

On the other hand, Smith decided, Mauritania might be where the Crescent Shield, if that was who they were, or even the Black Flame, was headed next.

Still thinking about Elizondo and the other man, Smith dropped low and crept through the night's shadows to the second window, which was also barred. He raised up and looked inside.

This time the room was small and empty, a bedroom with a simple iron cot made up for sleeping. There was a side table and chair, and on the cot lay a wooden tray that held an untouched meal. Smith heard a noise in the room, but from off to the side, out of sight. It sounded as if a chair had scraped across the floor. He moved to the side of the window and listened as footsteps sounded.

Someone was walking slowly, heavily, toward the cot. Excitement surged through him. It was Thérèse Chambord. He had been afraid she was as dead as her father. Air seemed to catch in his throat as he studied her.

She was dressed as he had last seen her, in her white satin evening suit, but it was smudged with dirt, and one sleeve was torn. Her lovely face was bruised and dirty, too, and her long black hair was snarled. It had been at least twenty-four hours since she was kidnapped, and judging by her appearance, she had fought her kidnappers more than once. Her face looked older, as if the last day had stolen her youth and enthusiasm.

As he watched, she sat heavily on the edge of the iron cot. She shoved away her dinner tray with a gesture of disgust and leaned forward, her head falling into her hands, her elbows resting on her knees, the picture of despair.

Smith checked the night, concerned one of the sentries might surprise him. The only sound was the low sighing of the wind through the distant woods. Above him, clouds drifted over the moon, and darkness deepened over the farmyard. A welcome help against discovery.

He started to tap on her window. And stopped. The door to the room

GALWAY COUNTY LIBRARIES

opened, and in walked the short, stout man Smith had seen pace the front room as he spoke with Elizondo. His Savile Row suit was elegant, his face composed, and his demeanor certain. He was a man who led, who had opinions that mattered to himself. There was a smile on his face, but it was a cold smile that had no impact on his eyes. Smith studied him. This nameless man was important to the group in the house.

As the man stepped into the room, another appeared behind. Smith stared. An older man, several inches over six feet tall. He was stooped, as if he had spent his lifetime talking to much shorter people or hunched over a desk . . . or a laboratory bench. In his early sixties, he had thinning black hair that was more than half gray, and a long, lean face aged into sharp planes and ridges. A face and characteristic stoop that Smith knew only from the photographs Fred Klein had supplied him, but had been burned into his mind forever by the bombing of the Pasteur Institute.

Thérèse Chambord stared up as he walked into the room. Her right hand searched blindly behind until she grabbed the end of the iron bed for support. She, too, was shocked. But the tall man was not. Eagerness filled his face, and he rushed to Thérèse. The great French scientist Dr. Émile Chambord pulled his daughter to her feet and enfolded her in his arms.

PART TWO

Chapter Fourteen

Aboard the Aircraft Carrier Charles de Gaulle
The Mediterranean Sea

Two hundred miles south-southwest of Toulon, France, the nuclear-powered *Charles de Gaulle* cruised silently through the night, a great beast of the sea, sleek, graceful, and lethal. Only its running lights were on, and its matching pair of PWR Type K15 nuclear-pressure water reactors propelled the carrier at a steady twenty-seven knots, leaving behind an iridescent wake as straight as a razor cut.

The *Charles de Gaulle* was the newest and largest addition to the navies of Western Europe, and anyone observing, who knew the telltale signs, would realize something significant was happening aboard that Wednesday night. For in the air above, ten Rafale M fighter jets and three E-2C Hawkeye early-warning aircraft were aloft, creating an aerial screen, while the crewmen on duty at the Aster 15 surface-to-air missiles and the eight Giat 20F2 20mm guns were on full alert.

Belowdecks in a small, secure conference room, five military men, wearing the uniforms of general officers in the armies of the key European Union nations, were listening with varying degrees of concern to their host, who was not only a French general but also Deputy Supreme Allied Commander in Europe for NATO—Le Comte Roland la Porte. Hulking and regal, the general stood with his pointer poised before a large map of Europe as he surveyed his fellow generals with his unblinking pale blue eyes.

"This, gentlemen," he said, tapping the chart with his pointer, "shows all the new multinational consortiums that have arisen across Europe to manufacture advanced military weapons and systems."

To his annoyance, he was addressing his guests in English, an insult to French, the historic language of diplomats, the mother tongue of Western civilization. But the truth was, more than half of the EU's military leaders did not speak French well enough to understand him.

So in English, but definitely with a French accent, the massive general continued: "BAE Systems in the UK. EADS in France, Germany, and Spain. Finmeccanica in Italy. Thales in France and the UK. Astrium in Sweden, which, as you know, is a coalition of both BAE and EADS. European Military Aviation in the UK and Italy. So far, these corporations have further combined with others, as well as among themselves, to produce the Eurofighter aircraft, the NH-90 military transport helicopter, the Tiger combat helicopter, the Stormshadow cruise missile, and the Meteor air-to-air missile. Under discussions that we hope will come to fruition are the Galileo global-positioning system and the Sostar airborne ground-surveillance system."

La Porte slapped the pointer against his palm for emphasis. "I think you will agree that it is an impressive list of cooperation and accomplishment. Add to it the recent political support for pooling all of our research and development funds to create a European program to match Washington's, and I think we can all see the military handwriting on the wall."

There was silence as the generals glanced warily among themselves. Finally, Lieutenant General Sir Arnold Moore, in his dry, clipped, very British voice, asked, "Aside from increasing European trade at the expense of the United States, what's your point, Roland?" General Moore had cobwebbed cheeks, a high forehead, and the same long, narrow aquiline nose that reminded those who knew English history of the first Lancaster king, Henry IV.

The French general turned his gaze upon the British general approvingly. He liked that question and had hoped someone would ask. "Quite simply, Sir Arnold, I believe we are swiftly approaching the time when we can and must have a fully combined European military, so strong that it will no longer need the Americans. Any Americans at all. Completely independent from them. We are ready to resume our rightful leadership role."

As the Englishman registered doubt about what he was hearing, General Valentin González of Spain narrowed his eyes, cautious. He was a dapper, swarthy man with a jaunty tilt to his general's cap. "You mean an army beyond the sixty thousand combined troops that we now have under the command of the Rapid Reaction Force, General La Porte? After all, the EU controls *it*. Don't we already have basically what you're proposing?"

"*Non!*" La Porte said bluntly. "It's not enough. The Rapid Reaction Force is intended only for deployment on humanitarian, rescue, and peacekeeping missions, and even then it still requires U.S. weapons, support systems, and communications systems so it can operate. Besides, it's too damn small to handle any major problems. What I'm arguing for here is the full integration of the militaries of all our member nations, the entire two million soldiers, so that we have all the capabilities of a self-sufficient army, navy, and air force."

"But to what purpose, Roland?" Sir Arnold wanted to know. He crossed his arms and frowned. "Why? Aren't we all NATO allies anyway, working for a peaceful world? Competing in many ways, yes, but with our military enemies in common?"

"Our interests are not always the same as those of the United States." La Porte stepped closer to the group, his enormous girth momentarily intimidating. "In fact, in my opinion, they are far from the same now, as I have been trying to convince the EU for some years. Europe was, and is, too great to be a mere satellite of the United States."

Sir Arnold repressed a chuckle. "Remind your own country of that, Roland. After all, this grand aircraft carrier, this futuristic French warship that's carrying us, has made-in-the-USA steam catapults and arresting cables, since nothing else is available. And the Hawkeye surveillance and early-warning planes that you've got up there circling are also made in the United States. Rather critical points, wouldn't you say?"

Italian General Ruggiero Inzaghi had been listening carefully. He had large dark eyes, as hard as flint, and a wide mouth that was habitually set in a straight, no-nonsense line. He had been studying the big French-man, but now he turned to the Englishman. "I think General La Porte has a point. The Americans often brush off our immediate and long-range needs, especially when they don't easily coincide with what they think they want."

The Spaniard, General Valentin González, wagged a finger at the Italian. "Your own problem in Albania some years ago wouldn't be on your mind, would it, Ruggie? As I recall, it wasn't just the United States that had no interest in such a minor matter. Neither did the rest of Europe."

General Inzaghi retorted, "With a fully integrated European army, we'd back each other with *all* our concerns."

"As do each of the American states, which once were so contentious that they fought a long, savage civil war among themselves," La Porte pointed out. "They still disagree, but they're all one on the larger issues. Consider, gentlemen, that we Europeans have an economy one-third *larger* than that of the United States, and most of our citizens enjoy levels of medical, educational, and social benefits that are superior, too. There are more of us, and we're better off. Yet we still can't engage in a crucial military operation alone. That was made painfully clear by our inability to deal with the crises in the Balkans. Once more, we had to go to Washington with our hats in our hands. It's too humiliating. Are we to remain stepchildren forever to a nation that owes its very existence to us?"

The only general in the conference room who still had taken no part in the discussion, preferring, it seemed, to watch and listen, was Bundeswehr General Otto Bittrich. As usual, the expression on his rawboned face was thoughtful. His blond hair was nearly white now, but his ruddy complexion seemed decades younger than his fifty-two years. He cleared his throat, his Prussian expression severe.

"The Kosovo campaign occurred in an area that's cost Europe millions of dead over the centuries," he said with a sweep of his gaze to make certain that he had their undivided attention, "a tumultuous region, dangerous to all our interests. The Balkans are, after all, our powder keg. Everyone knows this. Yet to do what was necessary to control the fighting in Kosovo and stabilize Europe again, it was Washington that had to provide eighty-five percent of the equipment and systems." The German general's voice rose with indignation. "Yes, our member nations have some two million soldiers, fully operational air forces, and excellent navies, all well equipped to fight . . . *but what good are they?* They stay home and inspect the space between their toes. *Useless!* We could go back into the past and fight World War Two again, *ja.* We could even destroy cities with dumb bombs now. But without the Americans, as General La Porte has correctly said, we can't transport troops and matériel to a modern war, much less fight it. We have no operational planning capability. No command structures. Technically, electronically, logistically, and strategically, we're mastodons. I am, in truth, embarrassed by this. Aren't you, too?"

But the Britisher, Sir Arnold, held his ground, asking lightly, "Could we all really get along in a unified European army? Could we actually plan operations together, allow multinational communications? Face it, my friends, it isn't only the Americans who have interests different from ours. We, too, disagree, especially politically. And that's where the approval of such an independent military force would have to come from."

General Inzaghi sat up straighter, annoyed. "About getting along, Sir Arnold," he retorted, "our politicians may have difficulty, but I assure you that our soldiers don't. The Rapid Reaction Force is already stationed outside Mostar in Bosnia—the Salamander Division, seven thousand men strong, in Italian, French, German, and Spanish battle groups. General La Porte's own countryman—General Robert Meille—is in charge."

"And the Eurocorp," the Spaniard González pointed out. "Don't forget them. Fifty thousand Spanish, German, Belgian, and French troops."

"At the moment, under Bundeswehr command," General Bittrich added with satisfaction.

"Yes," Inzaghi said, nodding. "The multinational Italian, Spanish, French, and Portuguese troops under a single command to protect our Mediterranean coastline."

The missing nation in all these multi-European military organizations became glaringly clear as each was enumerated. There was a heavy silence, in which no one mentioned that when Britain took part in a joint operation, it was invariably only with the Americans, where they were the second-largest contingent and therefore at least second in command.

Sir Arnold only smiled. A political as well as a military man, he continued to speak lightly: "And are those combined units how all of you envision the structure of this Pan-European army? Bits and pieces stuck together with schoolboy's paste? I'd hardly call them unified."

La Porte hesitated, then said carefully, "The exact structure of any European combined military would have to be worked out, of course. I envision more than one possibility, Arnold. Naturally, we'd want Britain's full input and—"

Otto Bittrich broke in. "For myself, I see a centrally organized and highly integrated force where the influence of individual states is blurred if not nonexistent. In short, a truly independent European army under a rotating joint command, answerable to no individual nation, but to the EU Parliament alone. That way, political control is assured, where all nations have members, and majority rules. Anything less would be a eunuch."

But General González looked troubled. He complained in a Spanish accent, "You're talking of more than an army, General Bittrich. You're imagining a United Europe, which to some of us is very, very different from a European Union."

"A United Europe will almost certainly result from a true European military, I should say," the British general remarked pointedly.

Bittrich and La Porte both brushed that aside, and Bittrich said angrily, "That's not at all what I said, General Moore. I speak militarily, not politically. As a trading bloc and a geographical entity, Europe has common interests that are of little importance to the United States. In fact, many times our interests are opposed to the United States. The EU shares everything from a currency to regulations on hunting migratory birds. Surely it's time to spread that umbrella. We should *not* depend on the bloody American military any longer!"

"For myself," La Porte put in with a gruff laugh, "and I believe you will all admit that no one is more protective of his national identity and importance than is a Frenchman, especially one like myself . . . I believe a true United Europe must come. Perhaps a thousand years from now, but it's inevitable. Still, I doubt a united military will force it to happen any sooner."

"Well," the Briton snapped, all lightness abruptly gone, "my own nation's views on the matter are clear. No totally integrated European army.

No European cap badges. No European flag. None. Any British contribution to the Rapid Reaction Force, or a self-contained army, must remain firmly under British control, deployed at the bidding of the British prime minister." Sir Arnold took an angry breath and asked, "And exactly where would the money come from for the transport planes such a 'no U.S. involvement' military would need? Also for the cargo ships and aircraft, the communications systems, the laser-guided munitions, the electronic jamming units, the military planning system, the fully modernized command structure? Certainly not from Britain!"

La Porte said confidently, "The money will be there, Sir Arnold, when the need becomes so clear that even the politicians can evade the future no longer. When they understand that the fate of Europe is at stake."

Sir Arnold was watching the French general intently. "Do you perhaps envision a time when we'd want to go to war with the United States?"

A hush spread around the room, while La Porte paced, his face in a sudden scowl, his ponderous body impressive for its agility. "We already *are* at war with the Americans, in every aspect of life and business except militarily. But militarily, we *cannot* be. We are too weak, too dependent on all their systems, hardware, and even the most modern weapons. We have soldiers and arms that we can't properly equip, move, or control, without Washington." He stopped pacing to face them, allowing his stern, unblinking eyes to examine each face. "For example, what would happen if there was some extreme crisis with Russia or China, and the American systems upon which we depend were all rendered useless or worse? What if Washington lost control of its own command and control systems? Where would we be then? If, for any reason, the Americans became defenseless, if only for a short time, then we would, too. In fact, we'd be even more defenseless."

Sir Arnold's eyes suddenly narrowed in his leathery face. "Do you know something the rest of us don't, Roland?"

Roland la Porte met his gaze. "I know nothing more than you, Sir Arnold, and I'm insulted you'd even raise the question. If anyone would know more, it'd be you. We French do *not* have a 'special relationship' with the Americans, unlike you English. But yesterday's invasion of the American energy networks could have easily been far worse, which certainly underlines my point."

General Moore stared at La Porte a full thirty seconds more. Then he seemed to think of something else. He relaxed, smiled, and stood up. "I believe our business here is over. As for the fate and future of Europe, we in Britain consider it tied permanently to that of the United States, whether we like it or not."

"Ah, yes." La Porte smiled a humorless smile. "The concept of your George Orwell, I believe."

General Moore, the Englishman, flushed a livid red, locked eyes again with La Porte, then turned on his heel and marched out of the conference room.

"What was that all about?" General Inzaghi wanted to know, his black marble eyes suspicious.

Otto Bittrich said grimly, "The English novel *1984*. In it, England was Air Strip One for a Pan-American and British Commonwealth entity called Oceania, united happily forever. At the same time, Europe and Russia were joined together and formed Eurasia. What was left over was called Eastasia—China, India, Central Asia, and all the Oriental countries. Personally, I'd say Britain already is America's Air Strip One, and we must proceed without them."

"Exactly how *do* we proceed?" González asked.

La Porte had the answer: "We must each convince our nations and EU delegates that a future European military is the only way to protect Europe's identity. And our greatness. In fact, that is our destiny."

"You are speaking about the *principle* of such an army, General La Porte, yes?" General González said.

"Of course, Valentin." General La Porte's eyes were dreamy. "I'm an idealist, it's true. But it's a principle we must start to work toward now. If the Americans can't protect their own utility systems, how can they continue to protect ours? We must grow up, be on our own."

∎

Captain Darius Bonnard stood out of the night wind as the last of the five generals' helicopters—General Inzaghi's—rose up against the night sky. The salty Mediterranean air was crisp, invigorating, and he breathed deeply as he listened to the loud chop of the blades.

The big bird flew north, in the direction of the Italian coast. Once it was safely out of range, the *Charles de Gaulle* altered course, sliding quietly through the sea in a long arc as it headed back to the French coast and Toulon. Still, the Frenchman continued to watch the Italian helicopter as its lights faded, the roar of its rotors dimmed.

But he was not so much watching as mulling over the meeting of the generals, which had been instructive. He had sat at the back of the room, quiet and unobtrusive, where he had missed nothing. General La Porte's compelling arguments for a European military had pleased him, as had discovering that most of the other generals were already thinking along the same lines. But the general's implication that he knew more about the recent breakdowns in American electronic systems than was common knowledge had worried him.

Bonnard sensed trouble on the horizon. He pulled meditatively on his lower lip as he thought about the British general, Sir Arnold Moore. The English bulldog was stubborn, obviously an American pawn, and altogether too paranoid. What La Porte had said had alarmed his English sensibilities, and he would soon be reporting possible plots to his prime minister, the War Office, and MI6. Measures would have to be taken, and quickly.

Again the captain looked out to sea, where the retreating helicopters formed four tiny dots. Sir Arnold Moore would be handled. He smiled. There were only three more days. Just three days to control all aspects. Not long at all, but in other ways, perhaps, an eternity.

Chapter Fifteen

Toledo, Spain

As Smith watched through the barred window, Émile Chambord tenderly pressed his wrinkled cheek down onto the top of his daughter's head, closed his eyes, and murmured something, a prayer perhaps. Thérèse clung to him as if he had come back from the dead, and in a way he had. He kissed her hair and turned furious eyes onto the short, stout man who had entered the room first.

Smith could hear Chambord clearly through the window glass as he snarled, "You damned monster!"

"I'm truly hurt, Dr. Chambord," the other man said, his round face pleasant. "I thought you'd welcome your daughter's company, since you'll be with us for some time. You seemed so lonely that I feared your emotions were causing you to take your mind off your work. That'd be unfortunate for all of us."

"Get out of here, Mauritania! Have the decency at least to leave me alone with my daughter!"

So that was what *Mauritania* meant. It was the name of this soft-looking man, who smiled but did not mean it, who was fueled by some kind of iridescent vision.

Mauritania shrugged. "As you wish. I'm sure the lady is hungry. She's forgotten to eat tonight again." He glanced at the untouched meal on the wooden tray. "We'll have a quick dinner soon, now that our business here is finished, and you can both join us." He bowed in polite farewell and left, closing the door behind him. Smith heard it lock.

Émile Chambord threw one more angry look over his shoulder and then stepped back from Thérèse, his hands firmly on her shoulders. "Let me look at you, daughter. Are you all right? They didn't hurt you? If they did, I'll—"

He stopped as a burst of gunshots sounded. A violent fusillade by small arms somewhere outdoors, near the front of the house. Inside, running feet hammered, and doors crashed open. In the barred room, Dr. Chambord and Thérèse stared first at the door and then at each other. Thérèse's face was frightened, while Dr. Chambord appeared more concerned than scared. He frowned at the door. A tough old man.

Smith had no idea what was happening, but this was a distraction he could not lose. Now that he had found them both alive, he must get them out. They had been through enough, and without Émile Chambord, the DNA machine might be useless to the terrorists. He did not know whether Chambord had been forced to operate his molecular computer for them, or perhaps they had another expert and had kidnapped Chambord to keep him from duplicating his triumph.

Whatever the truth, Smith needed to get the Chambords out of their hands. As he pulled on the window's iron bars to see whether any were loose, Thérèse caught sight of him.

"Jon! What are *you* doing here?" She ran to the window and tried to raise the glass. As she struggled, she turned back to her father. "It's Dr. Jon Smith, an American. He's a friend of your new collaborator, Dr. Zellerbach." She studied the window, and her eyes grew large and appalled. "The wood part of it's nailed shut, Jon. *I can't open it.*"

Bursts of gunfire continued to crackle in the distance as Smith gave up on the bars. They were set firmly in an iron frame. "I'll explain everything later, Thérèse. Where's the DNA computer?"

"I don't know!"

Chambord growled, "It's not here. What are you—"

There was no more time for talk. "Stand back!" He held up his Sig Sauer. "I've got to shoot the frame loose."

Thérèse stared at the weapon. She looked from it to Jon's face and then back at the gun. She nodded and ran back out of the way.

But before Jon could fire, the door to the room flung open, and the short, heavy man known as Mauritania stood there. "What's all this shouting?" His gaze froze at the window. On Smith. They looked into each other's eyes. Mauritania drew a pistol, fell flat onto his belly, fired, and bellowed, "Abu Auda! I need you!"

Smith peeled away just in time. The bullet smashed through the glass. He burned to return fire, but if he shot blindly into the room, he might hit one of the Chambords. Clenching his jaw, he waited until another bullet blasted through the window, and then he quickly raised up, Sig Sauer first, one eye peering into the room, ready to shoot.

But it was empty, and the door was wide open, showing an equally empty hall. Émile and Thérèse Chambord were gone. As quickly as he had found them, they had disappeared.

Smith ran toward the third window. Perhaps they had been moved to this room. But just as he reached the window and discovered an empty office inside, the tall Fulani in the long white robes, who had patrolled earlier, appeared from around the back of the farmhouse, gun up and ready. Right behind him came three more armed men, and all had that alert look of soldiers at war.

Smith went into an instant shoulder roll as bullets thudded into the ground, following him. He returned fire through the dark night, thankful for the thickening spring cloud layer that blocked the moon. His bullet hit one of the men in the midsection. The man doubled over and fell, and in those few seconds Smith's other pursuers shifted their attention to their wounded comrade. That was when Smith leaped up and sprinted.

More bullets chased him, whining past and hitting the ground, tufts of weeds shattering up into the air. He ran a zigzag pattern, faster than he had ever run in his life. Marksmanship was more than being able to shoot straight and hit the target. It was psychology, reflexes, and being experienced enough to predict what the target was going to do next. An erratic pattern was good defense. As Smith's weary body complained, he saw he was approaching the windbreak.

With a final burst of speed, he threw himself into the growth of trees. The musky odors of decaying leaves and wet soil filled his head. Again he shoulder-rolled, came up in a tight ball on his haunches, whirled around, and pointed his Sig Sauer back at his assailants. He squeezed off a series of rounds, a hailstorm of bullets, and he did not care where they landed. His barrage was enough that the tall leader and the others fell to the ground for cover, and maybe he had hit two of them. But then, they had run straight at him, perfect marks.

Smith tore away through the woods, heading around toward the front of the house, where the initial gunfire had started. He listened. The shots were sometimes sporadic, sometimes intense. Behind him in the trees, there was no sign of pursuit.

Then he saw it: In the front of the farmyard, pandemonium had broken out. Figures lay stretched out on the ground, weapons up and pointed at the windbreak. At least twenty of them. As Smith watched, rapid muzzle flashes burst from the other side of a thick oak, while out in the yard, someone screamed in agony.

In his white burnoose, the lead extremist came running around through the open area, shouting orders. He crouched next to the corral and bawled an instruction in violent Arabic back at the house. Moments later all the house's lights went out, its windows suddenly inky black pits, and a spotlight mounted at the left corner just beneath the roof blazed to life, illuminating the yard and rotating mechanically from some remote control until it focused on the windbreak, where it homed in on the oak tree.

Now that his men were no longer back-lighted, the white-robed leader waved them forward.

In response, a furious burst of automatic fire erupted from the woods. Two attackers fell, grunting, cursing, one clutching an arm and the other a shoulder. The rest plummeted to the earth again and raised up on their elbows to return fire. Only the bedouin leader remained a target, kneeling in plain sight as he coolly shot his old British assault rifle and cursed the others in vivid Arabic. With the gunman's total attention directed at the oak bathed in merciless light, Smith dropped lower and scrambled closer to see who was firing from behind it.

He parted a cluster of Spanish broom and peered through at a single figure, who knelt behind the tree, reloading a Heckler & Koch MP5K compact submachine gun with a fresh banana clip. The spotlight illuminated the front and sides of the tree, leaving the back in shadow. Still, he could see enough to be shocked a third time that night: It was the unattractive, dark-haired woman he had spotted yesterday outside the Pasteur Institute, the same woman who later walked right past where he sat in the café but had shown no interest in him.

She was no longer wearing the dowdy, ill-fitting clothes and plain shoes of Paris. Instead, she was dressed in a slim, black jumpsuit, a black watch cap rolled up above her ears, and snug black boots. A change that revealed a far from frumpish shape, and also suited the requirements of her current activity. As Smith watched, she moved as calmly and smoothly as if she were on a firing range, releasing a series of careful bursts of three as she swept the MP5K across the semicircle in front of her. There was a precision, but at the same time a controlled carelessness to her work, as if her instincts were as well honed as her craft, which was impressive. As she released her last burst, somewhere to the left, there was another shriek of pain, and she jumped up and ran back, retreating deeper into the woods.

Smith followed, fast and low to the ground, attracted by the fact that not only were she and he fighting on the same side, but he suddenly realized there was something about her that was familiar, something that had little to do with the events of today or yesterday. Her coolness and skill, the shape of her body, the intuitive risk-taking while at the same time the almost machinelike exactness. The right move at the right time.

As he watched, she dropped again, this time behind bushes. Simultaneously, bursts of gunfire and a round of swearing showed that the terrorists had arrived at the oak and found she had flown.

Smith remained motionless, hidden behind a poplar tree, as the sense of familiarity grew. Her face was wrong, her hair was wrong, and yet? Her body in the slim coveralls, the way she held her head, the sure, powerful hands. And then there were her movements. He had seen it all before. It *had* to be her. What she was doing? Being *here*. CIA was in on this, that was certain. *Randi Russell*.

He smiled briefly, feeling the same surge of attraction he experienced every time he saw her under any circumstance. That was because of her close resemblance to her sister, Sophia. At least he always accounted for it that way, knowing he was not being completely honest with himself.

She glanced away over her shoulder, clearly planning her next move, a certain angry desperation on her face. He would have to help her, despite the fact that if they survived, she would interfere with his investigation. In fact, she already had. But her chances of getting away alone were minimal.

The terrorists had stopped their frontal assault and were moving around her in two arms, while holding her pinned down from in front. Smith could hear the men padding through the murky woods on both flanks. She glanced nervously right and left, listening, too, her desperation deepening. It was like the jaws of a trap closing in on her, and if she was caught alone, she would be unable to recover.

The first man slipped into view. It was time to remind the Fulani and his men that they were dealing with more than just one opponent.

Smith unscrewed his Sig Sauer's silencer and opened fire. As the sound of his gunshot cracked like a thunderbolt in the quiet, woodsy air, the terrorist spun back, clutching his wounded firing arm. Another man appeared suddenly to the first one's right, still not understanding the danger. Quickly, Smith shot again. As the new man screamed and fell, there was a babble of shouts, scurrying feet scrambling for cover, and the angry voice of the leader. Almost simultaneously, Russell squeezed off three bullets aimed at assailants on her other side, where Smith could not see.

More shouts followed, and then more noise of feet in retreat. Smith turned to run when a flash of white attracted his attention, from the direction of the farmhouse. He looked more closely and saw the dark Fulani had arisen to his full, erect height and was standing defiant in his white robes at the edge of the windbreak. His voice was furious as he raged at his people to hold their ground.

Then Smith heard another sound and turned again: Randi Russell was speeding toward him. "Never thought I'd be glad to see you." Her whisper was filled with both relief and annoyance. "Come on. *Let's get out of here.*"

"Seems like every time we meet, you're on the run."

She glowered at him, and they bent low and bolted in the direction of the main road.

He was on her heels. "What did you do to your face?"

She did not answer as they tore through the timber. Their pursuers were momentarily disorganized, and that was going to be their only break. They had to make time while they could. They pounded onward, ducking under tree branches, dodging patches of scrub, terrifying the wildlife with their ferocious pace.

At last they dove over a stone wall, scrambled back up to their feet, and ran onward, gasping for breath, sweating, until, finally, they found the main blacktop road. They lurked inside the woods and studied the road both ways, weapons ready.

"See anything?" she asked.

"Not two-legged and armed."

"Smart-ass." In the shadowy trees, she looked at him as a crooked smile of greeting curled up the corners of his mouth. He had a great face, one she had always liked. His high, flat cheekbones and chiseled chin were very male. She pushed that from her mind as she continued to study the road, the woods, the shadows.

Jon said, "We'd better move on back toward Toledo, try to keep ahead of them. And I really do want to know about your face. Please don't tell me it's plastic surgery, I'd be devastated." They trotted off again, alongside each other now on the dark road.

"Hold out your hand."

"I have a feeling I shouldn't." He stuck out his free hand anyway.

She reached inside her upper lip, left side, right side, and removed inserts. She extended her hand, intending to drop them onto his palm.

He yanked his hand away. "Thanks, but no thanks."

She grinned, unzipped a pocket on her web belt, and slipped them inside. "The wig stays on. It's bad enough you're running around in that neon Hawaiian shirt. At least it's a dark blue. My blond hair would be like a beacon."

She really was good; she knew how to use very little cosmetic change to great effect. With the inserts, her features had been lumpy and wide, making her eyes seem too close together, and her chin too small. But now her face was the one he remembered. Her wide-set eyes, straight nose, and high forehead radiated a kind of sexy intelligence that he found intriguing, even when she was her usual prickly self.

He was thinking about all that as he watched for the terrorists. He half-expected a truckload of them to roar down the road, a machine gun attached on top, when he heard engines thunder to life behind them from the direction of the farmhouse.

"Hear that?" he asked.

"I'm not deaf."

The noise changed, and the *chop-chop* of rotors was added to the booming engines. Soon, from behind them in the direction of the farmhouse, three helicopters rose into the night like the shadows of giant birds, one after the other, their red and green navigational lights blinking as they circled and headed south. Dark, bruised-looking clouds scudded across the sky. The moon peeked out and disappeared, and so did the helicopters.

"We've just been abandoned," she complained. "Damnation!"

"Shouldn't that be 'amen'? That was a damn close call for you."

She bristled. "Maybe, but I've been tailing M. Mauritania for two weeks, and now I've lost him, and I damn well don't know who the rest of them were, much less where they've gone."

"They're an Islamic terrorist group called the Crescent Shield. They're the ones who bombed the Pasteur Institute, or had it done by a front group to cover their tracks."

"What front group?"

"The Black Flame."

"Never heard of them."

"Not surprising. They've been out of action for at least ten years. This operation was their attempt to raise money so they could get back to their game. Tell your people the next time you check in, and they can warn the Spanish authorities. The Black Flame also kidnapped Chambord and his daughter. But it's the Crescent Shield who's holding them prisoner, and they have Chambord's DNA computer, too."

Randi stopped running as if she had hit a wall. "Chambord's alive?"

"He was in that farmhouse, so was his daughter."

"The computer?"

"Not there."

They resumed moving, this time walking in silence, busy with their own thoughts.

Jon said, "You're part of the search for the DNA computer?"

"Of course, but peripherally," Randi told him. "We've got people out investigating all known terrorist leaders. I was already surveilling Mauritania, because he'd reemerged from whatever hole he'd been hiding in the last three years. I tailed him from Algiers to Paris. Then the Pasteur was bombed, it looked as if a DNA computer had been stolen, and all of us were put on high alert. But I never saw him make contact with any other known terrorist except that big Fulani, Abu Auda. They're friends from the old days of Al Qaeda."

"Just who or what is this Mauritania that he was on the CIA's to-be-watched list?"

"You'll hear him called *Monsieur* Mauritania," Randi corrected. "It's a sign of respect, and he insists on it. We think his real name's Khalid al-Shanquiti, although sometimes he goes by Mahfouz Oud al-Walidi. He was a top lieutenant of Bin Laden but left before Bin Laden moved his people to Afghanistan. Mauritania keeps a damn low profile, almost never shows up on intelligence radar, and tends to operate more in Algeria than anywhere else, when we do spot him. What do you know about this Crescent Shield group?"

"Only what I saw in that farmhouse. They seem to be experienced, well trained, and efficient—at least their leaders are. From the number of languages I heard, I'd say they're from just about every country that has Islamic fundamentalists. Pan-Islamic, and damn well organized."

"They would be, with Mauritania in charge. Organized and smart." She turned her X-ray eyes on Smith. "Now let's talk about you. Clearly you're part of the hunt for the molecular computer, too, or you wouldn't have appeared at that farmhouse in the nick of time to save my skin, and know what you know. When I spotted you in Paris, the story Langley told me was you'd flown to Paris to hold poor Marty's hand. Now—"

"Why was the CIA having me watched?"

She snorted. "You know the services spy on each other. You could be an agent working for a foreign power, right? Supposedly you don't work for CIA, FBI, NSA, or even army intelligence, no matter what anyone says, and the 'I'm only here for poor Marty' story is obviously bull. You had me fooled in Paris all right, but not here, so who the hell do you work for?"

Smith feigned indignation. "Marty was almost killed by that bomb, Randi." Inwardly he cursed Fred Klein and this secret life to which he had agreed. Covert-One was so clandestine—black code—that even Randi, despite all her CIA credentials, could not learn about it. "You know how it is with me," he continued with a self-deprecating shrug. "I can't *not* find out who nearly killed Marty. And we both know that won't satisfy me. I'll want to stop them, too. But then again, what else would a real friend do?"

They stopped at the base of a long, low hill and gazed up. It was such a gentle incline that Smith had not even noticed it while he was following Elizondo. But now, for the return trip, the upward slope seemed long and hard. They looked at it as if they could make it go away.

"Nuts," she told him. "Last time I heard, Marty was in a coma. If he needs you anywhere, it's in the hospital, bugging the doctors. So give me a break. Once it was personal, like with the Hades virus, because of Sophia. But *now?* So who do you really work for? What don't I know that I should?"

They had stood there long enough, he decided. "Come on. Let's go back. We've got to check the farmhouse. If it's empty, maybe they've left something to tell us where they've gone. If there's still someone there, we'd better question them and find out what they know." He turned around, retracing their steps, and she sighed and caught up. "It's all about Marty," he told her. "Really. You're too suspicious. All that CIA training, I suppose. My grandmother used to warn me to not look for filth in a clean handkerchief. Didn't your grandmother ever tell you something useful like that?"

She opened her mouth to retort. Instead, she said, "*Shhh.* Listen." She cocked her head.

He heard it, too—the low purr of a powerful car engine. But no headlights. They darted off the road and into a grove of olive trees. The sound was coming toward them, down the hill, heading toward the farmhouse. Abruptly, the engine stopped, and all he could hear was something strange, something he could not quite identify.

"What the devil is that?" Randi whispered.

Then he knew. "Rolling car wheels," he whispered back. "See it? It's that black, moving lump on the road. You can almost make it out."

She understood. "A black car, no headlights, no engine. Coasting down the hill. Crescent Shield?"

"Could be."

They made quick plans, and Jon darted across the road to an olive tree that stood alone, probably cut off from the little grove when the road was put in.

The vehicle emerged from the dark like a mechanical apparition. It was a large, old-fashioned touring car of the type favored by Nazi officers during World War II. The top was open, and it looked as if it could have glided straight out of an old newsreel. There was only one person inside. Jon held up his Sig Sauer to signal Randi. She nodded back: The Crescent Shield would not have sent one man to attack them.

As the elegant touring car continued coasting, it had gained speed and now was just a hundred feet away. Randi pointed to herself and then at Jon and nodded toward the car. Jon got the message: She was tired of walking. He grinned and nodded back: So was he.

As the car passed, still dark and silent, they jumped onto the old running boards on either side. With his free hand, Jon grabbed the top of the door, and with the other he pointed his Sig Sauer at the driver's hat. Amazingly, the driver did not look up. In fact, he did not react at all. And then Jon saw that the man wore a black suit and clerical collar. He was an Episcopal minister—Anglican over here.

Randi grimaced across the car at him. She had noticed, too. She rolled her eyes, her message clear: It was not good international relations to steal a car from a parson.

"Feeling a shade guilty, are we?" the British voice boomed, still not looking up. "I expect you would've managed eventually to get back to Toledo by yourselves, but it would've taken too bloody long, and, as you Americans say, time it is awasting."

There was no mistaking that voice. "Peter!" Jon grumbled. "Are there any agencies *not* chasing the DNA computer?" He and Randi climbed into the backseat of the open car.

"Not bloody likely, my lad. Our world has the wind up. Don't blame them, actually. Nasty scenario."

Randi demanded, "Where the hell did you come from?"

"Same place you did, Randi girl. Watched your little dustup from a hill above the farmhouse."

"You mean you were there? You saw it all," Randi exploded, "and you didn't help?"

Peter Howell smiled. "You handled the situation nicely without me. Gave me a chance to observe our nameless friends and saved you the trouble of going back, which, of course, you were already on your way to do."

Jon and Randi looked at each other. "Okay," Jon said, "what did happen after we got away?"

"They bunked lock, stock, and barrel in their helicopters."

"You went down to search?" Randi asked.

"Naturally," Peter said. "Food still warm in the kitchen, waiting to be served. But the house was empty of people, dead or alive, and no clues to who'd been there or where they'd gone. No maps in the house, no papers, absolutely nothing, except great heaps of burned paper in the fireplace. And, of course, there was no sign of the beastly machine itself."

"They have it all right," Jon assured him, "but it was never there, or at least that's what Chambord believed." As Peter turned the car around in a wide place on the road, Jon and Randi filled him in on what they had learned about the Crescent Shield, Mauritania, the Chambords, and the DNA computer.

Chapter Sixteen

Elizondo Ibargüengoitia licked his lips and dropped his gaze. His wiry body was hunched, the red beret askew, his demeanor harried. "We thought you were leaving Toledo, M. Mauritania. You say you have another job for us? The money is good?"

"The others left, Elizondo. I'll join them soon. There was too much I still had to do here. Yes, the rewards for this new job are impressive, I assure you. Are you and your people interested?"

"Of course!"

They were inside the vast, echoing Cathedral, in the famed chapel of the White Madonna with its white statues, columns, and rococo stone and plaster decorations. Abu Auda was leaning against the wall next to the Christian icon Mary and the infant Jesus, where his white burnoose seemed to mimic the statue itself.

As Mauritania talked to the three Basques—Elizondo, Zumaia, and Iturbi—he smiled, leaned on a cane, and studied Elizondo's face.

Elizondo nodded eagerly. "What's the job?"

"All in good time, Elizondo," Mauritania said. "All in good time. First, please describe for me how you killed the American Colonel Smith. You're certain his body's in the river? You're *positive* he's dead?"

Elizondo looked regretful. "When I shot him, he fell into the river.

Iturbi tried to pull his body out, but the current captured him, and he was gone. We would've preferred to bury him, of course, where he wouldn't be found. With luck, his corpse will float all the way to Lisbon. No one there will know who he is."

Mauritania nodded solemnly, as if considering whether there would be problems when the corpse was eventually recovered. "All of this is strange, Elizondo. You see, Abu Auda there"—he nodded at the silent terrorist—"assures me that one of the two people who attacked us at the farmhouse after you left was the same Colonel Smith. That makes it unlikely you killed him."

Elizondo's complexion turned as bloodless as the statue. "He's wrong. He was shot. We shot—"

"He's quite certain," Mauritania interrupted, sounding genuinely puzzled. "Abu Auda came to know Colonel Smith in Paris. In fact, one of Abu's men was there when you kidnapped the woman. So, you see . . ."

Now Elizondo understood. He pulled his knife from his belt and lunged at Mauritania. At the same time, Zumaia yanked out his pistol, and Iturbi spun away to escape.

But Mauritania whipped his cane up with the speed of a striking snake, and a narrow blade shot out from the tip. It glinted in the dim light of the chapel and then disappeared as Elizondo impaled himself on its point with his frantic charge. Mauritania, his face red with anger, twisted the blade and ripped it up in an arc through the vital organs. Elizondo collapsed, holding his own entrails, staring in surprise at Mauritania. He pitched forward, dead.

At the same time, Zumaia had managed to half-turn, his pistol firing a single unaimed shot before Abu Auda's scimitar slashed through his throat. Blood spurted, and he sprawled forward.

Iturbi tried to run, but Abu Auda smoothly reversed his powerful wrist and thrust the blade backhanded so deep into the fleeing Basque's back that the point exited through his chest. With both hands, the giant Fulani lifted the sword a few inches and, with it, the dying Basque. Abu Auda's green-brown eyes flashed with anger as he watched Iturbi wriggle like a rabbit on a spit. When the man slumped dead on the blade, Abu Auda pulled the scimitar out.

Mauritania wiped his narrow sword on a white altar cloth and touched the button on the cane that retracted the blade. Abu Auda washed his sword in the font of holy water and dried it on his burnoose. His desert robes were now not only dirty but bloody.

Abu Auda sighed. "It's been a long time since I've washed in the blood of my enemies, Khalid. It feels good."

Mauritania nodded, understanding. "We mustn't linger. There's still much to do before we strike."

The two men stepped over the dead Basques and slipped through the Cathedral and out into the night.

·

An hour later, Jon, Randi, and Peter were on the highway, driving away from Toledo. First they had stopped in the city, where Jon had retrieved his laptop and bag from the trunk of his rented Renault. The car was untouched, containing only the cut ropes. With luck, Bixente had escaped back to his life as a shepherd. As Jon loaded his belongings into the touring car, Peter and Randi put the top on it, and they sped away, Peter driving. Now as the spires and towers of the fabled city of El Greco faded in the distance, Peter slowed to just beneath the national speed limit of 120 kilometers an hour. They did not need to attract police attention.

Randi settled into the rear of the classic touring car, where the old seat still gave off a scent of expensive leather. She listened as Jon and Peter discussed in the front seat which route to take to Madrid, where they would report in and regroup.

"Just don't go back the same way Jon drove, in case the Basques were tailing him." She repressed her irritation as Peter took her advice. Why was she so testy around Jon? At first she had blamed him for her fiancé Mike's death in Somalia, and later for Sophia's tragic murder, but she had since grown to respect him. She wanted to put the past behind her, but it nagged like an unfulfilled promise. The odd part was she felt he would like to forget about it, too. They were frozen by too much history between them.

"God knows what we'll find next," Peter said. "Let's hope it's the molecular computer." The "retired" SAS trooper and MI6 spy was muscular and lean, perhaps just a shade too lean under his priest's costume.

His hands were curved brown claws on the steering wheel, and his face was narrow, the color and texture of leather dried out by years of wind and sun. It was so deeply lined that his eyes seemed embedded in canyons. But even in the night, those eyes remained sharp and guarded. Then they suddenly twinkled, amused. "Oh, and Jon, my friend, you seriously owe me for this little scratch. But I suppose I owe you for a bump on your noggin, too."

Peter reached up and lifted off his churchly black hat to reveal a bandage wrapped around the top of his head.

Jon stared at the bandage and shook his head as Peter adjusted the hat back onto his head. "I'll be damned. So you were the Algerian orderly at the Pompidou who caused all the trouble." He remembered a flitting sense of familiarity as the orderly had run backward down the hospital corridor, waving a mini-submachine gun in warning to keep everyone at bay. It was Peter's head that had left the trace of blood on the banister. "So you were there to protect Marty, not to kill him. That's why when you finally shot, it was high."

"All true." Peter nodded. "Happened to be in the hospital keeping an eye on our friend when I heard he had a 'family' visitor. Since Marty has no close family left, if you don't count the dog we picked up on the Hades thing, I got the wind up and flew up there *didi mau* with my little Sterling. Saw you spot me and had to bunk or blow my whole pantomime."

From the back, Randi said, "Which means SAS or MI6 is watching Marty."

"Ah, a trifle old for the Special Air boys, but MI6 does still find me useful from time to time. Whitehall is salivating over this DNA gadget."

"They called on you?"

"I know a bit about the DNA potential, and I've worked fairly often with the French, which is not MI6's best feature. One of the perks of being retired, out of the game, so to speak, is that I get to go my own way a bit. If they think they need me, they have to come to me. Then whenever I don't want to play, I gather my toys and toddle back to my lair in the Sierras with Stan. Drives them silly, of course."

Randi repressed a smile. Peter often referred to his age disparagingly, maybe to distract people from his actual abilities, which would shame many a thirty-something.

Jon frowned. "But why not identify yourself to me? Why let me chase you? Hell, you made me jump over a gurney!"

Peter grinned. "That was a pretty sight. Worth anything just to witness that." He paused. His voice grew serious as he admitted, "Never sure, are we? Couldn't know why you were there, eh? Downing Street and the Oval Office don't always back the same pony. Better to find out first who's doing what."

Jon continued to frown. "But after that, I saw you go into General Henze's *pension*. The one where he wasn't supposed to be. Sounds as if you were interested in the same pony there."

"You spotted me? Don't like that very much. Others could have as well."

"I didn't have a clue it was you. Either time, if that helps."

Considerable satisfaction was in Peter's voice as he decided, "That was the idea, wasn't it?"

"Especially when you're visiting an American general," Jon said, studying his friend.

"He's NATO, too, you see. Have to make nice with the EU."

"And tell the NATO general what?"

"Classified, my boy. Strict orders."

With that Peter was clearly going to say no more, friends or no friends.

To those accustomed to the heavy traffic of Madrid, the highway was almost an empty parking lot. A few cars roared past, speeding, but Peter was behaving himself and kept the town car under control. Near the lush, green city of Aranjuez, a former summer retreat for Spain's kings and queens, he left the N400 and turned the car north toward the A4 and Madrid, which was now fifty kilometers distant. The moon peeked out, spreading a silver glow across fields of newly planted strawberries, tomatoes, sugar beets, and wheat, as Randi leaned forward, resting her forearms on the back of the seat.

"Okay, Jon, who the hell do you work for?" The moment she said it, she regretted it. Irritable *and* confrontational. But dammit, she wanted to know. "Tell me it's not my dear, devious bosses at Langley lying through their teeth again."

"I'm here on my own, Randi. Peter believes me, right, Peter?"

Peter smiled behind the wheel. "It do stink a bit, you know. Not that I especially care, but I see Randi's point about her people. Behind her back and all that. Shouldn't like it myself."

Among Randi's finer traits was a laserlike focus, and she would worry a bone of contention with the tenacity of a pit bull. He had resisted long enough, it was time to trot out his believable lie.

"Okay, you're right," Jon told her. "There's something else going on, but it's *not* Langley. It's the army. Army intelligence sent me to find out whether Dr. Chambord actually did create a prototype operational DNA computer. And if he did, whether it and his research notes were stolen and the bombing a coverup."

She shook her head. "Langley never found you on the army intelligence roster."

"It's a one-shot. If they go high enough, they'll find me." He was confident of Fred Klein's deviousness.

She seemed to believe him this time, and for a moment he felt guilty. "See?" she said. "That wasn't so hard. Be careful, though—truth can become addictive."

"Never heard it put that way," Peter said dryly.

Jon had a clear impression that Peter did not believe a word of his fiction, but at the same time, Peter did not care, either.

To the Brit, his own assignment came first, and he returned to it. "Let's get back to the mission. Since Chambord is alive and kidnapped, then something's not shipshape at the Paris police."

"You mean the fingerprint identification," Jon understood. "I've thought about that. The only way I can figure the Black Flame and Crescent Shield made that happen was a simple reverse. They planted a corpse in the Pasteur before they blew it up. Put the corpse right on top of the bomb, except for the lower arms and hands the police found. They must've cut those off and planted them far enough away that at least one had a good chance of being recoverable, but close enough to be battered by the explosion. Then they had someone substitute the corpse's prints for Chambord's in his file. They also could've substituted DNA information, in case less identifiable body parts survived. Once the Paris police had a reason to make an identification one way or the other, they'd be satisfied. They'd have bigger problems to deal with, such as the DNA computer."

Randi thought about it. "The terrorists must've sweated blood when it took so long for the remains to be found. Not that it mattered much, since the police would assume they hadn't found his body yet."

"Wonder how they managed to sneak a corpse in at all? Could have scuttled their entire plan had they been spotted," Peter said. "Curious."

"I think," Jon suggested slowly, "the corpse simply walked in with them, unknowing, or maybe he was a dedicated martyr for Islam, counting on a guaranteed place in heaven."

"Good God," Randi breathed.

"Another type of suicide bomber," Peter said. "What's the world becoming?"

They were silent with the implications. Finally, Jon asked, "We've both told you how we got here, Peter. How about you?"

"Fair enough question. After the bombing, MI6 spotted a known Basque separatist in Paris, Elizondo Ibargüengoitia. The Second Bureau had missed him. MI6 factored that information into what the French told Whitehall about the other Basque that they did pick up, and it seemed like a chance to steal a march on the Second Bureau that was too good to miss. As it happened, I'd crossed berets with Elizondo more than once, so my assignment was to tail the bugger and see what mischief I might uncover." He stared ahead at the highway. "My nose for chicanery also tells me Whitehall would not be averse to snatching the thingamajig for Queen and country, eh, and my unofficial status could give deniability should the grab go wrong."

"As I expect would every other government and military," Jon observed, "including my own."

While Randi and Peter pondered this, Jon leaned back and let his head rest against the leather seat. He gazed out the windshield. The moon was lower in the sky, leaving a vast sweep of stars in the La Mancha sky. When he looked at such a brilliant display, he knew the earth and the universe would always be here. When he dealt with his fellow species, he was not as sure.

His gaze still up on the stars, he said, "You know, it's obvious we're all under the usual strict orders to play it close, tell nothing to anyone, especially agents of any other country on the same quest." He glanced at Peter and then back at Randi. "All of us have said the insane rivalry, even within our own governments, will destroy us. This one has all the potential for an Armageddon. My guess is that the Crescent Shield is planning a big bang somewhere. Probably against the United States. Maybe against Britain. Don't you both think it's time to cooperate? We know we can trust each other."

Randi hesitated, then gave a sharp nod. "I agree. Mauritania's gone to a lot more trouble than usual to cover his tracks, even to using another terrorist group as a cover, and now we know he has both the molecular computer *and* Chambord. The threat is too enormous to hold back, no matter what Langley or the army thinks."

Peter's careful eyes became less closed. He gave a short nod. "Right, cooperation it is. Bugger Whitehall and Washington."

"Good," Jon said. "Now, Peter, why were you really talking to General Henze?"

"It wasn't Henze, it was Jerry Matthias."

"The general's master sergeant?" Jon was surprised.

Peter nodded. "He used to be special forces. We met in the Iraqi desert some years back, and I wanted to see what I could pump out of him."

"About what?"

"Some odd shenanigans at NATO."

"What 'shenanigans'?" Randi demanded. "You're being difficult again."

Peter sighed. "Sorry, old habit. All right, I uncovered a phone call to Elizondo Ibargüengoitia from inside NATO. When I traced the number, it was from a maintenance office that had supposedly been locked at the time."

Randi was shocked. "The Black Flame, or Crescent Shield, has a spy inside NATO?"

"That'd be one answer," Peter agreed.

"Or someone *at* NATO," Jon speculated, "was, or is, working with the Black Flame or Crescent Shield to get the molecular computer."

"That'd be another answer," Peter agreed. "Sergeant Matthias is a former Green Beret and now the majordomo for your General Henze. I'd hoped he'd kept his eyes open from old habit. Unfortunately, he'd seen nothing especially suspicious. Still, the Black Flame was a live lead, so that's when I left to go after them in Toledo."

"I'll bet the Black Flame's no longer a live lead," Randi said. "Anyone want to give me odds their leadership's dead?"

"I don't like to bet against a sure thing," Peter said. "The Mauritanian. Smart bloke like that, he's figured out how you found him, Jon. With luck, he doesn't know about me."

"The Black Flame is a cover that went bad," Jon agreed. "Mauritania would've kept them in the dark, knowing they could turn on him, extort him, interfere in any number of ways with his plans. What he didn't figure on was that they'd lead someone like me to him. He's got to have killed them by now, and not just for retribution but to make sure they can't hurt him anymore."

As he thought that, Jon's mind returned to Marty. He realized that the better part of a day had passed since he had checked on him. The welfare of his oldest friend preyed upon his mind, and he pulled out his cell phone.

Randi looked across at him. "Who're you calling?"

"The hospital. Maybe Marty's awake."

Peter gave a curt nod of agreement. "With, one hopes, an earful to tell us that will help with the daunting task of relocating Mauritania and his Crescent Shield."

But the word from the Pompidou Hospital was not what Jon had hoped: little change in Marty's condition. They continued to be hopeful, but Dr. Zellerbach's progress had not accelerated.

Chapter
Seventeen

Gibraltar

Disturbed, Lieutenant General Sir Arnold Moore sat alone in the backseat of the Royal Air Force station commander's staff car and pondered the secret meeting in the conference room aboard the *Charles de Gaulle* that he had just left. What was going on? Why had his old ally and friend Roland la Porte *really* assembled them? As the bright lights of planes landing and taking off from the crown colony's airport streaked past, he stared ahead unseeing, worriedly analyzing the evening's discussion. Ultimately, it all ended up on the shoulders of General La Porte.

Everyone recognized that the French had a strong nostalgia for past glory, but everyone also knew that they were a practical lot, and that, at La Porte's lofty government level at least, *la gloire* was something of a joke. Although La Porte, both privately and as NATO's second in command, favored the combined European Rapid Reaction Force, Sir Arnold had always believed it was for rational reasons . . . that it would ease the pressure on NATO, which depended so heavily on the United States when intervening in disagreements small and large around the planet. In fact, La Porte was known to emphasize that reasoning with Washington.

But now the French general had shifted to overt anti-Americanism. Or had he? Was the European integrated military that he proposed simply a logical extension of his desire to relieve Americans of the burden to do most of the job? Sir Arnold fervently hoped so, because the other justification could be the first salvo in a dangerous vision of Europe as a second—and rival—superpower to the Americans in this new, post–Cold War, terrorist-filled world. It was never wise to divide one's fronts, which both Hitler and Napoleon had learned to their chagrin. Now, more than ever, it seemed to Sir Arnold that the civilized world must stand united.

Despite the anti-American rhetoric, Sir Arnold would certainly have accepted the former view had it not been for what appeared to have been La Porte's fleeting suggestion that America could soon face an electronic attack that would shut down all its command and communication controls. Of course—horrifyingly—that would make the U.S. military helpless, as well as any European force that depended on it.

Taken together with the scattered electronic crashes in those secret systems that were already occurring—which Sir Arnold should have been the only one there to know about—he was more than startled. He was deeply alarmed.

Had La Porte learned about them, too? If so, how was that possible?

Sir Arnold had the information only because President Castilla had personally informed the prime minister, explaining that the U.K. was the only ally he was alerting, while the only NATO official he was telling was its supreme European commander, General Henze.

So how had French General La Porte learned of the terrifying electronic attacks?

Sir Arnold dug his knuckles into his forehead. He had a dreadful headache, and he knew the cause: He was worried that La Porte was somehow connected to whoever was causing the electronic crashes, and that was why and how he had the information.

The British general could barely consider the possibility. The whole thing was unthinkable, preposterous, and yet he could not ignore the logic of it. He could not escape his worried conclusions about La Porte. He must not speak of them to anyone but the PM himself. And it must be in person.

This kind of speculation, which might be wrong but would still tarnish a good man's reputation, could be trusted to not just anyone. Which was why he sat alone in the backseat of the dark command car, waiting for his personal driver and pilot to oversee the servicing and refueling of the Tornado F3 jet that would speed them to London.

As he waited, he continued to mull the entire bizarre meeting. Had he been mistaken? Was he overreacting? But every time he raised those questions, he was more convinced: He was worried about what La Porte's hints implied, and the ghastly danger they suggested.

He was rehearsing the words he would use to communicate these conclusions to the PM when Stebbins tapped on the closed car window. He opened the door.

Sir Arnold looked up. "We ready, George?"

"Sir!" Staff Sergeant George Stebbins inclined his head to signal the affirmative.

"A simple yes would do nicely, George. You're not a company sergeant major in the Grenadiers now, you know." He climbed out of the car, briefcase in hand.

"Nossir. Thank you, sir."

Sir Arnold sighed and shook his head. You could get the man out of the guards, but you could almost never get the guards out of the man. "You think, former Sergeant Major Stebbins, that when your warrant is final, you could forget the household brigade, just a little?"

Stebbins finally smiled. "S'pose I could try, sir."

Sir Arnold chuckled. "All right, Stebbins. I appreciate a straight answer and an honest effort. So what do you say to our finding out if you remember how to fly that thing out there?"

They entered the station ready room to put on their insulated suits and helmets for the high-level flight, and twenty minutes later, Stebbins, in the pilot's seat, was taxiing the sleek jet across the dark airfield to the runway. In the navigator's seat directly behind Stebbins sat Sir Arnold, who continued to rehearse the shocking news that he must deliver to the PM, certainly to the defense minister as well, and probably to old Colin Campbell, who was commander in chief now.

The supersonic Tornado took off and soon left behind Gibraltar, the southernmost point of Europe. It streaked high through the sky, far above the clouds. The dramatic panorama of stars against the black velvet sky always made Sir Arnold choke up, because he believed in God. Surely no other force could have created such beauty. He was alternately thinking about that and worrying what General La Porte was up to when, out of hearing of anyone on earth, the aircraft exploded in a massive burst of flame. From below, the fireball looked simply like another shooting star.

Madrid, Spain

Madrid had a vibrant energy all its own, and residents and visitors alike reveled in it, particularly at night. Palpitating music and a festive spirit infused the air. From rushing taxis to unrepentant fun, Madrileños were a tolerant people, occasionally known to flaunt their anarchist streak in a search for a wild time amid the cobbled streets and pretty fountains under big, old trees.

Peter left the borrowed touring car in the garage of its owner, a trusted friend, then led Jon and Randi onto the metro. Carrying their few pieces of luggage, they kept careful watch everywhere, fighting off the conflicting emotions of urgency and mental exhaustion, although Randi and Jon had each taken good naps during the drive, while Peter, the stalwart Brit, had already had more sleep than either of them and so had driven them on in to Madrid.

With relief, they disembarked at the San Bernardo metro station and entered the Malasaña, known to locals as the Barrio de Maravillas, or District of Miracles. Here in the city's colorful bohemian quarter, nightlife was in abundance, and they passed bars, restaurants, and clubs, some a bit decayed but always charming. But then, this was a haven for not only artists and writers but expatriate yuppies who toted their dreams and assumptions with them around the world. Everywhere Jon, Randi, and Peter walked, lively music vibrated out into the streets.

The MI6 safe house was on Calle Dominguin, not far from Plaza del Dos de Mayo, the hub of this spirited area. It was a six-story stone building in a row of identical attached and semiattached stone buildings, with painted wood shutters, shuttered doors that opened onto traditional iron balconies, and shops and restaurants on the street level below. The odors of liquor and cigarette smoke drifted along the street as Jon, Randi, and Peter arrived at the address. Advertisements for Langostino Plancha and Gambas al Ajillo showed in the dark windows of the first-floor shop.

They stopped at an inconspicuous door, and Jon and Randi kept watch as Peter unlocked it. With a final look all around, they slipped inside and upstairs.

The place was decorated with comfortable furniture that had seen better days, but then, a safe house's purpose had nothing to do with being a decorator's showplace. They chose bedrooms, changed into casual trousers and shirts, and met in the second-floor living room.

Jon announced, "I'd better contact army intelligence." He used his cell phone to dial Fred Klein. As the phone's electronic codes and numbers were scanned and cleared, there were the usual clicks, silences, and hums.

Finally, Fred's voice announced simply: "Not a word. Hang up. *Now.*"

The line went dead, and Jon quickly switched off the phone. Startled, dismayed, he muttered, "Damn. There's more trouble." He repeated what his "army contact" had said.

"Maybe it'll be different with Langley," Randi said, and dialed her cell phone. The phone in far-off Virginia rang for a long time, and she grimaced and shrugged at Jon and Peter. "Nothing yet."

At last there was a short, sharp series of clicks. "Russell?"

"Who did you expect?"

"Hang up."

Randi clicked the cell phone off. "What the hell could it be?"

"Sounds to me as if someone's compromised your secure dedicated electronic intelligence communications systems," Peter decided. "Which could also mean those at SIS in London, including MI5 and MI6."

Randi swallowed hard. "Good God. At least they didn't learn anything from us."

"Ah," Peter told her, "but I'm afraid they might have."

"Yes," Jon said, understanding. "They could know now where you and I both are, Randi, assuming they're interested, know who they're tracking, and have the DNA computer up and running."

"That's a lot of 'ifs,' Jon. You said the machine wasn't at the farmhouse, and the last we saw of Mauritania's people, they were taking off in helicopters."

"All too true," Peter said. "But I doubt the prototype's ever far away from Mauritania, which makes me think they had a second safe house nearby and used that farmhouse to meet and pay off Elizondo and his

Basques and store the Chambords. Which is why *I* will *not* call London. Too bloody close to Madrid. I think we need to assume for the time being that all our electronics are under siege. Which means it's entirely possible they have a bead on you two now. They don't necessarily know about me, but if I whip out my cell phone and report into MI6, there's the chance they'll figure out about me faster than a hare across the highlands, and about MI6."

"It's ridiculous to have to hop on planes and fly home to report in person," Randi decided. "But it's true we used to do business this way, with messengers hand-carrying information back and forth. Good Lord, we could be going back to the Dark Ages in intelligence."

"Goes to show how dependent we've become on our oh-so-convenient electronic communications," Peter said. "Still, we must somehow figure out how to contact our superiors about the Crescent Shield, Mauritania, the DNA machine, and the Chambords. They must be told."

"True." Jon pushed his cell phone back into his pocket with a gesture of finality. "But until we can, we're going to have to operate on our own. Looks to me as if Mauritania himself is our best hope to track. Where he likes to operate, hide out. What his mental quirks are." In intelligence, quirks, patterns, and habits were often a fugitive's weak spots, revealing to experienced analyses far more than anyone might guess. "And then there's the elusive Captain Darius Bonnard. As General La Porte's aide, he's got damned high access and cover. And he of course could've made the phone call from NATO."

Peter's leathery face showed deep worry lines. "All true. And Randi's probably right about the wisdom of getting back to old-fashioned intelligence communications." He suggested, "London's a lot closer than Washington. If need be, I can flog myself over there to check in."

"Our embassies in Madrid will have fully coded communications," Randi said. "But considering the last assault when every code was cracked, the embassies' communications are probably compromised, too."

"Right. Anything electronic is out," Peter said.

Jon paced in front of a stone fireplace that looked as if it'd had no fire in years. "Maybe they didn't disrupt everything everywhere," he said cautiously.

Peter looked at him sharply. "You have an idea, Jon?"

"Is there a real phone in this house? Nothing electronic."

"On the third floor, in the office. That just might work."

Randi glared from one to the other. "You two mind telling me what you're talking about?"

Jon was halfway up the stairs as Peter said, "Regular phone wires. A direct call. Fiber-optics, don't you know."

"Of course." She followed Jon, Peter close behind. "Even if the Crescent Shield had the technology or the time to tap a cable, they'd still have all the problems of sorting through the dreck. A technician told me once that so much data went through fiber-optics lines that to tap into it was like getting sprayed in the face by a high-pressure hose." She had been told a cable as narrow as her wrist could carry an astronomical forty thousand phone conversations all at once, comparable to the entire trans-Atlantic voice traffic handled by satellites back in Cold War days. The way fiber-optics worked was to translate phone calls, faxes, e-mail messages, and data files into beams of light that traveled through a single strand of glass as thin as a human hair. Most undersea cables contained eight such strands, or fibers. But extracting the data required gaining access to the minute light beams in the ocean's black, high-pressure depths—a dangerous, almost impossible task.

Peter grumbled agreement: "Even if they had the time and technology to tap a cable, would they waste their time listening in to a million long-distance phone calls, give or take, discussing in detail Aunt Sarah's bunions and the Queen Mum's shocking gin intake? I doubt it."

"Exactly," Randi agreed.

As soon as the threesome reached the bare-bones office, Jon tapped his calling card number into the telephone on the desk. Then he entered the number he wanted in Washington. As he waited for it to ring, he pulled out the desk chair and sat. Peter leaned on a nearby desk, and Randi fell into an old, padded rocker.

A brisk female voice answered. "Colonel Hakkim's office."

"It's Jon Smith, Debbie. I need to talk to Newton. It's urgent."

"Hold on."

The strange vacuum of hold, and a man's concerned voice: "Jon? What's up?"

"I'm in Madrid, and I need a favor. Could you send someone over to

E block to the Leased Facilities Division and office 2E377, and have him tell the woman there to tell her boss to call Zapata at this number?" He read the number of the safe house phone. "Make sure whoever you send uses that name—Zapata. Can you do it?"

"Should I ask what this is all about or who's really in that office?"

"No."

"Then I'll go myself."

"Thanks, Newton."

Newton's voice was cool and calm, but Jon heard anxiety, too. "You'll have to tell me the whole story when you get back."

"Count on it." Jon hung up and checked his watch. "It should take him about ten minutes. E block's a long way from his office. Figure another two minutes for contingencies. Twelve minutes, tops."

Randi said, "Leased Facilities Division? A cover for army intelligence, no doubt?"

"No doubt," Jon said noncommittally.

Peter pressed a finger to his lips and padded to the shuttered front window, which was next to the shuttered door that opened onto the balcony. He angled the slats open a fraction wider and looked down at the dark street. He stood there motionless as the pulsing night sounds of the city drifted up from below—the rumble of heavy traffic on the Gran Via, voices calling from windows down to the street, the slam of a car door, a drunk's serenade, a guitar's liquid chords.

Peter left the window and sank onto the sofa, relieved. "False alarm—I think."

"What's wrong?" Randi asked.

"I thought I heard an odd sound from the street. It's something I've run across a few times before and learned rather quickly to heed."

"I didn't hear anything unusual," Jon said.

"You're not meant to, my boy. It's a blowing sound, with a tiny whistle at the center. It seems to be far away, the call of a weak whippoorwill, that simply fades away. In reality, it's a muted whistle no one actually hears. Resembles a random night sound—the wind, an animal turning in sleep, the earth itself creaking as if it really were set in a three-pronged nest. I heard it more than once in northern Iran on the border of the old Soviet Union's central Asian republics, and in the 1980s I heard it in

Afghanistan during that barbarous blowup. It's a signal used by the central Asian Muslim tribes. Rather close to night signals your Iroquois and Apache used."

"The Crescent Shield?" Jon asked.

"Could be. But there was no answer to the call. Since I didn't hear it a second time, I was probably mistaken."

"How often have you been wrong on a matter like that, Peter?" Jon said.

The ring of the telephone made them jump. Jon grabbed the receiver.

Fred Klein's voice said, "We got everything back online, but the computer warfare specialists tell us that all the electronic encryption codes may have been cracked, so no one's to use any electronic communication until further notice. Nothing that goes through the air either, because that would be easy for them to tap into. Meanwhile, they're changing all the codes and developing emergency measures to protect them better. We've told them we think there's a DNA computer out there, and they've got to do more than try. Why Madrid? What did you find in Toledo?"

Without preamble, Jon reported, "The Black Flame was a hired front. The Crescent Shield seems to be the real power behind everything. And Émile Chambord is alive. Unfortunately, the Crescent Shield has both him and his daughter and the DNA computer."

There was a stunned silence. Klein said, "You *saw* Chambord? How do you know about the computer?"

"I saw and talked to both Chambord and his daughter. The computer wasn't at that site."

"Chambord alive explains how quickly they got the machine working, and makes the worldwide danger a hell of a lot worse. Especially if they have the daughter, too. They'll use her to control him."

"Yeah," Jon said.

Another silence. Klein said, "You should've killed Chambord, Colonel."

"The DNA computer wasn't there, Fred. I tried for the save, to get him out of there alive so he could build one for us to fight back. How do we know what they've forced Chambord to tell them? Maybe enough for another scientist to duplicate his work."

"What if you don't get a second chance, Jon? What if we don't find him or the machine in time?"

"We will."

"That's what I tell the president. But we both know there are no miracles, and the next time will be harder."

It was Jon's turn to be silent. Then, "I made a judgment call. That's what you pay me for. If in my judgment I can't pull Chambord out, or destroy the computer, I'll kill him. That make you happy?"

Klein's voice was as flat and hard as poured concrete. "Can I count on you, Colonel? Or do I have to send someone else?"

"There's no one else who knows what I know. Not in the beginning, and especially not now."

If the phone had been a television phone, they would have been staring each other down. Finally there was a slow outlet of breath in the far-off Pentagon. "Tell me about this Crescent Shield. Never heard of them."

"That's because they're newer and have stayed out of sight," Jon told him, repeating what Randi had said. "They're pan-Islamic, apparently pulled together for this specific attack by a man named Mauritania. He's—"

"I know who he is, Jon. Only too well. Part Arab, part Berber, and with rage over the fate of his poor country and its starving people to add to his endemic Muslim and Third World rage about corporate globalization."

"Which, in truth, motivates these terrorists more than their religion."

"Yeah," Klein said. "What's your next step?"

"I'm with Randi Russell and Peter Howell now." He filled Klein in on how Randi and Peter had shown up at the farmhouse of the Crescent Shield.

There was another surprised hesitation. "Howell and Russell? CIA and MI6? What have you told them?"

"They're right here," Jon said, letting him know he could say no more.

"You haven't told them about Covert-One?" Klein demanded.

"Of course not." Jon kept the irritation from his voice.

"All right. Cooperate, but keep the confidence. Understood?"

Jon decided to let the admonition pass. "We need anything and everything you can dig up about Mauritania's personal history. Any patterns he's shown. Where he's most likely to hole up, where we should look for him."

Klein regrouped and said, "I can tell you one thing. He'll have chosen a secure hole to hide in and a carefully planned target we won't like one bit."

"How long will the electronic communications be compromised?"

"No way to tell. Could be until we find that computer. Meanwhile, we'll switch to couriers and drops, verbal and manual codes, and a dedicated surface phone line over secure diplomatic fiberoptic phone cables where we can monitor for any break-ins and fix them in seconds. We used to get a lot of intelligence accomplished that way in the old days, and we can do it again. The DNA computer won't help them there. That was smart to get to me through Colonel Hakkim. Here's the new secure private phone number they'll have up as fast as they can, so you can call direct next time."

Klein relayed the number, and Jon memorized it.

Klein continued, "What about General Henze and that hospital orderly who tried to kill Zellerbach?"

"False alarm. Turns out the 'orderly' was Peter guarding Marty for MI6. He ran because he couldn't taint his operation. He went to Henze's *pension* to interview Henze's sergeant, not the general." Jon explained what Peter had wanted with Sergeant Matthias.

"A phone call out of NATO headquarters? Damn, that doesn't sound good to me. How do we know Howell isn't lying?"

"He isn't," Jon snapped flatly, "and there are a lot of people at NATO. I'm already wondering about one of them, a Captain Bonnard. The Black Flame expected me in Toledo, so either I was tailed or they were tipped. Bonnard is the personal aide to a French general, Roland la Porte. He's the—"

"I know who he is. Deputy supreme commander."

"Right. Bonnard is the one who gave La Porte the data about the fingerprints and DNA analysis in Chambord's file, proving he was dead. He also brought La Porte the file on the Black Flame and Toledo. His position with the general is ideal. Just where anyone would put a spy if they could. He'd have access to just about whatever he wanted in NATO, France, and most of Europe, in the name of the general."

"I'll see what I can dig up on Bonnard and on Sergeant Matthias. Meanwhile, you'd better go back to Henze. NATO's got Europe's most complete data on current terrorist groups and alliances. Whatever I can dig up here, I'll shoot over to Henze."

"That's it?" Jon asked.

"That's all . . . no, wait! Damn. Because of Chambord and the Crescent Shield, I almost forgot. I just got a call from Paris that Marty Zellerbach started talking an hour ago. Out of the blue. Full sentences. Then he fell back asleep. Not much, and he's not completely coherent yet. That could be the Asperger's Syndrome, I suppose. But stop in Paris on your way to Brussels."

Excitement rushed through Jon. "I'll be there in two hours or less." He hung up and turned, almost laughing with relief. "Marty's out of the coma!"

"Jon, that's wonderful!" Randi flung her arms around his neck in a joyous hug.

He hugged back and swung her up off her feet.

From the sofa, Peter cocked his head, listening closely. . . . And jumped up. "*Quiet!*" He ran back to the window and leaned toward it, listening intently. His thin, muscular body was like a coiled spring, taut, nervous.

"Did you hear it again?" Randi's whisper was tense.

He gave one sharp nod. He whispered back, "That same breathing whistle on the wind in the night. It was there. This time I'm certain. A signal. We'd better—"

Above them, there was a faint clink of metal striking stone. Jon padded to the staircase and pressed his ear against the wall, feeling for vibrations.

"Someone's on the roof," he warned.

And then all three heard it: A strange sound, like a breathy whistle through the teeth of someone in restless sleep. Or perhaps from a lonely nightbird far away. Not just from below, but from above. They were surrounded.

Chapter Eighteen

The harsh, splintering sound of a door being forced open below signaled the attack.

Randi jerked her head up. "The stairs!"

Her weapon aimed ahead of her, she sprinted from the office, her blond hair flashing with white light as she bolted past Jon.

Peter's leathery face was grim as he sped toward the shutters that covered the balcony door, snapping off lights as he ran. "Check the back windows."

As gloom descended, Jon raced through the bedroom behind the office to the rear, while at the stairwell Randi peered down and opened up with her H&K MP5K in careful bursts of three. There was a scream from below, followed by the sound of feet and two wild shots. She held her fire.

In the sudden vacuum of sound, Jon checked out the windows. Beneath the safe house, the back patio appeared inhabited only by benches and plants awash in moonlight and shadows. He studied the area, looking for movement, but then heard a muted shuffle in the office behind him.

As he tore back to investigate, there was a choking gasp. Jon stopped just inside the door. Peter was crouched over the fallen figure of a man in black street clothes, wearing heavy black gloves, and a flat hat like those worn by Afghan *mujahedeen*. His head and face were completely hidden by a black balaclava.

"Glad you haven't lost your touch." Jon stepped past Peter to check the balcony. It was empty, except for a nylon rope that dangled from the roof. "Not particularly clever, but it got him inside."

Peter wiped the blood from his old Fairbairn-Sykes stiletto on the attacker's pants. "Fellow thought he was quiet as a dormouse." He peeled up the balaclava, revealing brown, sun-dried skin, a beard trimmed short, and an expression of outrage. "I've got a plan. If I'm right about *their* plan, it should give us a chance."

"And if you're wrong?"

There was another burst of gunfire from Randi on the stairs followed by another cry of pain from below. Eerie silence again settled over the safe house.

Peter shrugged. "Then we're probably cooked, as the goose said to the gander."

Jon hunched down beside him in the shadows. "Tell me what you have in mind."

"We're in a box, true. But they're in a bind, because we've shown sharp teeth, and the gunshots will bring the police. They know that. They must make their move soon. Any forced action leads to carelessness and thus errors. They attacked openly from the street level, which I think was cover to send our dead friend here"—he gestured at the corpse at his feet—"to hold the balcony, while others would come down from the roof to trap us between them and the bottom assault team."

"So why don't we hear a charge down the stairs from up top? What are they waiting for?"

"I suspect for a signal from the forward reconnoiterer—this poor sod here. A weakness in their plan, and now we can take advantage of that weakness." Peter put on the dead man's balaclava and flat Afghan hat. He stepped out onto the balcony.

Seconds later, Jon heard the soft night-whistle signal once more. This time it came from Peter. Soon after, a door creaked upstairs. An old door, warped and damaged by the weather where it opened onto the roof, as was true of so many Madrid buildings.

Peter stepped back into the room. "That should do it."

Jon ran into the room he had chosen as his bedroom, aimed his Sig Sauer at his laptop, and fired. He was going on the run, and the laptop could hold him back. He sped back across the landing and told Randi, "Fire a burst, and get in here."

Randi shot one volley, then a second, and bolted back into the office, where she joined Jon on the balcony. Peter was already climbing the rope, while Jon steadied it with both hands, one foot anchoring it.

Randi gazed down warily. The street was deserted, but she could almost feel the eyes of terrified innocents hiding in doorways and behind windows, poised to flee, but also drawn almost hypnotically to witness others' violence and danger. It was that atavistic grip of the hunt, the ancient will to survive that lurked in the Cro-Magnon brain and influenced so many human actions.

Jon looked up and saw that Peter had reached the top. "You next," he breathed into her ear. "Go."

She slung her submachine gun over her back and jumped up onto the balcony railing. She grabbed the rope, and—as Jon continued to steady it—climbed. She saw Peter extend his head over the roof parapet to make sure she followed safely. He touched his forehead in salute and vanished, his teeth white in a Cheshire cat grin. She climbed harder, faster, worried because Jon was exposed where he stood alone on the balcony, but it could not be helped.

Meanwhile, as Jon held the rope, he surveyed carefully all around for trouble. His Sig Sauer seemed very far away, although it was simply tucked into his holster. He looked up, noting Randi's rapid progress. His chest tight, he saw what an easy target she was for anyone who spotted her. As he was thinking that, footsteps sounded: They were searching the rooms on the floor directly above him. They would be down to this floor any moment. And now the undulating wail of police cars had begun. Yes, they were heading in this direction.

With relief he saw Randi had disappeared onto the roof. He jumped up and climbed, hand over hand as fast as he could, his fingers and palms burning on the corded nylon. He had been lucky so far, but now he must be on the roof before the terrorists discovered their dead comrade, and before the police arrived. Second only to staying alive was not being caught by the police.

Alarmed oaths in Arabic came from inside the house below as the terrorists found the body of their comrade and the destroyed laptop. At that moment, Jon reached the roof. He gave a powerful final pull, surged over the edge, and flopped onto the shallow slope of red tiles, still holding to the rope to keep from sliding backward. With a tug, the rope moved, dragging him up toward the ridge line. He could see the top of Peter's head. As he slid over headfirst and started to fall, Randi grabbed his shoulders to keep him from nose-diving onto flagstones. He shoulder-rolled up onto his feet and looked around. They were in a small, roof-top garden.

"Nice job." Peter sliced through the rope, and the cut end rushed back over the rooftop. A shout of rage rose from below, followed by a despairing shriek and crash.

Without another word, the three agents leaped, grabbed the peak of the rooftop, and pulled themselves up to their feet. Straddling it, they ran carefully, one after the other, Jon in the lead, jumping gaps and dodging birds' nests as fast as they could without slipping and falling the six stories to the ground. They were five attached roofs away from the safe house when their pursuers burst up and out to the rooftop garden behind them.

As a fusillade of shots buzzed, whined, and ricocheted around them, they dropped flat on the other side of the incline, only their fingers exposed to the gunfire as they gripped the rough tiles that crowned the peak. Below, police cars were roaring onto Calle Dominguin. There were angry Spanish shouts and running feet.

"¡Cuidado!"

"¡Vamos a sondear el ambiente!"

As the police consulted below, Jon was thinking about their attackers. "They'll try to get ahead of us, break into any building they can, and find a way to get up here and cut us off."

Randi said nothing. The street lamps had been shot out, and the two police cars were parked side by side in the middle of the street, their headlights on bright, doors wide open. "It's the Policía Municipal," she decided as the men ran behind the cars for protection, shotguns pointing out and around like porcupine quills, while one grabbed his radio phone and shouted into it. "He's probably summoning shock units of the Nacionals or the Guardia Civil antiterrorist units. We should be out of here when they arrive. They'll have too much firepower, and too many inconvenient questions."

"I'll second that," Peter agreed.

Randi listened. "They say they've got a witness who saw our attackers, and the police have deduced terrorists may be behind the trouble tonight."

"That'll take some of the heat off us."

Jon saw a head pop up above the balcony railing on the safe house five buildings back. The terrorist fired a burst from an Uzi. Jon quickly pulled himself up so that his armpits were caught on the ridge, aimed carefully, and returned fire. There was a yelp and a curse as the terrorist pulled back inside the safe house, his arm bloody.

"They'll try to hold us here until their buddies get ahead of us," Jon said.

"Then we best be on our way." Peter's pale gaze swept the area. "You see that taller apartment building at the end of this row? If we can reach it and climb up to the roof, it looks as if it leads to those two other apartment buildings. We may be able to get to the next street from there, where it'll be easier to lose them."

The heads of two terrorists rose above the wall that rimmed the safe house's roof garden. Jon, Randi, and Peter immediately dropped back behind the ridge, and the terrorists laid down a line of withering fire. But as soon as there was a pause, the trio rose again, returned fire, and when the terrorists ducked, the agents jumped up and ran. They had almost reached the taller apartment building that was their goal when another hail of bullets and polyglot shouts burst out from the rear. Gunshots slammed into the building's wall, shattered windows, and raised shouts of terror from within the apartments.

"Inside!" Jon made a headlong dive through a shattered apartment window. Two terrified women in nightgowns sat bolt upright in twin beds and screamed, sheets pulled tight against their throats, eyes wide in horror.

Randi and Peter dove in after him, and as Peter rolled to his feet, he bowed to the frightened women and apologized in flawless Castilian, "Lo siento," as he rushed after Randi and Jon, through the apartment, and out into a broad corridor. One of them was leaving a trail of blood drops.

They passed the elevator and ran up the fire stairs, not pausing to check for wounds until they reached a fire exit that opened onto a wide, flat roof.

"Who's hurt?" Jon puffed. "Randi?"

"It looks like all of us, especially you." She pointed.

There were long, bloody furrows on Jon's left arm and shoulder under his ripped shirt and a narrower slash on his left cheek where he had gone headfirst through the shattered window with its jagged wedges of glass. Randi and Peter had lesser cuts, a few bruises, and a couple of bloody creases from the gunfire.

While Jon ripped the left sleeve off his shirt and Randi used it to bind the deeper gashes on his arm, Peter was scrutinizing the street below where it intersected with Calle Dominguin.

Randi studied the long, broad roof behind them as she bandaged. "We could hold off an attack from where we are, but there's no point. Our situation would only get worse, especially once more police arrive."

Peter spoke from the parapet, still looking down: "It's going to be a dicey thing, one way or the other. Looks like the buggers are circling the block to head us off, and there appears to be enough of them to cover all exits."

Randi cocked her head, listening. "We'd better do something quick. They're starting up after us."

Randi finished wrapping Jon's wounds, and Peter ran from the parapet to join them. Randi pulled open the roof door. Three masked terrorists armed with an Uzi, an AK-74, and what looked like an old Luger pistol were halfway up the stairs. In the lead was a burly ruffian with a black beard so great that it sprouted out from beneath his black balaclava.

Without hesitation, Randi squeezed off a short burst of her MP5K, sending the fellow falling back onto the two behind him. One of them, in baggy jeans and a T-shirt as black as his balaclava, leaped over his fallen comrade, firing up as he climbed. Randi cut him down, too, while the third tripped over his own feet as he frantically escaped.

Peter broke into a run. "The next roof!"

They sprinted across the building, jumped the short space to the next one, and ran on. A series of shots sounded far behind from the third terrorist, who had braved coming out onto the roof and was now blazing away with the old Luger with little chance to hit them at this distance even if they had been standing still.

"Damn!" Randi skidded to a stop, staring ahead.

Three roofs away, on a building on the street that paralleled Calle Dominguin, four figures had emerged. Their silhouettes, rifles cradled in their arms, stood out against the stars.

"Listen!" Jon said.

Behind them on Calle Dominguin, heavy vehicles had arrived. Now there was the clatter of booted feet jumping down to the pavement, of officers bawling orders in Spanish. The antiterrorist units were on site. Seconds later, that soft sighing whistle seemed to come from nowhere and hang suspended in the night air. Before the signal had faded, the four silhouettes on the distant roof spun around, ran back to the door, and were gone.

Peter looked behind. The terrorist with the Luger had retreated, too. "The bloody thugs are bunking," he said, relieved. "Now all we have to do is get past the police. Which, I'm afraid, will not be easy, especially if they really are the antiterrorist Guardia Civil units."

"We'll go separately," Jon decided. "A change of clothes would be helpful."

Peter eyed Randi. "Especially the lady's black tights and all."

Randi turned her cool gaze on him. "The lady will take care of herself, thank you. Let's agree where we'll go next. For me, it's Paris, Marty, and my CIA station chief."

"I'm for Paris, too," Peter said.

"Where will you go, Jon?" Randi asked innocently. "To report to your army intelligence bosses?"

Jon could hear Klein's voice in his ear: *Tell them nothing*. He said, "Let's just say I'll catch up with you in Brussels, after I've been to NATO headquarters."

"Right. Sure." But Randi smiled. "Okay, after we do what we have to, we'll meet in Brussels, Jon. I know the proprietor of the Café Egmont in old town. Drop a message there when you're ready. That goes for both of you."

They said "good luck" all around. Randi ran lightly toward the building's rooftop exit door, a stunning figure in her tight black working clothes and pale blond hair. The men watched her, then Peter jogged toward the fire escape, his lean, lined face inscrutable. Left alone, Jon walked to the parapet and stared down. The antiterrorist units, with their heavier weapons and flak jackets, were spreading out. There were no alarms, no shooting, no activity of any kind beyond their methodical dispersal. As for the terrorists, they appeared to have vanished.

Jon ran across the rooftops to the farthest building he could reach and took the interior stairs down. At each door, he paused to listen. On the third floor he found what he wanted: Inside, a television was on. He heard the volume decrease, a window creak open, and a man's voice shout down to the street, "*¿Que paso, Antonio?*"

A voice called up in Spanish, "Didn't you hear all the shooting, Cela? There was a terrorist battle. The police are all over the area."

"*Después de todo lo ocurrido, eso nada más me faltaba. ¡Adios!*"

Jon heard the window close and waited for the man to speak to anyone else in the apartment. But the only sound was of the television, the volume again raised.

Jon knocked sharply and announced in peremptory Spanish, "*Policía.* We need to speak with you."

He heard swearing. Soon the door was flung open, and a heavy man in a dressing gown with a potbelly glowered at him. "I been home here all—"

Jon pressed the muzzle of his Sig Sauer into the man's stomach. "Sorry. Inside, *por favor.*"

Five minutes later, dressed in a pair of pants and a sports jacket from the man's closet, a white shirt with the collar open, and the dressing gown over everything—all far too big in the waist—Jon tied and gagged the Spaniard and left. He sauntered down the stairs to the street, where he joined a group of alarmed residents who were watching the police unit as it stopped before the apartment building. In their dark combat gear, the officers rushed in, leaving two behind to interrogate the onlookers. After a few questions, the pair sent one resident after another back into their buildings.

When the officers finally reached Jon, he told them he had seen nothing and no one, and lived in the previous building, which they had already searched. The police officer ordered him back to his "own" building, and moved on to the next interview. When Jon was sure the officer's back was turned, he crossed the street into the shadows of the far sidewalk, rounded the corner, and discarded the dressing gown.

At the San Bernardo metro station, he took the next train, where he picked up a discarded copy of *El País*, one of Madrid's daily newspapers, from one of the seats, and buried his face in it, using his peripheral vision to watch for tails. Soon he transferred to line eight, and from there he rode out to Aeropuerto de Barajas. Just before entering the terminal, he found a large waste bin. He checked quickly to make certain he had still not been detected. Then he dropped his Sig Sauer into the soiled paper cups and wrappers and, with a pang of regret, watched it sink. He tossed the newspaper on top.

With nothing but his stolen clothes, wallet, passport, and cell phone, he bought a ticket for the next Brussels flight. After he phoned Fred Klein using the new number that was thankfully up and running and arranged to have a change of clothes, a uniform, and a weapon delivered to him in Brussels, he sat down in the waiting room, where he read his detective novel.

The Brussels flight was departing from the next gate, but he saw no sign of Randi. About ten minutes before his plane was to board, a tall Muslim woman wearing the traditional black head covering and long black robes—a *pushi* and *abaya*, not the chador, which covered the eyes as well as the head and body—sat down across the aisle from him. He watched her unobtrusively. She sat immobile, her hands hardly visible, looking at no one. Her face was modestly lowered.

Then he heard that same strange, soft sound that seemed almost a part of the wind. It gave him a start. Obviously there was no wind inside this modern, bustling airlines terminal, at least none that was natural. He looked sharply at the woman who was swathed in black, instantly regretting that he no longer had his Sig Sauer.

She seemed to sense his interest. She looked up, gazed boldly into his eyes, and winked. And humbly bowed her head. Jon repressed a smile. Peter had fooled him. The faint strains of a whistled tune reached his ears—"Rule Britannia." The old SAS trooper loved his little jokes and amusements.

When his flight was finally called, Jon was still scanning all around for

Randi, his stomach tight with worry. She had been first to leave. She should have arrived here by now.

■

After leaving Peter and Jon, Randi had run down the central staircase, stopping to knock on doors until she found an apartment on the first floor where there was no response. She picked the lock, hurried inside, and discovered a closet filled with flamboyant women's clothes. She chose a tight skirt that flared wide below the hips and looked as if it had been designed for the swirl of a flamenco dancer. Quickly she put it on as well as a peasant blouse and high-heeled black pumps. She shook out her hair so it was loose and fluffy around her head, and then she hung her MP5K submachine gun under the skirt from her waist.

The apartment building was quiet, and she was just beginning to relax, when she reached the front entry hall with its fake palms and expensive oriental carpeting. But through the glass panel on the front door she could see five masked men running toward her, glancing warily back over their shoulders as if they were being chased. She felt a burst of fear. *The terrorists.*

She retrieved her weapon, wheeled around, yanked open a door beneath the stairs, and dashed down into a dark basement. Breathing hard, she listened intently. As the basement door opened above again, she sprinted away from the light, batting aside spiderwebs. Feet clattered down. The door closed, and sooty darkness spread. Men grumbled in Arabic, and she realized from their conversation that they had not noticed her. The five were here because they were hiding, too.

Out on the street, some kind of heavy vehicle screeched to a stop, booted feet pounded the pavement, and orders were given in Spanish. The Guardia Civil shock troops had arrived, and they were spreading out to hunt for the terrorists.

Inside the basement, the men's voices were angry now, continuing low in Arabic:

"Who are *you*, Abu Auda, to tell us to die for Allah? You've never even seen Mecca or Medina. You may speak our language, but not a single drop of the blood of the prophets runs in your veins. You're a *Fulani*, a mongrel."

A deep voice, hard and tight, sneered, "You're a coward who doesn't deserve the name of Ibrahim. If you believe in the Prophet, how can you be so afraid to die a martyr's death?"

"Afraid to die? No, black one. That's not it at all. We were beaten today. But that's just today. There'll be better times. To die senselessly is an affront to Islam."

A third voice said contemptuously, "You tremble like a timid woman, Ibrahim."

And a fourth: "I stand with Ibrahim. He's proved himself over more years than you've lived. We're warriors, not fanatics. Let the mullahs and imams prattle of jihad and martyrdom. *I* speak of victory, and a Spanish prison has many doors for those who'll fight on for Allah."

The deep voice asked quietly, "You'll surrender, then? You, too, Ibrahim? And Ali as well?"

"It's wise," the first voice, Ibrahim, announced with a tremor of fear. "M. Mauritania will find some way to free us quickly, because he needs all his fighters to strike his great blows against our enemies."

The contemptuous voice was impatient. "You know there's no time to free any of us. We've got to fight our way out now like men, or die for Allah."

More angry arguments from the trio who favored surrender were abruptly cut off by three low, sharp sounds. Silenced gunfire. Probably from the same weapon. Randi listened as the silence stretched for what seemed minutes but was probably only seconds. She kept her MP5K aimed into the impenetrable darkness toward the sounds of the shots. Her stomach tightened into a knot.

At last the voice that had spoken third, the man who claimed to be ready to die, asked softly, "So you'll kill me, too, Abu Auda? I was the only one who dared to stand with you against the other three."

"It's unfortunate. But you look too much like an Arab, and you don't speak Spanish. All men can be made to reveal what they know under the right circumstances. You're a risk. However, a single black man such as myself who *does* speak Spanish can perhaps escape."

Randi could almost hear the other man nod. "I'll greet Allah in your name, Abu Auda. Praise Allah!"

The final silenced shot made Randi jump. She wanted to see the face of the man whom they had called the Fulani, the black one, who could kill a friend as easily as an enemy. *Abu Auda.*

She backed away as his footsteps approached. Chills shot along her spine. She followed the sounds with her weapon trained and heard an exhalation of breath, almost a sigh of relief, as a door opened into the night about ten feet to her right. Moonlight shone in, and she stared at the terrorist who had opened it—a giant black man who was dressed like an ordinary Spanish worker. He stepped outside and lifted his face toward the heavens as if saying a silent prayer of gratitude for his freedom. When he turned to grasp the door handle, light from a window caught in his eyes, and they flashed an odd brown-green.

Before the door had closed, she remembered where she had seen him: He was the white-robed bedouin who had led the attack against her at the farmhouse outside Toledo. Now she had a name for him, too: Abu Auda. She ached to open fire, but dared not. In any case, she had better uses for him.

She turned abruptly. Light had appeared on the other side of the basement again. The door above the stairs had been opened, and booted feet were pounding down into the cellar—the Guardia Civil.

She forced herself to count to ten, then she pulled open the outside cellar door, glanced quickly around, stepped out into a courtyard, and closed the door. Somewhere a dog barked, while out on the street a car cruised past. She dismissed the sounds of normalcy.

It was only a matter of time until the Guardia Civil found the door and tried it. She ran toward a gate. It was the courtyard's only exit, and she hoped to find the terrorist beyond it. Just as she rushed through and into an alley, she heard the cellar door open behind her. She put on a burst of speed, disgusted with the clumsiness of the high heels. She tightened her ankles and raced determinedly onward to the street, waiting for the sounds of shouts and pounding feet behind her.

But they never came. She must have been sufficiently fast that they had not seen her. Breathing deeply, she looked around. There was no sign of Abu Auda. She slowed, hooked her MP5K up under her flared skirt again, and stepped out onto the street. For a moment, excitement coursed through her as she saw Abu Auda again. He was approaching the corner . . . but police stationed there stopped him. Aching to capture and interrogate him herself, she watched as one of the officers examined his papers. But the inspection was only cursory: After all, a black man with Spanish papers could not be an Arab terrorist.

Randi rushed through the street's yellow pools of lamplight, but they were already letting him pass. The police turned to stare at her, their faces grim. She was next. She did not mind their questions, because she had good fake ID. What concerned her was the delay of having to deal with them.

As she watched Abu Auda turn the corner and disappear, she thought quickly. And began to swing her hips. She swayed toward them in her best imitation of the fiery Carmen, heels clicking on the street rhythmically.

As she approached, their expressions grew interested. She smiled widely, spun on her toes, and flipped the back of her skirt at them just enough for a flash of panties but not enough to show the weapon that dangled in front. They grinned and whistled in salute, and she passed by, holding her breath, heart thudding against her ribs, until one demanded her phone number. With snapping eyes, she gave him a phony one.

As the others pounded him on the back in congratulations, she sauntered off and around the same corner that Abu Auda had taken. And stopped, gazing all around, searching the lamplight and shadows of the street for him. But he was nowhere in sight. She had gone through the checkpoint faster than he had, but not fast enough. Disappointed, she moved on, looking everywhere, until finally she reached the next intersection and was forced to believe she had been too slow, or—more likely—he was already gone.

She hailed a taxi and told the driver to take her to the airport. Sitting back in the dim interior, she considered what she had learned: First, the black Crescent Shield leader from the Fulani tribe was named Abu Auda and he spoke Spanish and Arabic. Second, whatever the Crescent Shield planned to do were to be massive blows. Third—and most worrisome— was that it would happen soon. Very soon.

Chapter Nineteen

Paris, France
Thursday, May 8

In the ultramodern Pompidou Hospital, Marty Zellerbach had been moved to a private room, where Legionnaires now guarded his door. Peter Howell pulled up a chair to Marty's bed and said cheerfully, "Well, old friend, this is a fine mess you've gotten yourself into. Can't leave you on your own for long, can I? That's right . . . Howell here. Peter Howell, who taught you all that you know about firearms. Oh, don't try to deny it or claim weapons are vulgar and stupid. I know better." Smiling to himself, he paused, remembering. . . .

It had been night, black night, in a large state park outside Syracuse, New York. He and Marty were trapped in his RV at the edge of the woods, surrounded by hired thugs whose gunfire had shot out all the windows. He threw Marty an assault rifle. "When I say point, just pull the trigger, my boy. Imagine the weapon's simply a joystick."

He could see Marty's expression of distaste as he examined the rifle and grumbled to himself, "There are some things I never wanted to learn." He gave a pained sigh. "Naturally, I understand this primitive machine. Child's play."

Marty was as good as his word. When Peter told him to fire, Marty nodded and squeezed the trigger. The weapon bucked hard, and Marty fought to keep his balance and to keep his eyes open. His barrage shredded leaves and pine needles, ripped bark, sawed through branches, and created so much havoc that their attackers had been momentarily stopped. Which was just what Peter had needed to slip away and go for help.

Peter liked to think of himself as a peaceful man, but the truth was, he enjoyed action. To his way of thinking, he was just an old English bulldog, who relished getting his fangs into something worthwhile. He leaned over the bed's railing and told Marty, "Took to bloody combat like a duck to water, you did." It was far from true, but it was the sort of annoying statement that always got a rise out of Marty.

Peter waited, hoping Marty's eyes would snap open and he would say something insulting. When nothing happened, he turned to look back at Dr. Dubost, who was standing at the end of the bed, entering information into Marty's computer chart. Peter raised his eyebrows questioningly.

"It's a small relapse," the doctor explained in French. "They're to be expected."

"They'll diminish with time?"

"*Oui*. All the signs are there. Now I'm off, *monsieur*, to see other patients. Please continue your conversation with Dr. Zellerbach, by all means. Your ebullience is charming, and it can't but help."

Peter scowled. "Ebullience" did not strike him as an accurate description, but then the French were known to be slightly off kilter in their understanding of a lot of things. He said a polite *adieu* and turned back to Marty. "Alone at last," he muttered, suddenly feeling tired and very worried.

He had dozed on the jet ride from Madrid, giving him more consecutive hours of sleep than he had on many assignments, but it was the worry itself that nagged him. He had been thinking about the Crescent Shield, that it appeared to be pan-Islamic. There was no shortage of countries in the Third World that hated the United States and, to a lesser extent, Britain, claiming great damage from their driving capitalism, that their brand of globalization ignored local customs and businesses and destroyed the environment, and that their cultural arrogance crushed sensible protest. He was reminded of that old died-in-the-wool

Tory, Winston Churchill, who had explained blithely—and accurately—
that His Majesty's government did not base its practices and policies on
the whims of locals. Whether the Crescent Shield were fundamentalists
or not religious at all seemed less worrisome to him than the poverty that
gave rise to so much terrorism.

The voice that brought him out of his uneasy reverie was not Marty's:
"You couldn't wait for me?"

Automatically, Peter grabbed for his gun and turned. And relaxed. It
was Randi Russell, marching into the private room, the credentials she
had shown the guard at the door still in her hand.

"To where, may I ask," Peter admonished, "did you disappear?"

Randi put away her ID, and Peter met her in the middle of the room.
She related what she had seen and done since they separated in Madrid.
The sexy flamenco outfit she described was gone, and now she was
dressed in serviceable twill slacks, a white button-down shirt, and a tailored black jacket. Her blond hair was pulled back into a stubby ponytail,
and her brown eyes were worried as she told him, "I got to Barajas about
ten minutes after the two of you had flown out."

"You had Jon's wind up a bit. The poor sod was anxious about you."

At that, she grinned. "Was he now?"

"Save it for Jon, my girl," Peter declared. "For me, I never doubted.
You say Abu Auda was leading them?" He looked grim. "Possibly some
Nigerian warlord is helping the Crescent Shield. It gets murkier with
every new detail."

"It sure does," Randi agreed. "But the most vital piece of information
I overheard was that whatever they're planning is going to happen soon.
Two days, at the most."

"Then we'd best get a move on," Peter told her. "Check in with your
station chief yet?"

"Not before I saw Marty. Is he asleep?"

"Relapsed." Peter sighed wearily. "With any luck, he'll wake again
soon. When he does, I shall be here in case he can tell us anything we
haven't learned."

"Is this your chair?" She headed for the armchair he had moved next
to Marty's bed. "Mind if I use it?" She sat without waiting for an answer.

"Certainly," he said. "Be my guest."

She ignored the sarcasm and picked up Marty's hand. It had a natural warmth that was reassuring. She leaned forward and kissed his pudgy cheek. "He looks good," she told Peter. Then she said to Marty, "Hi, Marty. It's Randi, and I just want you to know how great you look. As if you're going to wake up any moment and say something wonderfully disagreeable to Peter."

But Marty was silent, his jaw relaxed, his high forehead uncreased, as if he had never had an unpleasant experience. But that was far from the truth. After the Hades problem had been resolved, and Marty had returned to his solitary life in his bungalow hidden behind high hedges in Washington, he might have left bullets and terrifying escapes behind, but he still had to deal with the normal activities of everyday life. For someone with Asperger's, they could be overwhelming. Which was why Marty had designed his home as a mini fortress.

When Randi had arrived to visit him the first time, he had put her through her paces, demanding she identify herself even though he could see her in his surveillance camera. But then he had unlocked the barred interior cage, hugged her, and stepped back bashfully to welcome her into his cottage, where all the windows were protected by steel bars and thick drapes. "I don't have visitors, you know," he explained in his high, slow, precise voice. "I don't like them. How about some coffee and a cookie?" His eyes made glittering contact and then skittered away again.

He made instant Yuban decaf, handed her an Oreo cookie, and took her into a computer room where a formidable Cray mainframe and other computer equipment of every possible description filled all wall space and most of the floor, while the few pieces of furniture looked like Salvation Army discards, although Marty was a multimillionaire. She knew from Jon that Marty had tested at the genius level since the age of five. He had two Ph.D.s—one in quantum physics and mathematics, of course, and the other in literature.

He had launched into a description of a new computer virus that had caused some $6 billion in damage. "This was a particularly nasty one," he explained earnestly. "It was self-replicating—we call them worms— and it e-mailed itself to tens of millions of users and jammed e-mail systems around the globe. But the guy who started it left behind his digital fingerprint—a thirty-two-digit Globally Unique ID—we call them

GUIDs—that identified his computer." He rubbed his hands gleefully. "See, GUIDs are sometimes embedded in the computer code of files saved in Microsoft Office programs. They're hard to find, but he should've made real sure his was erased. Once I located his GUID, I tracked it to files all over the Internet until I finally pinpointed one that actually contained his name. His *whole name*—can you believe it?—in an e-mail to his girlfriend. Dumb. He lives in Cleveland, and the FBI says they have enough evidence to arrest him now." The smile on Marty's face had been radiant with triumph.

As she remembered all this, Randi leaned over Marty's hospital bed to give him another kiss, this one on the other cheek. She stroked it tenderly, hoping he would stir. "You've got to get better soon, Marty, dear," she told him at last. "You're my favorite person to eat Oreo cookies with." Her eyes felt moist. At last she stood up. "Take good care of him, Peter."

"I will."

She headed toward the door. "I'm off to check in with my station chief and find out what he can tell me about Mauritania and the DNA computer hunt. Then it's Brussels. In case Jon does call here, remind him I'll look for a message at the Café Egmont."

He smiled. "A message drop, just like the old days when tradecraft really mattered. Damn me, but it feels good."

"You're a dinosaur, Peter."

"That I am," he agreed cheerfully, "that I am." And more soberly, "Off with you. I'd say there appears to be considerable urgency, and your country's the most likely target."

Before Randi was out the door, Peter was back in his chair beside the silent Marty, talking and joshing, the quirkiness of their friendship in every light, bantering word.

St. Francesc, Isla de Formentera

Captain Darius Bonnard sat in the fishermen's café on the rustic waterfront, eating a plate of *langosta a la parrilla* and gazing across the flat, spare landscape of the last and smallest of the main Balearic Islands toward the port of La Savina. Two of the islands in the chain—Mallorca and Ibiza—were synonymous with tourism and had once been the main vacation destination of well-to-do Britishers, while this one, La Isla de Formentera, had remained a little-known, underdeveloped, almost perfectly flat Mediterranean paradise. Captain Bonnard's ostensible mission here was to bring back for his general's table a generous supply of the famous local mayonnaise, first created in Maó, the picturesque capital of the fourth island, Menorca.

He had finished his meal of lobster and the same ubiquitous mayonnaise and was sipping a glass of light local white wine, when the real reason for his trip sat down across the table.

Mauritania's small face and blue eyes shone with triumph. "The test was a complete success," he enthused in French. "The smug Americans never knew what hit them, as they say in their barbaric language. We're exactly on schedule."

"No problems?"

"There is a problem with the DNA replicator that Chambord tells me needs to be corrected. Unfortunate, but not disastrous."

Bonnard smiled and raised his glass. "*Santé!*" he toasted. "Cheers! Excellent news. And you? How goes your end?"

Mauritania frowned, and his gaze bore into Bonnard. "At the moment, my largest concern is you. If exploding the jet that was carrying General Moore was your work, as I think it was, it was a blunder."

"It was necessary." Bonnard drained his wineglass. "My general, whose stupid nationalistic convictions enable me to work so well with you, has the unfortunate habit of exaggerating his position in order to impress doubters. This time he alarmed Sir Arnold Moore. We don't need a suspicious British general alerting his government, which in turn is guaranteed to warn the Americans as well. Then both would be up in arms about a nonexistent danger that might easily be tracked back to us."

"His sudden death will do precisely that."

"Relax, my revolutionary friend. Had Sir Arnold reached Britain, he would've revealed the meeting on the *Charles de Gaulle* and what my general suggested. *That* would've been a serious problem. But now the prime minister knows only that one of his generals was flying to London to speak to him on a delicate matter and has now disappeared. He and his staff will speculate about it. Was it a private matter? A public matter?

All of this will give us time, since their vaunted MI6 will have to dig around until it finds out what and why. They'll probably never succeed. But if they do, enough days will have passed that by then"—Bonnard shrugged—"we won't care, will we?"

Mauritania thought for a time and smiled. "Perhaps you do know what you're doing, Captain. When you first approached me to join you, I wasn't convinced of that."

"Then why did you agree to the plan?"

"Because you had the money. Because the plan was good, and our purpose the same. So we will smite the enemy together. But I still fear your action against the English general will draw attention."

"If we didn't have the full attention of Europe and the Americans before, your tests have assured we do now."

Mauritania admitted grudgingly, "Perhaps. When will you come to us? We may want you soon, particularly if Chambord's back needs more stiffening."

"When it's safe. When I won't be missed."

Mauritania stood. "Very well. Two days, no more."

"I'll be there long before. Count on it."

Mauritania walked from the café to his bicycle, parked near the water. Out on the Mediterranean, white sails were unfurled against the blue sea. Above him, seagulls rode the salty air. A scattering of cafés, bars, and gift shops dotted the open area, with the Spanish flag whipping smartly overhead. As he pedaled away from the annoyingly Western scene, his cell phone rang. It was Abu Auda.

Mauritania asked, "You were successful in Madrid?"

"We weren't," Abu Auda told him, his voice angry and frustrated. He did not tolerate failure in anyone, including himself. "We lost many men. They are clever, those three, and the police arrived so quickly that we were unable to finish our mission. I was forced to eliminate four of our own." He described the confrontation in the Madrid basement.

Mauritania muttered an Arabic oath he knew would shock the puritanical desert warrior, but he did not care.

"It was not entirely a loss," Abu Auda said, his mind more on his chagrin at having failed than on Mauritania's flouting of their religion. "We slowed and separated them."

"Where did they go, Abu Auda?"

"There was no way to find out."

Mauritania's voice rose. "Do you feel safe with them free to plot against us?"

"We were unable to hunt them because of the police," Abu Auda said, controlling his temper. "I was fortunate to escape at all."

Mauritania swore again and heard Abu Auda give a disapproving grunt. He hung up and muttered in English that he did not give a tinker's damn about Abu Auda's religious sensibilities, which were mostly humbug anyway and never prevented Abu Auda from being as devious as a snake striking its own tail when it suited him. What mattered was that the mysterious Smith, the old Englishman from the western Iraqi desert, and the shameless CIA woman were still out there.

Paris, France

The frumpy brunette who emerged from the entrance to the Concorde métro stop onto the rue de Rivoli bore a striking resemblance to the woman who had followed Jon Smith from the Pasteur Institute except that this woman wore a pastel pantsuit common to many tourists and walked with the hurrying steps of most Americans. She crossed the rue Royale into the avenue Gabriel, passed the Hôtel Crillon, and turned onto the grounds of the American embassy. Once inside, she acted distraught as she described an emergency at home in North Platte, Nebraska. She had to get home, but her passport had been stolen.

She was sympathetically referred to a room on the second floor, and she almost ran up the stairs. Inside the room, a short, heavy man in an impeccable dark blue pin-stripe suit was waiting at a conference table.

"Hello, Aaron," Randi said as she sat down at the table, facing him.

Aaron Isaacs, CIA station chief in Paris, said, "You've been out of touch almost forty-eight hours. Where's Mauritania?"

"Gone." Randi told him all that had happened in Toledo and Madrid.

"You uncovered all that? Chambord alive, the DNA computer in the hands of some group calling itself the Crescent Shield? So why did the DCI have to get it from the White House and army intelligence?"

"Because I didn't uncover all that. At least not without help. Jon Smith and Peter Howell were there, too."

"MI6? The DCI's going to go apoplectic."

"Sorry about that. Most of it came from Smith. He got the name of the group, he saw Chambord and his daughter alive. Even talked to them. Chambord told him the Crescent Shield had the computer. All I did was find out Mauritania was bossing the terrorists."

"Who the hell's this Smith?"

"Remember the one I worked with on the Hades virus?"

"That guy? I thought he was an army doctor."

"He is. He's also a cell and microbiology researcher at USAMRIID, a combat doctor in the field, and a lieutenant colonel. The army grabbed him to work on this because of his field experience and his knowledge of DNA computer research."

"You believe all that?"

"Sometimes. It's not important. What can you give me on Mauritania and the DNA computer hunt I don't have?"

"You say the last you saw Mauritania was heading south from Toledo?"

"Yes."

"You know he's from Africa. Most of his strikes with Al Qaeda and other groups have been launched from Africa or Spain. Most of the men he's lost over the years in one group or another have been arrested in Spain. With him and his group heading south, North Africa seems a logical destination, especially after a rumor Langley picked up that says Mauritania may be married to at least one Algerian woman and could have a home in Algiers."

"Now we're getting someplace. Names? Places?"

"Not yet. Our assets are trawling for specifics. With luck, we'll know something soon."

Randi nodded. "How about a terrorist named Abu Auda? A giant Fulani, older, maybe late fifties? Odd green-brown eyes?"

Isaacs frowned. "Never heard the name. I'll have Langley run it." He picked up a phone that stood on the table near him. "Cassie? Send this through to Langley top priority." He gave her the data on Abu Auda and hung up. "Want to know what we've come up with in the Pasteur bombing?"

"Something new? Damn, Aaron, spit it out."

Isaacs gave a grim smile. "We got a clandestine call from a Mossad agent here in Paris, and maybe it's pure gold. It seems there's a Filipino postdoctoral researcher at the Pasteur, whose cousin tried to plant a bomb in the Mossad's Tel Aviv HQ. The guy was from Mindanao, where the Abu Sayaaf group of the Moro Islamic Liberation Front was an ally of the Bin Laden faction and Ayman al-Zawahiri. The researcher has no known terrorist connections and has been away from Mindanao a long time."

"Then what made Mossad alert you to the family relationship?"

"The researcher called in sick to the Pasteur that night. He was supposed to be there, according to his boss, who was badly injured in the blast. That was because he was needed for some important experiment they were conducting."

"Where's their lab, if the boss was so badly hurt?"

"On the floor below Chambord's laboratory. Everyone in that lab was killed or maimed."

"Mossad thinks he was the inside man?"

"There's no evidence, but I passed it on to Langley, and they think it's a hot lead. The Pasteur's security isn't state-of-the-art, but it's good enough to keep out bombers, unless the bomber has some kind of internal contact. Particularly since my people believe the terrorists took not only a resisting Chambord, but the entire experimental setup for his DNA computer. And they did it all just minutes before the bomb went off."

"What about the researcher's supposed illness?"

"On the surface, legitimate. He consulted a doctor for chest pains and was advised to stay home a few days. Of course, chest pains and even heart irregularities can be chemically produced."

"They can, and relatively easily. Okay, where is this guy? Does he have a name?"

"Dr. Akbar Suleiman. As I said, he's postdoc and lives in Paris. We asked the Paris police to check, and they say he's on leave from the Pasteur until his lab can be rebuilt. Mossad says he's still in the city. I have his address."

Randi took the sheet of paper and stood up. "Tell Langley I'm going to be working on Mauritania and the DNA computer with Jon Smith and Peter Howell. Tell them I want authorization to commandeer any asset we have, anywhere."

Aaron nodded. "Done." The phone rang. Aaron listened. Then,

"Thanks, Cassie." He hung up and shrugged. "Nothing on an Abu Auda at all. Must keep a really low profile."

Randi left, heading for De Gaulle again, then Brussels and Jon. If this Dr. Akbar Suleiman was part of the Crescent Shield, and they could find him, maybe he would lead them to Mauritania. She doubted there would be a third chance. Not in time.

Chapter Twenty

Brussels, Belgium

At the airport thirteen kilometers outside Brussels in Zaventem, Jon rented another Renault and picked up the supplies Fred Klein had arranged to be waiting for him. Among them was a uniform, which he put on in preparation for his next destination. Carrying a small overnight bag in which were packed civilian clothes and a 9mm Walther, he drove onto the RO heading west. It was raining steadily, a gray, dismal downpour. Once past Brussels, he left the trunk road and took smaller highways and back roads, watching behind to be certain he was not being tailed.

The countryside was green, flat, and bleak through the sheets of early May rain. Well-tended farms stretched into the distance to a horizon flatter than the great prairie of the American West or the steppes of Russia. In this low-lying land, the various roads crossed many small rivers and canals. Traffic was relatively heavy as he drove in the general direction of the French border—not as thick as in Los Angeles or London at rush hour, but far more than the wide-open interstates of Montana or Wyoming.

From time to time he stopped at a country inn or simply pulled off into a grove of trees to search the sky for helicopters or light aircraft that might be tracking him. When he was satisfied no one followed, he drove on using the same tactics until at last he reached the outskirts of Mons, fifty-five kilometers southwest of Brussels. Wars and soldiers had been part of the history of Mons, or "Bergen" in Flemish, for more than two thousand years, since the days Roman legions first established a fortified camp here on their empire's northern border. Here, too, the generals of Louis XIV engaged in one of their long series of bloody battles against their perpetual nemesis, John Churchill, duke of Marlborough. Mons had also been a bruising battlefield for the armies of the French Revolution, as well as for the heavily outnumbered British Expeditionary Force, which fought its first major engagement of World War I here.

All in all, this was a fitting location for the Supreme Headquarters of Allied Powers in Europe (SHAPE)—the military arm of NATO, and the main office of the Supreme Allied Commander of Europe, the SACEUR himself, General Carlos Henze, U.S.A. Located a few kilometers outside the historic town, the entrance to the parklike campus was a simple kiosk standing before an array of flagpoles flying the banners of all the NATO member nations, plus the United Nations. In the background was a flat-roofed, two-story pale brown building, and behind that rose more unprepossessing buildings.

When Smith presented his credentials at the kiosk, he stated his business as reporting to the chief medical officer. Because of the heightened security of the twenty-first century, one of the military policemen on duty called the chief medical officer's office to confirm the appointment, while another scrutinized Jon, his army uniform, and especially his photo ID and army medical credentials.

When the guards were satisfied, Smith drove onto the right arm of the V-shaped road, parked in the designated lot, and walked to the main entrance, where a steel-beamed marquee like those on a no-frills hotel announced proudly: SUPREME HEADQUARTERS ALLIED POWERS EUROPE. Above that was SHAPE's green-and-gold official shield. Inside, the receptionist directed him to the second floor, where Master Sergeant Matthias met him with a sharp salute. Dressed in full uniform, with rows of stripes and battle ribbons, Matthias escorted him through endless corridors to General Carlos Henze's office.

The wiry general was as blunt as ever: "Is all this damned cloak-and-dagger necessary, Colonel?"

Smith saluted and said, "Don't look at me, sir. It's not my idea."

Henze glared, returned the salute, and grumbled, "Civilians." He waved Smith to a leather chair that faced his desk. "The president's people filled me in. Here's the data they sent over." He pushed file folders toward him, holding back one file. "My staff couldn't locate damn all about any Crescent Shield. Even the CIA knew zip. Looks like you've found a brand-new gang of Arab thugs, Colonel. I had my doubts, but maybe you know what you're doing. Now what?"

"Not Arabs alone, sir. Militants from all parts of the Muslim world: Arabs from many countries, Afghans, a Fulani from northern Nigeria . . . who knows who else. Their leader appears to have been originally from Mauritania. Islam is a world of many nations and ethnic groups, and I'm not even certain they're all Muslims."

As the rail-thin general listened, the four stars on his uniform seemed to glint belligerently as if to defy the terrorists, the bleak day outside his rain-swept windows, and the fruit salad climbing from his pocket nearly to his shoulder. His gaze was intense, as if he were seeing every country, every ethnic group, analyzing every implication. This was no longer a potential threat. It was real. So real and worrisome that Henze rotated his chair around to face his window in his usual back-turned act.

"Indonesia? Malaysia?" the general's voice rumbled. "Turkey?"

"Not so far. But I wouldn't be surprised if there were recruits from all of them, and we have indications some of the Central Asian tribes and countries could be involved as well."

Henze whipped his chair back around to stare at Smith. "*Indications?*"

"An MI6 man I know identified an unusual auditory night signal as being from Central Asia, similar to the night signals of our woodland Indians."

"The old Soviet Republics? Tajiks? Uzbeks? Kirghiz and Kazak?"

Jon nodded, and Henze stroked his nose, deep in thought. He picked up a thinner file from his desk and tossed it across the desk. "The president wanted you to have this, too. It's the complete official NATO dossier on Captain Darius Bonnard, plus what the Oval Office dug up from the French. You're suspicious of General La Porte's top aide? A trusted man who works right here? Practically in my lap?"

"I'm suspicious of everyone, General."

"Even me?"

Remembering his earlier suspicions about the "orderly's" visit to Henze's *pension* in Paris, Jon's smile was thin. "Not so far."

"But I'm not above suspicion?"

Jon hesitated, then decided to be as blunt as the general. "No, sir."

"God in heaven," Henze breathed. He leaned back and studied Jon, his fierce focus reminding Jon of a laser beam. "Yesterday when you and I talked, we knew zip. Now we know the doohickey is for real, the big Kahuna who created it is alive and kicking, and the gang that has them and the daughter is both multinational and multiethnic. So answer what I asked earlier: Now what?"

"Now we find them."

"How?"

"I don't know yet."

"*You don't know yet?*" Henze stared at Smith. "When the hell *will* you know?"

"When I do."

Henze's mouth opened, his bony face turned almost purple. "Is that supposed to satisfy me?"

"It's that kind of war, General. I wish I could give you more, a lot more. I have ideas, leads, hunches, but nothing I can honestly say will do the job, much less how and when."

The general continued to stare at Smith, but his high color receded. "I don't like this kind of war. I don't like it one damn all."

"Neither do I. But it's the way it is right now."

Henze nodded to himself, his focus turned inward. He was the supreme commander of NATO in Europe, with all of the highly mechanized, cyber-smart armies of the member nations at his disposal. Yet he was feeling powerless in the face of this new enemy—little known, without territory or tribe, with hardly a way of life to protect. Only an apocalyptic vision and impossible-to-satisfy grievances.

He rubbed his eyes, looking tired. "I went through one kind of 'new' war, Colonel Smith, and it damn near destroyed me. After Vietnam, I'm not sure I can handle another 'new' one. Maybe it's just as well. Time for a new kind of commander."

"We'll get it done," Jon said.

Henze nodded. "We have to win." Looking drained, he indicated Jon should pick up the file folders.

Jon took them, saluted, and left. In the corridor, he paused and decided to take the files to Brussels, where he was to meet Randi. He could study them there. As he walked off, he heard his name called. He turned to see General the Count Roland la Porte striding toward him with a broad smile.

"*Bonjour*, General La Porte."

Doors seemed to rattle on their hinges as the massive general cruised past. "Ah, Colonel Smith. The man who's given us all the great shock. We must speak at once. Come, my office is near. We will have coffee, *non?*"

Jon agreed they would have coffee, and he followed La Porte into his office. The general sat in a large red leather armchair in the style of a British club chair. It looked as if it were the only piece of furniture besides the desk chair that would not crumble under his oversized body. He assigned Jon another delicate occasional chair from the Louis Quinze period. Soon a nervous young French lieutenant served coffee.

"So, our Émile is alive after all, which is *magnifique*, but the kidnappers have him, which is not so *magnifique*. You could not be mistaken, Colonel?"

"Afraid not."

La Porte nodded, scowling. "Then we've been duped. The remains found in the bombed Pasteur building were not there by accident, nor the fingerprints and DNA profile in his Sûreté file, and the Basques were only a front, a charade to hide the real terrorists. Is that so?"

"Yes," Jon acknowledged. "The actual perpetrators call themselves the Crescent Shield. A multiethnic, multinational Muslim extremist group led by a man who calls himself M. Mauritania."

The general gulped angrily at his coffee. "The information I was given, and then gave to you, appears to have misled you on many counts. I apologize for this."

"Actually, it was following the trail of the Basques that revealed most of what we know now, so in the end you turned out to be of great help, General."

"*Merci.* I take comfort in that outcome."

Jon put down his cup. "May I ask where your aide, Captain Bonnard, is?"

"Darius? I sent him on a mission to the South of France."

Not far from Spain. "Where exactly, General?"

La Porte stared at Jon, frowned. "Our naval base at Toulon and then on to Menorca for an errand. Why? What are these questions about Darius?"

"How well do you know Captain Bonnard?"

"*Well?*" La Porte was astonished. "You suspect Darius of . . . ? No, no, that's impossible. I can't think such a treason."

"He gave you the information you gave me."

"Impossible." The general glared in anger. "How well do I know Darius? As a father knows his son. He's been with me six years. He has a spotless record with many decorations and commendations for courage and daring from before the first time we were together—when he was a platoon commander for me in the Fourth Dragoons in the Iraq War. Earlier, he was a *poilu* in the Second Foreign Legion Infantry Regiment operating in North Africa at the request of nations that were our former colonies and still called on us from time to time for aid. He was commissioned from the ranks. How can you suspect such an honored man?"

"An enlisted man in the Legion? He's not French?"

"Of course he's French!" La Porte snapped. His broad face seemed to freeze, and a look of discomfort took hold on it, squeezing his features. "It's true his father was German. Darius was German-born, but his mother was French, and he took her name when he was commissioned."

"What do you know of his private life?"

"Everything. He's married to a fine young woman from a good family with many years of service to France. He's a student of our history, as am I."

La Porte swept his arm in a wide circle to encompass the entire office, and Jon saw that the walls were covered with paintings, photographs, drawings, maps, all of great moments in French history. There was one exception, a photograph of the painting of the red-stone castle Jon had seen first in the general's Paris mansion.

But the general was still talking. "History is more than the story of a nation, a people. Real history chronicles a country's soul, so that to not know the history is to not know the nation or the people. If we do not know the past, Colonel, we are doomed to repeat it, *non?* How can a man devoted to his country's history betray it? *Impossible.*"

Jon listened with a growing sense that La Porte was talking too much, defending Bonnard too hard, as if to convince himself. Was the general realizing deep down that what he saw as impossible might just be possible? There was more than a little doubt in the general's final few words. "No, I cannot believe it. Not Darius."

But Jon could, and as he left the office, he glanced back at the general in his great, thronelike chair. La Porte was brooding, and there was dread in his unfocused gaze.

Paris, France

Peter Howell dozed on the narrow cot he had insisted the hospital move into Marty's private room, when a bee or wasp or some kind of annoying flying stinger buzzed his ear. He slapped hard and awakened to the pain in his head where he had clouted himself . . . and the harsh, insistent ringing of the room telephone on the stand next to his pillow.

Across the room, Marty stirred, mumbling.

Peter glanced at him and grabbed the phone. "Howell."

"Sleeping were we, Peter?"

"An unfortunate necessity at intervals even for a field operative, no matter how inconvenient for you nine-to-five civil servants who get to spend every night in your own bloody beds, or your mistress's."

In London, Sir Gareth Southgate chuckled. But there was no real amusement in the sound, for it had been his unenviable task, as the head of MI6, to manage Peter Howell long past when he should have seen the maverick's backside. But nothing about the retired agent was normal, including his pleasure in being troublesome. The fact was, Peter Howell was a brilliant operative, which made him useful in emergencies. Therefore, jocularity and a very rigid lip were the methods Southgate had chosen to deal with him.

But now Southgate's chuckle died in his throat. "How is Dr. Zellerbach, Peter?"

"Unchanged. What the devil do you want?"

Southgate kept his voice light, but added an overtone of gravity: "To give you some disturbing information, and to ask your oh-so-insightful opinion on the matter."

In the hospital room, Marty stirred again. He appeared restless. Peter looked at him hopefully. When Marty seemed to fall back into slumber, Peter returned his attention to the conversation with Southgate. Once he knew he had gotten under any of the bosses' skins, he became quite civil. *Noblesse oblige.* "I am, as we say in California, all ears."

"How nice of you," Southgate commented. "This will be ultrasecret. PM's eyes only. In fact, I'm making this call using a brand-new scrambler and encryption code, to make bloody damn sure the terrorists haven't had a chance to break through it yet. And I'll never use it again, not until we get that monstrous DNA computer under our control. Do you read me clearly, Peter?"

Peter growled, "Then you'd best not tell me, old boy."

Southgate's testiness rose closer to the surface. "I beg your pardon?"

"The rules haven't changed. What I do on an assignment is my decision. Should I, in my judgment, need to share the information to achieve the goal, then I will. And you may tell the PM that."

Sir Gareth's voice rose. "Do you enjoy being an arrogant bastard, Peter?"

"Immensely. Now tell me what you want me to know or push off, right?" Peter figured it was only logical that officials a great deal higher up than the head of MI6 had invited him to this party, which meant Southgate was powerless to fire him. He smiled as he envisioned Southgate's frustration.

Southgate's voice was brittle: "General Sir Arnold Moore and his pilot are missing and presumed dead on a flight from Gibraltar to London. He was flying home to present a report of utmost urgency to the PM. All he would tell the PM over even the most secure electronic connection was that it involved the—and I quote—'recent electronic disruptions in America.' For that reason, I have been instructed to relay the information on to you."

Peter was instantly sobered. "Did General Moore give any hint of how or where he had encountered what he wanted to tell the PM?"

"None." Southgate, too, abandoned the feud. "We've checked every source we have, and what we know is that the general was supposed to be at his country estate in Kent. Instead, he flew to Gibraltar from London with his own pilot. After that, he and the pilot took a helicopter and returned some six hours later. During those six hours, he was out of contact."

"Gibraltar station doesn't know where he flew?"

"No one does. His pilot, of course, vanished with him."

Peter digested this news. "All right, I need to remain here until I can question Dr. Zellerbach. Meanwhile, put everyone you can on finding out where Moore went. Once I've spoken to Zellerbach, I'll head south and root around. A helicopter has a limited flight range, so we should be able to narrow the general's destinations."

"Very well. I . . . hold on." Southgate's voice faded as he turned to speak with someone else. The two voices continued for some seconds before the chief of MI6 resumed his conversation with Peter: "We've just received a report that debris from Moore's Tornado have been found at sea off Lisbon. The fuselage showed signs of an explosion. I imagine we can consider both him and the pilot dead."

Peter agreed. "An accident seems unlikely, considering everything. Keep your people digging, and I'll be in touch."

Southgate bit off a remark that Howell was also one of his people, subject to orders. But it was not true. Inwardly, he sighed. "Very good. And, Peter? Try to tell as few people as possible, eh?"

Peter hung up. *Pompous ass.* He thanked his stars he had always managed to remain out of a position of authority. All it did was go to a perfectly decent man's brain and impede oxygen, progress, and results. On second thought, decent men rarely sought or received authority. You had to be a solemn fool before you wanted that sort of agony.

"My goodness." A shaky voice was speaking behind him: "Peter . . . Peter *Howell?* Is that you, Peter?"

Peter leaped from his cot and ran to Marty's bedside.

Marty blinked and rubbed his eyes. "Am I then . . . dead? Surely I must be. Yes, I must be in hell." He gazed worriedly into Peter's face. "Otherwise, I wouldn't be seeing Lucifer. I should've known. Where else would I meet that insufferable Englishman but in hell?"

"That's more like it." Peter smiled broadly. "Hello, Marty, you silly fellow. You gave us quite a turn."

Marty peered worriedly around his hospital room. "It looks pleasant enough, but I'm not tricked. It's an illusion." He cringed. "I see flames behind these innocent walls. Orange, yellow, red. Boiling fire from the hubs of hell! Blinding! Don't think you can hold Marty Zellerbach!" He threw back his sheets, and Peter grabbed his shoulders.

As he struggled to hold Marty in bed, Peter roared, "Guard! Get the nurse! Get the damn doctor! Get somebody!"

The door snapped open, and the guard looked in and saw what was happening. "Be right back."

Marty pressed into Peter's hands, not struggling now so much as simply using the full weight of his stout body to push determinedly toward freedom. "Arrogant Lucifer! I'll be out of your clutches before you can blink. Reality and illusion. *Zounds*, who do you think you're dealing with? Oh, it'll be fun to match wits with the archfiend. There's no way you can win. I'll fly from here on the wings of a red-tailed hawk. No way . . . no . . . no . . ."

"Shhh, boy," Peter said, trying to calm him. "I'm not Lucifer. Not really. Remember old Peter? We had some good times, we did."

But Marty continued to rave, caught in the grip of the extreme manic stage of his Asperger's Syndrome. The nurse ran in, followed by Dr. Dubost. While she and Peter held Marty down, the doctor injected him with an aqueous solution of Mideral, the drug that controlled his manic stage.

" . . . I must fly away . . . Satan can't outwit me! Not me! I will . . ."

While Peter and the nurse continued to restrain Marty, the doctor nodded approval. "Try to keep him as quiet as possible. He's been in the coma a long time, and we don't want any relapses. The Mideral will take effect soon."

Peter talked quietly as Marty continued to rant, building his schemes and castles in the sky, all centered on the delusion that he was in Pluto's underworld and had to outwit the devil himself. Soon he grew less physical and no longer tried to escape, and eventually his eyes turned dull, his lids drooped, and he began to nod.

The nurse smiled at Peter and stepped back. "You're a good friend to him, Mr. Howell. A lot of people would've run screaming from the room."

Peter frowned. "That so? Don't have much backbone, do they?"

"Or heart." She patted him on the shoulder and left.

For the first time, Peter regretted not having electronic communications or being able to bounce cell calls off a satellite. He wanted to let Jon and Randi know about Marty, while at the same time, he should call his contacts in the South of France, along the Costa Brava into Spain, and all the places a helicopter from Gibraltar could have flown to see what he could learn about General Moore's last few hours. But they were best reachable by their cell phones.

Frustrated, he sat down, sighed, and let his head fall forward into his hands. That was when he heard light steps behind him. Soft, evasive footsteps, and he had not even heard the door open.

"Randi?" As he started to turn, he reached for the Browning Hi-Power 9mm in his belt. That tread was not Randi's. . . . And he was too late. Before the weapon was in his hand, the cold metal of the intruder's gun muzzle pressed firmly into the back of his head. He froze. Whoever it was, was skilled. Frighteningly adept, and not alone.

Chapter
Twenty-one

Brussels, Belgium

Smith closed the cover of the last file folder, ordered a second Chimay ale, and sat back. He had dropped a note at the Café Egmont, telling Randi to meet him at the café Le Cerf Agile, where he was seated at a sidewalk table. It was his favorite café in the rue St-Catherine area of the lower city, not far from the bourse and what had once been the banks of the river Senne when this part of Brussels was a port to hundreds of fishing vessels. As this was still a fish-market area, seafood remained the order of the day in bistros here, even though the river had long ago been boxed inside a manmade channel and bricked over to become the boulevard Anspach.

But the fish, the hidden river, and the food were far from Smith's mind as he took a long draft of his dark ale and looked around. No other patrons were sitting outside, since dark clouds still rolled occasionally across the sky. But the rain had stopped an hour ago, and when Smith had asked, the maître d' had wiped off this table and the two accompanying chairs. The other patrons had decided to take no chances that the heavens would open again in another deluge, which was fine with Jon.

He liked being out here alone, out of range of prying eyes and ears. He had changed out of his uniform after he left SHAPE and now looked like any tourist in his tan cotton slacks, open-necked tartan shirt, dark-blue sports jacket, and athletic shoes. The shoes were important, in case he had to run. The jacket was important, to hide his pistol. And the black trench coat he had slung over the back of his chair was important, because it helped him to blend with the night.

But now, as the sun fought the clouds for dominance of the afternoon sky, Jon was thinking about what he had learned at NATO. The file on Captain Darius Bonnard was revealing. Either La Porte did not know or he was protecting Bonnard by withholding the fact that Bonnard's current wife—the Frenchwoman that La Porte had so admired—was not Bonnard's first: While serving in the legion, he had married an Algerian woman. Whether he had converted to Islam was unknown. However, even after being commissioned, he took all his leave time in Algiers, where the wife and her family lived. There was no information about why Bonnard had divorced her. Since there were no divorce documents in the file either, Jon was suspicious. Like sleeper spies or moles, terrorists often established new identities in target countries while maintaining entirely different lives elsewhere.

So Darius Bonnard, favored aide to NATO's Deputy Supreme Allied Commander, was a German serving in the French army, once married to an Algerian woman, now away somewhere in the South of France—not all that far from Toledo.

Still pondering, Jon reached for his ale and gazed up just in time to see Randi paying off a taxi a half block away from the café. He sat back, smiling, holding his glass and admiring the view. She was dressed conservatively in dark slacks and a fitted jacket, her hair pulled back casually in a ponytail. With her easy movements and slender figure, for a moment she looked like a teenager. She hurried toward him, vigorous and beautiful, and he realized he no longer thought of Sophia every time he saw her. It gave him an odd feeling.

She reached the table. "You look as if you've seen a ghost. Worried about me? Sweet, but completely unnecessary."

"Where the hell were you?" he managed to growl through his smile.

She sat and peered around for a waiter. "I'll give you a full report in a minute. I've just come from Paris. I thought you'd like to know that I stopped to see Marty—"

He sat up straighter. "How is he?"

"He was asleep again and still hadn't told Peter a thing." As she filled him in about the relapses, she watched worry pinch his high-planed face and darken his navy-blue eyes. Jon could look like a predatory monster when things were going badly, especially if it was in the middle of action, but right now he was a man whose main concern was his friend. With his tousled dark hair and worry-wrinkled brow and the scratches on his face from when they were chased in Madrid, she found him almost endearing.

"It's all so much harder now that we can't use our cell phones," Jon grumbled. "Otherwise, Peter would've called to tell me all this himself."

"Everything's a lot harder without our cell phones and modems." She shot him a look of warning. The waiter was coming to their table. They stopped their conversation as she ordered a Chimay, too, but the Grand Reserve. As soon as the waiter was out of earshot, she asked, "Have you learned anything?"

"A few things." Jon described the file information about Darius Bonnard and his meeting with General La Porte. "La Porte might not know about the Algerian connection, or he could be covering for Bonnard out of loyalty. What did you get?"

"Maybe what we need." She was excited as she told him what she had learned from Aaron Isaacs, finishing with Dr. Akbar Suleiman's illness.

"You're right. This is promising. Where is the guy?"

"He's postdoc and lives in Paris. Mossad says he's still in the city. I have his address."

"What are we waiting for?"

Randi smiled grimly. "For me to finish my ale."

Somewhere on the Coast of North Africa
From time to time, a cool breeze blew through the large, whitewashed room of the sprawling Mediterranean villa, making the gauzy curtains billow. The villa had been designed to take advantage of even the lightest wind. Currents of air drifted continuously through the open arches that separated the rooms from the hallway at the isolated coastal estate.

Deep inside an alcove, Dr. Émile Chambord worked over the ultrathin tubing and connections between his keyboard and the conglomeration of gel packs in their tray, feeder machine, flexible metal plate, monitor, and electronic printer that Mauritania and his men had carefully transported all the way here from his lab at the Pasteur. Chambord liked the alcove because it was sheltered from the constant breeze. Both temperature control and a complete lack of vibration were vital to the operation of his delicate prototype DNA computer.

Chambord was concentrating. At his fingertips was his life's work—his secret molecular computer. While he made adjustments, he thought about the future, both electronic and political. He believed that this rudimentary DNA computer was the beginning of changes most people were not educated enough to imagine, much less appreciate. Controlling molecules with the deftness and precision that physicists used to control electrons would revolutionize the world, ultimately leading to the subatomic realm, where matter behaved very differently from what people saw with their eyes or heard with their ears or touched with their skin.

Electrons and atoms did not act with the straightforwardness of the billiard balls in Newton's classic physics. Instead, they showed characteristics closer to fuzzy wavelike entities. At the atomic level, waves could behave like particles, while particles had waves associated with them. An electron could travel many different routes simultaneously, as if it were really a spread-out phenomenon like a wave. Similarly, an atomic computer would be able to calculate along many different paths simultaneously, too. Perhaps even among different dimensions. The fundamental assumptions of our world would be forever proved wrong.

At its most basic, today's computer was simply a set of wires arranged in one direction, a layer of switches, and a second set of wires aligned in the opposite direction. The wires and switches were configured to fabricate logic gates . . . but the kinds of wires and switches made all the difference. Chambord had succeeded in using DNA molecules to function as AND and OR logic gates, the basic computational language of electronic computers. In earlier experimental DNA machines created by other scientists, one of the insurmountable problems had been that the rotaxane molecules, which was what they used for gates, could be set only once, making them suitable for read-only memory, not random-access memory, which required constant switching.

That had been the so-called impossible niche that Chambord had filled: He had created a different molecule with the properties that would make a DNA computer work. The molecule was synthetic, and he called it Francane, in honor of France.

As Chambord turned from his apparatus to make mathematical calculations in his notebook, Thérèse appeared in the archway. "Why do you help them?" Her eyes were angry but she controlled her voice as she studied her father. He looked very tired as he bent over his calculations.

He sighed, looked up, and turned. "What else can I do?"

Her full lips were pale, all the dynamic red lipstick worn off days ago. Unbrushed and uncombed, her black hair no longer hung in a satin sheet. She still wore the slim white evening suit, but now it was torn and dirty. The high-necked, off-white silk blouse was flecked with blood and what looked like grease, and the high-heeled, ivory pumps were gone. Her shoes were bedouin slippers. They were her one concession; she had refused to accept even a change of clothes from her captors.

"You could say no," she told him tiredly. "None of them can operate your molecular computer. They'd be helpless."

"And I'd be dead. More important, so would you."

"They'll kill us anyway."

"No! They've promised."

Thérèse heard the desperation, the grasping at straws. "*Promised?*" She laughed. "The promise of terrorists, kidnappers, *murderers?*"

Chambord closed his mouth, refused to answer. He returned to his work, checking the connections of his computer.

"They're going to do something terrible," she said. "People will die. You know that."

"I don't know that at all."

She stared at his profile. "You've made a deal. *For me.* That's it, isn't it? Your soul in exchange for my life."

"I've made no deal." Still her father did not look up again.

She continued to stare, trying to fathom what he must be feeling, thinking. What he was going through. "But that's what you'll do. You'll make them let me go before you help them accomplish whatever it is they want."

Chambord was silent. Then he said quietly, "I won't let them murder you."

"Isn't that my choice?"

Now her father whirled in his chair. "No! It's *my* choice."

There were soft footsteps behind Thérèse. She flinched as Mauritania arrived at the archway, gazing from her to her father and back again. Armed and glowering, Abu Auda stood sentry behind.

Mauritania was solemn. "You are wrong, Mademoiselle Chambord. When our mission is accomplished, I have no further need of your father, and we will announce our triumph to the world so the Great Satan can know who brings his downfall. There will be no reason to care what you *or* your father can tell. *No one* is going to die, unless they refuse to help us complete the mission."

Thérèse sneered. "Perhaps you can fool him, but not me. I know lies when I hear them."

"It pains me that you do not trust us, but I have no time to persuade you." Mauritania looked at Chambord. "How much longer before you are again ready?"

"I told you I needed two days."

Mauritania's small eyes narrowed. "They are nearly passed." He had not raised his voice since he arrived, but that did not dispel the menace that burned from his gaze.

Paris, France

The towering Tour Montparnasse with its complement of other tall, up-scale buildings along the boulevard Montparnasse receded as Smith, Randi, and Hakim Gatta, a terrified lab assistant from L'Institut Pasteur, walked deeper into the back streets of Paris, where the new bohemians worked and lived among the spirits of the old. The sun had set, and the last glowing embers of the day gave the sky a somber gray-and-yellow cast. Black shadows stretched across overgrown spring gardens and cob-bled streets, and the scents of liquor, marijuana, and oil paints mingled in the air.

At last the nervous little bottle-washer, Hakim, muttered in French, "This is the street. Can . . . I leave . . . leave now?" He was a little over five feet tall with a mass of curly black hair, soft brown skin, and furtive black eyes. He lived above Dr. Akbar Suleiman.

"Not yet," Randi told him. She pulled him back into the shadows, where Jon followed in three quick steps. "Which building is it?"

"N-number fifteen."

Jon said, "Which apartment?"

"Th-third floor. In back. You promised you'd pay me, and I could go."

"The alley is the only other way out?"

Hakim nodded eagerly. "The front entrance, or the alley. There's no other way."

Jon told Randi, "You take the alley, I'll go in."

"Who put you in charge?"

Hakim started to back away. She grabbed his collar and showed him her gun. He flinched and stopped moving.

Jon watched. "Sorry. You have a better idea?"

Randi shook her head reluctantly. "You're right, but ask next time. Remember that discussion we had about politeness? We'd better move. No telling how long he'll be there if he learns we were inquiring about him at the Pasteur. You've got your walkie-talkie?"

"Of course." Jon patted the pocket of his black trench coat. He hurried off along the narrow sidewalk. The lighted windows of the four-, five-, and six-story apartment houses were beacons above the deep valley of the street. At No. 15, he leaned back casually against the building and watched. Men and women were sauntering off to bars and bistros or perhaps home. A few couples, young and old, held hands, enjoying the spring twilight and each other. Jon waited until no one was close enough to observe him, and he made his move.

The building's outer door was ajar, and there was no concierge. He took out his Walther, slipped inside, and climbed the stairs to the third floor. The door of the rear apartment was closed. He listened and after a moment heard the sound of a radio in a distant room. Somewhere inside, someone had turned on a water tap and he could hear water rushing into a basin. He tried the door, but it was locked. He stepped back and examined it—a standard spring lock. If there were a dead bolt and it was locked, too, he would have a lot harder time getting in. On the other hand, most people were careless, not engaging the dead bolt until they went to bed.

He took out his small case of picklocks and went to work. He was still working when the water stopped running. There was a thunderous noise, and a fusillade from inside tore through the door inches above Jon's head. As needlelike pieces of wood shot through the air, pain seared Jon's side, and he dove to the floor, striking his left shoulder. *Damn, he'd been hit.* A wave of dizziness swept through him. He scrambled up to a sitting position, leaning back against the wall across from the shattered door, his Walther out and covering it. His side throbbed painfully, but he ignored it. He stared at the door.

When no one came out, he finally unbuttoned his coat and pulled up his shirt. A bullet had torn through his clothes and the flesh above his waist, leaving a purple gouge. It was bleeding, but not badly, and nothing serious had been damaged. He would deal with it later. He left the shirt out; the black fabric of his trench coat hid the blood and bullet holes.

He stood up, the Walther ready, stepped aside, and tossed his case of picklocks against the door. Another fusillade smashed and splintered more of the wood and metal, this time destroying the lock. Screams, shouts, and curses from above and below filled the stairwell.

With his right shoulder, Jon slammed through the door, dove to the side, rolled, and came up with his pistol in both hands. And stared.

A small, attractive woman sat cross-legged on a shabby couch facing the door, a large AK-47 in her hands, the weapon still aimed at the door. In apparent shock, she stared at it as if she had not seen him smash through.

"Put the weapon down!" Jon commanded in French. *"Down! Now!"*

Suddenly the woman snarled, leaped up, and swung the Kalashnikov toward him. He kicked, knocking the assault rifle from her hands. Grabbing her arm, he turned her around and pushed her ahead of him as he searched the apartment room by room.

There was no one else there. He put the Walther to the tiny woman's head and snarled in French, "Where is Dr. Suleiman?"

"Where you won't find him, *chien!*"

"What is he, your boyfriend?"

Her eyes snapped. "Jealous?"

Jon took a walkie-talkie two-way radio from his trench-coat pocket and spoke low, "He's not here, but he was. Be careful."

He returned the walkie-talkie to his pocket, ripped up a bedsheet to tie the woman securely to a kitchen chair, and hurried from the apartment, letting the door lock behind him. He ran down the stairs and out into the street.

•

In the cobbled alley behind the apartment building that stank of urine and old wine, Randi stared up at the darkened windows of the third floor, her Beretta ready. Beside her, Hakim Gatta shifted nervously from foot to foot, a frightened rabbit eager to bolt for cover. They were waiting beneath a linden tree where the shadows were pitch-black. Above them, a slice of the night sky was visible, the stars just beginning to show, distant pinpricks among the clouds.

Randi prodded him with the Beretta. "You're sure he was up there?"

"Yes. I *told* you. He was there when I left." He ran the fingers of one hand, then the other through his mop of curly black hair. "They shouldn't've of told you I lived in the same building."

Randi ignored him, calculating. "And you're positive this is the only way out?"

"I told you!" Hakim almost screamed.

"*Quiet.*" She looked down, shooting him a fierce look.

He lowered his voice and was complaining to himself when the violent fusillade of shots from above reverberated through the alley.

"Down!"

The little man collapsed to the cobblestones, whimpering. She dropped down, too, and strained to hear more movement from inside the building. There was nothing, and then a second noisy volley echoed from upstairs, followed by what sounded like wood exploding.

Randi glared at the cowering Hakim. "There'd better not be another way out."

"I told you the truth! I swear, I—"

At the sound of pounding feet, Randi looked up. The apartment building's rear door burst open, and a man blasted out at full speed. But within four steps he slowed to a fast walk, a 9mm pistol in his hand but held low to his side where it would be less noticeable. He was jumpy, and his head turned constantly as he looked for danger up and down the alley.

Randi's radio crackled. She pulled Hakim close, clamped her hand over his mouth, and listened as Jon reported, "He's not here, but he was. Be careful."

"I've got him. Meet me in front if you can."

Chapter Twenty-two

As Randi watched, the man turned and hurried toward the far end of the alley, braking occasionally as if he seemed to realize that rushing would draw attention. He was escaping, but not running in panic. Randi handed euros to Hakim and warned him to stay down and silent until she and the man were gone. He nodded eagerly, his eyes wide with fear.

She stood up, and as she padded forward, she pulled her miniature walkie-talkie from her jacket pocket. She carried it in her left hand. In her right was her Beretta.

The fleeing man stopped where the alley met the street. He scanned left and right. Randi flattened back against the wall, not breathing. In the light of passing headlights, she saw that he was short and slender, with straight black hair worn down to his shoulders. In his late twenties, she guessed. Well-dressed in a blue Western blazer, white shirt, striped tie, gray slacks, and black oxfords. He had alert, intelligent dark eyes and the longer, high-cheeked Filipino-Malaysian face that was typical of the Moros of Mindanao. So this was Dr. Akbar Suleiman, worried and scared. He continued his patient surveillance, but he did not leave the mouth of the alley.

Randi spoke into her walkie-talkie: "He's waiting for something. Get as close to the rue Combray as you can."

She had barely closed the walkie-talkie when a small, black Subaru sedan screeched to a halt in front of Dr. Suleiman. A rear door swung open, and he leaped inside. Before the door could slam, the Subaru drove off. Randi ran down the alley and arrived just as a second car, an equally black Ford Crown Victoria, skidded to a stop. Jon ran from the front of the building and around to the street side of the car. He and Randi jumped into the backseat together.

The driver sped off in the same direction as the Subaru. Randi leaned forward behind the driver. "Has Max got the Subaru?"

"Square in his sights," Aaron Isaacs told her.

"Great. Follow them."

Aaron nodded. "That Smith with you, or Howell?"

She introduced them. "Lieutenant Colonel Jon Smith, M.D., at the moment attached to army intelligence. Jon, meet Aaron Isaacs, our chief in Paris."

Jon could feel Isaacs's eyes studying him, trying to analyze what he saw, assess the truth of his story. Suspicion was the CIA's trade.

Isaacs's radio crackled, and a disembodied male voice reported, "The Subaru's stopping in front of the Hôtel St-Sulpice, near Carrefour de L'Odéon. Two men are getting out and entering the hotel. The Subaru's driving off. Instructions?"

Randi leaned over the seat, and Aaron handed her his mike. "Follow the Subaru, Max."

"You got it, little lady."

"Go to hell, Max."

Aaron glanced back. "The hotel?"

"You read my mind," she told him.

Three minutes later, the Crown Victoria pulled to a stop a half block from the Hôtel St-Sulpice. Randi studied the building. "Tell me about it, Aaron."

"Cheap. Eight floors. Used to cater to the usual bohemian crowd of the quarter, then to North Africans, now mostly to low-rent tourists. No side or rear exits or entrances. Front only."

The car's built-in radio crackled again, and Max's voice reappeared: "The Subaru is a rental from a chauffeur service. Reservation made by phone. No info on the passenger or the pickup."

"Come back here to the hotel to get Aaron. We'll keep his Crown Victoria."

Max said instantly, "Does that mean no date tonight, Randi?"

Randi was losing patience. "Talk like a good boy, or I'll tell your wife."

"Oh, yeah. You're right. I'm married." And the radio went dead.

Randi shook her head. While she and Aaron talked over their respective assignments, Jon was thinking about Marty. He broke into the CIA dialogue: "Marty should be awake by now, Randi. Plus we could use Peter with us on this."

"Dr. Suleiman could come out anytime," she objected.

"True, but if Max drives me to the hospital, I can get there and back quickly. In case of trouble, you and Max can use the radios to confer, and I'll take a walkie-talkie so he can call in the hospital."

"What about not using anything wireless?" Randi objected.

Jon shook his head. "Wherever they have the DNA computer, it's not likely to be focused on local Paris police calls that don't use a satellite. For one thing, they can't have any idea Suleiman's on the run yet. No, it's almost impossible we'd be overheard or tracked. So if Suleiman moves before I get back, let me know. Peter, Max, and I'll join you there."

Randi agreed, and Aaron announced he would stay on the job with Randi until Jon and Max returned. The two Langley agents continued their discussion, and when Max arrived in a Chrysler Imperial, Jon said good-bye and climbed into the front passenger seat next to Max.

"You got a med kit here?" Jon asked as the car wove through traffic, heading southwest toward the hospital.

"Sure. Glove compartment. Why?"

"Nothing much. Just a scratch." He cleaned the bullet wound on his side and applied antibiotic cream to it. He taped a bandage to his side, made sure it was secure, then packed the med supplies back into the kit. He returned it to the glove compartment as they neared the hospital.

■

Jon moved quickly through the cavernous galleria of the mammoth Pompidou Hospital, past the palm trees and gift shop, and up the escalators to the ICU. He was eager to see Marty, feeling optimistic. Surely by now Marty would be awake, perhaps even feeling like his usual stubborn self. At the desk that guarded the ICU, Jon identified himself to a nurse he had not seen before.

"Your name's on the list, Doctor, but Dr. Zellerbach has been moved to a private room on the fourth floor. Didn't anyone tell you?"

"I've been out of the city. Is Dr. Dubost still here?"

"Sorry, Doctor. He's gone for the night. Unless there's an emergency, of course."

"Of course. Then give me Dr. Zellerbach's room number."

On the fourth floor, the first sight he had of the door to Marty's new private room made his stomach drop. There was not a single guard out-side. He glanced all around, but saw no sign of anyone else watching the room from anywhere. Where were the Sûreté? MI6? He slid his hand inside his coat, grabbed his Walther, and held it at the ready just inside his trench coat. Fearing the worst, he passed nurses, doctors, attendants, and patients, his gaze blotting them from his mind as he closed in on Marty's door.

He tested it to see whether it was fully closed. It was. With his left hand, he slowly turned the knob until he felt it click open. Holding his weapon in both hands, he used his foot to nudge open the door just enough so he could slip inside, the Walther extended in front, sweeping the room.

His breath seemed to catch in his throat. The room was empty. The bed's covers were thrown back, the bottom sheet rumpled as if by a restless patient. No Marty. No Peter. No guards. No plainclothes or MI6 in disguise. His nerves almost vibrating with alertness, he walked deeper into the room and stopped. On the far side of the bed lay two corpses. Jon did not have to examine them to know they were beyond his or anyone's help. Blood had pooled around them. Although it appeared to be thickening at the edges, it was relatively fresh. Both were dressed in doctors' scrubs, complete with booties and masks. He could tell by their body shapes that neither man was Marty or Peter.

He exhaled and knelt. Each had been stabbed once by a two-edged knife handled by an expert. This could easily be Peter's work. But where were he and Marty? Where were the guards? Jon rose slowly. Clearly no one in the hospital was aware of what had happened. No panic, no alarm, no hint Marty was not where he was supposed to be. The guards were gone, two men were murdered, and Peter and Marty had vanished, all without causing a stir, or, apparently, being noticed at all.

His walkie-talkie beeped on his belt. He switched it on. "Smith. What's up, Max?"

"Randi reports the bird has a companion and is moving. She and Aaron are going after them. She says we should hit the road. She'll direct us to wherever they follow the guy."

"On my way."

His distraught gaze took in the silent private room once more. Peter was good, even good enough to have pulled off all of this without anyone's knowing, although Jon had no idea exactly how he had done it and managed to hide and escape with a sick patient like Marty. But what had happened to the two Legionnaires at the door? To all the plainclothes people who should have been here?

Just as Peter could have accomplished all this, so could the terrorists. The terrorists could have lured away the sentries and guards, killed and hidden them, captured Peter and Marty, and killed them somewhere else. For a long moment, he did not move.

He could not lose a quarry who could lead them to the DNA computer. He would alert the Paris police, the CIA, and Fred Klein to what he had found here and hope they could track Marty and Peter.

He jammed the walkie-talkie back into his pocket, sheathed his gun, and ran out to where Max waited with the Chrysler door open.

•

The small black bakery van turned right onto the boulevard St-Michel. At the wheel of the Crown Victoria, Aaron slowed, let the van pull ahead while still keeping it in sight. It continued steadily south.

Randi guessed, "He's heading for the Périphérique." It was the broad road that circled inner Paris. She relayed her guess to Max, Jon, and Peter, who were, she hoped, already on the road and closing in.

"I think you're right," Aaron agreed. He tightened the distance between his car and the van, beginning to worry he might miss a sudden turn.

They had been following this new lead perhaps ten minutes. It had all begun when the bakery van had pulled up outside the Hôtel St-

Sulpice. The driver had jumped out and opened the side doors as if to unload a delivery of bread. Instead, Dr. Akbar Suleiman and a second man ran from the hotel entrance and climbed inside. The driver looked both ways as he slammed the doors shut. Then he carefully walked around, checking, climbed inside, and drove off.

"Damn," Randi swore.

Aaron tensed. "What do you want to do?"

"No choice. We've got to follow."

When the van reached the boulevard Périphérique, it turned onto it and headed west. Aaron kept it in sight, while Randi radioed each change of direction to Max, who was driving the other car. Soon the van blended onto the A10 toll road, and many miles later when the A11 split off west to Chartres and the distant sea, the van remained on the A10, now heading south.

The night sky was a foreboding canopy of black, the stars hidden by clouds, as the van continued at a constant pace past the ancient city of Orléans and over the legendary Loire River. Hours had passed. It veered suddenly west again, this time onto a two-lane local road, the D51. Abruptly, without bothering to slow, it turned sharply again onto an un-numbered back road, which it followed for several miles until it finally sped into a drive hidden by dense trees and brush.

It was a tribute to Aaron's driving that he had not lost them or apparently been spotted. When Randi congratulated him, he shrugged modestly.

He pulled off onto a shoulder. "What now?"

"We get close and watch." She was already stepping out of the car.

"Might be best to wait for Max and your friends. They're not far behind."

"You stay here. I'm going in."

She did not hear the rest of his protest. She could see the lights of a farmhouse through the trees. Moving carefully, she headed into the timber and threaded her way through the vegetation until she found what appeared to be an animal trail. With relief, she hurried along it. Unlike the one outside Toledo, this farmhouse had little open ground around it. It appeared to be more like a hunting lodge or rustic retreat for weary city workers. There were no helicopters, but there were two other cars, and two armed men leaning against the front corners of the country lodge.

Randi watched silhouettes crossing and recrossing on the other side of the window blinds, their arms gesticulating violently. It looked like an argument. Raised voices came faintly to her ears.

A hand fell on her shoulder, and a voice whispered, "How many are there?"

She turned. "Hello, Jon. Just in time. There were three men in the bakery van, and there were two cars already here. There are two guards outside, and there has to be at least one more inside—whoever they came here to meet."

"Two cars? Probably more than one waiting for your wandering trio inside then."

"It's possible." She looked behind him. "Where's Peter?"

"Wish I knew." He told her what had happened at the hospital. Her heart sank as she listened. He went on. "If there were only two terrorists, and Peter killed them, then maybe he was able to figure out a way to get Marty out of there, and they're somewhere safe. After all, neither of the dead men's guns had been fired, and I found no shell casings. So, it's possible." He shook his head worriedly. "But if there were more terrorists, they could've knocked out Peter, or used knives, too. I don't like to think what they've done to Marty and Peter if that's what really happened."

"I don't like it either." The front door to the lodge opened. "We've got movement. Look."

A rectangle of bright light spilled out into the night. Dr. Akbar Suleiman stormed angrily outdoors, turning to continue arguing with someone behind. His voice carried through the night, speaking French: "I tell you my escape was clean. There was no way they could've followed me. I don't even know how they found me in the first place!"

"That's what worries me."

Jon and Randi looked at each other, recognizing the voice.

The speaker followed Suleiman from the house. It was Abu Auda. "How can you be sure they did *not* follow you?"

Suleiman waved his arms to encompass the estate. "Do you see them here anywhere? Do you? Of course, you don't. Ergo, they didn't follow me!"

"People who could find you, Moro, would not let you, or us, see them."

Suleiman sneered. "What then? I should allow myself to be arrested?"

"No, you would've told them everything. But it would've been better had you followed normal procedure and contacted us first so we could pursue a plan that was safer than bolting to your own friends like a panicked puppy straight to its pack."

"Well," Suleiman said sarcastically, "I didn't. Are we going to talk unproductively all night, since you're so sure they could arrive any minute and overwhelm us?"

The terrorist's eyes blazed. He barked orders in Arabic. The man who had left the hotel in Paris with Suleiman joined them from the house, followed by the driver of the bakery van and a third armed man—an Uzbek from the look of his face and Central Asian cap. The bakery driver got into the van and drove off on the rutted dirt road that led back to the rural highway.

"Let's go," Randi whispered.

She and Jon sped through the woods to where Aaron and Max waited in their cars, which were now hidden off the road in brush.

"What's up?" Aaron asked, quickly climbing out.

Max joined him and was staring at Randi as if he were a starving Neanderthal and she were the only meat he had seen in a year.

Randi ignored him. "Neither of you can quit now. They're using two cars. No way we can know which one Suleiman's in." She did not add that they could not know which car Abu Auda was in either. Of the two, he could be the more important quarry. "We'll have to split up, tail one car each."

"And damn carefully," Jon added. "Abu Auda is suspicious someone followed Suleiman, and he'll be alert."

Aaron and Max grumbled about their own work and a night of lost sleep, but Randi's mission took top priority.

Jon got in beside Max, while Randi rejoined Aaron. Moments later, the two cars carrying the terrorists left the dirt road for the country highway. Shortly afterward, Aaron and Max drove their cars out to pursue. They kept back almost out of sight, spotting taillights sporadically. It was difficult surveillance and risky, and they could easily lose their prey. But when the two Langley cars finally reached the A6, the four agents saw the terrorists' cars clearly. Once on the toll highway, it would be simpler to follow.

But then one of the cars took the ramp south, the other the ramp north. Aaron and Max separated, following as agreed. Jon settled in next to Max, bone-weary already. It was going to be a long night.

Chapter Twenty-three

Washington, D.C.

The tense meeting that morning of the president, his senior staff, and the Joint Chiefs was interrupted by the abrupt opening of the door between the Oval Office and that of the president's executive secretary. The secretary—Mrs. Pike, frizzy-haired and known for her brusqueness— gazed questioningly into the room.

Irritation creased Sam Castilla's forehead, but if Estelle was interrupting, he knew it had to be important. Still, these last few days had been nerve-racking and his nights sleepless, so he snapped, "I thought I said no interruptions, Estelle."

"I know, sir. Sorry, but General Henze's on the line."

The president nodded, smiled a mute apology to Mrs. Pike, and picked up the receiver. "Carlos? How's everything over there?" He gazed at the cluster of people sitting and standing around the Oval Office. The name "Carlos" told them it was General Henze, and they had grown even more alert.

"Almost nothing new in Europe, Mr. President," General Henze reported. His voice was resolute, but the president heard an undertow of anger as well. "There hasn't been a single breakdown or interruption anywhere on the continent for more than twenty-four hours."

The president decided to ignore the anger for the time being. "A bleak ray of sunshine, but at least it's something. What about locating the terrorists?"

"Again nothing so far." Henze hesitated. "May I be frank, sir?"

"I insist on it. What's the problem, Carlos?"

"I had a meeting with Lieutenant Colonel Jon Smith—the army doctor you sent over to handle the search. He wasn't reassuring. He's shooting in the dark, Mr. President. Not only does he suspect that a trusted aide to General La Porte is mixed up with the crazies, he flat out said even I wasn't above suspicion. In short, he knows damn little."

Inwardly, the president sighed. "It seems to me his progress has been impressive."

"He's dug up a lot. That's true, but I don't see he's any closer to the damned dingus. I think he's spinning his turbans. Shooting off half-cocked, and I'm damned concerned. Shouldn't we put everything we have on this, not just one lone man, no matter how good he may be?"

From the sound of it, the president decided, the general would be a lot happier sending the entire 82nd Airborne and all of the 1st Air Cav to search the Middle East, house-to-house, for the terrorists. Of course, the downside of that could be World War III, but the general had not thought that far ahead.

"I'll take your thoughts and objections under advisement, General, with my thanks," the president told him. "If I decide to change horses, I'll let you know. But don't forget Langley's on the job, too, as is MI6."

There was stony silence. Then: "Yes, sir. Of course."

The president nodded to himself. The general would toe the line for a while at least. "Continue to keep me informed. Thank you, Carlos."

After he hung up, President Castilla hunched his big shoulders, dropped his chin onto his tented fingers, and peered through his titanium glasses outdoors into the relentless morning storm. The sky was so dismal and gray with rain he could not see beyond the Rose Garden, which did not improve his frame of mind. He was more than uneasy himself, even scared, that Covert-One had not found the molecular computer.

But he could not let his misgivings show, at least not yet. He turned to focus on the advisers and military leaders who were seated on the chairs and sofa and standing against the mantel, waiting. His gaze lowered to linger on the Great Seal of the United States that was woven into the carpet in the middle of the group, and he told himself the United States of America was not beaten yet, and it would not be beaten.

He said calmly, "As you heard, that was General Henze from NATO. Everything's been quiet over there, too. No attack for twenty-four hours."

"I don't like it," Chief of Staff Charles Ouray said. "Why would the people with the DNA computer stop harassing us now? Threatening us? Do they have all they wanted?" In his early sixties, he had an almost lineless, triangular face and a low, gruff voice. He crossed his arms and frowned. "I seriously doubt it."

"Or perhaps our countermeasures are stopping them," National Security Adviser Powell-Hill suggested hopefully. Slender, businesslike, and no-nonsense as usual, she was immaculately turned out, this time in a Donna Karan suit. "With luck, all the backup systems we've brought online have stumped them."

Lieutenant General Ivan Guerrero, army chief of staff, leaned forward and nodded in vigorous agreement. His square-fingered hands were clasped between his knees, and he looked up and around at the group, studying them with a cool, calculating gaze that was more than confident, it radiated the certainty that was too-often prized over intellect in military command. "We've got our backups installed down to the onboard targeting systems in our tanks. I think we've outwitted the bastards, whoever the hell they are, *and* their diabolical molecular computer."

"I agree," Air Force General Bruce Kelly said from where he stood beside the fireplace. His florid face was firm as he looked at General Guerrero and then at the others. Although he enjoyed his liquor perhaps too much, he also was shrewd and tireless in the pursuit of a goal.

The marine chief, Lieutenant General Clason Oda, who had just recently risen to his position and was still in a honeymoon of popularity, chimed in with his confidence that the countermeasures had worked and stymied the terrorists. "Good old-fashioned American know-how at work," he concluded, beaming at the cliché.

As his people continued to discuss backup systems, President Castilla listened without joining in, hearing both the voices and the rain outside, drumming an ominous counterpoint to their optimism.

When their discussion ended, Castilla cleared his throat. "Your efforts and thoughts are encouraging, ladies and gentlemen. Still, I must offer another explanation, one which you won't like but that we must pay attention to. Our intelligence sources overseas have suggested an entirely different scenario. They believe that rather than our defenses beating off cyber attacks over the last day, there have simply been no attacks."

Admiral Brose, the Joint Chiefs' chairman, frowned. "What does that signify to you, Mr. President? That they've backed off? They've made their point and are going back into their holes?"

"I wish it did, Stevens. I truly wish it did. But no. One part of the explanation may be some most welcome successes by our intelligence people themselves. I'm glad to report we now know the name of the group that has the DNA computer. It's the Crescent Shield. Our people may have delayed their plans."

"The Crescent Shield?" NSA Powell-Hill said. "I've never heard of them. Arabs?"

The president shook his head. "Pan-Islamic. No one has heard of them. They appear new, although with many veteran leaders and players."

"What's the second part of the explanation for their inaction, sir?" Admiral Brose asked.

The president's expression grew more sober. "That they need no more practice. They've tested all they're going to, because they've learned whatever it was they wanted to learn about their system and about us. They've also put us out of business, since we're scrambling to put alternate programs into place. In fact, they likely have accomplished exactly what they set out to do by this point. My guess is they're ready to act. This is the quiet before the killer storm, lulling us before they launch some deadly strike—or strikes, God help us—at our people."

"When?" Admiral Brose wanted to know.

"Probably within the next eight to forty-eight hours."

The silence was long and tense. No one made eye contact.

At last, Admiral Brose admitted, "I see your logic, sir. What do you suggest?"

The president said forcefully, "That we return to our posts and go the limit. Nothing held back. Not even the most experimental and even potentially dangerous new defense systems. We have to be prepared to stop anything they throw at us, from bacteria to a nuclear bomb."

Emily Powell-Hill's perfect eyebrows shot up. "With all due respect, sir," she protested, "these are terrorists, not global nuclear powers. I doubt they can inflict anywhere near all that."

"Really, Emily? Are you willing to stake the lives of possibly millions of Americans on that as well as you and your family's lives?"

"Yes. I am, sir," she said stubbornly.

The president tented his fingers again, rested his heavy chin on the tips, and smiled a quiet but thin smile. "Brave woman, and brave security adviser. I made a good choice. But I'm the president, Emily, and I don't have the luxury of blind courage or of rolling the dice. The potential costs are simply too high." His gaze swept the room, including all of them, no matter the differences of opinion. "It's our country, and we're all in this together. We've got the burden, but we also have some opportunities here to defend and fight back. We'd be irresponsible and mule-stupid to do less than everything we can. Now, let's go to work."

As they filed out, already discussing the steps they would take, Admiral Brose stayed behind. Once the door was closed, he spoke wearily across the room: "The media's getting suspicious, Sam. There've been leaks, and they're sniffing around hard. With the possibility of an imminent strike, shouldn't we have the press in and start briefing them? If you want, I can do it. That way you can keep out of it. You know the drill—'an informed government source.' We can test the public's response, and prepare them for the worst, too, which isn't a bad idea."

The admiral studied the president, who suddenly looked as exhausted as the admiral felt. The president's broad shoulders were slumped, and jowls seemed to have come from nowhere to age his face ten years. Worried not only about the future but about his leader, Stevens Brose waited for an answer.

Sam Castilla shook his head. "Not yet. Give me another day. Then we'll have to do it. I don't want to start a panic. At least not yet."

"I understand. Thank you for hearing us out, Mr. President."

"You're welcome, Admiral."

Looking doubtful, the chairman of the Joint Chiefs opened the door and left. As soon as President Castilla was alone, he stood up behind his pine-table desk and paced. Outside on the colonnade, a Secret Service sentry gazed back once, his attention attracted by the movement. As soon as he saw that there was no danger, his gaze swept back over the White House grounds and the rainy sky above.

The president noted the attention, the approving look that indicated normalcy, and shook his head grimly. Nothing was normal. Everything had gone to hell in a pretty wicker handbasket. In the eighteen months since he had established Covert-One, Fred Klein and his team had never failed him. Was this to be the first time?

Paris, France

Tucked away on the short rue Duluth in the Sixteenth Arrondissement, the building looked like a typical town mansion of Baron Haussmann's Paris. But the elegant, if unremarkable, facade concealed one of the most exclusive and expensive private hospitals in Paris. Here the rich and infamous came for cosmetic surgery, less to fight the scoring of age than to recapture an imagined youth. Discreet and accustomed to the demands of the elite for the utmost secrecy and security, it was the perfect place to hide, if you knew the right people to convince.

Marty Zellerbach's private room was airy and comfortable, with a vase of fresh pink peonies on a low table before the window. Peter Howell sat beside the bed where Marty lay propped up. Marty's eyes were open and clear, but a bit dulled, as was to be expected when he was on a fresh dose of Mideral, the quick-acting wonder drug that enabled him to sit quietly through onerous tasks like changing lightbulbs, paying bills, or visiting with a friend. Asperger's sufferers were often written off as "nerds" and "geeks," oddballs and eccentrics, or behaviorally disturbed. Some scientists estimated that as many as one in two hundred fifty people had at least a mild case. There was no cure for Asperger's, and the only help for people with more severe cases like Marty's was medication, usually in the form of stimulants for the central nervous system, such as Mideral.

The shock of events had worn off, and now Marty was acting courtly but gloomy. His soft, chubby frame was collapsed back like a weary rag doll against the white mountain of pillows. There were bandages on his forehead and arms from scrapes he had received as a result of the explosion at the Pasteur.

"My goodness, Peter." Marty's eyes skittered around the room, avoiding Peter. "It was dreadful. All that gore in the hospital room. If our lives hadn't been at stake, I would've been even more horrified."

"You could say thank you, Marty."

"I didn't? That's remiss of me. But then, Peter, you're a fighting machine. You've said so yourself. I suppose I simply took you at your word. Just another day of work for you and your sort."

Peter straightened. "*My* sort?"

Marty ignored Peter's glare. "I suppose the civilized world does need you, although I often cannot imagine why—"

"Marty, old boy, don't tell me you're a pacificist."

"Ah, yes. Bertrand Russell, Gandhi, William Penn. Very good company. Interesting, too. Men who really *thought*. I could quote you passages of their speeches. *Long* passages." He glanced at Peter with teasing green eyes.

"Don't bother. Need I remind you that you now know how to use a weapon? An automatic rifle, at that."

Marty shuddered. "Caught." Then he smiled, ready to give Peter his due. "Well, I suppose there are times when fighting is appropriate."

"Bloody damn right. I could've trotted on out and abandoned you for those two goons in the hospital to carve up into dainty morsels. But you'll notice that I didn't."

Marty's expression changed completely. He stared, appalled. "You have a point, Peter. *Thank you.*"

"Well done. Now should we get to business?"

Peter exhibited a bandaged cheek, left arm, and left hand, the result of the grim, quiet battle in Marty's room at the Pompidou Hospital. Marty had awakened in time to witness it all. After Peter had dispatched the two attackers, he'd located an attendant's uniform and a laundry basket on wheels, convinced Marty to crawl inside, and piled linens on top of him. Then he'd donned the attendant's uniform. The Legionnaire guards on the door had disappeared, and Peter deduced they must have been bribed, or murdered, or were themselves terrorists. But where were MI6 and the Sûreté? But he had no time to think about that.

Fearing more of the extremists could be nearby, he had wheeled Marty out of the hospital and straight to his rental car for the trip to this private clinic, which was run by Dr. Lochiel Cameron, an old friend of Peter's from the Falkland Wars.

"Of course. You asked what happened in the lab." Marty clasped his cheeks with both hands, remembering. "Oh, my. Such a terrible experience. Émile—you know, Émile Chambord?"

"I know who he is. Go on."

"Émile said he wouldn't be working that night. So I hadn't planned to go into the lab either. Then I remembered I'd left my paper on differential equations there, so I had to return for it." He paused, and his plump face quivered. "Appalling!" His eyes widened in a strange mixture of fear and elation. "Wait! There was something else. *Yes*. I want to tell you about . . . about everything. I've been trying to tell you . . ."

"We know, Marty. Jon's been with you nearly every day. Randi came to see you, too. What was it you wanted to tell us?"

"Jon? And Randi as well?" Marty clutched Peter's arm and pulled him close. "Peter, listen. I must tell you. Émile wasn't in the lab, but of course I expected that. *But neither was the prototype!* Worst of all, there was a body on the floor. A *corpse!* I ran out and almost got to the stairs, when"—his eyes grew haunted—"there was this ear-shattering noise, and a hand seemed to lift me, throw me . . . I screamed. I know that I screamed . . ."

Peter grabbed the little genius in a bear hug. "It's okay, Marty. It's over. You're fine. Perfectly safe now. It's all over. You're all right." Perhaps it was the hug, or his reassuring words, or just that Marty had finally been able to relate what he had been trying to say for four days, but Peter felt Marty calm.

At the same time, Peter was deeply disappointed. Marty had told him nothing new, only that Chambord and the DNA computer had not been in the lab when the bomb exploded, but a corpse was, all of which they had figured out. But at least Marty was alive and recovering, and for that Peter was more than grateful. He released him and watched him sink back.

Marty gave a wan smile. "I guess the trauma affected me more than I realized. One never knows how one will react, does one? You say I've been in a coma?"

"Since the bombing, lad."

Marty's face spread in worry. "Where's Émile, Peter? Did he visit me, too?"

"Bad news there. The terrorists who blew up the Pasteur kidnapped him and took the DNA computer. They also kidnapped his daughter. Can you tell me whether the prototype actually works? We figured it does. True?"

"Oh, dear. Those heathens have Émile and Thérèse *and* the DNA computer! This is worrisome. Yes, Émile and I considered it finished. There were a few minor tests to run before we made a formal announcement. We planned to do them the next morning. This concerns me, Peter. Do you know what someone can do with our prototype, especially if they have Émile to operate it? Oh, my! What will happen to Émile and Thérèse? Too ghastly to consider!"

"We've had a graphic demonstration of what the computer can do." Peter filled in Marty about the various electronic attacks. As he described them, Marty's face flushed with anger and he clenched his fists, something Peter had never seen Marty, who really did hate violence, do.

"How impossibly awful! I must help. We must save the Chambords! We must get back the prototype! Get me my slacks . . ."

"Whoa, you're by no means recovered, my boy. Besides, you don't have anything here but that darling hospital gown of yours." As Marty opened his mouth to complain, Peter hurried on. "Now you just lie back again, lad. Perhaps in a few days, right?" He paused. "I have a critical question for you. Can you build a DNA computer, something so we can fight back?"

"No, Peter. I'm sorry. What happened is . . . I didn't just hop on a plane and arrive unannounced at Émile's lab. No, he called me in Washington and intrigued me with his great secret, his molecular computer. He needed me to show him how to make the most out of operating it. So that was my end of our partnership. Émile's, of course, was creating the machine himself. Everything was in his notes. Do you have his notes?"

"No one's been able to find them."

"I was afraid that was the situation."

After Peter had reassured Marty that everything possible was being done, he made two calls, using the standard phone by Marty's bedside. That finished, he and Marty talked longer.

As he prepared to leave, Peter said soberly, "You're in excellent hands here, Marty. Lochiel's a hell of a doctor and a soldier. He'll make sure no one can get to you, and he'll monitor your health. A coma's nothing to fool around with. Even an overeducated egghead like you knows that. Meanwhile, I have a bit of work to do myself, then I'll be back before you can say Jack the Ripper."

" 'Jack the Ripper.' Very funny." Marty gave a small nod of the head in tribute. "Personally, I prefer Pete the Sticker."

"Oh?"

"Much more appropriate, Peter. After all, that nasty, sharp stiletto of yours saved our lives in the hospital. Ergo: Pete the Sticker."

"There's that."

As Peter returned the smile, the two men accidentally looked into each other's eyes. Both smiled wider. Then they averted their gazes.

"I suppose I'll be all right," Marty grumbled. "Goodness knows, I'm safer here than with you and all the trouble you can get yourself into." Then he brightened. "I forgot. It puzzles me."

"What puzzles you?"

"The painting. Well, not really a painting . . . a print copy of a painting. It was Émile's, and it was missing, too. I wonder why? Why on earth would terrorists want that?"

"What print, Marty?" Peter was impatient. He was already making plans in his mind. "Missing from where?"

"Émile's laboratory. It was his print of the famous *The Grand Army Retreats from Moscow* painting. You know it. Everyone does. It's the one in which Napoleon is riding his white horse, his chin sunk on his chest, with his ragged troops trudging through the snow behind him. They've been badly beaten. I think it was after the battle for Moscow. Now, why would terrorists steal *that*? It wasn't valuable. Just a print, after all. Not the real painting."

Peter shook his head. "I don't know, Marty."

"Odd, isn't it?" Marty mused. He stroked his chin, looking for a meaning.

Washington, D.C.

Fred Klein sat in the presidential bedroom, chewing again on the stem of his unlit pipe. There had been moments in the last few days when his jaw had been so tight he had nearly bitten through the stem. He had faced other crises of great magnitude and desperation, but never anything as tense and uncertain as this. It was the sense of impotence, the knowledge that if the enemy wanted to use the DNA computer there would be no defense against it. All their mighty weapons, built so carefully and expensively over the last half century, were useless, although they gave a feeling of security to the uninformed and unimaginative. In the end, all they had were the intelligence services. A few agents following a faint trail, like a single hunter in a planet-sized wilderness.

President Castilla came in from his sitting room, shed his suit jacket, loosened his tie, and flopped into a heavy leather armchair. "That was Pat Remia over at 10 Downing. Seems they've lost a top general—General Moore—and they think it's the doing of our terrorists." He leaned back, resting his head against the chair, his eyes closed.

"I know," Klein said. The light behind him reflected on his face, emphasizing the receding hairline and the deepening ravines in his face.

"Did you hear what General Henze thinks of our tactics? Our progress?"

Klein nodded.

"And?"

"He's wrong."

The president shook his head and pursed his lips. "I'm worried, Fred. General Henze says he's unimpressed by Smith's prospects for finding these people again, and I have to admit from what you've told me I'm concerned myself."

"In clandestine operations, Sam, progress is sometimes hard to see. We've got all our intelligence resources out there working on various aspects of this. Plus, Smith's teamed up with a couple of highly seasoned fellow agents. One from CIA, and one from MI6. It's unofficial, of course. But through them he can tap directly into CIA and MI6 resources. Because of all the communications problems, I haven't been as much help to him as I'd ordinarily be."

"Do they know about Covert-One?"

"Absolutely not."

The president crossed his hands over his wide girth. The room filled with silence. At last he looked across at Klein. "Thanks, Fred. Stay in touch. Close touch."

Klein stood up and headed toward the door. "I will. Thank you, Mr. President."

Chapter
Twenty-four

Es Caló, Isla de Formentera
Friday, May 9

From where he lay on the low, sun-bleached hill, Jon raised his head just enough to see the Far de la Mola lighthouse, which loomed to the east on the highest point of this windswept island. All around spread pristine beaches that led down to clear, unspoiled waters. Since the island was not only largely undeveloped but essentially flat, he and Max had used every possible rock and thicket of the tough native brush for cover as they crawled closer to the three terrorists whom they had been following through the long night.

The trio—Dr. Akbar Suleiman, the other man from the Hôtel St-Sulpice, and one of the armed guards from the lodge—had parked their car above a narrow strip of sand, where they paced impatiently and stared out at a large, fast-looking motorboat that swung at anchor a hundred yards offshore.

In the small hours of the morning, the terrorists' Mercedes had crossed south into Spain, with Jon and Max tailing. It had been a long drive. By dawn, they were heading past Barcelona, the tips of the towers of the great Gaudi church of the Sagrada Familia to the right, and the seventeenth-century castle on the hill of Montjuic to the left. The extremists' car continued on, approaching El Prat Airport, and then past the major terminals. Finally it slowed and turned into an area of corporate, private, and charter facilities, where it parked in front of a helicopter charter service.

As the terrorists entered the heliport terminal, Jon and Max waited, their car far back, its motor idling. There was still no sign of the second car or of Abu Auda.

Jon asked, "The Company has a presence in Barcelona, right?"

"Possibly," Max acknowledged.

"Then get a chopper here and fast," Jon told him.

Soon after that, Dr. Suleiman and the others lifted off in a chartered civilian Bell 407. When a Seahawk helicopter arrived, Jon and Max had pursued the Bell across the Mediterranean to here, the southernmost main Balearic Island, where they were now lying among rocks and brush above the strip of beach.

As Jon watched, a large rubber raft splashed over the side of the motorboat that was anchored offshore. Jon had only minutes to decide what to do. If he lost the terrorists, it could take days, maybe weeks, to track the destination of the fast craft, which looked like a converted PT boat. Tailing a helicopter in another helicopter was not in itself inherently suspicious. After all, that was how they had followed the extremists here. More than one chopper could be going to the same place, and the tailing craft could hang far enough back in a clear sky to be almost invisible. Plus, the noise of distant engines would be drowned out by the quarry's own engines, and the question of fuel would not come up. But a helicopter following a boat, forced to fly circles because of its far greater speed, would instantly cause alarm. And there was no certainty the tracking helicopter would have enough fuel.

"I'm getting aboard that boat," he told Max. "You cover me, and wait for Randi to show. If she doesn't, fly back to Barcelona and contact her wherever she is. Tell her what I'm doing, and that she should throw out a dragnet for the boat. If she can't find it, sit tight, and I'll contact her."

Max gave a short nod. Then he resumed studying the speedboat swinging lazily on the swell of the blue water. "It looks damn chancy to me."

"Can't be helped."

Jon crawled backward until out of sight of the shore. Running, he circled to the far side of a rocky promontory, stripped to his shorts, and tied his trousers, Walther, and stiletto around his waist with his belt. From there, he trotted down to the sand and out into the shimmering sea. The water was cool, not yet as warm as it would be in summer. He dove in and swam underwater as far as he could, surfaced carefully, and looked around. The raft was to his left, halfway to shore, with a single crew member steering the small outboard motor toward the waiting trio on the beach. From what Jon could see, the deck of the old PT boat appeared deserted. He took a deep breath and submerged.

As he swam below the blue surface, came up, and submerged again, he considered options. The boat would be operated by no more than a crew of five, plus a captain. At least one crew member was on his way ashore, and no one else had appeared ondeck. Where were the others? He had to get aboard and find clothes and a safe hiding place. It was not going to be easy, but there was no alternative.

He surfaced beside the boat, its white hull rising and falling with the swell. The stern slapped the water as it came down again, the power of it creating a small wake that pushed Jon off. He took a deep breath, dove again, and came up on the vessel's ocean side, hidden from shore. He paddled to where a rope-and-board ladder hung and treaded water as he strained to hear voices or movement aboard, but the only sounds anywhere were the excited cries of seagulls heading in to the island and the regular slapping of the boat's stern.

His nerves were on edge. Although there was no indication anyone was on the boat, he had no guarantee of that. His stiletto in his teeth, he timed the rhythm of the swell and caught the ladder as the boat slammed down. It was a balancing act, but he scrambled up the ladder, reached the deck, and raised his head.

No one was visible. He listened to his heart thunder, and then he climbed higher, crawled onto the deck, and fell prone, trying to be unnoticeable both on the boat and from the island. As he waited, he took his bearings. What he noted first was that not only was the large rubber raft gone, so was the usual dinghy. That was good news.

Watching and listening, he crab-walked, bare feet padding quietly on the wood, to the main hatch, where he slipped below. In the dim light, he worked his way forward along a narrow gangway between small rooms like the officers' quarters on a submarine. He was aware of every creak of the boat, of every groan of a joist, as he waited for the sound of a human voice or footstep.

There were five identical cubicles, one for each crewman, and a sixth at least twice as large for the captain. He found a pair of athletic shoes that would fit him. By the personal items lying around, all the cubicles appeared occupied. Individual quarters were a luxury afforded to few on a small, narrow boat built for speed. This many could mean long periods at sea and hazardous duty. Which also could mean a laundry. Even terrorists needed to wash their clothes, especially Muslims, for whom cleanliness was a commandment.

All the way forward, Jon found a tiny laundry with a compact washer and dryer and a pile of dirty garments. Clothes lost here were less likely to be missed. He grabbed a shirt and socks to go with the pants he had brought. He dressed quickly and worked his way back aft, where he discovered another necessity for a long time spent at sea—stacked barrels of diesel fuel. And farther back an answer—a large hold with wall brackets and straps to keep cargo steady in heavy seas. There were traces of white powder on the slats of floorboards designed to keep cargo dry even if the sea washed aboard. The powder looked like heroin or cocaine. Most likely, this boat smuggled drugs and, from the heavy straps, maybe guns, too.

All of this told him a great deal, but the emptiness of the cargo compartment revealed more: Today's trip was special, not usual business.

He froze. There was the faint but definite noise of a boat's motor, and it was approaching. He needed a hiding place. He could not use the cargo hold, since it was empty. The tiny cabins were out, since men were assigned there. He had passed the galley aft, which was a possibility. Still, someone would probably get hungry even on a short trip. Thinking rapidly, he hurried back along the narrow passage. Above him, the noise of feet landing on the deck made his pulse accelerate. Voices sounded uncomfortably close above his head.

His chest tight, he finally located a large storage locker all the way forward. It was crammed with ropes, chains, canvas, hatch covers, engine parts, and other supplies needed to maintain a seagoing boat under hard use. As he monitored the noises of the boarding crew, he shoved matériel around until he had a snug hole. Feet sounded in the corridor outside his hiding spot. He scrambled into the hole and pulled a hatch cover over to roof it. He crossed his legs and sank down, nerves pulsing, his back against the bulkhead. His trousers were wet and clammy.

Voices shouted above, and two pairs of feet stopped outside his door. A conversation commenced in Arabic. Suddenly one of the men laughed, then the other, and with relief he listened to the pair move away. As their voices faded, the boat's powerful engines—oversized, he judged—roared into throbbing life, shaking the entire craft. The anchor rose and clanged against the side, and he felt the boat swing.

The momentum threw him into a coil of rough ropes at his side, and then acceleration slammed him back against the bulkhead. As the boat leaped ahead, gaining speed, he was already beginning to ache. Still, he smiled. He was alive, his Walther was in his hand, and there was promise that on the other side of the ride he would find answers.

■

Randi stood below the lighthouse of Far de la Mola, the statue of the famous French author Jules Verne nearby, and stared out across the sea to where the faint shape of the sleek motorboat rode steadily south. "He got on the boat okay?"

"He did," Max told her. "After everyone was aboard, and she weighed anchor, I saw nothing going on. No big disturbance or fight, so I'd say he found a place to hide. What happened to the SUV you were tailing?"

"They led us to Barcelona, too, but we lost them in the city."

"You think they lost you deliberately?"

"Yes. We were made." She grimaced with disgust. "Then Salinger, the station chief in Madrid, relayed the information that you'd called for a helicopter. It took us time to pin down the right charter service and squeeze the destination out of them. Then we flew here."

"This could be bad for Jon."

Randi nodded anxiously as she stared out to sea where the speeding boat had disappeared into the gray mists on the horizon. "I know. Even if Jon arrives safely all the way to wherever they're going, he's in trouble."

"What the hell do we do?"

"Get the Seahawk refueled so we can fly to North Africa."

"It's got extra tanks, so it can make it the way it is. But if we try to follow the boat, they'll spot us for sure."

"We won't follow," Randi decided. "We'll locate them and fly straight on to Africa. They'll see us. No doubt about it. But when we fly past without showing interest, they'll figure we're just another chopper on a trip."

"Why fly over them at all?"

"To make sure they're heading for Africa and not Spain, or even Corsica."

"Then what?" Max waited.

"Then we send out everything we can to find them." Her dark eyes turned worriedly back out to sea.

Marseille, France

The fisherman's bar stood among other weather-beaten buildings above the ranked fishing vessels that were moored along the quays. Twilight had fallen, and the waterfront was crowded with the usual roistering throngs that signaled the boats had come in and the fish market was in full swing. Inside the old bar, French and Arabic were the primary languages in the cacophony of loud talk.

A short, stocky man threaded through shifting gray curtains of cigarette smoke. He had the rolling gait of a seaman who had just stepped ashore. He wore jeans, a stained T-shirt revealing muscular arms, and a merchant sailor's cap with a soft white crown, a black rim, and a shiny black peak.

When he reached the copper-topped bar, he leaned toward the bartender and spoke in broken French: "I'm supposed to meet a boat captain named Marius."

The bartender scowled at the bad French. He looked the stranger up and down and finally announced, "Englishman?"

"*Oui,* yes."

"Off that container ship come in yesterday from Japan?"

"Yes."

"You should learn better French, you come in here."

"I'll take that under consideration," the Englishman said, undisturbed. "What about Marius?"

A typical Marseille feisty character, the bartender glared for a moment, then jerked his head toward a beaded curtain that separated the boisterous main room from a backroom. The English "sailor," whose name was Carsten Le Saux and who actually spoke excellent French and was not a sailor at all, thanked the bartender in even worse French and ambled back through the curtain to sit across a scarred table from the only occupant of the room.

As if by a miracle, Le Saux's French improved. "Captain Marius?"

The man at the table was whiplike, of medium height, with the usual thick, dark, Gallic hair worn down to his shoulders and hacked off with a knife. His sleeveless shirt revealed a body that seemed to consist of nothing but bone and muscle. He tossed back a *marc*, a very cheap brandy, pushed the empty glass away, and sat back is if waiting for something momentous to occur.

Le Saux smiled with his mouth, not his eyes, as he waved to a waiter in a white apron, who was swabbing dirt around on an empty table. "*Deux marcs, s'il vous plaît.*"

Captain Marius said, "You're the one who called?"

"That's right."

"You said there were dollars? One hundred of them?"

Carsten Le Saux reached into his trouser pocket and produced a hundred-dollar bill. As he laid it on the table, the captain nodded but did not pick it up. Their *marcs* arrived. The captain reached for his.

The two men sipped slowly. At last Le Saux said, "I've heard you and your boat had a close call at sea a few nights ago."

"Where did you hear? From who?"

"From a source. He was convincing. He said you were almost run down by some large vessel. A rather unpleasant experience, I expect."

Captain Marius studied the hundred-dollar bill. He picked it up and folded it into an ancient leather pocket purse he produced from somewhere. "It was two nights ago. Fishing had been bad, so I sailed out to a bank I know and most others don't. It was where my father would go when there was no catch closer in." He took a half-crushed packet of cigarettes printed in Arabic from his shirt pocket and extracted a pair of bent, foul-smelling, Algerian cigarettes.

Le Saux took one. Marius lit both, blew a toxic cloud into the air of the curtained room, and leaned closer. His voice was intense, as if he were still shaken by the event. "It came out of nowhere. Like a skyscraper or a mountain. More like a mountain, because it was a behemoth. Only moving. A moving, mountainous behemoth, bearing down on my little boat. No lights inside or outside, so it was darker than the night itself. Later I saw it did have its running lights on, but who could see them so far above, eh?" He sat back and shrugged, as if it no longer mattered. "It missed us to port. We were nearly swamped, but here I am."

"The *Charles de Gaulle?*"

"Or the *Flying Dutchman, hein?*"

Carsten Le Saux also sat back, thoughtful. "Why would she be running dark? Were there destroyers? Other ships?"

"I saw none."

"What was her course?"

"From her wake, I'd say south-southwest."

Le Saux nodded. He waved to the waiter again and ordered another pair of *marcs*. He pushed back his chair, rose, and smiled down at the fishing boat captain. "*Merci.* Be careful out there." He paid the waiter as he left.

Twilight had turned into indigo night. On the crowded waterfront, the pungent odors of fish and alcohol filled the air. Le Saux paused to gaze at the rows of masts and listen to the lulling sound of ropes slapping against wood hulls. The ancient harbor had supported one city or another here since the days of the Greeks in the seventh century B.C. He turned and gazed around as if he were a tourist, then he walked quickly along above the quays. To his left, on a hill high above Marseille, stood the ornate basilica of Notre-Dame-de-la-Garde, the modern city's guardian, aglow with light.

At last, he turned into an old brick building on a narrow side street and climbed the stairs to a two-room apartment on the fourth floor. Once inside, he sat on the bed, picked up the phone, and dialed.

"Howell."

Le Saux grumbled, "How about a pleasant 'good evening'? I retract that. Considering your generally surly nature, I would accept a simple 'hello.' "

A distant snort at the far end of the line. "Where the devil are you, Carsten?"

"Marseille."

"And?"

"And the *De Gaulle* was at sea southwest of Marseille a few hours before General Moore reappeared at Gibraltar. I checked before I talked to the captain of the fishing boat and also discovered there were no NATO or French naval exercises scheduled at the time. Actually, none this week at all. The *De Gaulle* was heading farther south and west toward the Spanish coast. And get this, she was running dark."

"Dark, was she? Interesting. Good job, Carsten. Thanks."

"It cost me two hundred American."

"More likely one hundred, but I'll send the hundred in pounds."

"Generosity is its own reward, Peter."

"Would it were so, would it were so. Keep your ears open, I need to know why the *De Gaulle* was out there."

Chapter
Twenty-five

The Mediterranean, Near Algeria

For hours, the fast motorboat slammed through the waves. Trapped like an animal in a cage, Jon kept himself sharp by playing games with himself, seeing how perfectly and with how much detail he could reconstruct the past. . . . The too-brief time with Sophia . . . his work as a virus hunter at USAMRIID . . . the long-ago stint in East Berlin undercover. And, too, there was the fatal mistake in Somalia, when he had failed to identify the virus that eventually killed Randi's fiancé, a fine army officer. He still felt guilty, even though he knew that it had been a diagnostic error any doctor could have made, and many had.

The years pressed in on Jon, and as time dragged and the boat continued to batter him, he began to wonder whether this journey would ever end. He fell into an uncomfortable sleep. When the door to the storage room opened, he was instantly alert. He released the safety on his Walther. Someone entered, and he could hear what sounded like a search. The minutes passed slowly, and he felt a trickle of sweat run down his side. The frustrated crewman muttered to himself in Arabic. Jon strained to understand, finally realizing the man was looking for a certain wrench.

Fighting a rising tide of claustrophobia, Jon tried to envision the storage room, wondering whether he had inadvertently hidden the damn wrench. Inwardly he swore, and almost simultaneously he heard the crewman curse, too, aloud. But the crewman's tone was excited, not frustrated, because he had found the tool. Soon his footsteps retreated across the storage room and out the door.

As the door settled back into its frame, Jon let out a long stream of air. He wiped the back of his arm across his forehead, put the safety back on his gun, and slumped against the bulkhead with relief. Almost instantly, the boat slammed into another wave.

He checked his wristwatch again and again. In the sixth hour, the motorboat's throbbing engines suddenly racheted down, and the boat slowed. Soon it glided to a floating stop, and there was the metallic creak of the anchor being released. Its chain rattled out, and the hook hit the sea bottom quickly. Which meant they were in shallows. The sharp shrieks of seagulls told him they were near land.

There was quiet activity on deck. A brace of soft splashes, followed by a flurry of padded scrambling sounds over the side. There were no shouted orders. The crew was being as quiet as they could. Jon heard the creak of oars and the controlled splash of paddles, and then the noises faded. Had both the dinghy and the rubber raft been launched? He hoped so.

He waited. The boat rose and fell rhythmically, without the teeth-jarring crashes of heavy waves. As the sea washed against the hull, the vessel seemed to sigh, its wood and metal joists and panels settling in to rest. Silence permeated the craft.

He eased the hatch cover open over his head and stood up slowly, waiting for the feeling to return to his limbs. He stretched, his gaze on the line of light under the door. At last he climbed from his hole. As he advanced through the dark room toward the door, his knee struck some kind of machine part, knocking it to the floor with a clang.

He froze and listened. There was no sound on the deck above. Still, he did not move. He waited. A minute. Two. But no one came along the belowdecks passageway.

He inhaled, opened the door, and peered out in both directions. The corridor was clear. He stepped into it, closed the door, and headed forward toward the gangway. He did not realize it at the time, but he had lowered his guard, allowing himself to rely on his sense of the boat's silence and emptiness, the way he had initially found it.

That was when a powerful-looking man stepped out from one of the small sleeping cubicles, pointing a pistol at Jon. He had a fez on his head and a nasty look on his beard-stubbled face.

"Who the fuck are you? Where'd you come from?" His English had some kind of Middle Eastern accent. Egyptian?

Exasperated, frustrated, Jon lunged. He grabbed the terrorist's gun wrist with his left hand while he used his right to draw his stiletto.

Taken aback by the suddenness of the assault, the man tried to pull free. He jerked back, off balance. Jon slammed a fist toward his jaw, but the fellow recovered, dodged, and jammed his pistol into Jon's side, his finger on the trigger.

Jon twisted away just in time. The man pulled the trigger, the gunfire like a cannon blast in the confines of the boat. The bullet shot past Jon and into one of the cubicles, where it thudded into a wall. Before his attacker could aim and fire again, Jon plunged his stiletto into the man's chest.

The terrorist went down, landing hard on his knees, his black eyes blazing. With a grunt, he keeled forward onto his face.

As Jon kicked the pistol—a 9mm Glock—out of the man's hand, he drew his Walther from his waistband and stepped back. The man lay motionless, blood trickling out from beneath him.

Jon crouched and felt his pulse. He was dead.

When he stood again, Jon was shaking. After a long bout of forced inactivity, his nerves and muscles had been required to surge into sudden, violent action. He shook the way a racing car did when slammed from high speed to a sudden stop. He had not intended to kill the man. In fact, he did not like to kill at all, but he'd had no choice.

Once his quaking passed, he stepped over the corpse and climbed up the gangway to the deck. Afternoon sunlight came to greet him.

His eyes just above the opening, he surveyed the deck. He could see no one. Built for speed, the boat had few structures to catch the wind. The deck was flat and clear all the way to the bridge, which was unoccupied. The dinghy and rubber raft were gone.

Warily, he crawled up and moved forward to the bridge, from where he could view the rest of the boat. It was empty, too. In the bridge well, he found a pair of binoculars. To the west, the sun was a ball of lemon fire low in the sky. The air was cooling rapidly, but then, according to his watch, it was past six o'clock in Paris. Judging by the amount of time spent on the ride here and the speed at which he guessed the vessel had been traveling, he figured he was likely still in the same time zone or, at the most, one zone over.

Through the binoculars, he scanned the shore, aglow in the cooling light. There was a fine, smooth beach with what looked like plastic greenhouses. Other greenhouses had been built in rows behind it, reaching inland. Nearby, a citrus grove ran from the coast into the distance. He could see oranges ripening in the leafy branches. There was a large promontory, too, that jutted out into the sea. It appeared to be entirely enclosed by a long white wall at least ten feet high. The high height impressed him, and he studied the promontory. Dark olive trees and palms stood stark against the wall, and he could see some kind of domed building behind.

He moved the binoculars. Far to the right, modern cars sped along what looked like a good highway, close to the sea. He moved the binoculars again, this time sweeping the distance. Behind everything rose a line of hills, while taller hills loomed in the distance.

Jon lowered the binoculars, mulling over the clues.... This was not France. It could be southern Spain, but he doubted it. No, this had the feel of North Africa, and from the lushness, the greenhouses, the wide sandy beaches, the palms, the hills, the highway, the newer cars, in fact the prosperous appearance of it all, and the speed and time of the journey, his judgment was that he was anchored off Algeria, probably not far from Algiers.

He raised his binoculars to study the far-off wall again. The rays of the afternoon sun had grown even longer and now bounced off the tall white barrier as if it were chrome, half-blinding him. The light danced with dust motes, too, which made what he could see of the wall hazy and indistinct. It seemed almost to undulate. With so much visual interference, he could not make out the buildings behind it. He studied the beach, but there was no dinghy or rubber raft resting there.

Pursing his lips, he lowered the binoculars and contemplated the setup. He was intrigued by that tall, very solid-looking wall that seemed to enclose the promontory.

He hurried belowdecks to the storage room, where he remembered seeing a plastic bucket. He stripped to his shorts again and folded his clothes, Walther, and stiletto into the bucket. Back topside, he carried his belongings down the swaying rope ladder to the darkening sea. He slid into the cool water, and, pushing the bucket in front of him, swam toward the coast, creating as little ripple as possible, since white water reflected sunlight and could attract attention.

He was tired as he closed in on landfall, wearied by the stress of events as well as by the day's rough travel. But as he stopped to tread water so he could scrutinize the white wall, fresh energy coursed through him. The wall was higher than he had gauged—at least fourteen feet. Even more interesting was the sharp, rolled concertina wire that ridged its top like a crown of thorns. Someone had gone to a great deal of trouble to discourage trespassers.

Contemplating that, he swam quietly on toward the end of the promontory, the temperature of the seawater and air dropping as twilight spread like an inky hand. The point's terminus was overgrown with what looked like an impenetrable mass of vegetation and palm trees. He continued swimming on around but still saw no sign of buildings.

Then he smiled soberly to himself: There on the beach lay the dinghy and rubber raft, pulled close up to the thick growth. This was progress.

The strength of his stroke improved, and he continued farther on until he spotted a place where the wilderness ran so close to the sea it almost seemed to drop into it, and the white wall had ended in tribute to the density of nature's green wall. Again he stopped to tread water, this time watching the coastline for movement. After a time, he pushed his bucket ashore toward the thick vegetation and crawled up onto the sand, still warm from the day's sun. He lay there a full minute, feeling his heart pound against the beach, absorbing the comfort of the warmth.

At last, he pulled himself up and ran barefoot into the vegetation where he soon found a tiny glade, dark and shadowy, filled with the scents of rich earth and growing plants. Under a date palm, he dressed quickly, stuck his Walther into his waistband, strapped the stiletto into a sheath Velcroed to his calf, and hid the bucket.

He moved through the trees and bushes, keeping the beach in sight, until he ran into a dirt trail. He crouched to study it. There were footprints with treads characteristic of athletic shoes like the ones he wore. The most recent prints—a jumble of several different sets of feet—led away from where the raft and dinghy were tied.

Encouraged, he took out his Walther and followed the trail inland for another fifteen yards until it ended at a vast open area in the grip of night's growing shadows. There were olive trees and date palms and beyond them a rise of land. On it stood a large white villa crowned by a white dome inlaid with mosaic tiles. He had seen that dome from the boat.

The sprawling villa appeared completely isolated, and at first glance it seemed deserted, too. No one worked or strolled in the gardens, and no one sat in the blue, wrought-iron furniture that was arranged artistically on the long terrace. Neither could he see anyone through the open French doors. No cars or other vehicles were visible. The only movement was from gauzy curtains, billowing from the open windows. But then voices came from somewhere in the distance. They were raised in unison in a marchlike rhythm, while an occasional gunshot echoed faintly from somewhere far away. Obviously, there was more here than the ordinary visitor might expect.

As if to prove the point, a man wearing a British camouflage uniform and with an Afghan puggaree on his head appeared at the far corner of the house. He carried an AK-47 slung casually over his shoulder.

Jon felt his pulse increase. He sank down behind a bush to watch as a second guard appeared from the villa's other corner. This man was bareheaded, dressed in denims and a flannel shirt, and looked Oriental. He cradled a U.S. M60E3 light machine gun in the crook of his left arm. The pair crossed paths below the terrace steps and continued on in opposite directions around the house, patrolling.

Jon made no move. Moments later, a third guard appeared, this one from inside the house. As well armed as the others, he stood on the terrace, cradling his assault rifle, his gaze sweeping the grounds, and then he returned inside. Five minutes later, the pair circling the villa reappeared, soon followed by a fourth sentry, who emerged from the villa onto the terrace. They were using four guards.

Now that Jon was beginning to see a pattern, it was time to work his way inside the villa. He circled back through the dense green growth until he found what appeared to be a secluded door near the building's front. Here the rambling mansion was closer to the junglelike forest than at any other point. He still saw no cars or even a driveway, which was probably on the other side of the villa. The distant voices raised in a chanting chorus sent a chill up his spine. He could make out the Arabic words now, and they were a litany of hate for Israel and America, the Great Satan.

The instant the guard walked around the rear corner and out of sight, Jon stepped from the thick cover and sprinted to the hidden corner of the house. The door was unlocked. Considering the myriad access points through open windows to what seemed like every room, it was hardly a surprise. Still, he maintained his caution, and he opened the door an inch at a time. Through the widening gap, he saw a polished tile floor, expensive Arab furniture, modern abstract paintings that were far from traditional but would not offend Islamic sensibilities, small curtained alcoves for quiet reading and meditating, and no humans.

He eased inside, the Walther out in both hands. Another room, similar to the first, was clearly visible through a traditional Moorish archway. In this land, which had been overrun and occupied by a long series of conquerors and settlers, it was the Arabs who had left the most lasting influence. They were also still a majority. Despite the tenacity of the Berber tribes and the power of French bureaucrats and residents, some Arabs were still trying to take Algeria back to full Islamic control, a goal that had proved long, difficult, and particularly bloody. It also accounted for why so many Islamic residents supported and even harbored fundamentalist killers.

The next room was as empty as the first, and he continued to move cautiously through more cool, shadowed rooms. He encountered no one. Then he heard voices ahead.

Redoubling his caution, he closed in, the words growing steadily clearer. At last, he recognized a voice—Mauritania's. He had found a Crescent Shield hideout of some kind. Perhaps even a headquarters. Nervy and excited, he slid into a corner and listened. There was an echoing quality to the voices that told him they were in a large room with a high ceiling, higher than the ones he had passed through.

He moved again until the voices were obviously coming from the next archway. He flattened back against the wall next to it and peered around at the backs of some dozen men who were gathered in a great room under the building's soaring dome. They were a wildly disparate group—bedouins in their long robes, Indonesians wearing the latest in Levi's and designer T-shirts, Afghans in pyjama pants with their trademark long-tailed puggarees wrapped around their heads. All carried weapons, which ranged from the most modern assault rifles to battered old AK-47s. At the front of the room, the small, deceptively mild-looking Mauritania was perched on the edge of an oak library table, dressed in long white robes. He was talking in French. The crowd of men were listening with rapt attention.

"Dr. Suleiman has arrived and is resting," he announced. "He will report to me soon, and the moment Abu Auda arrives, the countdown will begin."

The gathered terrorists erupted in excited cries of *Alahu Akbar* and other exclamations in a myriad of languages, most of which Jon did not understand. They waved their weapons overhead and shook them.

Mauritania continued, "They'll call us terrorists, but we're not. We're guerrillas, soldiers in the service of God, and with God's help we'll triumph." He raised the palms of his hands, silencing the tumult. "We've tested the Frenchman's device. We've misdirected attention to America. And now we'll blind and silence the Americans so they can't warn their Jewish lackeys when the Russian tactical missile is stolen and sent on its glorious way to wipe the Zionists from our sacred land!"

The roar this time was so great, the fierce cries so loud and intense, that the dome seemed to shake.

As the noise subsided, Mauritania's fair eyes darkened, and his face grew solemn. "It'll be a great explosion," he promised. "It'll destroy them all. But the Great Satan's reach is long, too, and many of our people will be killed as well. This saddens me. That we'll lose a single son of Mohammed stabs me to the heart. But it must be done to cleanse the land, to end this bastard nation of Zion. We will erase the heart of Israel. Our people who die will be martyrs and go straight into God's arms, in glory forever."

Shouts burst forth again. Where he crouched in the next room, Jon's blood was chilled. It was a nuclear attack, and it was not aimed at the

United States. The target was Israel. From what Mauritania had said, the DNA computer was going to reprogram an old Soviet medium-range tactical nuclear missile and drop it on Jerusalem, "the heart of Israel," erasing millions in that country as well as many others in neighboring nations, all Arab countries, sacrificed for Mauritania's sick dreams.

Jon spun away from the wall. He had no more time. He had to find Dr. Chambord and destroy the DNA computer. They must be somewhere in this sprawling, whitewashed building. Peter, Marty, and Thérèse might be here, too. Hoping he would find all of them, he circled through more empty rooms, searching.

The Naval Base, Toulon, France
In the spring twilight, Maître Principal Marcel Dalio left the Toulon naval base through the security gate. He was a nondescript man in many ways, of average height and weight, and circumspect in his demeanor. But his craggy face made him a standout. Although he was a virile fifty-year-old, he looked a good twenty years older. It came from the years at sea in the constant sun, wind, and salt air. The elements had etched his face into a Grand Canyon of ravines, crevices, and mesas.

As he walked along, his great face, handsome in its dramatic character, turned to take in all the sights of the Toulon harbor with its fishing boats, private yachts, and cruise ships, which were just beginning the season. Then his gaze swept out to sea where his own ship, the mighty carrier *Charles de Gaulle*, rode at anchor. He was proud to be a *maître principal*, similar to a chief petty officer in the American navy, and even prouder to serve on the grand *De Gaulle*.

Soon Dalio reached his favorite bistro, on a narrow back street off the quai Stalingrad. The proprietor greeted him by name, bowed, and ceremoniously led him to his favorite secluded table at the rear.

"What is best today, César?" Dalio asked.

"Madame has outdone herself with the *daube de boeuf*, Maître Principal."

"Then bring it, by all means. And a nice Côte du Rhône."

Dalio sat back and glanced around the provincial bistro. As the naval petty officer had expected, since the season was spring the restaurant was not yet crowded. No one showed interest in him or his uniform. Tourists tended to stare at a uniformed Frenchman in Toulon, since many came principally to see the naval base, hoping to have a good view of the warships and, if very lucky, an onboard tour.

When his food and wine arrived, Dalio ate his *daube de boeuf* slowly, savoring the heavy flavor of the mutton stew as only the proprietor's wife could create it. He made short work of his Côte du Rhône, its lovely mulberry color glistening like blood in his wineglass. He finished with a *tarte au citron* and lingered over his demitasse coffee. At last he left for the *pissoir* at the rear. Like all those near the quai Stalingrad, this bistro catered to tourists most of the year. For the sensibilities of the well-paying American crowd, it had not only installed separate facilities for men and women, it also included stalls in both.

Inside the door, Dalio noted with relief that the *pissoir* appeared empty. He bent over to check that all the stalls were, too. Satisfied, he locked himself inside the one he had been told to use, lowered his trousers, and sat. He waited.

Moments later, another man entered the next stall and spoke softly in French. "Marcel?"

"*Oui.*"

"Relax, old friend, you'll be revealing no state secrets."

"You know I wouldn't do that anyway, Peter."

"True," Peter Howell acknowledged. "What did you discover?"

"Apparently—" Dalio paused as a man entered the men's room. As soon as the fellow washed his hands and left, Dalio continued, "The official word was that we had orders from NATO to demonstrate our drill for running dark to a committee of EU and NATO generals."

"Which NATO generals?"

"One was our Deputy Supreme Commander, General Roland la Porte."

"The others?"

"Didn't recognize them," the *maître principal* told him, "but by their uniforms, they were German, Spanish, English, and Italian."

Two more men pushed into the facility, laughing raucously while holding a loud, half-drunken conversation. In the stalls, Peter and Marcel Dalio remained silent while they endured the stumbling, slurring inanity.

In Peter's mind, he was gauging whether their behavior was real or an act for his and Marcel's benefit.

When the pair left, having at last worked out who would attempt to seduce the redhead on the barstool next to them, Peter sighed. "Bloody boors. Very good, Marcel. You've given me the official line. What's the unofficial?"

"Yes, I thought you might ask about that. A couple of the stewards told me the generals never went out on deck. They spent their whole time in a closed meeting below, and then they left the ship right after the meeting ended."

Peter came alert. "How'd they get off the ship?"

"Helicopters."

"They flew to the ship on their own choppers and left in them, too?"

Dalio nodded. Then he remembered Peter could not see him. So he said, "That's what the stewards thought. I was below most of the cruise so didn't see any of it."

So that's where General Moore was, Peter thought. But why? "Did any of the stewards know what the meeting was about?"

"Not that they mentioned."

Peter stroked his nose. "See if you can find out, and if you do, contact me through this phone number." Under the partition he slid a card on which he had written the phone number of an MI6 contact drop.

"All right," Dalio agreed.

"*Merci beaucoup*, Marcel. I owe you."

"I'll remember that," the *maître principal* said. "I hope I never have to collect."

Peter left first, and then Dalio, who returned to his table to enjoy a second pot of demitasse coffee. He glanced idly around the entire restaurant once more. He saw no one he knew or anyone who looked suspicious. Peter himself, of course, was nowhere to be seen.

The Western Mediterranean, Aboard Missile Cruiser USS *Saratoga*
The combat information center of the AEGIS Weapons System cruiser was a dark, cluttered cave. It had the almost-odorless, highly filtered smell of all U.S. government locations where millions of taxpayer dollars in electronic equipment were at work. Randi sat behind a communications

technician, watching mechanical hands sweep across luminous radar and sonar screens, while she listened to Max's voice on the radio shout above the throb of the Seahawk helicopter's rotors.

The chopper was patrolling along the Algerian coast, and Max had radioed to let her know he had found the boat on which Jon had stowed.

"It's the same boat," he bellowed.

"You're sure?" Randi pursed her lips and considered the tiny blip on the radar screen relayed from the Seahawk.

"*Definite.* I spent a lot of time studying it while Jon was swimming out to it and then after he boarded."

"Any sign of people? Of Jon?"

"No one and nothing," Max's voice shouted.

"It's getting dark out there. How far away are you?"

"Over a mile, but I'm using binoculars, and I can see it clear. No raft or dinghy on the boat."

"Where could they have gone?"

"There's a big villa on a finger of land that juts out into the Mediterranean. About a half mile inland are a bunch of low buildings that could be barracks. Looks like there's a parade ground, too. The whole thing's pretty isolated. The main road turns off before it gets near the place, and then it passes far south."

"You can't see *any* people? *Any* activity?"

"Nothing."

"Okay, come on back." Randi mulled the information. At last, she turned to the young petty officer who had been assigned to help her. "I need to talk to the captain."

She found Captain Lainson having coffee in his quarters with his executive officer, Commander Schroeder. They had been ordered to detach from their carrier group to shepherd what appeared to be a minor clandestine CIA mission, and this had put neither officer in a good mood. But they sat straighter and listened with obvious interest as Randi described her plans and needs.

"I think we can insert you and stand ready easily enough, Agent Russell," Commander Schroeder assured her.

"This is cleared with Washington and NATO, I presume?" Captain Lainson questioned.

She said firmly, "Langley assures me it is."

The captain nodded, his face noncommittal. "We'll insert you, that's fine. But I'll have to go through the Pentagon for the rest."

"Do it fast. We don't know yet exactly what kind of disaster we're facing, but it won't be minor. If we don't end the threat, the loss of just a carrier battle group could look like a victory." Randi could see skepticism vie with uneasiness in the officers' eyes. She left them to their work and returned to her makeshift quarters to change.

Chapter
Twenty-six

Outside Algiers, Algeria

After a careful search, Jon found what looked like the bedroom wing of the sprawling villa, where there were actual doors on some of the rooms. The doors were carved, heavy wood, with solid brass fittings that looked as if they might date back to the days of the first Arab and Berber dynasties.

Jon stopped at a side corridor with magnificent mosaics that began their designs on the floor and wrapped completely up the walls and across the ceiling. Every square inch was covered with bits of perfectly placed semiprecious stones and glazed tiles, many with gold leaf. Whatever rooms were off this passage had been set off, secluded, and they must have belonged to someone important. Perhaps they still did.

He moved cautiously down the jewel-like hall. It was like being inside a long treasure box. At the end, he stopped. Here was the only door, and it was not only closed, it was locked from the outside by an antique sliding bolt that looked as sturdy as the day it had been forged. The door itself had filigreed fittings and was intricately carved, elegant, and massive. He pressed his ear to it. What he heard made his heart accelerate—the clicks of a keyboard.

He slid open the bolt and turned the handle with slow, steady pressure until he felt rather than heard the door's interior latch open. He pressed the door in a few inches until he could see a room furnished comfortably with Western overstuffed chairs, simple tables, a bed, and a desk. There was also an archway that opened onto a whitewashed corridor.

But the center of gravity, the heart of the room, the point where Jon's gaze was riveted was the long, thin back of Émile Chambord, who was stooped over the desk, working at a keyboard that was connected to a strange, clumsy-looking apparatus. Jon recognized it instantly: *The DNA computer.*

He forgot where he was, the danger of it all. Transfixed by the science, he studied the machine: There was a glass tray, and inside lay a collection of silvery blue gel packs, which must contain the vital DNA polymers. Connected by ultrathin tubing, the gel packs were submerged in a foam-like jelly, which would prevent vibration and keep the readout stream stable. The tray appeared to be temperature controlled, which was also crucial since molecular interaction was highly temperature sensitive. There was a small digital readout for set-point adjustment.

Nearby, another machine with an open, glass face was linked to the gel packs by more of the thin tubing. Through the glass he could see a series of small pumps and glass canisters. That had to be the DNA synthesizer—the feeder station for the gel packs. Small lights blinked on its control panel.

Excited, Jon drank in the rest of Chambord's miraculous creation. A "lid" sat on top of the tray, and at the interface between it and the packs of DNA was what appeared to be a thin plate of soft metal coated with a biofilm—probably another type of molecular polymer. He deduced it must be a sensor device, absorbing the DNA chemical energy, changing its conformation, and emitting light as a result.

What an ingenious idea—a molecular switch that was based on light. Chambord was using the DNA molecules not only to compute; another class of molecules in the sensor *detected* the computation. A brilliant solution to what had been an impossible problem.

In awe, Jon forced himself to take a deep breath. He reminded himself of the reason he was here, the danger this machine presented to the world. Considering that it was still in enemy territory, Fred Klein would want him to destroy it instantly. But Chambord's prototype was not only scientifically beautiful, it was ground-breaking. It would revolutionize the future and could make life better and easier for masses of people. It would be years before anyone else came close to approximating what was here right now in this room.

As Jon argued with himself, he eased the door farther open and slid into the room. Using the handle, he held the latch bolt open and closed the door. As the bolt slid gently home, he decided he would give himself one serious chance to get the prototype out safely. If he failed, if he had no other option . . . he would wreck it.

Still having made no sound, he looked for a lock on this side of the door, but there was none. He turned and studied the airy room, lighted by electricity even though the villa dated back long before its invention. The windows were open onto the night, and filmy curtains floated in on a light breeze. But the windows were barred.

He focused on the archway, which showed what appeared to be another hallway and the edge of another archway that opened onto yet another room. The layout suggested a complex of rooms reachable from the rest of the house only by the door behind him, locked from the outside. He nodded to himself. This would once have been the quarters of the favorite wife of a Berber noble or perhaps of the queen of a *seraglio*—harem—of a Turkish official from the old Ottoman Empire.

He started across the room to Chambord, when the scientist suddenly turned. A pistol was in his bony hand, pointed at Jon.

A cry in French came from the archway: "No, Papa! You know who this is. It's our friend, Dr. Smith. He tried to help us escape in Toledo. Put down the gun, Papa!"

The pistol held steady, still aimed across the room at Jon. Chambord frowned, his cadaverous face suspicious.

"Remember?" Thérèse continued. "He's Dr. Zellerbach's friend. He visited me in Paris. He was trying to find out who bombed the Pasteur."

The pistol relaxed a hair. "He's more than a doctor. We saw that at the farmhouse in Toledo."

Jon smiled and said in French, "I really am a medical doctor, Dr. Chambord. But I'm also here to rescue you and your daughter."

"Ah?" A puzzled wrinkle appeared between Chambord's eyes, but his great, bony face still peered suspiciously. "You could be speaking lies.

First, you tell my daughter you're just a friend of Martin's, and now you say you're here to save us." The pistol jerked up again. "How could you find us? *Twice!* You're one of them. It's a *trick!*"

"No, Papa!"

As Thérèse ran between Jon and her father, Jon dove behind a large couch covered with an Oriental rug and came up with his Walther in both hands. Thérèse stared unbelieving at Jon.

"I'm not one of them, Dr. Chambord, but I wasn't totally honest with Thérèse in Paris, and for that I apologize. I'm also a U.S. Army officer. It's Lieutenant Colonel Jon Smith, M.D., and I'm here to help you. Just as I was trying to help you in Toledo. It's the truth, I swear. But we must move quickly. Almost everyone's in the dome room, but I don't know for how long."

"An American lieutenant colonel?" Thérèse said. "Then . . ."

Jon nodded. "Yes, my real mission—my assignment—was to find your father and his computer. To stop his kidnappers from using his work."

Thérèse turned on her father. Her slender, dirt-smudged face was insistent. "He came to help us!"

"Alone?" Chambord shook his head. "Impossible. How can you help us *alone?*"

Jon stood up slowly. "We'll figure out how to get out of here together. I'm asking you to trust me." He lowered his pistol. "You're safe with me."

Chambord considered him. He glanced at his daughter's determined expression. At last he let his pistol fall to his side. "You have some proof, I suppose?"

"Afraid not. Too chancy."

"That's all very well, young man, but all she can tell me is that you're a friend of Martin's, which is what you told her. That doesn't give me much confidence you can help us escape. These people are dangerous. I have Thérèse to consider."

Jon said, "I'm here, Dr. Chambord. That's got to be worth something. Plus, as you pointed out, I've found you twice. If I got in here, I can get you out. Where did you find that pistol? That may come in handy."

Chambord gave a humorless smile. "Everyone thinks I'm a helpless old man. *They* think that. So they're not as alert as they should be. In one of the many cars they used to transport me, someone left a gun. Naturally, I took it. They've had no reason to search me since."

Thérèse put a hand over her mouth. "What were you going to do with it, Papa?"

Chambord avoided her gaze. "Perhaps we shouldn't talk about that. I have the gun, and we may need it."

Jon said, "Help me dismantle your computer and answer some questions. Quickly."

As Chambord turned the machine off, Jon asked, "How many are in the villa? What's the access like? Is there a road out? Cars? What kind of security in addition to the guards outside?"

Analyzing information was familiar territory for Chambord. As they disengaged wires and tubes, he said, "The only access I saw was a gravel road that connected with the coast highway. The highway runs between Algiers and Tunisia, but it's more than a mile inland. The road ends at what appears to be a small training camp for new recruits. The car that brought us here is parked there with some former British military vehicles. I saw a helipad near the training center, and I believe there were two old helicopters parked on it. I can't say exactly how many men are in the house. At least a half dozen are guarding it, probably more. They're always arriving and departing. Then, of course, there are the new recruits as well as a cadre at the training facility."

As Jon listened, he controlled his frustration with Chambord, who was working slowly, methodically as they took apart the prototype. Too slowly.

Jon weighed options. Those cars parked near the helipad would work, if they could sneak out to them without being detected. Jon told them both, "Okay, here's what we're going to do . . ."

■

Under the high dome of the villa's great hall, spotlights bathed the mosaics in a warm glow as Mauritania interrogated an exhausted Dr. Akbar Suleiman. They spoke in French, since the Filipino did not know Arabic. While Suleiman stood in front of him, Mauritania remained seated on the large table, his short legs dangling and swinging like those of a boy sitting on the limb of a tree. He enjoyed his small size, his deceptive softness, the stupidity of those who believed in the superficiality of physical strength.

"Then what you're saying is that Smith broke into your apartment without warning?"

Suleiman shook his head. "No, no! A friend at the Pasteur alerted me, but only a half hour earlier. I had to make my emergency calls, tell my girlfriend what to do, and there was no time to escape sooner."

"You should've been more prepared. Or at least called us, not handled it yourself. You knew the risks."

"Who would've thought they'd locate me at all?"

"How *did* they?"

"I don't know for sure."

Mauritania said thoughtfully, "The address in your hospital file was incorrect, as instructed?"

"Of course."

"Then someone knew where you lived and sent them to you. You're sure there was no one else? He was wholly alone?"

"I neither saw nor heard anyone else," Suleiman repeated wearily. The trip had been long, and he did not sail well.

"You're certain no one followed you once you escaped your apartment?"

Suleiman grumbled, "Your black man asked me that, and I told him the same as I tell you. My arrangements were foolproof. No one *could* follow."

There was a sudden commotion, and Captain Darius Bonnard entered angrily, with two armed bedouins and the towering Abu Auda himself immediately after. Mauritania saw Bonnard's rage and Abu Auda's fierce gaze, which bored across the great room and into Dr. Akbar Suleiman.

Abu Auda snarled, "His 'black man' asks you no more, Moro. A car followed me all the way to Barcelona, where I was able to lose it at last, but only with difficulty. No one had followed me until then. So where did the car come from, eh? From *you*, Suleiman. You must've been surveilled when you ran away from Paris, which meant you led them to me at the lodge. And you, fool, didn't even know it!"

Bonnard's anger had built even higher. His face was violent red as he told Mauritania, "We have evidence Suleiman brought them from Barcelona to Formentera to here. At the very least, he's compromised us!"

As Suleiman blanched, Mauritania asked quickly, "Here? How do you know this?"

"We don't speak idly, Khalid." Abu Auda scowled at Suleiman.

Captain Bonnard switched to French. "One of your men is dead on the motor launch, and he didn't die by stabbing himself. Suleiman brought an extra passenger, who's no longer on the boat."

"Jon Smith?"

Bonnard shrugged, but his face remained furious. "We'll know soon. Your soldiers are searching."

"I'll send more." Mauritania snapped his fingers, and all of the men poured out of the hall.

·

In the dark night, the lightless SH-60B Seahawk helicopter hovered low over an open area near plastic greenhouses and citrus groves a mile from the villa. The air whipped Randi's face as she stood in the open doorway and hooked the rescue cable onto her harness. She was wearing night combat camos with a black watch cap covering her blond hair. She carried equipment attached to her mesh belt and wore a backpack with more equipment. She gazed down, thinking about Jon, wondering where he was and whether he was all right. Then her mind moved to the mission itself, because in the end that was most important. More important than either hers or Jon's life. The DNA computer must be destroyed so that whatever madness the terrorists planned was stopped.

She gripped her harness and nodded her readiness. The crewman at the hoist watched the pilot, who finally nodded that he had the chopper in position, hovering. The signal given, Randi jumped into the dark void. The crewman let out the hoist as she descended. She fought the terror of falling, of the failure of equipment, blocked all her fears from her mind until, at last, she bent her knees and rolled onto the ground. Quickly she unhooked the harness. There was no need to bury it. They would know she was here soon anyway.

She bent to the small transmitter. "*Saratoga*, do you read me? Come in *Saratoga*."

With a clean, clear sound, a voice from the cruiser's combat information center responded, "We read you, Seahawk 2."

"This could take an hour, maybe more."

"Understood. Standing by."

Randi shut off the radio and stowed it in a pocket of her camos, unslung her MP5K mini-submachine gun from her shoulder, and loped off. She avoided the main road and the beach. Instead, she worked her way through the citrus groves and past the greenhouses, their plastic coverings stirring with the wind. The moon hung low on the horizon, its milky light reflecting eerily on the plastic. In the distance, surf pounded the beach, rhythmic as a heartbeat. Above her, the stars had come out, but the sky seemed more black than usual. Nothing moved on the highway or out at sea, and there were no houses in sight. Only the ghostly orange and lemon trees, and the shifting glitter of the greenhouses.

At last she heard two cars speeding along the highway, their motors loud assaults in the quiet night. They roared past, and abruptly their tires screeched and burned rubber as they made the sharp turn inland that Max had identified from the air. In a few minutes, the engines stopped, cut off as if a curtain of silence had fallen over them. Randi knew the only residence ahead was the villa. The speed indicated someone had felt an urgent need to get to the villa.

She accelerated into a serious run and soon reached the high white wall, where she discovered it was topped by coils of razor wire. An open space of almost ten yards had been cut between the vegetation and the wall as far as she could see, which meant she would not be helped out by overhanging branches. She unslung the backpack she had loaded on the *Saratoga* with equipment flown to her by the CIA and pulled out a small air pistol, a miniature titanium barbed dart, and a roll of thin nylon-covered wire. She attached the wire to a miniature ring on the dart, inserted the dart into the pistol barrel, and searched until she found a thick old olive tree some ten feet inside the wall.

She stood back and fired. The dart landed where she wanted—into the tree. She returned the pistol to her backpack, put on padded leather gloves, and, grasping the wire, she swarmed hand over hand up to the top of the wall. Once there, she hooked the wire to her belt, returned the gloves to the backpack, and brought out a miniature pair of wire cutters. She clipped a three-foot opening in the razor wire, returned the cutters, and slid over the wall and dropped to the ground.

High-tech security was extremely expensive, and terrorists could rarely afford it. Fundamentalists who became terrorists maintained such an extreme secrecy that their paranoia prevented them from seeking out the necessary hardware, the sales of which were often too closely monitored for their tastes. At least, that was the theory, and she could only hope it was correct—and be cautious as hell.

With that in mind, she released the wire from the dart, pulled the coil over the wall after it, and returned everything to her backpack. She melted through the vegetation toward the unseen villa.

·

Dr. Émile Chambord paused, his hands on the lid of the glass tray. "It's possible. Yes, I believe you're right, Colonel. We should be able to escape that way. It appears you're indeed more than a physician."

"We've got to go immediately. No telling when they'll discover I'm here." He nodded at the computer, which was only partially disassembled. "There's no more time. We'll take the gel packs and leave the rest—"

There was a noise out in the corridor, the door flung open, and Abu Auda and three armed terrorists rushed in, weapons raised. Thérèse cried out, and Dr. Chambord attempted to jump in front of her to protect her with his pistol. Instead, the scientist stumbled heavily into Jon, destroying his balance.

Jon recovered, grabbed for his Walther, and spun. It was too late to destroy the DNA prototype, but he could damage it so that Chambord would need days to make it operational again. That would buy Randi and Peter time to find it, if he were not around to help.

But before Jon's gun could home in on the gel packs, Abu Auda and his men jumped him, knocked the pistol away, and wrestled him to the floor.

"Really, Doctor." Mauritania had followed his men into the room. He pulled Chambord's pistol away from him. "This is hardly your style. I don't know whether to be impressed or shocked."

Abu Auda jumped to his feet and pointed his assault rifle down at Jon's head where he lay on the floor tiles. "You've given us enough trouble."

"*Stop*," Mauritania ordered. "Don't kill him. Think, Abu Auda. An army doctor is one thing, but the American colonel we saw in action in Toledo who's managed to find us again is quite another. We may have need of him before this is finished. Who knows how valuable he may be to the Americans?"

Abu Auda did not move, the rifle still at Jon's head. His erect, angry posture radiated intent to kill. Mauritania said his name again. He looked at Mauritania. His eyes blinked thoughtfully, and the fire in them slowly banked.

At last, he decided, "Wasting a resource is a sin."

"Yes."

Abu Auda gestured with disgust, and his men hauled Smith to his feet. "Let me see the doctor's gun." Mauritania handed him Chambord's pistol, and he examined it. "It's one of ours. Someone will pay for this carelessness."

Mauritania's attention returned to Smith. "Destroying the computer would've been a futile gesture in any event, Colonel Smith. Dr. Chambord would simply have had to build us another."

"Never," Thérèse Chambord insisted and pulled away from Mauritania.

"She hasn't been friendly, Colonel Smith. Pity." He glanced back at her. "You underestimate your power, my dear. Your father would build us another. After all, we have you, and we have him. Your life, his own life, and all the work he will do in the future. Much too high a price to save a few people from a bad day, wouldn't you say? After all, the Americans would not be as concerned about you or me. We'd be a small ancillary cost—'collateral damage,' they call it—while they took what they wanted."

"He'll never build you another!" Thérèse raged. "Why do you think he stole your pistol!"

"Ah?" Mauritania raised an eyebrow at the scientist. "A Roman act, Dr. Chambord? You'd fall onto your sword before you'd help us in our dastardly attack? How foolish, but how brave to consider such a gesture. My congratulations." He looked at Jon. "And you are equally foolish, Colonel, to think you could stop us for any length of time by putting a few bullets into the doctor's creation." The terrorist leader sighed almost sadly. "Please give us credit for some intelligence. Accidents are always possible, so naturally we have the materials at hand for the doctor to rebuild, should you decide to martyr yourself even now." He shook his head. "That's perhaps you Americans' worst sin—hubris. Your so-smug assumption of your own superiority in all things, from your borrowed technology to your unexamined beliefs and assumed invulnerability. A smug assumption you often extend to include your friends, the Jews."

"This isn't religious or even cultural with you, Mauritania," Jon told him. "You're just like every other aspiring dictator. Look at you. This is profoundly personal. And disgusting."

Mauritania's pale eyes were alight, and his small body bristled with energy. There was an air about him of almost godlike invincibility, as if he alone had seen heaven and had been charged with the mission of not simply spreading God's word, but enforcing it.

"This from a heathen," Mauritania mocked. "Your greedy nation has turned the Middle East into a series of puppet monarchies. You gorge on our resources while the world struggles to find food for the next meal. That's your pattern everywhere. You're the richest nation the planet's ever known, but you manipulate and hoard and then wonder why no one thanks you, much less likes you. Because of you, one of every three people doesn't have enough to eat, and one billion are actually starving. Are we to be grateful?"

"Let's talk about all the innocents that'll be killed in your attack on Israel," Jon retorted. "The Koran says, 'You shall not kill any man whom God has forbidden you to kill, except for a just cause.' That's from your sacred writings, Mauritania. There's no *justness* in your cause, just cold-eyed, selfish ambition. You're fooling no one but the poor souls you've lied to so they'd follow you."

Thérèse accused, "You're hiding behind a god you've invented."

Mauritania ignored her. He told Jon, "For us, the man protects his women. They are not to be on public display for all to touch with their eyes."

But Jon was no longer listening, nor was he watching Thérèse and Mauritania. He was focused on Émile Chambord, who had said nothing since Mauritania, Abu Auda, and their men had rushed in. The scientist stood exactly where he had been when he tried to protect Thérèse. He was silent, looking at no one in particular, not even at his daughter. He seemed almost unconcerned. Perhaps he was in shock, paralyzed. Or maybe his thoughts were no longer here in this room, but somewhere else where there were no worries and the future was safe. Watching Chambord made Jon uneasy.

"We talk too much," Abu Auda announced and beckoned his men forward. "Take them out and lock them in the punishment cell. If even one should escape," he warned his followers, "I'll have all your eyes."

Mauritania stopped Abu Auda. "Leave Chambord. We have work to do, do we not, Doctor? Tomorrow will see a changed world, a new beginning for mankind." The little terrorist leader chortled with genuine pleasure.

Chapter Twenty-seven

Randi watched the two armed sentries cross at the front of the villa, followed by another who came out of the entrance. The two who crossed were walking easily, relaxed, laughing to each other. The solitary sentry stopped on the terrace outside the front door and stared appreciatively up at the moonlit night, savoring the citrus-scented breeze and the cool weather and the few clouds that were floating gently across the starry sky.

There was a laxness about them, as if they had been doing this too long with nothing happening. They were *expecting* nothing to happen. This told her the Crescent Shield had spotted neither her insertion nor her climb over the wall. As she had hoped, there were no motion detectors, closed-circuit cameras, or optical scanners mounted at the perimeter. The villa itself could be another matter.

She had reconnoitered the area, finding barracks and a training camp, a road out to the east-west coastal highway, and a helipad with one dark old U.S. Army Huey, and one equally old Hughes OH-6 Loach scout, guarded by a single sleepy terrorist wearing a white turban. Now she circled past the villa's front and through the vegetation, hidden by it from both the arid area of olive trees and the sea. She stopped to study the villa again, which lay like a reclining white phantom, most of its windows dark, only its mosaic dome glowing like some alien spaceship.

She was looking for a weak point. What she saw was a fourth guard standing outside the rear entrance as relaxed as his three comrades.

Until a small man wearing American denim jeans, Levi's from the look of them, and a loud checked shirt ran out the rear door. Southeast Asian, probably Malaysian, and in a great hurry. He spoke briefly and sharply to the sentry, who immediately looked around alertly, nervously, and the small man reentered the house at a run. The sentry peered out into the night, his assault rifle up and traversing as he scanned the vegetation at the rear of the villa.

Something had happened. Were they looking for Jon? Found him?

Moving faster, she continued through the vegetation to the western side of the grounds, where she discovered that the villa had a wing. It jutted out of the otherwise symmetrical building and was blocked from viewing on the east by the villa itself. The wing had no exterior doors, and the windows were barred—elaborate, wrought-iron bars that appeared centuries old. The only entrance to the wing must be from inside the house, and Randi felt a sudden physical sensation, a small, involuntary shudder that combined both anticipation and disgust. She recognized what the wing had been—the female quarters of the old villa, the harem. The bars and lack of doors were not only to keep intruders out, but to keep the women locked in, prisoners.

As she slipped closer, she heard voices from somewhere inside. She circled on and saw light in three windows. The voices came from behind the lighted windows, and they were angry, speaking both French and Arabic. The words were indecipherable, but one of the voices belonged to a woman. Thérèse Chambord? If it were her, she would know her from the briefing photograph she had been shown. As soon as she reached the first window, she eagerly raised up and peered in past the bars.

Mauritania, Abu Auda, and two armed terrorists were standing in the room, all pointing weapons. Even from outside, she could feel the tension. Mauritania was speaking to someone, but she could not see who it was. Ducking low, she crawled to the next window and again arose. Excited, she saw that it was Thérèse Chambord and her father. She angled a bit and, with relief, spotted Jon, too. But the joy of finding them disappeared in the terrible danger in which all three were, under the guns of Mauritania and his men.

As she watched, Abu Auda gestured violently and announced in French, "We talk too much. Take them out and lock them in the punishment cell. If even one should escape, I'll have all your eyes."

Abu Auda's men herded the three toward the door.

Mauritania said, "Leave Chambord. We have work to do, do we not, Doctor? Tomorrow will see a changed world, and a new beginning for mankind."

The terrorist's laughter sent chills along Randi's spine. But not as great a chill as a decision she knew she had to make. With Jon and Thérèse Chambord taken away, only Mauritania and Dr. Chambord, who stood near an apparatus that might or might not be the DNA computer, remained in the room. She examined the bars on the window. They were as substantial as they had appeared from the distance.

She knew her job. In seconds, she considered her options: She had a clear shot at both men but a difficult one at the apparatus. The moment she killed one man, the other would drop to the floor out of sight. Even Chambord would know to do that. A burst from her weapon might damage the apparatus, but she had heard nothing to confirm to her that it was the actual prototype, and she did not know enough science to be confident this was it.

If it really were the computer, there was the chance Chambord could repair or rebuild it quickly. Which meant the logical choice was to kill Chambord. On the other hand, Mauritania might have someone else with enough scientific training to operate the DNA computer, even if he could not build one. Then the choices would be between killing Mauritania and damaging the prototype.

Which was the best course? Would give the best outcome?

Chambord alive might eventually mean the world would have the DNA computer, or perhaps the United States alone would. Much would depend on who rescued Chambord. Langley really wanted the computer.

On the other hand, any attack by her could sign Thérèse Chambord's and Jon's death warrants. And if the apparatus really was *not* the molecular machine, her gunfire would call everyone down on her and end whatever chance she had to save the situation or them.

She lowered her MP5K. She had, after all, a backup plan that was dangerous but would take care of all contingencies. It would eliminate the computer, wherever it was in the villa. The problem was, it might mean the deaths of everyone.

She had to take the chance. Watching for sentries, she ran low, toward the front of the villa. In the distance, she could hear the surf pounding the sand. It seemed to echo the pounding of her heart. At the corner, she peered around at the front terrace and entry. Abu Auda and two of his men were marching Jon and Thérèse across the terrace and down to the bare ground in the direction of the distant barracks. When they were far enough ahead, she followed.

∎

Jon surveyed the dark trees, looking for a way to break Thérèse and himself free. Abu Auda and his men had taken them through a tangerine grove to a square wooden building in a clearing some fifty yards behind the barracks. The scent of citrus seemed cloying, overpowering.

As one of his bedouins opened the heavy door, Abu Auda kicked Jon into a dark room. "You've caused us too much trouble, American. Usually I would've killed you by now. Be grateful to Khalid, for he thinks greater than I. You'll cause us no more trouble in here, and the female can think upon her sins."

The guards pushed Thérèse in after Jon and slammed the door. The key turned in the lock, and there was a *clang* as an additional iron bar was slid home and then a *click* as it was padlocked.

"*Mon Dieu.*" Thérèse sighed.

Jon said in English, "This wasn't how I pictured our next time alone together." He gazed around the single cell. Moonlight slanted in from a barred window high in the wall, sending a rectangular pattern across the concrete floor. Its color was pale, indicating recently poured cement. There were no other windows, and the wood door was massive.

"No," she agreed. Despite her torn white suit and dirty face, there was a beauty and dignity to her that remained untouched. "I'd hoped you would come to the theater to see me work, and then we'd have a late dinner."

"I would've liked that."

"Seeing me work, or the late dinner?"

"Both . . . the dinner and drinks—and later, the most." He smiled.

"Yes." She smiled back, and then her expression grew solemn. "It's odd how life can change so quickly, so unexpectedly."

"Isn't it?"

She cocked her head and gazed at him curiously. "You say that as if you're a man who's lost much."

"Do I?" He did not want to talk about Sophia. Not here, not now. The shadowy cell smelled dry, almost sandy, as if the Algerian heat had baked the moisture forever from the wood structure. "We have to get out of here. We can't leave the computer or your father in their hands."

"But how?"

There was nothing in the room to stand on. The single cot was fastened to the wrong wall, and there was no other furniture. He looked up at the window again, and calculated its height as no more than nine feet. "I'll boost you up so you can test the bars. Maybe one or two are loose. That'd be a happy piece of luck."

He made a stirrup of his hands and hoisted her up to his shoulders.

She strained at the bars, examined them, and announced in a discouraged voice, "They've been sunk through three horizontal boards bolted together, and then bolted to iron plates. They're not new."

Old bars in a prison built long ago, perhaps to punish Arab slaves or the prisoners of the pirates who once ruled here along with what was once a local bey of the Ottoman Empire.

"You don't feel even a creak?" he asked hopefully.

"No. They're solid."

Jon helped her down, and they turned their attention to the wood door. Its advanced age might help. But it, too, showed no weakness, and it was double locked from the outside. Even its hinges were outside. The slave owners and the pirates had apparently been worried more about a prisoner breaking out than anyone breaking in to free someone. And now, without outside help, he and Thérèse would not get out either.

Then he heard a faint, odd sound—like tiny chewing. A small animal tentatively biting into wood. He listened, but could not pinpoint the source.

"Jon!"

The whisper was so low at first he thought he was hallucinating, hearing voices conjured up by his own desperate thoughts of escape.

"Jon, dammit!"

He whirled and looked up at the window. All he saw was the dark sky. The whisper came again. "Idiot! The back wall."

Then he knew the voice. He hurried across the cell and crouched low against the back wall. "Randi?"

"Who did you expect, the marines?"

"I could hope. Why are we whispering?"

"Because Abu Auda and his men are all around. It's a trap, you're the bait, and I'm the quarry. Me or anyone else who comes to rescue you at this dinkus little jail."

"How did you manage to get through?" Once again he found himself admiring her abilities, her tradecraft skills.

The whisper came after a hesitation. "I had to kill two of Abu Auda's men. The night's dark, and that helped. But Abu Auda will miss them soon, and then we're cooked."

"In here, I don't have a lot of options. I'm open to suggestions."

"The padlock on the door's good, but the lock's a piece of junk. The hinges are old, but not rusted enough to do us much good. The hinges are oiled, and I can take them off. The screws holding the bar are outside. If I remove them, I think you can push the door out from the backside."

"Sounds like a possibility. Traditional, but good."

"Yeah. That's what I thought, until I had to kill the two guys. They're in the grove near the front. So I've had to come up with an alternate plan. There's a lot of wood rot back here."

Jon heard the noise in the wall again, muffled. "Are you digging into it?"

"Right. I tested with my knife, and the rot goes deep enough that I think I can cut a nice exit hole. It'll be a lot quieter and maybe quicker."

Inside the room, Jon and Thérèse listened to the noises that sounded like some small animal chewing. The noises went on, faster and faster.

Randi whispered at last, "Okay, big man, shove from your side. Shove hard."

Thérèse knelt beside him, and together they strained against the wall where they had heard Randi work. For several seconds, nothing happened. Then the wood gave under their hands in a cloudburst of sawdust. Dry wood, riddled with termite and other insect tunnels, turned into dust, and the rotten boards shot out. Randi caught them and lowered them silently to the ground.

Jon and Thérèse slipped through and into the languid night air. Jon looked quickly around. The grove of tangerine trees rustled with wind, and the moon was just rising low in the sky.

Randi was crouching just inside the citrus grove, her expression tense, her MP5K held at the ready. She was gazing past the jail and across the grassy open ground to the grove on the other side. The open area was dusky and vague in the night, and the distant trees impenetrable. She motioned them to follow.

She rolled over onto her belly and elbows, her MP5K cradled in the crooks of her arms, and crawled off into the grass. Imitating Randi, Thérèse followed. Jon brought up the rear. Their progress was silent, maddeningly slow. The moon was rising higher, already beginning to shine low through the grove that surrounded the jail.

At last they reached the shadows of the forward trees. They did not pause to rest but crawled on past the dead body of one of the terrorists Randi had killed, and then the second one, until finally they reached a growth of date palms well past where Abu Auda had set his trap.

Randi sat up against a palm trunk. "We should be safe here a couple of minutes. No longer. They've got people out everywhere."

Somewhere nearby, insects made a clicking sound. Above them, stars glittered occasionally through the palm fronds.

"Nice save." Jon rose to his haunches.

"*Merci beaucoup.*" Thérèse sat cross-legged.

As the three faced one another, Randi smiled at Thérèse. "At last we meet. I'm glad you're alive."

"I, too, as you can imagine," Thérèse said with gratitude. "Thank you for coming. But we must get my father. Who knows what terrible things they're planning for him to do!"

Jon gave Randi an innocent smile. "I don't suppose you have an extra gun for me?"

Randi looked disapproving. Jon noted her black eyes, the sculpted face, a fringe of blond hair peeking out from beneath her black watch cap.

She said, "I still don't know who you're really working for, but in the Company we come prepared." She produced a 9mm Sig Sauer of the exact model Jon had been forced to leave in the trash basket at Madrid airport, complete with silencer.

"Thank you," he said sincerely. As he checked the cartridges and saw that it was fully loaded, he told the two women what he had overheard in the dome room.

"Mauritania's planning a *nuclear* strike against Jerusalem?" Randi was shocked.

Jon nodded. "It sounds like a Russian medium-range tactical warhead, probably to minimize damage to the Arab countries around, but they're going to be hurt, too. Bad. The fallout will probably be worse than at Chernobyl."

"*Mon Dieu*," Thérèse whispered, horrified. "All those poor people!"

Randi's eyes glinted. "I was inserted here from a missile cruiser out there about seventy miles. The USS *Saratoga*. I've got a dedicated radio, and they're standing by for my call. That's because we've got a real plan here. It's not pretty, but it'll stop these guys from any nuclear strikes, whether it's against Jerusalem, New York City, or Brussels. We can go a couple of ways with it. If we can rescue Chambord and the computer, then they'll come in and extract all of us. We like that option most." She asked for confirmation that the apparatus she had seen in the room with Jon, Mauritania, Abu Auda, and the Chambords was the molecular prototype. When Jon said it was, she nodded. "If worse comes to worst . . ." She hesitated and looked at Thérèse.

"It can't be any more unpleasant than what we've already been through, or what Mauritania plans, Mlle. Russell."

"We can't let the DNA computer remain in their hands," Randi said gravely. "There's no wiggle room about that. No options."

Thérèse's gaze narrowed, and she frowned. "So?"

"If it comes to it, the *Saratoga* has a Standard Missile SM-2 aimed square on the dome of the villa. Its purpose is to eliminate the DNA computer."

"And the terrorists," Thérèse breathed. "They will die, too?"

"If they're here, yes. Whoever's there will die." There was no emotion in Randi's voice.

Jon had been watching the two women. He told Randi, "She understands."

Thérèse swallowed and nodded. "But my father. He was ready to stop them. He even stole a gun." She turned toward the trail that led back to the villa. "You can't kill him!"

"We don't want to kill him or anyone—" Randi began.

Jon said, "Let's go with a combination of the options. I don't want to take the time to try to get the computer out of there. But we can rescue Chambord, and then your people can extract us."

"I like that," Thérèse said. "That's what I want, too. But if worse comes to worst"—her face seemed to pale in the moonlight—"you must do what you have to, to prevent a catastrophe."

Randi checked her watch. "I can give you ten minutes." She pulled a short-range walkie-talkie from her backpack. "Take this. When you've got Chambord and you're exiting the villa, call me. Then I'll notify the *Saratoga* that it's their turn."

"Right." He attached the walkie-talkie to his belt.

"I'm going with you," Thérèse told Jon.

"Don't be stupid. You're not trained. You'd just be—"

"You may need my help with my father. Besides, you can't stop me. What will you do, shoot me to keep me here?" She looked at Randi. "Give me a gun. I know how to use one, and I'll hold up my end."

Randi cocked her head, considering. She nodded. "Take my Beretta. It's silenced. Here, take it, and go!"

∎

Jon timed the passage of the guards, and when they turned the corner, he led Thérèse in a fast run. They landed on either side of the front door and flattened themselves back. The interior guard emerged through the doorway. A single blow from Jon's new Sig Sauer dropped him. Jon dragged the unconscious terrorist into the house as Thérèse closed the door carefully, making only a small noise. He could hear a loud discussion from the direction of the dome room. It sounded as if a war council were in progress.

He signaled Thérèse, and they sprinted across the broad tiled entry into the west wing of the old villa, not stopping until they reached the sharp turn toward the rear. They paused there, and Jon peered around the corner. He whispered in Thérèse's ear: "No guards. Come on."

They dashed down the side hallway that was completely lined in magnificent mosaics, their pistols ready to fire if discovered. They stopped again, this time at the door to the former women's quarters.

Jon was puzzled. "Still there's no sign of a guard. Why's that?" he whispered.

"Perhaps he's in the room with Papa."

"You're probably right." Jon tried the door. "It's open. You go first. Tell them you were set free and sent back to make him work even harder. The guard may believe that."

She nodded, understanding. "Here, take the gun. We don't want to make them suspicious."

Jon considered, then took the Beretta.

She straightened her shoulders and pushed the door open. She stepped in, crying out in French as she ran to him, the consummate actress: "Papa, are you all right? M. Mauritania said I should return—"

Émile Chambord rotated in his desk chair and stared at Thérèse as if he were seeing a ghost. Then he saw Jon slip in behind her, the two weapons in his hands, sweeping the room in search of guards. But there were none.

Mystified, Jon looked at Chambord. "Why aren't you being guarded?"

The scientist shrugged. "Why would they need to watch me now? They had you and Thérèse. I wasn't going to destroy the prototype or escape and leave her, was I?"

Jon motioned sharply. "Let's get you out of here. Come on."

Chambord hesitated. "What about my computer? Are we leaving it?"

"Leave it, Father," Thérèse cried. "*Hurry.*"

Jon looked at his watch. "We've got only five minutes left. There's no more time." He grabbed Chambord's arm and pulled the scientist until he started hurrying on his own. They ran down the corridors, from one to another until at last they reached the grand foyer. There were accusatory voices outside the front door. Either the unconscious guard had awakened, or he had been discovered.

"To the back!" Jon ordered.

They had gone halfway when they heard more angry voices, these from the distant dome room, and then the noise of many running feet. Jon shoved his Sig Sauer into his waistband next to where he had put Thérèse's Beretta. He pulled out the short-range walkie-talkie and pushed the Chambords to a window at the side of the villa.

"We'll go this way. *Hurry!*" Herding them, he flicked on the walkie-talkie. Urgently he relayed the good news to Randi in a whisper: "We've got Chambord. We're fine and will be out in a couple of minutes. *Call in the strike.*"

■

Randi had moved closer to the villa and was now crouched under a canopy of leaves in the shadows of the fragrant orange grove. She looked at her watch again, dreading the advance of the digital numbers. *Damn.* Heartsick, she saw that the ten minutes she had given Jon were up. The moon was behind a dark cloud, and the temperature was dropping. Still, she had broken out in a sweat. There were lights in the three windows of the female annex and under the towering dome, but she saw nothing else noteworthy, heard nothing.

She looked at her watch again. Eleven minutes. She ripped up a handful of grass, roots and all, and hurled it into the night.

Then her walkie-talkie gave a low crackle, and her pulse raced with hope as Jon's voice reported in and finally whispered, "Call in the strike."

With a thrill of relief, she told him where she was hiding. "You've got five minutes. Once I call in—"

"I understand." There was a hesitation. "Thanks, Randi. Good luck."

Her voice seemed to catch in her throat. "You, too, soldier."

As she cut the connection, she turned her face up to the cloudy night sky, closed her eyes, and gave a silent prayer of thanks. Then she did her job: She bent to her radio transmitter and made the death call to the *Saratoga.*

■

Jon stood at the villa's window, waiting for Thérèse to crawl through. She froze, staring at her father. Jon looked back.

Chambord had produced a pistol. He was pointing it at Jon. "Step away from him, child," Chambord said, the pistol leveled steadily at Jon's chest. "Lower your weapon, Colonel." He'd had it in his jacket pocket.

"Papa! What are you doing?"

"Shhh, child. Don't worry. I'm making things right." He took a walkie-talkie from his other pocket. "I'm serious about your weapon, Colonel Smith. Put it down, or I'll shoot you dead."

"Dr. Chambord—" Jon tried, puzzled. He let his weapon drift down, but he did not release it.

Chambord said into the walkie-talkie, "West side. *Get everyone out here.*"

Jon saw the shine in Chambord's eyes. The glow of excitement. They were the eyes of a fanatic. He remembered the detached, almost dreamy expression he had seen on the scientist's face when Mauritania had discovered them. With a flash of insight, Jon understood: "You weren't kidnapped. You're *with* them. That's why all the work to make you look dead. That's why there was no guard on you just now. It was all an act with Mauritania, to make Thérèse *think* you were a prisoner."

Dr. Chambord spoke with disdain: "I'm not with them, Colonel Smith, *they're with me.*"

"Father?" Thérèse questioned, her face full of disbelief.

But before Chambord could respond, Abu Auda, three of his men, and Mauritania appeared on the run. Jon raised his weapon and grabbed Thérèse's from his belt.

■

Randi checked her watch. *Four minutes.* Suddenly there was noise from the building. Shouts and running feet. She held her breath as shots rang out, followed by a burst of automatic fire. Jon and Thérèse had no automatic weapons. She was afraid to think, but there was only one possibility: Jon and the Chambords had somehow been discovered. She shook her head, denying it, as two more bursts of automatic fire spit noisily in the distance.

She leaped to her feet and tore across the grounds toward the villa. Then came another awful sound: From inside, she could hear triumphant laughter. Shouts of victory, praising Allah. The infidels were dead!

She froze. Unable to think, to feel. It could not be. But all of the gunfire after the two initial early single shots had been automatic. They had killed Jon and Thérèse.

A great sorrow washed over her, and then a towering rage. She told herself sternly she had no time for either. It was all about the DNA computer. That it must not remain in the terrorists' hands. . . . Too much was at stake. Too many other lives.

She turned on her heel and ran away from the villa, racing as if all of the hounds of hell were pursuing. Trying not to see Jon's face, the dark blue eyes, the laughter, the outrage, all of the intelligence. His handsome face with the high, flat cheekbones. How his jaw would knot when he was angry—

When the missile landed, the explosion threw her forward ten feet. The percussive blast was thunderous all around her head and inside it and a windy heat at her back. It was almost as if she had been hurled away by an angry demon. As debris shot through the air and fell in a dangerous rain, she crawled under the branches of an olive tree and covered her head with her arms.

■

Randi sat with her back to the perimeter wall, watching red and yellow flames lick up toward the dark sky from where the white villa had stood nearly a mile away. She spoke into the radio. "Call the Pentagon. The DNA computer is destroyed, and Dr. Chambord with it. There's no more danger."

"Roger, Agent Russell. Good work."

Her voice was dull. "Also tell them Lieutenant Colonel Jonathan Smith, M.D., U.S. Army, died in the explosion, as well as Dr. Chambord's daughter, Thérèse. Then get me out."

She switched off the transmitter and gazed up at the slowly moving clouds. The moon peeked out, a silver orb, and then it was gone. The stink of death and burning debris filled the air. She thought about Jon. He had taken a chance and known the risk. It had come out against him, but he would not complain. Then she began to cry.

PART THREE

Chapter
Twenty-eight

Beirut, Lebanon

CIA agent Jeff Moussad moved warily through the rubble of South Beirut, an officially denied area. The air was dusty, and the mountains of brick and mortar on either side reflected the sad story of the long civil war that had torn apart Lebanon and destroyed Beirut's reputation as the Paris of the East. Although the downtown heart of the city was rebuilding, and several hundred international firms had returned, little progress was in evidence here in this largely lawless no-man's-land of the grim past.

Jeff was armed and in disguise, on assignment to contact an important asset, whose identity and location had been discovered in the notes of a fellow CIA agent who had died in the infamous attack on the Pentagon of September 11. His difficult mission—akin to finding a needle in a silo of needles—was largely possible because of new sources of intelligence that the U.S. government had been developing in everything from familiar tools like the U-2 spy planes and the constellation of secret spy satellites orbiting overhead, to commercial satellite photos and remote-controlled spy drones.

Since there were no road markers, Jeff was relying on a specially programmed Palm Pilot to find his way to the right cave carved into the debris of what had once been some kind of building. He paused in dark shadow to check the Palm Pilot again. The viewing screen showed the streets and alleys of this section in live video relayed from one of a new family of pilotless aerial drones. Those upgraded, unmanned aircraft provided real-time images of an area over vast distances through satellite communications. This was a major improvement from when a drone could provide up-to-the-minute intelligence only if a radio signal could be beamed directly back to the base from where it took off.

Because of the changing geographical chaos here in South Beirut, a stranger would be easily confused. But with the live video feed and the directional lines that told exactly which turns to make, Jeff followed a sure path for perhaps a quarter of a mile. But then gunfire exploded nearby, followed by footsteps behind him. His pulse accelerated, and he darted quickly into the shadow of a smoke-blackened tank that had been twisted and burned in some long-ago firefight. Straining to hear, he pulled out his pistol. He needed to get to the asset's lair quickly, before he was discovered.

He checked his Palm Pilot. His destination was not much farther. But as he studied the next turn, the unthinkable happened. The Palm Pilot went dark. He stared at it, stunned, his chest tight. He had no idea where he was. Cursing under his breath, knowing he was lost, he hit buttons, and the usual fake information that he carried in the Palm Pilot appeared—phone numbers, appointments. But there was no communication from the drone to tell him where to go later, or how to return to base. The connection had died.

Frantically, he tried to remember the exact location of the next turn. When he was sure he remembered correctly, he moved on past a collapsed building, rounded the corner, and crossed toward what he hoped was his final destination. As he emerged onto a leveled area, he looked nervously for the cave entrance. He never found it. What he did see was the muzzle flashes of four assault rifles . . . and nothing more.

Fort Belvoir, Virginia

Just south of Washington, D.C., stood historic Fort Belvoir, now a state-of-the-art site for some one hundred tenant organizations—a Who's Who of the Department of Defense. Among its most clandestine residents was the main receiving station for satellite information for the National Reconnaissance Office (NRO). Created in 1960 to design, launch, and operate U.S. spy satellites, the NRO was so highly secret that it was not even officially acknowledged until the 1990s. Large and powerful, the NRO's multibillion-dollar annual budget exceeded the yearly spending of any of the nation's three most powerful espionage kingdoms—the CIA, the FBI, and the NSA.

Here in the rolling hills of suburban Virginia, the NRO's information-receiving station was a hotbed of cutting-edge electronics and analytical manpower. One of the civilian analysts was Donna Lindhorst, raven-haired, freckle-faced, and exhausted from the last six days of being on high alert. Today she was monitoring a missile-launch facility in North Korea, a country that was not only considered a serious potential threat to the United States and its allies, but one that had made development of longer-range missiles a high priority.

A longtime NRO employee, Donna knew that spy satellites had roamed the skies for some forty years, many orbiting a hundred miles above the planet. Traveling at mach 25, these billion-dollar birds flew over every spot on the face of the Earth twice a day, taking digital snapshots of places that the CIA, government policymakers, and the military high command wanted to see. At any one time, at least five were overhead. From civil war in the Sudan to environmental disasters in China, America's satellites provided a steady river of black-and-white images.

The missile-launch facility in North Korea that Donna was studying was high-danger priority right now. All the United States needed was for some rogue nation to take advantage of the current uncertain electronic situation. And that was what might be happening right now. Donna's throat was dry with fear, because the images she was monitoring indicated a heat plume like those emitted by rocket launches.

She studied the screen nervously, cuing the satellite to focus on the area longer. Known in the spy trade as an Advanced Keyhole-class satellite, it could take a photo every five seconds and relay it almost instantly through Milstar satellites to her monitor. This placed enormous demands on data relay and image processing, but she had to know whether that plume was real. If it were, it could be an early warning of a missile attack.

She leaned anxiously forward, running digital scans, reading the data, homing in until . . . The screen went blank. All the photos were gone. She froze a moment in utter shock, then pushed her chair back and stared terrified at the wall of screens. All were blank. Nothing was coming through. If the North Koreans wanted to mount a nuclear attack against America, nothing would stop them.

Washington, D.C.

The mood in the offices and all along the corridors of the West Wing was of quiet jubilation, a rare Thanksgiving in May. In the Oval Office itself, President Castilla had allowed himself a smile, unusual these past few harrowing days, as he shared the same measured exultation with his room full of advisers.

"I don't know exactly how you did it, sir." National Security Adviser Emily Powell-Hill beamed. "But you really pulled it off."

"*We* pulled it off, Emily."

The president stood up and walked from around his desk to sit on the sofa beside her, a casual act of fellowship he seldom indulged in. He felt lighter today, as if a crippling load had been lifted from his shoulders. He peered through his glasses, favoring everyone with his warm smile, gratified to see the relief on their faces as well. Still, this was no cause for real celebration. Good people had died in that missile attack against the Algerian villa.

He continued, "It was everyone here, plus the intelligence services. We owe a great deal to those selfless heroes who work in the lap of the enemy without any public recognition."

"From what Captain Lainson of the *Saratoga* told me," Admiral Stevens Brose said, nodding to the DCI—the Director of Central Intelligence, "it was CIA operatives who finally got those bastards and destroyed that damned DNA computer."

The DCI nodded modestly. "It was primarily Agent Russell. One of my best people. She did her job."

"Yes," the president agreed, "there's no doubt the CIA and others, who must remain nameless, saved our bacon—this time." His expression grew solemn as he gazed around at his Joint Chiefs, the NSA, the head of the NRO, the DCI, and his chief of staff. "Now we must prepare for the future. The molecular computer is no longer theoretical, people, and a quantum computer will be next. It's inevitable. Who knows what else science will develop to threaten our defenses, and to help humanity, I might add? We have to start right now, learning how to deal with all of them."

"As I understand it, Mr. President," Emily Powell-Hill pointed out, "Dr. Chambord, his computer, and all his research were lost in the attack. My information tells me no one else is close to duplicating his feat. So we have some leeway."

"Perhaps we do, Emily," the president acknowledged. "Still, my best sources in the scientific community tell me that once a breakthrough like this has been made, the pace of development by everyone else is accelerated." He contemplated them, and his voice was forceful as he continued. "In any case, we must build foolproof defenses against a DNA computer and all other potential scientific developments that could become threats to our security."

There was a general silence in the Oval Office as they solemnly considered the task ahead and their own responsibilities. The quiet was shattered by the sharp ringing of the telephone on the president's desk. Sam Castilla hesitated, staring across the room at the phone that would ring only if the matter were of great importance.

He put his big hands on his knees, stood up, walked over, and picked up the receiver. "Yes?"

It was Fred Klein. "We need to meet, Mr. President."

"Now?"

"Yessir. Now."

Paris, France

In the exclusive private hospital for patients undergoing plastic surgery, Randi, Marty, and Peter had gathered in Marty's spacious room. The muted noises of traffic from outside seemed particularly loud as the painful conversation paused, and tears streamed down Marty's cheeks.

Jon was dead. The news ripped at his heart. He had loved Jon as only two friends of such dissimilar talents and interests could love each other, bound by the elusive quality of mutual respect and seasoned by the years.

For Marty, the loss was so large as to be inexpressible. Jon had always been there. He could not imagine living in a world that had no Jon.

Randi sat down beside the bed and took his hand. With her other hand, she wiped the tears from her own cheeks. Across the room, Peter stood against the door, stone-faced, only his slightly reddened skin betraying his grief.

"He was doing his job," Randi told Marty gently. "A job he wanted to do. You can't ask for more than that."

"He . . . he was a real hero," Marty stammered. His face quivered as he struggled to find the right words. Emotions were difficult for him to express, a language he did not fully have. "Did I ever tell you how much I admired Bertrand Russell? I'm very careful about my heroes. But Russell was extraordinary. I'll never forget the first time I read his *Principles of Mathematics*. I think I was ten, and it really startled me. Oh, my. The *implications*. It opened everything to me! That was when he took math out of the realm of abstract philosophy and gave it a precise framework."

Peter and Randi exchanged a look. Neither knew what he was talking about.

Marty was nodding to himself, his tears splashing helplessly out onto the bedclothes. "It had so many ideas that were exciting to think about. Of course, Martin Luther King, Jr., William Faulkner, and Mickey Mantle were pretty heroic, too." His gaze roamed the room as if looking for a safe place to alight. "But Jon was always my biggest hero. Absolutely, positively *biggest*. Since we were little. But I never told him. He could do everything I couldn't, and I could do everything he couldn't. And he liked that. So did I. How often can anyone find that? Losing him is like losing my legs or my arms, only worse." He gulped. "I'm going to . . . miss him so much."

Randi squeezed his hand. "We all are, Mart. I was so sure he'd get out in time. *He* was sure. But . . . ." Her chest contracted, and she fought back a sob. She bowed her head, her heart aching. She had failed, and Jon was dead. She cried softly.

Peter said gruffly, "He knew what he was doing. We all know the risk. Someone has to do it so the businessmen and housewives and shop girls and bloody playboys and millionaires can sleep in peace in their own beds."

Randi heard the bitterness in the old MI6 agent's voice. It was his way of expressing his loss. Where he stood he was alone, as in reality he always was, the wounds on his cheek, left arm, and left hand half-healed and unbandaged, livid in his repressed rage at the death of his friend.

"I wanted to help this time, too," Marty said in that slow, halting voice that resulted from his medication.

"He knew, lad," Peter told him.

A sad silence filled the room. The traffic noises rose in volume again. Somewhere far off, an ambulance siren screamed.

Finally Peter said in gross understatement, "Things don't always work out the way we want."

The telephone beside Marty's bed rang, and all three stared at it. Peter picked it up. "Howell here. I told you never to . . . what? Yes. When? You're sure? All right. Yes, I'm on it."

He set the receiver into its cradle and turned to his friends, his face a grim mask as if he had seen a vision of horror. "Top secret. Straight from Downing Street. Someone has taken control of all the U.S. military satellites in space and locked the Pentagon and NASA out. Can you think of any way they could've done that *without* a DNA computer?"

Randi blinked. She grabbed tissues from the box beside Marty's bed and blew her nose. "They got the computer out of the villa? *No*, they couldn't have. What the hell does it mean?"

"Damned if I know, except that the danger isn't over. We have to start finding them all over again."

Randi shook her head. "They *couldn't* have gotten the prototype out. There was nowhere near enough time for that. But . . ." She stared at Peter. "Maybe Chambord somehow survived? That's the only thing that makes sense. And if Chambord . . ."

Marty sat straight up in the bed, his distraught face quivering with hope. "Jon may be alive, too!"

"Hold on, both of you. That doesn't necessarily follow. The Crescent Shield would've done everything to get Chambord away safely. But they wouldn't have given a ragman's damn about Jon or Ms. Chambord. In fact, you heard automatic fire, Randi. Who else could it have been aimed at? You said in your report that Jon had to have died either in a firefight or when the missile hit. The bloody bastards were cheering. Victorious. Nothing changes that."

"You're right. It doesn't, dammit." Randi grimaced. "Still, it opens a possibility we can't just ignore. If he's alive—"

Marty threw back his covers and jumped out of bed, swaying and holding to the frame, suddenly weak. "I don't care what *either* of you says. *Jon's alive!*" His pronouncement was firm. He had made up his mind, dismissing the news that was too painful to believe. "We must listen to Randi. He could desperately need us. Why, when I think of what he might be suffering, lying wounded and alone somewhere in the hot Algerian desert . . . or perhaps as we speak those ghastly terrorists are preparing to kill him! We must find him!" His medication was wearing off, and life was looking more possible. A superman armed with a computer and the power of genius.

"Calm down, my boy. You know how you tend to take flight beyond the logical universe."

Marty drew his portly body up to its full height, which brought his indignant eyes on a level with Peter's breastbone. He announced with great restraint, "My universe is not only logical, but far beyond your insignificant powers of comprehension, you ignorant Brit!"

"Quite possibly," Peter said dryly. "Still, remember we're working now in my universe. Say Jon *is* alive. From what Randi's reported, he's a prisoner. Or at the very least wounded, pursued, and in hiding. The question becomes where is he, and can we get in touch with him? Except possibly for short distances and brief contact, our electronic communications were locked out when the satellites were taken over."

Marty opened his mouth to make some sharp response, then his face screwed up in helpless frustration as he tried to make his still-slowed brain function on the problem as he wanted it to function.

Randi wondered, "If he did manage to escape—especially if Chambord is with him—the Crescent Shield would've pursued. Mauritania would make sure of that. Probably sent that killer, Abu Auda, after them. From what I've seen, Abu Auda knows what he's doing. So if Jon and any of the others are alive, they're probably still in Algeria."

"But if he didn't escape," Peter reasoned, "if none did—and from what just happened to the American satellites I'd say the Crescent Shield still has Dr. Chambord in its hands—then Jon's a prisoner. And we have no earthly idea where."

∎

Impatient and more worried than ever, Fred Klein sat on the scarred wooden bench that the president had transferred from his private office in his Taos ranch to this private office in the upstairs residence suite of the White House. He peered around at the massive bookcases, not really seeing them as he thought about what he needed to discuss. He desperately wanted to light his pipe. It was still in the breast pocket of his baggy wool suit jacket, the stem poking up. He crossed his legs, the top one almost instantly swinging like the arm of a metronome.

When the president entered, he saw the agitation of the chief of Covert-One. "I'm sorry for your loss, Fred. I know how much you valued Dr. Smith."

"The condolences may be premature, sir." Klein cleared his throat. "As well as the celebration of our so-called victory in Algeria."

The president's back stiffened. He walked to the old roll-top desk, his favorite from Taos, and sat. "Tell me."

"The team of rangers we sent in right after the missile attack never found the bodies of Colonel Smith, Dr. Chambord, or Thérèse Chambord."

"It's probably too soon. In any case, the bodies could've been either badly burned or blown into fragments."

"Some were, that's true. But we sent in our own DNA experts as soon as I got Agent Russell's report, and the Algerian army and police sent in more people. So far, we have no matches to our three. None. Plus, there were no female parts. If Ms. Chambord survived, where is she? Where's her father? Where's Colonel Smith? If Jon were alive, he would've reported to me. If Chambord and his daughter had survived, they would certainly have been heard from by now."

"Unless they were prisoners. That's what you're getting at, isn't it?" The president could not remain seated. He arose stiffly and paced across the Navajo rugs. "You think there's a chance some of the terrorists escaped, and that they took our three with them?"

"That's what worries me. Otherwise . . ."

"Otherwise, you'd be celebrating Smith's and the Chambords' survival. Yes, I see what you mean. But it's all circumstantial. Speculative."

"I deal in circumstance and speculation, sir. All intelligence services do, if they're going about their jobs properly. It's up to us to see dangers before they occur. Possibly I'm wrong, and their bodies will be found." He clasped his hands and leaned forward. "But for all three to be unaccounted for is too much to be ignored, Sam."

"What are you going to do?"

"Keep searching the ruins and testing, but—"

The telephone rang, and the president snapped up the receiver. "Yes?" He grimaced, the lines on his forehead knitting. He barked, "Come up to my private office, Chuck. Yes, *now*." He hung up and closed his eyes a moment as if trying to wipe away the contents of the call.

Klein waited, his general unease heightened.

Castilla said in a tired voice, "Someone has just readjusted the computer processors aboard all of our military and private satellites so we can't retrieve data. *All* the satellites. *No* data. It's a catastrophic systems failure. What's even worse, no one on the ground can get them programmed back to the way they were."

"*We're blind from space?*" Klein bit off a curse. "It sounds like the DNA computer again, dammit. But *how?* That's the one thing Russell was sure of. The missile struck the villa, and the computer was inside. Smith told her he and Chambord were about to escape, all three of them, and to call in the strike. Even if Smith and Chambord hadn't destroyed it already, it should've gone up with the building."

"I agree. It should've. It's the logical conclusion. Get into the other room now, Fred. Chuck's going to be here in a moment."

Just as Klein slipped away, Charles Ouray, the president's chief of staff, hurried into the office. "They're still trying, but NASA says whoever readjusted the computers has locked us out. Completely. We can't break through! It's causing problems everywhere."

"I'd better hear what they are."

"For a while, it looked as if the North Koreans were sending off a missile strike, but we had a contact on the ground that said it was just a heavy fog that was masking the heat from a truck that was near the missile silo in question. We lost an agent in South Beirut, Jeffrey Moussad. His 3-D directional finder failed. We believe he's been killed. Also, there was a near-miss in the Pacific with one of our carriers and a submarine. Even Echelon's ears are deaf." In the Echelon program, the United States and Britain intercepted calls handled by satellites as well as tapping intercontinental undersea telephone cables.

The president forced himself to take a deep breath. "Reconvene the Joint Chiefs. They're probably not out of the building yet. If they are, get Admiral Brose and tell him to instruct the others to assume the worst—an immediate attack on the United States. Anything from biological warfare to a nuclear missile. Scramble every defense, and everything we don't have, officially."

"The experimental antimissile system, sir? But our allies—"

"I'll talk to them. They've got to know, so they can alert their own people. We feed a lot of them information off our satellites anyway. Hell, many buy time, too. Their systems have to be reflecting a loss of data, some of it dramatic. If I don't call them, they're going to call me. I'll put it up to some wild-haired hacker, the best we've ever seen. They'll believe it for a while. Meanwhile, we scramble everything. At least the secret experimental system should be totally secure because no one knows we have it, and it should be able to handle everything short of a massive missile attack, which terrorists won't be able to mount. No one but the Brits and Moscow can do that, and they're on our side this time, thank God. For any other kinds of strikes, we'll have to rely on our conventional military, the FBI, and the police every damn where. And Chuck, this doesn't get leaked to the press. Our allies won't want their media people to get wind of it either. This makes none of us look good. Get going, Chuck."

Ouray ran out, and the president opened the other door. Klein's face was gray with worry as he returned to the room.

"You heard?" the president asked.

"Damn right."

"Find out where the hellish thing is, Fred, and this time *finish it!*"

Chapter
Twenty-nine

Paris, France

When Marty fell asleep again in his hospital room, Peter slipped away to contact local MI6. Randi waited ten minutes and left, too. But her journey was much shorter—down to the phone booth she had spotted off the main lobby. She hovered at the top of the fire stairs, waiting as a few employees came and went, serving the rich patients who would soon emerge with new faces or new bodies or both. As soon as the lobby was clear, she padded down to it. Lilacs, peonies, and jonquils were arranged in showy springtime displays in tall cut-glass vases. The place was as fragrant as a florist's, but it was making a lot more money.

Enclosed in the glass booth, she dialed her Langley chief, Doug Kennedy, on a secure undersea fiber-optic cable line.

Doug's voice was grim. "I've got bad news. In fact, rotten news. The surveillance and communications satellites are still offline. Worse, we've lost *everything* in orbit, both military and civilian. NASA and the Pentagon are working like demons with every tool they have, and they're making up the rest as they go along. So far, we're zilch, kaput, aloha, and good luck. Without those satellites, we're blind, deaf, and dumb."

"I get your point. What do you think I'm working on? I told you the prototype had been destroyed, period. The only thing that makes sense is that Chambord survived, although I still can't figure out how. I also can't figure out how he could've built a new prototype so fast."

"Because he's a genius, that's how."

"Even geniuses have only two arms and ten fingers and need time and materials—and a place to work. A stable place. Which brings me to my reason for calling your august self."

"Hold the sarcasm, Russell. It gets you into trouble. What do you want?"

"Check with every asset we have on the ground within a two-hundred-mile radius of the villa and find out if they noticed, heard of, or even suspect any unusual traffic on the roads and in the ports, no matter how small, all along the coast near the villa for twelve hours after the explosion. Then do the same with everything we have, sea and air, over the Mediterranean, in the same time frame."

"That's *all?*"

She ignored the acid tone. "For now, yes. It could tell us for sure if Chambord survived." She paused. "Or whether we're dealing with some unknown factor, which scares the hell out of me. If he did survive, we need to know that, and where he went."

"I'm convinced."

"Yesterday, okay?"

"If not sooner. What about you?"

"I've got some other leads, unofficial, you understand?" It was total bravado. The only possible leads she had were from Peter's highly developed, far-flung, idiosyncratic private assets, and Marty's brain at its most manic.

"Don't we all. Good luck, Russell." He ended the connection.

Aloft Somewhere over Europe
Gagged and blindfolded, Jon Smith sat upright in a passenger seat at the back of a helicopter, his hands bound behind him. He was anxious and worried, his wounds aching, but still he was recording in his mind as much information as possible, while twisting his wrists against the ropes. Every once in a while, he felt the bonds loosen a bit more. It gave him hope, but Abu Auda or his men could easily discover what he had been

up to when they reached wherever they were going, if he had not broken free by then.

He was in a helicopter, a large one. He could feel the throb of twin, high-powered engines. From their size, the placement of the door through which he had been shoved aboard, and the interior arrangement that he had deduced by stumbling against each row of seats as he was pushed to the rear, he figured the chopper was a Sikorsky S-70 model, known by several names—the Seahawk in the navy, Black Hawk in the army, Pave Hawk in the air force, and Jayhawk in the coast guard.

S-70s were troop carriers and logistical aircraft, but they often carried out other duties like medical evacuation and command-and-control. He had flown in enough while in the field and during his command days—courtesy of both the army and air force, with a navy chopper or two thrown in—to remember the details well.

After he had decided all this, he overheard Abu Auda talking nearby with one of his men. Their conversation had confirmed that it was a Sikorsky all right, but it was the S-70A model, the export version of the multimission Black Hawk. Maybe a leftover from Desert Storm, or acquired through some fellow terrorist whose day job was in the procurement division of some Islamic country's army. In any case, it meant the chopper could easily be armed for combat, which made Jon even more uneasy. Shortly after that, Abu Auda had moved out of listening range.

Jon had been straining to hear any other talk for what he figured was nearly three hours, trying to pick up more information over the roar of the motors, but he had learned nothing useful. The chopper must be near the end of its fuel range. Then it would have to land. At the villa in Algeria, Mauritania had decided he could be useful in the future, and he must still think so, or they would have killed him. Eventually, they would get rid of him, or Abu Auda would get tired of dragging him along and kill him. Hostile witnesses made poor long-term companions.

As he was helplessly carried along in the big Sikorsky, he quit working on the ropes for a while, resting. The wound on his arm ached and burned. Still, it was superficial, more an annoyance than a danger, but it should be taken care of before infection set in. On the other hand, a much more pressing goal was simply surviving. Which brought his thoughts back again to Randi. He knew her only too well, and he was worried. Had she made it out of range before the missile hit? She would have waited for him and the Chambords as long as possible. When they had not appeared, her first instinct would have been to try to rescue them.

God in heaven, he hoped she had not. Even if she had finally realized she had to run for it, she might not have escaped in time. His mouth went dry as he recalled how close he and Thérèse had come to dying . . .

∎

. . . Near the window of the dark villa . . . armed guards all around . . . Jon and Thérèse disarmed . . .

Émile Chambord tells Mauritania, "The American has called in some kind of missile strike. We must leave. Tell your men to fire their weapons, make it sound like a fight. Then shout. Celebrate loudly as if you've killed Smith and my daughter. Hurry!"

They fire bursts. Scream their slogans. Race from the villa, herding Jon and Thérèse toward the helipad. They reach the barracks, and the world detonates behind them. They are flung into the air. Thrown to the ground. Deafened by an explosive roar that hammers with the rush of a shock wave and tears at their clothes, their hair, their limbs. Tree branches and palm fronds fly. A massive wood door cartwheels overhead and slams down onto one of Abu Auda's men, crushing him to death.

When the ground stops heaving, Jon staggers up, bleeding from a head wound. His left forearm burns with pain. He searches frantically for a weapon.

But Abu Auda trains his British-made assault rifle on Jon. "Don't try, Colonel."

The survivors crawl to their feet. Amazingly, most are still alive. Thérèse is bleeding from her right leg. Chambord hurries to her. "Thérèse! You're hurt."

She pushes him away. "I don't know who you are anymore. You must be mad!" She turns her back and helps Jon.

Chambord watches as she rips off the sleeve of her white suit. "What I do is for the future of France, child," he explains earnestly. "You'll under-stand soon."

"There's nothing to understand." She binds the wound on Jon's arm and then the one on her leg. The blood on Jon's forehead is a minor scratch.

Mauritania interrupts, "She'll have to understand later, Doctor." He gazes around with the canny expression of a feral animal. He seems to sniff the air as if he can read intelligence on it. "They may strike again. We must leave immediately."

One of the terrorists gives a loud bellow of dismay. Everyone converges, staring at the Huey helicopter. Its rotors have been broken by debris hurled in the blast. The chopper is grounded.

Chambord decides, "There's room for five of us in the scout helicopter. You, of course, M. Mauritania, and your pilot. Plus Captain Bonnard, Thérèse, and I." Mauritania begins to protest. He wants more of his own people. But Chambord shakes his head firmly. "No. I need Bonnard, and I won't leave my daughter behind. If I'm to build another prototype, I need to go where I can work. A new DNA computer is our most pressing priority. I regret there's room for no one else, but there it is."

Mauritania has to agree. He turns to his towering lieutenant, who has heard everything and is glowering with disapproval. "You'll remain behind to lead the others, Abu Auda. Make arrangements to be picked up. I'll have to take our Saudi pilot, Mohammed. He's our best. You'll rejoin us soon."

"What of the American, Smith? May I kill him now? It was he who—"

"No. If he's arranged for this missile strike, he must be even more important than I realized. You'll keep him safe, Abu Auda."

Thérèse Chambord protests vehemently, but they force her aboard. The compact helicopter rises, skirts the disaster site, and heads north toward Europe. Abu Auda orders Jon's hands bound, and the group moves at a brisk clip to the distant highway, where they are met by two covered pickup trucks. A long, jolting ride through the wind-swept inland desert finally ends at the noisy docks of Tunis. There they board a motorboat like the converted PT boat on which Jon stowed the day before. The ragtag group is exhausted, but their sense of urgency remains clear.

On the boat, they blindfold him. He sees none of the long trip across the Mediterranean. He falls asleep again despite the slamming of the boat against the waves, but as soon as the boat lands, he is instantly awake, craning his head to listen. They hustle him out ondeck, still blindfolded, where he hears many voices speaking Italian and guesses they must be in Italy. They board the Sikorsky helicopter to fly to an unnamed location that could be anywhere from Serbia to France . . .

■

Now as Jon sat blindfolded in the helicopter, waiting for them to either run out of gas or land, he wrestled with his tormenting thoughts: Was Randi alive? Where were Peter and Marty? From what Thérèse knew, she and her father had been the only prisoners in the villa until Jon arrived. Jon hoped they had not been captured, that Peter had somehow saved Marty, and that they were safe. His only comfort was that the molecular computer had been pulverized in the missile blast.

Now he must stop Émile Chambord before he built another. It had been a shock to learn Chambord had been working with the terrorists all along, apparently the instigator of an elaborate—and very successful—charade to fool not just national governments but also his daughter. In a perversion of a great scientific achievement, he was scheming to build another molecular computer so he could use it to destroy Israel. Why? Because his mother had been Algerian? Part of Islam? Jon remembered Fred Klein's report: *His mother raised him as a Muslim, but he showed little interest in religion as an adult.* There had seemed no reason to consider that bit of information salient, since Chambord had never shown religious tendencies.

As Jon thought about it all, he remembered Chambord's stint teaching in Cairo just before he returned to the Pasteur, and that Chambord's wife had died not long ago. A reacquaintance with Islam, plus the life-changing loss of a beloved spouse. Belief shifts in later years had happened to others, and they would happen again. Forgotten faith could reach out and reclaim, especially as one aged and faced personal tragedy.

Then there was Captain Darius Bonnard, who had a similar background: Married to an Algerian woman when he had been in the Foreign Legion. When commissioned, his leaves spent in Algiers with, maybe, a first wife he had never divorced. A double life? It certainly seemed more than possible now. And, too, there was his job—within whispering distance of the top echelons of NATO and the French military. He was one of the invisibles—the quiet, efficient aide to a general. Although he had far more access than most, he was seldom in the limelight, unlike his general.

Chambord's and Bonnard's lives made a new kind of sense when looked at with the hindsight of Chambord's shattering revelation: "I'm not with them . . . *they're with me!*"

The scientist's prototype was destroyed, but not his knowledge. Unless someone stopped him, he would build another. But that would take time. Smith held on to that morsel of hope. Time to find Chambord and to stop him. But first he had to escape. Behind him, he resumed trying to loosen the ropes that bound him.

Paris, France

Marty was awake, gratefully out of his hospital gown, and dressed in clothes Peter had brought back after making contact with MI6—a pair of shapeless dark brown cord pants, a black cashmere turtleneck despite the warmth of the hospital room, athletic shoes with racing stripes along the sides, and his ubiquitous tan windbreaker. He looked himself up and down and pronounced himself appropriately attired for anything short of a formal dinner with the prime minister.

Randi had returned to the room, too, and the three friends wrestled with the issue foremost in their minds—how to find Jon. Without any formal agreement, they had simply decided that Jon was alive. Eyes sparkling, Marty volunteered to go off his meds and devote himself to solving the problem.

Randi agreed. "Good idea."

"Sure you're up for it?" Peter questioned.

"Don't be a dolt, Peter." Marty looked offended. "Does a mastodon have tusks? Does an algebraic equation require an equals sign? Gee."

"Guess so," Peter decided.

The room phone rang. Randi picked it up. It was her boss at Langley, Doug Kennedy, on the secure scrambled surface phone line. He was not encouraging. She listened, asked some pointed questions, and as soon as she hung up, she reported what he had learned: The ground assets in Algeria said there was little unusual activity of any kind, not even smugglers, except perhaps in Tunis, where a known smuggler's high-speed boat had left some five hours after the strike for an unspecified destination with a dozen or so men on board. One of the men, however, was reported to be a European or American. There had been no women among them, which pretty much ruled out Émile Chambord, who was certainly traveling with Thérèse. He would not have left her, or at least Randi and Marty did not think he would. Peter was not so sure.

Marty made a face. "No one like Émile abandons a child, you ridiculous man."

"She's pushing forty," Peter noted dryly. "She's no child."

"To Émile she is," Marty corrected him.

There had been few U.S. ships or aircraft in the eastern Mediterranean at the time, the *Saratoga* having left its position the instant it launched its missile. It had turned off all surface-to-air radar so as not to allow back-tracing and had run dark, steaming straight north to put as much deniability as possible between it and the Algerian coast before the certain uproar from the Arab countries began.

"That could have been Jon on the smuggler's boat," Randi decided. "It was the kind of craft the Crescent Shield used to cross the Mediterranean to Algeria. On the other hand, the terrorists could have had some Americans among them."

"Of course it was Jon," Marty declared. "There can be no doubt."

Peter said, "We'll wait for what my people tell me, shall we?"

Marty was standing at the window, watching the Paris street below. His mind was in a race against time, soaring through the stratosphere of his imagination as he sought a solution for how to find Jon. He closed his eyes and sighed happily as lights flashed in a variety of vivid colors, and it seemed to him that he was lighter than air. He saw shapes and heard sounds in a kaleidoscope of excitement. His freed self was soaring toward the magical heights where creativity and intelligence joined, and ideas far beyond the scope of ordinary mortals were waiting to be born like infant stars.

When the phone rang, Marty jumped and frowned.

Peter headed for it. "My turn."

He was right. The information was delivered in a crisp London accent: A British submarine, running deep, had surfaced less than ten miles from the Algerian villa moments after the blast. In fact, it was the blast's shock wave, transmitted through the water and picked up by the sub's sonar, that had prompted its rise. With its radar fixed toward the villa, it had identified a small Hughes scout helicopter leaving the vicinity some fifteen minutes after the strike. Five minutes later, the sub dove again, concerned it might be discovered.

Meanwhile, on land, a passing MI6 informant had spotted two pickup trucks exiting the area, driving west toward Tunis. The informant had reported the news to his contact in hopes of being paid, which he had been, and handsomely. It was not cost-efficient to be niggardly in the spy trade. Finally, the captain of a British Airways jet en route from Gibraltar to Rome had observed a small helicopter of the same model flying from the direction of Oran toward the Spanish coast in an area where the captain had never seen a helicopter. Thus, he had entered it in his log. A quick check by MI6 revealed that no scheduled, or even authorized, helicopter flights had been made from Oran or any place near it that night.

"He's alive," Marty boomed. "There's now no doubt."

"Let's assume that's true," Peter said. "But we still have the problem of contacting him, and which course do we pursue? The unauthorized helicopter flying to Spain, or the smuggler's boat out of Tunis that carried a possible American?"

"Both," Randi decided. "Cover all bases."

Meanwhile, Marty had retreated blissfully again into the fertile fields of his mind. He could feel an idea forming. It was almost tactile, as if he could stroke it with his fingers and taste it on the tip of his tongue. His eyes snapped open, and he paced around the room, rubbing his hands with excitement. And skidded to a stop to do a little dance, his plump body as agile as an imp's. "The answer's been in front of us all along. Someday I need to study the nature of consciousness. Such a fascinating subject. I'm sure I could learn a thing or two—"

"Marty!" Randi said, exasperated. "What's your idea?"

He beamed. "We've been utter fools. We'll do as we did before— place a message on the Asperger's Web site—OASIS. After that unpleasant Hades mess, how could Jon forget that's how we stayed in touch before? Impossible for him to not remember. All we need do is compose a message that will baffle everyone but Jon." He screwed his florid face into a knot as he considered.

Peter and Randi waited. It did not take long.

Marty cackled with joy. "I have it! 'Coughing Lazarus: Sex-starved wolf seeks suitable mate. Must have own location. Eager to meet, ready to go. What do you want to do?' " He watched their reaction with eager eyes.

Randi shook her head. "I have no idea what that means."

"I'm at sea, too," Peter agreed, avoiding Marty's gaze.

Marty rubbed his hands together with satisfaction. "If *you* don't, no one else will either."

"That's all fine," Randi said, "but you'd better tell us the code anyway."

Peter said, "Just a moment, I'm beginning to see part of it. 'Coughing Lazarus' must refer to 'Smith'—Smith's Cough Drops, of course. And 'Lazarus' is Jon again, because like Lazarus we're hoping Jon's risen from the dead."

Randi chuckled. "So, 'Sex-starved wolf' implies a 'randy howl,' yes? Randi and Howell. 'Seeks suitable mate' is easy. A mate's a pal, a friend, and we're looking for our friend Jon. 'Must have own location' means we're asking where he is. 'Eager to meet, ready to go' is obvious. We want to meet him, and we'll go wherever necessary. But I don't quite get 'What do you want to do?' "

Marty arched his brows. "That," he announced, "was the easiest part. I thought better of you both. There's a famous movie line *everyone* knows: 'What do you want to do tonight—' "

"Of course," Peter said, recognizing it. "From the movie *Marty*. 'What do you want to do tonight, Marty?' So that means you."

Marty rubbed his hands. "Now we're getting someplace. So my message, translated, is simply: 'Jon Smith: Randi and Peter are looking for you. Where are you? They'll meet you wherever you say.' And it's signed Marty. Questions?"

"Wouldn't dare." Peter shook his head.

They hurried downstairs to the office of Peter's friend, Lochiel Cameron, the hospital's owner and chief surgeon. Dr. Cameron listened, left his chair, and Marty took over the desk, where Dr. Cameron's computer sat at the corner. Marty's fingers flew over the keyboard as he quickly found www.aspergersyndrome.org and entered his message. Then he leaped up and paced behind the chair, his eyes fixed on the screen.

Dr. Cameron glanced at Peter as if to ask whether he should administer a new dose of Mideral. Peter shook his head, all the while watching Marty for a sign that he was slipping dangerously near detachment from reality. As time passed, Marty paced faster, grew more agitated, waved his arms wildly, and muttered to himself in a voice that grew louder as the words grew more meaningless.

Peter finally nodded to Cameron. He told Marty, "Okay, lad. We've got to face it. You've had a good run, but it's time to pacify those nerve endings."

"What?" Marty spun around and narrowed his eyes.

"Peter's right," Randi agreed. "The doctor has your pill. Take it, Mart. That way you'll be in good shape if things get tense."

Marty frowned. He looked them both up and down with disdain. But at the same time, his quick mind registered their concern. He did not like it, but he knew that the medication bought him time for when he wanted to soar again.

"Oh, very well," he said grumpily. "Give me that awful pill."

An hour later, Marty had returned to sit quietly in front of the computer screen. Peter and Randi kept watch with him. There had been no answer from Jon.

Chapter Thirty

Aalst, Belgium

Outside the old market town of Aalst stood the country estate of the Brabant branch of the La Porte family. Although the town had grown into a bustling suburb of Brussels, the La Porte estate had retained its classic grandeur, an artifact from a long-ago time. It was called Hethuis, "Castle House," in honor of its—and the family's—medieval heritage. Today the walled courtyard was filled with the chauffeured sedans and limousines of NATO military leaders and members of the Council of European Nations, which was meeting this week in Brussels.

Inside the main house, General the Count Roland la Porte was holding court. Like his pedigreed estate, La Porte appeared large and magnificent where he stood before the walk-in fireplace in the baronial main room. Around him, period weapons, heraldic coats-of-arms, and the canvases of great Dutch and Flemish painters—everyone from Jan van Eyck to Peter Brueghel—hung from the dark, paneled walls.

EU Commissioner Enzo Ciccione, recently arrived from Rome, was giving his opinion in English: "These satellite problems of the Americans are frightening and have made many of us rethink our views, General La Porte. Perhaps we have indeed become too dependent upon the United States and its military. After all, NATO is essentially the same animal as the United States."

"Still, our relationship with the United States has been useful," La Porte responded in French, despite knowing that Ciccione did not speak the language. He paused as Ciccione's translator, who sat just behind him, finished his nearly simultaneous translation. "We weren't ready to assume our own destiny. Now, however, we've gained much-needed military experience in NATO operations. The point isn't simply to challenge the Americans, but to acknowledge our own growing power and importance. Which, of course, the Americans themselves have been urging us to do."

"Military strength also translates into economic clout in the international competition for markets," pointed out Commissioner Hans Brecht, who did speak French but chose to answer in English in deference to Ciccione. Brecht was from Vienna. "Again, as you've said, General, we're already competitors with the United States for world markets. It's unfortunate that we're so often constrained from going all out because of strategic political and military concerns."

"Your views are encouraging," La Porte acknowledged. "There are times when I fear we Europeans have lost the will to greatness that fueled our conquest of the world. We must never forget that we created not only the United States but all the other nations of the Western Hemisphere. Sadly, they now find themselves locked in the American sphere of ownership." He sighed and shook his large head. "There are times, gentlemen, when I think we, too, will soon be owned by the Americans. Vassal states. To my mind, Britain already is. Who will be next? All of us?"

The others had been listening carefully. Besides the Italian and Austrian commissioners, there were also Belgian and Danish members of the Council of European Nations as well as the same NATO military leaders who had gathered on the *Charles de Gaulle* just a few nights ago: Spanish general Valentin González, with his cautious eyes and the jaunty tilt to his army cap. Italian General Ruggiero Inzaghi of the flinty gaze and no-nonsense mouth. And German General Otto Bittrich, rawboned and thoughtful. Absent, of course, was British General Arnold Moore, whose untimely death had shaken them. Those who made the military their life found accidents offensive; if a soldier did not have the good luck to die at war, then he should be at least at home in his own bed with his medals and memories.

As General La Porte finished, they burst out with both agreements and objections.

General Bittrich was sitting apart, his bony face thoughtful as usual, but there was high intensity in his silence. He was watching no one but La Porte, and he had chosen a chair out of his easy line of sight for that reason. Under his thick, near-white hair, his ruddy face was so focused that he might be peering through a microscope at a specimen he was preparing to dissect.

But La Porte did not notice. He was concentrating on the speakers as they moved closer to seeing what he saw—a United States of Europe, or, as the EU organization called itself, Europa. Once more, he made his point: "We can argue forever, but in the end we all know that Europe, from the Baltic to the Mediterranean, from the Atlantic to, yes, the Urals and possibly beyond, must take charge of its future. We *must* have an independent, united military. We *are* Europa, we must *be* Europa!"

The giant room rang with the stirring call, but in the end it fell on wary, pragmatic ears.

Commissioner Ciccione lifted his chin as if his collar were too tight. "In a few years, you'll have my vote, General La Porte. But not now. The EU has neither the wealth nor the will for such an immense step. Besides, it's dangerous. Considering the political instabilities we're facing . . . the Balkans' quagmire, the continuing terrorist assaults everywhere, the shakiness of the Middle East, the problems in the various Stans . . . we can afford no such large risk."

There was a general murmur of agreement, although it was clear that, among some of the other council members and all of the generals, there was more than a little regret about not pursuing the idea.

La Porte's pale eyes flashed fire at the suggestion that he was too soon. "And I say we cannot *not* afford it! We *must* take our place militarily, economically, and politically. And now *is* the time. Soon you must vote. It's a grave responsibility, one that can make life better for everyone. I know when you face that moment of truth and must vote, you'll agree with me. You'll feel the destiny of Europa not as it has been for the past sixty years, but as it *can* be. *Must* be."

Ciccione looked around the room, meeting the others' gazes, until at last he shook his head. "I think I can speak for all of us when I say nothing can convince us yet, General. I regret it, but the hard truth is that the continent is simply not ready."

All eyes turned to General Bittrich, who was still studying La Porte. The German general said, "As for this recent attack on U.S. satellites that seems to concern the commissioners and our General La Porte so much, I think we'll find the Americans well prepared to resist and dispose of whoever is behind it."

As another murmur of agreement hummed through the room, General La Porte only smiled. He said mildly, "Perhaps, General Bittrich. Perhaps."

At that instant, the Prussian's gray eyes hardened into points of steel. As the others filed from the room into the sumptuous dining hall adjacent, Bittrich did not move.

Alone with La Porte, he stood and walked toward the Frenchman. "A tragic event, the death of General Moore."

La Porte nodded solemnly. His unblinking eyes studied the German. "I feel most guilty. Such a waste to lose him. If he hadn't come to our meeting on the *De Gaulle*—?" He gave a Gallic shrug of fate.

"Ah, so. *Ja*. But what was it Moore said before we disbanded? Now I recall. He wondered whether you knew something we did not."

"I believe he expressed a passing thought of that nature. He was, as I told him then, quite wrong." La Porte smiled.

"Of course." Bittrich smiled, too, and murmured as he walked away toward the dining hall with its table groaning with Flemish gourmet dishes, "Perhaps."

The Chartreuse Region of France

The chalet was modern, with a sharply pitched roof and a half-timbered exterior that blended into the majestic scenery beneath the snow-capped Alps. Nestled against sweet-smelling pines, the chalet was perched on a steep slope at the edge of broad fields and meadows in sight of La Grande Chartreuse, a famous Carthusian monastery. From one side of the house, the view was panoramic across the open area that dropped south, still spotted with winter snow and the fresh footprints of deer. The first blades of pale spring grasses were just beginning to show. To the north, thick pine forest rose up the mountainside, embracing the chalet.

All of this was important to Thérèse Chambord, who was locked in a room on the second floor. She gazed up at the only windows, which were placed high, as she pushed an old-fashioned frame bed beneath. Miserable and outraged, she dragged an empty bureau to the bed and wrestled it up onto it. She stepped back, put her hands on her hips, and shook her head, disgusted. Even with the bureau on top of the bed, the windows were still too far above to reach. She was carrying a thronelike chair toward the bed when she heard the door unlock.

Her father entered with a tray of food and stared dumbfounded as she stood up on the bed, preparing to hoist the chair atop the bureau. He set the tray on a side table and closed the door before she could climb down.

He shook his head. "That will do you no good, Thérèse. This house is on the edge of the mountainside, and your room overlooks a steep slope. Even should you manage to get through those windows, the drop is more than three stories. It alone could kill you. In any case, the windows are locked."

Thérèse glared down at him. "Smart of you. But I'll get away yet, and then I'll go to the police."

Chambord's lined face was sad. "I'd hoped you'd understand. That you'd trust me and join us in this crusade, child. I had expected to have time to explain all of this, but then this Jon Smith interfered and forced me to reveal myself. Selfish of me, I suppose, but . . ." He shrugged. "Even though you won't join us, I still can't let you escape. I brought you food. You'd better eat. We'll be leaving again soon."

Thérèse jumped down in fury. "Join your crusade? How can I be with you? You won't tell me what in the devil you're doing even now. All I see is that you're working with criminal terrorists who are planning a massacre using your computer. Murder! *Mass* murder."

"Our goal is good, child," Chambord said quietly, "and I'm not with these criminal terrorists, as you call them. As I told your friend Colonel Smith, they're with me. Captain Bonnard and I have a far different purpose than they."

"*What* purpose? *Tell me!* If you want me to trust you, you've got to trust me."

Chambord stepped to the door, looked back, and seemed to X-ray his daughter with his quick, sharp eyes. "Perhaps later, after it's all over and we've changed the future. Then you'll see, understand, and applaud. But not now. You aren't ready. I was mistaken."

He opened the door and left quickly, closing and locking it behind.

Thérèse swore and returned to the bed. She climbed up onto the bureau and then onto the chair. As the pyramid of furniture wobbled, she steadied herself against the wall. She stopped breathing, waiting for the pile beneath her to grow more solid. At last she summoned courage and straightened. *Success.* Her head reached the windows.

She looked out and, with a gasp, down. He had told the truth: The ground was too far below, and it dropped precipitously farther down from there. She glanced briefly at the breathtaking view across sweeping meadowlands and sighed. She pulled on the first window sash, but it was secure, with small padlocks attached to latches. Perhaps she could break the padlocks, but even if she did and managed to open a window, the drop was too far. She could not escape this way.

She peered out longingly at the beauty of the pastoral landscape that stretched out before her. In the distance, she could see the eleventh-century Chartreuse monastery, a lovely landmark in a green, beckoning land. Somewhere nearby, she had heard, was the city of Grenoble. It all made her feel like a caged bird, her wings clipped.

But she was no bird. She was a practical woman. She would need all her strength to stop her father from whatever he was planning. Besides, she was hungry. Carefully she climbed down to the bed, jumped to the floor, and carried the tray to another of the old throne chairs with its carved wood and tapestry upholstery. She ate a bowl of some kind of heavy peasant stew, thick with potatoes, cabbage, rabbit, and pork. She dipped dense slices of country bread into the stew and washed it all down with a carafe of red wine. It was light and pleasant, Beaujolais from the taste.

Only when she had finished and was sipping her last glass did she suddenly feel sad. What was her father doing? The terrorists clearly intended to attack Israel somehow, using his DNA computer. But why was he involved? His mother had been a Muslim, but he had never been religious, had never even visited Algeria that she knew, hated terrorists, and had nothing against Jews or Israel. He was a scientist, for heaven's sake. It was all he had ever been. Pure reasoning, logic, and clear thinking were his life. In his world, there was never room for social boundaries, racial barriers, or ethnic or religious distinctions. There was only truth and hard facts.

Then . . . what? What had happened, and what was this great future for France he saw? She was still trying to puzzle it out when she heard what sounded like a pickup arriving. Captain Bonnard and that sinister man they called Mauritania had left in one. Maybe they were returning now. Thérèse did not know where they had gone or why, but when they reappeared, it would be time to leave. Or so her father had told her.

Moments later, the key turned again in the lock, and Captain Bonnard entered. He was dressed in full uniform now, the staff-duty uniform of the French Foreign Legion complete with ribbons and regimental insignia and colors. His square face was grim, the firm chin high, his gaze clear, and his clipped blond hair hidden beneath his cap. He held his service pistol.

"He sent me, mademoiselle, because I'll shoot where he couldn't, you comprehend? I won't, of course, shoot to kill, but I'm an excellent marksman, and you can believe I won't allow your escape, *oui*?"

"You strike me as a man who would happily shoot a woman, Captain. Or a child, for that matter. The Legion is known for such things, *oui*?" she mocked him.

Bonnard's eyes went flat, but he made no response. Instead, he gestured with the pistol for her to precede him from the room. They went down the stairs to the chalet's timbered living room where Mauritania was leaning over a map spread out on a large table in the corner of the room. Her father stood behind, watching. There was a strange expression on his face that she could not place as well as a subdued excitement she had never seen, even when he made a research breakthrough.

Mauritania continued, "Please show me where this other hideout of yours is. I'll have more of my men meet us there."

Bonnard caught Thérèse's attention and pointed to a chair far from where Chambord and Mauritania stood. "Sit," he told her. "And remain there."

Thérèse settled uneasily into the chair, puzzled, as Bonnard approached the two men. She watched her father draw the same pistol she had seen in the villa. With surprise, she saw him make a quick movement and turn it on Mauritania.

His face and voice were as hard as granite. "You won't need that information, Mauritania. We know where it is. Come along. We're leaving now."

Mauritania had not looked up. "We can't go, Doctor. Abu Auda and my other men aren't here yet. There isn't space for all of us in the Bell helicopter, so we'll have to use their aircraft as well."

"That won't be necessary," Chambord said. "We won't be waiting for them."

Mauritania raised his gaze slowly from where he had been bent over, studying the map. He straightened and turned. When he saw the pistol in Chambord's hand, he went very still. He looked at Captain Bonnard, whose gun was now pointed at him as well.

"So?" Mauritania's brows raised a fraction, betraying only mild surprise at the two Frenchmen.

"You're an intelligent man, Mauritania. Don't attempt something you'll regret."

"I never do anything I'll regret, Doctor. May I ask what you think you're accomplishing?"

"Dispensing with your services. You've been useful. We thank you for all your good work, but from this moment on, you and your people will complicate the situation."

Mauritania seemed to consider that. "I take it you have a different plan. One you suspect we won't like."

"You'd agree to the initial stage. In fact, your brethren in other groups would be enthusiastic. But you, as you have often pointed out, are really guerrillas, not simple terrorists. You have concrete political goals, a narrow focus. Realistically, our focus is not yours, and therefore we need to dispense with you. To be more exact, with your men. You yourself will continue on with us, but as our 'guest' only. Eventually you will be of help to us."

"I doubt it." Mauritania's smooth facade cracked. "And who is to fly the helicopter? My pilot will do nothing unless I order it."

"Naturally. We expected that." Émile Chambord glanced at the French captain. "Bonnard, take Thérèse with you."

Bonnard grabbed her arm, pulled her up, and prodded her out the door.

Mauritania's light-colored eyes followed them. When the door closed, he looked up at Chambord.

Chambord nodded. "Yes, Captain Bonnard is a trained helicopter pilot. He'll fly us out of here."

Mauritania said nothing, but when two gunshots sounded in quick succession outside, he flinched.

Chambord showed no reaction at all. "After you, Mauritania."

He marched Mauritania to the chalet's entry, out the front door into the hazy mountain sunlight, and to a clearing among the pines where the Hughes scout helicopter was parked. Lying on the ground next to it was the body of the Saudi pilot, Mohammed. There were two bullet holes in his chest, and blood was thick on his clothes. Standing above him was Bonnard, who was now pointing his gun at Thérèse. A stricken look on her face, she held her hand over her mouth as if she were going to be sick.

Chambord studied her, searching for a sign that now she understood the seriousness of his purpose. He nodded to himself, satisfied, and turned to Bonnard. "The helicopter is refueled and serviced?"

"He had just finished."

"*Bon.* We'll be on our way." He smiled, a dreamy expression on his face. "By tomorrow, we will have changed history."

Bonnard climbed in first, followed by the stoic Mauritania and an ashen-faced Thérèse. Chambord entered last. As they buckled themselves in, and the rotors whined and turned, the scientist gave a final searching look across the sky. Moments later, the helicopter lifted off.

Chapter Thirty-one

Aloft Somewhere over Europe

The key was the hands. Escaping without free hands was possible only under exceptional and desperate circumstances. For the best odds, free hands were necessary. So when the terrorists had bound Jon's wrists behind him in the truck on the road to Tunis, he had placed them side by side in as straight a line as he could manage. In the fanatics' haste to escape the villa, they had not repositioned his wrists, and although they had bound them tight, the ruse had been partly successful. Since then, he had been twisting his arms and hands, expanding and contracting against the rope, over and over. Still, he had not gained enough slack. And time was running out.

The blindfold was another handicap. As he weighed all this, he felt his stomach drop. The Sikorsky was losing altitude, banking in a sweeping curve on the way to what felt like a landing. He had little time. With a sudden, blundering attack, he might destabilize the Sikorsky enough to bring it down, crash it. After all, it was designed to absorb crash-impact velocities, with crash-resistant seats and a crash-resistant, self-sealing fuel system. Still, the chances of his walking away would be only a hair above zero. And to crash the helicopter, he needed free hands.

If he could get free, and if he waited to attack just before landing, the helicopter would be low to the ground. He might survive without immobilizing injuries and be able to escape during the confusion. It was a long shot, but he saw no other option.

As the Sikorsky continued to descend, Jon worked frantically on the ropes, but there was no more give. Abruptly, at the front of the helicopter, Abu Auda said something angrily in Arabic. Others joined in, and the talk grew louder. Jon figured there were more than a dozen terrorists on-board. Soon everyone in the craft seemed to be arguing and comparing ideas about something they saw on the ground. Alarmed, they consulted in their many languages.

One of the voices demanded in English, "What's wrong?"

Above the noise of the rotors, Abu Auda shouted the bad news in French, with an occasional English word for those who did not under-stand that language: "Mauritania and the others aren't waiting for us at the chalet as planned. He isn't answering his radio either. There's an empty pickup near the chalet, but the scout helicopter's gone. Yes, there's someone lying in the clearing." He paused.

Jon felt tension rush through the vibrating craft as it continued its circling descent.

"Who is it?" someone called out.

"I can see him through my binoculars," Abu Auda told them. "It's Mohammed. There's blood on his chest." He hesitated. "He looks dead."

There was a furious outburst in Arabic, French, and all the other tongues. As Abu Auda shouted, trying to keep them under control, Jon continued to listen carefully. It became clear that Abu Auda had expected to find not only Mauritania but Dr. Chambord, Captain Bonnard, and Thérèse Chambord. The chalet was where Abu Auda was supposed to rendezvous with them, where Chambord would build another DNA com-puter.

A new voice raged, "You see what comes of trusting infidels, Fulani?"

"We told M. Mauritania not to work with them!"

Abu Auda sneered in his powerful basso voice, "You trusted their money, Abdullah. Our goal is a great one, and for that we needed the Frenchman's machine."

"So what do we have now? *Nothing!*"

An older voice asked, "Do you think it's a trap, Abu Auda?"

"I don't know what the devil it is. Get your weapons. Be ready to jump out the moment we touch down."

Jon was getting nowhere with the ropes around his wrists. But this could be his chance to escape, a better chance than risking death by crashing the aircraft. When it landed, Abu Auda and his men would have a great deal more on their minds than him. From the front, he appeared motionless. Only his twitching shoulder muscles hinted at the activity behind his back, where his hands and wrists continued their desperate struggle.

The helicopter shuddered and stood still in the air, rocking gently from side to side. He kept pulling and twisting his ropes. His skin burned from the abrasion, but he ignored it. The chopper settled into a straight but slow vertical descent. Abruptly, the whole craft pitched violently to the side. Jon lost his balance and toppled over, his shoulder thudding hard against the seat. Something sharp bit into his back. He heard shouts as the first few men jumped to the ground. More followed, and the chopper found its balance and touched down safely.

As the rotors slowed, Jon searched frantically for the sharp protrusion from the helicopter wall. He rubbed his back against the wall until again he felt the pain, and then a hot spot of blood on his back told him he had found it. Still lying on his side, he wiggled back against the wall, searching until his hands found the spot. He touched it gingerly. The wall's padding had separated, and a piece of sharp metal from the chopper's body was exposed when pressure was applied at the separating crack. Encouraged, he worked the ropes against it. As the engines cut back, a strange quietness settled into the craft and he felt the rope beginning to fray.

He continued rubbing against the knifelike metal until the rope abruptly split apart. He could feel blood on his hands where he had nicked himself. He unwound the rope from his wrists and lay quietly, his ears aching with the strain of listening. How many terrorists were left? They had been so eager to rush out that it seemed most had gone before the chopper actually landed.

Outside, there were more violent bellows and curses. Abu Auda shouted, "Spread out. Look for them. Search everywhere!"

"Here's a map of France!" someone yelled. "I found it in the chalet!"

More bellowed reports, more loud swearing. The hubbub outside moved away.

Jon tried to hear breathing inside the chopper, the smallest movement. Nothing. He inhaled deeply to calm his nerves, stripped off his blindfold, and dropped to the floor among the seats. He peered around. There was no one at the front. Twisting, he glanced behind and around. Again, no one. Still lying on the floor, he ripped off his gag and scanned the chopper for an extra assault rifle. A pistol. A knife someone had dropped. Anything. The stiletto he had Velcroed to his ankle had been taken when he was captured.

But again, there was nothing. He crawled to the pilot's and copilot's seats at the front. That was where he spotted an ungainly-looking pistol in a rack next to the copilot's seat. A flare gun.

Cautiously he raised up and peered out the windows. They had landed on a sloping field at the edge of a thick pine forest, near a half-timbered chalet with a high-peaked roof. The chalet was tall and narrow, which made it less visible from the air and two sides. Pine trees crowded close to the house and stretched away back up the slope toward a low mountain behind. Farther behind were snow-mantled peaks. Someone had said France. The Alps?

Two of the terrorist soldiers, their weapons slung, were picking up the body of Mauritania's dead pilot. Two more were searching out into the sloping meadow, while high above on a second-story deck stood Abu Auda with two older Saudis. They were scanning the distance.

But it was the endless forest that attracted Jon's attention. If he could slip out of the chopper and in among the pines, he would triple his odds of escaping. He needed to make his move now, while the terrorists were distracted. Every second increased the danger that Abu Auda and the others would give up their search, regroup, and remember him.

Low to the floor, he scuttled to the door on the copilot's side, which faced away from the chalet. His wounds forgotten, he slid over the edge and, holding on to a landing strut, he coiled toward the ground like a snake. Lying on his belly, he gazed under the chopper at the terrorists, who remained angrily busy. Satisfied, flare gun in hand, he crawled on his forearms toward the brown grass that edged the pine forest. Spring flowers were beginning to show among the grasses. The fresh scent of the moist mountain soil rose around his head. For a moment he felt dizzy, heady with freedom. But he dared not stop.

Crawling swiftly on, he reached the perimeter of the trees and slithered gratefully into the twilight forest, thick and hushed with fir trees. He was breathing hard. Beads of sweat had collected on his face. But he had seldom felt better. He crouched behind a tree trunk and studied the terrorists in the clearing and around the chalet. They still had not discovered he was missing. With a cold smile, he jumped up and loped off.

The first time he heard the sound ahead, he dodged behind a tree and dropped flat. His heart pounded as he stared through the lacy forest shadows. When he saw a head emerge from behind a pine tree, his heart pounded faster. The head wore an Afghan puggaree, long cloth tail and all. He had nearly blundered into an armed Afghan, who was still searching through the woods for any sign of Chambord, Mauritania, and the others.

The man turned slowly, his dark gaze examining the shadows. Had he heard Jon? It seemed so, since he lifted an old American M16A1 and aimed it in Jon's general direction. Jon held his breath, the flare pistol gripped in his hand. The last thing he wanted was to fire the thing. If the flare hit the Afghan, he would scream like a banshee. If it missed, the flare would ignite brighter than a Roman candle.

He watched the Afghan step carefully toward where he lay silent. The terrorist should have called for backup, but he had not. Perhaps he was unsure of what he had heard or whether he had heard anything at all. By the expressions playing across the man's face, it seemed as if he were talking himself out of his alarm. He had heard nothing. A rabbit. The wind. His countenance cleared, and his guard lowered. Now that his suspicions were eased, he approached faster. By the time he reached where Jon hid, he was moving at a fast clip.

Jon raised up and was on him before the fellow could react. Instantly, Jon swung the heavy flare pistol, knocking him to his knees. He clamped his hand over the man's mouth and crashed the weapon down onto his head. Blood spurted. The man struggled but was obviously stunned and confused by the initial blow. Jon hit him again, and the extremist collapsed limp into the forest duff. Breathing heavily, Jon stared down. His lungs ached, and his rib cage was tight. He ripped the M16 away and found the man's curved dagger.

He reached down to check the terrorist's pulse. He was dead. Jon stripped the extra M16 clips from the body, turned on his heel, and melted up through the forest again. As he settled into a distance-eating trot, thoughts flooded his mind. He tried to understand what had happened here before the helicopter had arrived. Why was the Saudi pilot murdered? From what Abu Auda had said, Chambord, Thérèse, Bonnard, and Mauritania had been at the chalet. Where had they gone now?

What came echoing back were Chambord's words: *I'm not with them, Colonel Smith, they're with me.* It stayed in his mind, teasing him with possibilities. The mosaic of odd pieces of what he had learned since Monday began to reassemble in his thoughts until they finally added to a question: Why would Chambord and Bonnard *not* be waiting? After all, the Crescent Shield was supposedly working for *him.*

Chambord was *not* part of the Crescent Shield. He had made a point of it, that *they* were with *him.*

As he ran on, Jon continued to puzzle over it all, trying to stretch the ideas out. And then, as if a mist had cleared, it began to make a crazy kind of sense: Just as the Black Flame had been a front for the Crescent Shield, the Crescent Shield could be a front for Chambord and the French captain Bonnard.

He could be wrong, but he did not think so. The longer he considered it, the more sense it made. He must get to Fred Klein and warn him as soon as possible. Klein and half the world's intelligence services were looking for criminals, but the wrong ones. Klein had to know, and Jon had to uncover where Chambord and Bonnard had gone and what devastation *they* were planning.

■

The first sign that Jon was in trouble again was explosive gunfire from the S-70A helicopter. It slashed over the treetops as Jon crossed a small clearing. Pine needles rained down, and the chopper banked steeply and climbed, turned, and came back for a second pass. By then, Jon was no longer in the open, and the chopper roared past overhead and down the slope. It was a ruse, Jon figured. They had seen him the first time and would land in another clearing lower on the slope. After that, the terrorists would spread up and out on foot and wait. If there were enough of them to cover a lot of territory, they could hope that he would come to them.

He had spent the last two hours working his way in a wide uphill loop.

When he had seen no more sign of the Crescent Shield forces, he had felt secure enough to turn downhill, where he would have better odds of running into a road. He guessed he was in southeastern France. If he were right, it could be anywhere from Mulhouse to Grenoble. Each hour that passed out of touch with civilization made time more pressing. Because he needed to reach a telephone, he had risked reversing course too soon. He had not moved far enough from the chalet, and so the chopper had spotted him.

He must stop playing into their hands. He turned but did not go straight uphill again. Instead, he angled across the face of the slope toward the chalet, hoping to catch Abu Auda by surprise. Also, the chalet must be near some kind of road. The sudden cawing of a flock of crows taking off from the tops of nearby pines was the first hint he had made another mistake. The second was the frantic scurrying of some frightened animal a hundred yards to his left.

He had underestimated Abu Auda. A ground force had trailed the helicopter, in case Jon did exactly what he had done. Jon dove into the crevices of a rock outcropping to his right, where he could watch the entire sweep of the forest ahead. How many men had Abu Auda assigned to the trailing force? Twelve men was all he had, unless reinforcements had arrived from somewhere. High above, the pine tops moaned in the wind. Somewhere in the distance, bees buzzed and birds sang. But no birds sang here. The woods were eerie with quiet, waiting, too. It would not be long.

Then the shadows beneath the lofty pines appeared to vibrate, undulate like a thin fog. Out of the fog, as if floating on the shadows themselves, emerged another Afghan. This one was not alone. Another terrorist materialized some fifty yards to Jon's right and twenty yards farther down the slope. A third was an equal distance away on the other side.

Jon saw no others. He smiled a humorless smile. There had been no reinforcements.

Three against one—and how many more from the helicopter coming up the slope behind? Probably six or seven. But if he acted quickly, they would not matter. This time, Abu Auda had miscalculated. He had not expected Jon to backtrack at such a sharp angle, which had brought him to the tailing threesome much sooner than they had estimated. Three against one, when the one was armed with an M16 and under cover, was not impossible.

Jon saw the first terrorist spot the rock outcropping and signal his companions to circle while he investigated. Jon figured they must know by now that he had the M16. Because Abu Auda was a strong commander, a thinker, he would have counted heads before they left the chalet. Which meant he would have discovered that he had an armed man missing. If they found the body, Auda would also be certain the M16 was gone.

Jon peered out carefully. The lead terrorist was advancing straight at the rocks. Jon's main consideration was how fast he could put all of them out of action or at least drive them to ground so he could slip away before they realized he was gone. But the first shot would bring the rest running. In all probability, someone would also alert the helicopter.

He waited until the other two were in line with the rocks, one on either side. By then, the lead man was less than twenty feet away. It was time. On edge, Jon raised up, squeezed off a quick cluster of three—two into the first terrorist and, swiftly moving the rifle, one into the man on the east. He shifted the rifle again and squeezed two more at the man on the west. Then he ran.

He had hit the first one dead center. He would not get up. The other two had gone down, too, but he was unsure how badly he had wounded them. As he ran, he listened anxiously for clues. He heard a distant yell . . . and nothing more. No running feet, no crashing through the bushes, no creaking of low tree branches. None of the noises of close pursuit.

Wary, seeking cover wherever he could, he raced on, angling downhill, until he heard the helicopter again. And dropped to a crouch beside a large pine. He watched up through small tunnels among the light-shimmering needles. Soon the chopper swept overhead, and Jon glimpsed a black face leaning out to scan below. Abu Auda.

The Sikorsky continued on. Jon could not remain here, because Abu Auda would not rely on aerial pursuit alone. Some of his men would still be on the ground, and Jon had to make a decision. But so did Abu Auda. He would have to guess which direction Jon ran.

As Jon listened intently for the sound of descent and landing, he tried to put himself in the killer's mind. Finally he decided that Abu Auda would expect him to head straight from his pursuers, trying to put as much distance between them as possible. Which meant, if he were right, that the chopper would land directly south. Jon turned and raced off to the right. Then he slowed and headed west down through the forest, trying to make as little noise as possible.

After less than an hour, the pine forest began to thin. Sweating, his wounds itching, Jon continued on across an open meadow and stopped in a fringe of trees, excited. A car was cruising past on an asphalt road below. He had heard no pursuit since turning west, and the occasional sound of the helicopter still searching the forest had been far off to his left, the south. He remained among the trees, hurrying north along the edge, hoping the road and the forest would meet or at least come much closer.

When he found a stream, he stopped and hunched beside it. Panting, he untied the white sleeve that Thérèse had used to bandage his arm after the missile strike at the villa. The wound was long but shallow. He washed it and his side, where a bullet had creased the skin; his forehead, where debris from the missile strike had scratched it; and his wrists. Some of the wounds were tinged with red, indicating small infections. Still, none was serious.

He splashed more of the cool spring water onto his hot, sweaty face, and, sighing, moved off again. The forest's sounds were normal here, the hushed quiet one would expect from a single person's moving through, not the utter stillness that told him many were intruding.

And then he paused. Hope filled him. Through the trees he could see a crossroads and a road sign. He looked all around and slipped cautiously from cover onto the asphalt. He tore across the road to the sign. At last he knew where he was: GRENOBLE 12KM. Not impossibly far, and he had been there before. But if he stayed on the road, he would be conspicuous. If the helicopter searched this far, he would be seen easily.

Making plans, he ran back into the forest and waited. When he heard the noise of a vehicle's engine, he smiled with relief. It was going in the right direction. He watched eagerly as it came around the bend—a farm truck this time. He abandoned his M16 with all its ammunition in the pines and kicked duff over them. Then he stuck the Afghan's curved knife into one jacket pocket and the flare gun into the other, and waved both arms.

The farmer stopped, and Jon climbed into the cab, greeting the fellow in French. He explained that he was a stranger in the area, visiting a friend who had gone into Grenoble earlier. They were to meet for dinner, but his car refused to start so he had decided to walk and hope for a Good Samaritan. He had taken a tumble in the woods, and that was why he was so disheveled.

The farmer clucked with sympathy and chatted away about the advantages of the region, pleased for Jon's company in this remote land of soaring peaks, wide open spaces, and few inhabitants. They drove on, but Jon did not relax. His careful gaze kept watch.

Grenoble, France

Nestled in the French Alps, Grenoble was a stunning city—old and historic, known for its fine winter sports, particularly in downhill skiing, and its medieval landmarks. The farmer dropped Jon on the left bank of the Isère River at the place Grenette, a bustling square lined with sidewalk cafés. Nearby was the place St-André, the heart of Grenoble. The warm sunshine had brought people out, and they sat at small, outdoor tables in their crisp shirtsleeves, sipping espresso.

As he studied them, Jon realized again how lousy his own clothes looked. They were dirty and smoke-streaked, and he had no idea whether he had managed to clean his face in the stream. He was already attracting the wrong kind of attention, something he definitely did not want. He still had his wallet, and as soon as he called Fred Klein, he would buy new clothes.

He turned, orienting himself, and walked toward the place St-André. That was where he found what he needed first—a public phone booth— and dialed Fred Klein.

Klein's voice was surprised. "So you *are* alive?"

"You sound disappointed."

"Don't get sentimental, Colonel," Klein said dryly. "We'll hug later. There are a few things going on that you should know at once." He described the latest electronic disaster—the blinded satellites. "I'd hoped the molecular computer was destroyed, and all we had was a nasty malfunction."

"You didn't believe that for a second. The damage is too widespread."

"Call it a naive hope."

"Did Randi Russell get away before the missile hit?"

"We wouldn't have known what really happened in Algeria if she hadn't. She's back in Paris. Where are you? Bring me up to date."

So Randi had made it. Jon slowly let his breath out. He reported the events since the missile strike and what he had learned.

Klein swore. "So you think the Crescent Shield's a front, *too?*"

"It makes sense. I can't see Darius Bonnard as an Islamic terrorist, no matter his Algerian connection. But he was in the right place at the right time to have made that surreptitious phone call from NATO. He or Chambord must've killed the Crescent Shield pilot at the chalet before we got there, and then they took off with Thérèse. Abu Auda was stunned. Outraged. Worried whether Mauritania was still alive. The way I read it, this was no sudden mutiny of the weak. This was the strong taking over as planned."

"You think Émile Chambord is behind everything?"

"Maybe, or maybe not. It could be Captain Bonnard, and he's holding Chambord and using the daughter as a lever," Jon said, worrying about Thérèse. He stared out at the street, watching for Abu Auda and his men. "Have you heard anything about Peter Howell and Marty?"

"According to my friends at Langley, they're all in Paris. Marty's awake."

Jon smiled. What a relief to know Marty was back. "Did he say anything useful about Émile Chambord?"

"Unfortunately, nothing we didn't already know. I'll have Randi sent to pick you up."

"Tell her I'll be waiting at the Fort de la Bastille at the top of the cable car lift."

Klein was silent again. "You know, Colonel, there could be someone we don't know about yet behind Chambord and Bonnard. It could even be the daughter."

Jon considered the idea. Not Thérèse, no. He did not believe that, but the rest of what Klein had said struck a chord. An idea began to form in his mind. An idea he had to chase down fast.

"Get me out of here, Fred."

Chapter
Thirty-two

Paris, France

In naval headquarters on the place de la Concorde, Senior Captain Liberâl Tassini toyed with the fine Mont Blanc pen on his desk as his steady gaze took in Peter Howell. "Odd you should be here asking that, Peter. May I inquire exactly what caused your interest?"

"Let's just say MI6 requested I look into the matter. I believe it may have something to do with a small problem involving one of our junior officers."

"And what would that small problem be?"

"Between you and me, Libby, I told them to just go through regular channels, but it appears it involves the son of someone important." Peter ducked his head, pretending embarrassment. "I'm only a messenger boy. One of the reasons I did a bunk from the service, eh? Temperament and all that. Just do me the favor of a simple answer, and I'll be off the hook and out of your sight."

"Can't be done, *bon ami.* Your question touches on a somewhat delicate and complicated situation of our own."

"You don't say. Well, puts my little query in its place, doesn't it. Sorry, I . . ."

Captain Tassini twirled the pen again on his desk. "On the contrary.

I would actually like to know exactly how this, ah, junior officer came to be concerned with whether a recent meeting on the *De Gaulle* was authorized or unauthorized."

"Well . . ." Peter chuckled conspiratorially. "All right, Libby. Seems the lad has put in a chit for expenses incurred for having attended such a meeting as a replacement pilot for one of our generals. His paymaster simply wants to know if the claim's legitimate."

Captain Tassini laughed aloud. "Does he, by heaven? What does the general say?"

"Touchy, that. Seems he died. Only a few days ago."

Tassini's eyes narrowed. "Really?"

"Afraid so. Not unusual with generals. Old, you know."

"Quite," Tassini said in English. "All right. At the moment, all I can tell you is that no such meeting was authorized on the *De Gaulle*, although one may actually have taken place. We're looking into it, too."

"Hmmm." Peter stood up. "Very well, I'll simply give the buggers the old 'can neither confirm nor deny' answer. The paymaster can reimburse the boy, or not. Up to him. But he'll get no official response."

"Hard on the boy," Tassini sympathized.

Peter headed for the door. "What was the *De Gaulle* doing out there anyway? What does her captain say about the meeting?"

Tassini leaned back and studied Peter again. At last he said, "He claims there was no meeting. Says he was out there to practice single-ship tactics in hostile waters at night, and that the order came from NATO. Rather a large problem for us, since no one at NATO appears to have issued it."

"Ouch. Well, glad it's not my kettle of fish, old man." Peter could feel Tassini's questioning gaze on his back as he left. He doubted that he had fooled his friend, but both of them had preserved face and, even more important, deniability.

Berlin, Germany

The Kurfürstendamm—the Ku'damm, as locals called it—was a bustling boulevard at the heart of new Berlin. Lined with crowded stores and high-rent offices, it was famous around the world. People in the know swore that the Ku'damm never slept. In one of its elegant restaurants, Pieke Exner wound her way among the white tablecloths and polished silverware toward her lunch date. It was their second in twelve hours, and she knew the young lieutenant was more than ready, he was eager.

That was obvious in the leap to his feet and the Prussian click of his heels that would have gotten him a dry reprimand from his boss, General Otto Bittrich. It was also obvious in his loosened tunic, showing the relaxed familiarity she had worked to produce in him all last evening before going home and leaving him if not panting, then breathing hard. These were the signs she had wanted to see. Still, she had more work to do. It was not his tunic she wanted loosened; it was his tongue.

She smiled and settled down into her chair. With a flourish, he helped her slide to the table. As he sat next to her, she notched her smile up to one of genuine warmth, as if she had been thinking about him ever since they had parted at her door. After he had gallantly ordered an expensive bottle of the best wine from the Rheingau, she resumed her chatter where they had left off, about her dreams of travel and love of all good things foreign.

As it turned out, she quickly saw that she had done her job too well, and the lieutenant was too busy thinking about her to take the bait. Lunch proceeded in that fashion through a *schnitzel*, a second bottle of the Rheingau, and an excellent strudel to the coffee and brandy. But as much as she plied him with smiles and warm hand holding, he never spoke about his work.

Running out of patience, she looked long and deeply into his eyes, managing to convey an intriguing range of emotions—shy, nervous, slightly frightened, adoring, brazenly eager, and in sexual heat, all at the same time. It was a gift, and older and wiser men than Lieutenant Joachim Bierhof had fallen for it.

He responded by quickly paying for the check, and they left. By the time they reached her apartment beyond the Brandenburg Gate and across the Spree River in the bohemian Prenzlauer Berg section of the former East Berlin, he was in no condition to think of anything but her, her glorious apartment, and her bed.

Once inside, he quickly pulled the shades against the afternoon sun and was soon naked and nuzzling Pieke's breasts, when she sighed and complained of how cold it was. A very cold May in Germany. How she would love to be with him in sunny Italy or Spain, or better yet . . . the glorious South of France.

Too busy with her breasts and pulling off her green thong bikini panties, Joachim muttered, "I was just there, the South of France. God, how I wish you'd been with me."

She laughed playfully. "But you had your general."

"He was out on that French carrier most of the night. Just him and our pilot. I walked on the quays alone. By myself. Had to eat alone. What a great bottle of wine I found. You would have liked it. God, how I wish . . . but we're here now, and . . ."

It was at this point that Pieke Exner fell off the bed, badly twisting her knee and back. She was unable to stand up without the lieutenant's reluctant and rather testy help. As he put her back into bed, she asked prettily to be covered to keep away the chills. She shivered. He turned up the heat and put another blanket over her. She held out her hand sadly.

She was, of course, devastated, and terribly disappointed as well as tearfully guilty: "You poor man. It must be terrible for you. I'm so sorry. Will . . . will . . . you be all right? I mean, you were so . . . so . . ."

Joachim Bierhof was, after all, an officer and a gentleman. He was forced to soothe her fears, declare he would be fine. She was much more to him than *that*.

She squeezed his hand and promised to meet him early tomorrow, if she felt up to it, right here in her apartment. "I'll call you tomorrow!" And promptly fell asleep.

There was nothing the lieutenant could do but dress and leave quietly, careful not to awaken her.

The moment the door closed and locked, she jumped out of bed, dressed, and dialed the telephone. She reported, "General Bittrich was in the South of France, just as you suspected. He spent half the night on a French aircraft carrier. Was that all you wanted to know, Peter?"

"You're a wonder, child," Peter Howell pronounced from Paris.

"You remember that."

Peter chuckled. "Hope the price wasn't too high, Angie, old girl."

"Jealous, Peter?"

"At my age, my dear, I'm remarkably flattered."

"At any age. Besides, you're ageless."

Peter laughed. "Not all of me seems to know that all the time. But we must talk further."

"A proposition, Mr. Howell?"

"Angie, you could entice the dead. And thanks again."

Angela Chadwick hung up, remade the bed, picked up her handbag, and left the apartment to return to her own place on the other side of the Brandenburg Gate.

Paris, France

Marty had a new laptop computer, which Peter had used Marty's credit card to buy. Left alone and on his meds, Marty was curled around it in his room in the clinic, sitting cross-legged on top of his bed's patchwork comforter. He had checked the OASIS Web site—Online Asperger's Syndrome Information and Support—fifteen times in the last two hours with no results.

Vacillating between despair and determined optimism, depressed in the sticky muck of his meds, Marty did not hear Randi or Peter enter the room until they spoke.

"Anything, Mart?" Randi asked before the door had closed.

Peter interrupted, "MI6 has heard nothing. Bloody irritating." He added a shade bitterly, "If we knew for whom Jon actually worked, we could contact them directly and maybe get some straight intelligence."

His gaze solemn, Marty stared at Randi. "What about the CIA, Randi?"

"No news," she admitted.

Marty frowned, and his fingers pounded the keyboard. "I'll check OASIS again."

"How long since you last tried?" Peter asked.

Two red spots of indignation appeared on Marty's cheeks. "If you think *I'm* obsessing, Peter, what about you? All those phone calls you keep making!"

Peter nodded and showed a brief smile.

Marty grumbled under his breath as he entered the OASIS Web site.

As soon as his screen filled with the opening page, he found himself relaxing a bit. It was like going home. Created for those with Asperger's Syndrome and their families, OASIS was full of information, plus there was a Web ring. Marty checked in often when his life was normal—well, normal for him. What the rest of the world considered normal he found painfully boring. He could not imagine why anyone would want to live like that. On the other hand, OASIS seemed to get the point. The folks who ran it knew what they were talking about. What a rarity, he mused to himself. He was looking forward to reading the new book *The Oasis Guide to Asperger Syndrome* by Patricia Romanowski Bashe and Barbara L. Kirby. It was waiting for him on his desk at home.

He scanned the messages on OASIS, but again there was nothing. He leaned back, closed his eyes, and heaved a big sigh.

"No word?" Peter asked.

"Darn it, no."

They were silent in their discouragement. When the phone rang, Randi snapped it up. It was Doug Kennedy, her Langley boss. As she listened, her eyes began to flash with excitement. "I know the place. Yes. What great news. Thanks, Doug. Don't worry. I'll handle it." As soon as she hung up, she turned to Marty and Peter. They were staring at her, waiting.

"Jon's *alive*. I know where he is!"

Grenoble, France

A cold Alpine wind blasted Jon's hair and chilled his face as he leaned over the parapet of the sixteenth-century Fort de la Bastille with other tourists, high above Grenoble. Despite the rising wind, they appeared to be enjoying the startling amalgam of medieval and ultramodern buildings far below. Known for its high-tech industries and fine universities, Grenoble spread out in a casual array from the confluence of the Drac and Isère rivers, while the dramatic Alps towered above, their snowy cloaks glinting in the afternoon sunshine.

Still, it was not the panorama on which Jon's attention had been fixed since he arrived at the old fort. It was the cable cars rising up from the city below.

He had been at the parapet several hours, dressed in new jeans, green pullover sweater, a medium-weight bomber jacket, and dark sunglasses. Inside the deep front pockets of his jacket were the Afghan's curved knife and the helicopter's flare gun, his only weapons. He was still savoring the good news that Randi was alive and Marty was awake and fine.

But he was uneasy. She should have been here by now, and he was increasingly aware that Abu Auda and his men could arrive any moment, too. It was inevitable that they would extend their search to Grenoble, the only major city near the Chartreuse villa. Jon knew far too much, and there was always the chance he had not yet made contact with his superiors. They could even have found the M16 rifle and ammunition he had buried under the duff close to the road that led here.

So now he stood shoulder-to-shoulder in the chilly mountain wind with other sightseers, unobtrusive in the lengthening afternoon shadows, as he leaned his arms on the parapet and studied each of the gondolas that regularly carried passengers up to the fort from the station at quay Stéphane-Jay. Designed to please tourists who wanted to see the sweeping views, the gondolas were see-through.

This, of course, also pleased Jon, because he could scrutinize each passenger through the gondolas' transparent shells. It was after five o'clock when he finally spotted not Randi, but one of the Crescent Shield killers. His heartbeat sped.

He wanted to attract no attention, so he continued his relaxed pose, a visitor enchanted like any other, while he quickly analyzed and placed the face: A clean-shaved Saudi who had been with the group of terrorists that had escaped from the villa. He was riding at the front of his gondola as it slowly rose to the fort. Although he was the only terrorist whom Jon recognized in the gondola, Jon doubted he was alone. More members of the Crescent Shield would be around somewhere.

Certain of the man's identity, Jon turned, stuck his hands nonchalantly into his jacket pockets where he could grip his weapons, and sauntered off toward the paths that wound down through the Parc Guy Pape to the city. He did not want to leave, in case Randi showed up. But where there was one Crescent Shield, there would be others, and he had to face the fact that Randi might never come.

Once he was beyond sight of the parapet, he walked faster. The number of tourists was decreasing. It was growing late, and the biting wind that whistled through the afternoon shadows had probably discouraged them. No longer noticing the chill, he left the fort, turned toward a downhill path, and broke into a steady trot. Which was when he saw five more Crescent Shield killers.

He fell back around a high hedge. They had been hiking up the route he was about to take down, and in the lead was Abu Auda himself. They were all wearing ordinary Western clothes. Abu Auda had on a beret and looked uncomfortable, a shark trying to walk on land. Jon reversed course and rushed around the rear of the fort to where there was another park area. He slipped behind a tall oak, scanned the area from where he had just come, and then the city and the rivers below.

He listened intently. Yes, he was right. There were quick footsteps behind, descending from a higher elevation. The steps were light but swift. He pulled out the flare gun and knife and whirled.

Randi flinched. She touched her finger to her lips.

"Randi!" he accused.

"Shhh. Be nice now."

He grinned with relief. "Bossy as ever."

Tall and athletically slender, she was more than a welcome sight. She had changed into dark trousers and a jacket zipped up only a third of the way, which made reaching for her weapons more convenient. There was a black watch cap on her head again, pulled down to her ears to hide her light-colored hair. She also wore dark, wraparound sunglasses secured at the back so they would not fall off if she had to go into action.

As she slipped into the shadow next to him, her face was alert but composed. "Peter's here, too. Two-person job, you know." She took out a mini radio and spoke into it: "I've got him. We're on our way."

"They're coming." He nodded back toward the Fort de la Bastille, where the clean-shaved Saudi was pointing toward where they were hidden. He was talking excitedly to Abu Auda. The men were showing no weapons. Not yet, at least.

"Come on!"

"Where to?"

"No time to explain." She sprinted.

The Crescent Shield broke into a run toward them, spreading out as

Abu Auda waved them right and left. Jon counted six, which meant there were five or so others somewhere, perhaps around here. As he rushed after Randi across the park and then higher, he wondered where those other two or three could be.

They ran onward, Randi in the lead, putting more and more distance between themselves and the Fort de la Bastille and the cable cars, as well as between themselves and the Crescent Shield. Breathing hard, he glanced back and could no longer see the terrorists. Then he heard a helicopter. *Damn.*

"It's their chopper!" he told Randi as he searched the sky. "I knew all of them weren't in the park."

"Keep running!" she yelled back.

They raced on, focused on escape, and then Jon saw it—not the Crescent Shield's Sikorsky, but another Hughes OH-6 Loach scout chopper. It looked like an oversized bumblebee as it settled down into an open spot twenty yards ahead and to their right. Randi swerved toward it, waving, as Peter, dressed in a black jumpsuit, dropped from the door. Next to Randi, Jon figured he had never seen a more welcome sight. Peter wore a black cap and reflecting sunglasses and held a British assault rifle up and ready.

Jon's relief was short-lived. There was a shout of anger behind them. From the left, one of the terrorists burst out from among the trees. He had somehow managed to circle more quickly than the others. His raised weapon focused on Randi as she closed in on the vibrating chopper. Peter jumped back onboard.

In a single smooth motion, Jon spun, aimed the flare gun, and fired. It made a huge noise, although it was drowned out by the helicopter. The flare burst out in a trail of smoke and hit the terrorist in the middle of his chest.

The projectile landed with such velocity that it flung the man back into the trees. He dropped his rifle and grabbed for the flare, which protruded from beneath his rib cage. He screamed, and the high-pitched noise sent chills up Jon's spine, because both knew what would happen next. The man's face was contorted in terror.

The flare exploded. As the terrorist's torso shattered, Jon dove into the helicopter after Randi. Peter did not wait for the door to be closed.

He lifted off. Abu Auda and his men abandoned pretense and loosed a fusillade of pistol and submachine gunfire. The bullets slashed around the helicopter, hitting the landing gear and ripping through the walls as Jon lay on his belly, hanging onto the seat legs, trying not to slide out the open door.

Randi grabbed the back of his waistband. "I've got you!"

Jon's hands were cold and sweaty, and he felt his fingers loosen. Even Randi would not be able to save him if he lost his grip. To make matters worse, Peter banked the chopper sharply to the right, trying to avoid the gunfire and get out of range. But the angle sent Jon sliding back toward the open door and certain death.

Randi swore and grabbed him under the arm with her other hand. Jon's slide paused. Still, the inexorable pull of gravity and the wind continued. Gunfire trailing, Peter pushed the chopper out over the rivers. Jon could feel his fingers loosening again. His breath was a raw rasp as he frantically tried to tighten his grip.

"We're out of range!" Peter bellowed.

It was none too soon. As Peter began to level the helicopter, Jon's fingers slipped off the chair struts. He grabbed for them, but all he could find was air. Randi fell on top of him, wrapped her legs around his waist, and seized the struts herself. The helicopter's angle had improved enough that she was able to stabilize him. He was vaguely aware of her on top of him, her weight firm, reassuring, the muscled legs tight, and somewhere in the back of his mind was the thought that under different circumstances he might enjoy this. And then the moment was gone. Terror returned.

Long seconds passed. Gravity shifted, and the pull was no longer on his feet, but along the length of his body. The helicopter was flying level at last. He remained motionless, stunned.

"Thank God that's over." Randi's voice was a hoarse croak as she clambered up, hopped over him, and slammed shut the door. "I'd rather never do that again."

The helicopter's interior was suddenly quieter. Jon's muscles trembled. Feeling weak, he struggled up and fell into the single rear seat. He looked up and saw Randi's face for the first time since he dove into the helicopter. Color was returning to it. She must have been white with fear.

"Strap yourself in," she ordered. And then she smiled a smile so broad and relieved that it lit up her whole face.

"Thank you." His throat was tight, and his heart was pounding like a jackhammer. "That's pretty inadequate, but I really mean it. Thank you." He quickly locked his seat belt.

"Works fine for me. You're welcome." As she started to turn back toward the front, her gaze caught his. For a long moment, they looked into each other's eyes, and understanding and forgiveness passed between them.

Chapter
Thirty-three

Heading northwest toward Paris, the helicopter left Grenoble behind. There was an appreciative silence inside as each privately acknowledged how close they had come to death. Alone in the back, Jon was emerging from his exhausted trance. He let out a deep sigh, releasing his mind and body of the stress and near-misses of the last few days. He unsnapped his belt and leaned forward between Peter and Randi, who sat in the twin pilots' seats.

Randi grinned and patted the top of his head. "Nice doggy."

Jon chuckled. She had an amusing way about her, and right now she seemed the most charming person in the world. There was nothing like friends, and two of his best were right here next to him. She had put earphones on over her watch cap, and her sunglasses moved from side to side as she gazed all around, looking for aircraft that might be following.

Peter wore earphones, too, and was watching his fuel gauge and the directional dials through his dark glasses. The lowering sun was off to their left, a fireball whose slanting rays illuminated the treetops and snowy fields below and ahead. Far ahead they could see the first sweep of the magnificent Rhône Valley, marked with its characteristic patchwork of vineyards.

The old OH-6's cabin was cramped, so with Jon leaning forward, the three of them were a cozy knot. He raised his voice above the noise of the rotors and announced, "I'm ready to be filled in. How's Marty doing?"

"The lad's not only out of his coma, he's chomping at the bit," Peter reported cheerfully. He described their escape to the plastic surgery clinic where he had hidden Marty since. "He's in good spirits now, once we told him you were, in fact, alive."

Jon smiled. "Too bad he wasn't more helpful about the DNA computer and Chambord."

"Yes," Randi said. "Now you. Tell us what happened at the villa in Algeria. When I heard the automatic fire, I was sure you'd been killed."

"Chambord hadn't been kidnapped at all," he told them. "He was with the Crescent Shield from the beginning. Actually, they'd been with him, or at least that's what he claims. It makes sense, knowing what I know now. He also created the deception that he was a prisoner, for Thérèse's benefit. He had no idea Mauritania had taken her, so he was as surprised to see her as she was to see him."

"Explains a lot," Peter said. "But how in blazes did they get the prototype out before the missile hit?"

"They didn't," Jon told them. "The missile destroyed it for certain. What I don't understand is how Chambord could've built another prototype and had it up and running soon enough to take over our satellites."

"I know," Randi agreed. "It's baffling. But our people say no other computer has the power, speed, or capacity to reprogram the satellites through all their codes, firewalls, and other defenses. In fact, most of our safeguards are still classified and supposedly impossible to discover, much less breach."

Peter checked the time, the distance they had come, and the fuel gauge. He said, "Perhaps you're both right. But why couldn't there be a second prototype?"

Jon and Randi exchanged a glance.

"That's an idea, Peter," Randi said.

Jon said slowly, "One already in existence. One that Chambord either had access to, had set up to be programmed remotely, or had trained someone else to operate on his instructions. Also, one that Mauritania appeared to know nothing about."

"Swell," Randi grumbled. "A second DNA computer. Just what we need."

"It makes a lot of sense, especially when combined with what I haven't brought up yet."

"That sounds ominous," Peter said. "Fill us in, Jon."

Jon stared ahead through the helicopter's windshield at the French countryside, threaded with small rivers and canals and dotted with neat farmhouses. "I told you I learned at the villa that Chambord had been part of the terrorism from the start," he said, "and that he probably helped plan the attack on us."

"Right. And?" Randi prompted.

"Hours ago, before I finally got away from Abu Auda, it began to make sense that not only did the Crescent Shield use the Basques for cover, Chambord and Bonnard have been using the Shield for cover, too. The Shield has a fairly large and flexible organization with terrorist skills, and it could do what Bonnard and Chambord couldn't do by themselves. But I think the Shield gave them something else as well . . . it's their stalking horse. A group to blame for whatever horror they're really planning. Who better to pin it on than an Islamic extremist group led by a man who was once a top lieutenant of Osama bin Laden? Which, by the way, is maybe why they took Mauritania with them. They could be planning to make them the fall guy."

Randi frowned. "So you're saying the two of them, Chambord and Bonnard, are behind all the electronic attacks on the U.S. But why? What possible motive could a world-renowned scientist and a respected French army officer have?"

Jon shrugged. "My guess is, their goal won't turn out to be dropping a mid-range tactical nuclear missile on Jerusalem or Tel Aviv. That makes political sense for the Crescent Shield, but not for a pair of Frenchmen like Chambord or Bonnard. I figure they're planning something else, most likely against the United States, since they've now taken out our satellites. But I still haven't been able to figure out why."

As the wind rushed past, and the helicopter's rotors beat a steady tattoo, the three friends fell silent.

"And the Shield knows nothing about what Bonnard and Chambord are planning?" Randi asked.

"From listening to all their talk, I'd say the idea that Bonnard and Chambord weren't *their* dupes never occurred to the Crescent Shield. That's what happens to fanatics, they see nothing but what they want to see."

Peter's hands tightened on the controls. "I expect you're right about the stalking horse. Could get nasty for whoever gets the blame for what they've done so far, never mind whatever Armageddon they're planning. Like what happened after the World Trade Center and the Pentagon were attacked. Our soldier and scientist wouldn't want responsibility for something like Afghanistan to come crashing down on their heads."

"Exactly," Jon acknowledged. "I think Chambord anticipates nations may converge again to hunt down the perpetrators this time, too. So he wants a patsy, someone the world is ready to believe would do it. Mauritania and the Crescent Shield are perfect for that. It's a little-known terrorist group, so who'll believe their denials, especially if it looks as if they've been caught red-handed? And then, too, all the evidence makes it look as if they kidnapped Chambord, which he'll swear to. He lies well enough that he'll be believed. Take it from me."

"What about Thérèse?" Randi said. "She knows the truth by now, right?"

"I don't know if she knows the whole truth, but she knows about her father. She's learned too much, which must be worrying Chambord. If push comes to shove, he might sacrifice her to save his plan. Or Bonnard will take the decision out of his hands and handle it himself."

"His own daughter." Randi shuddered.

"He's either unbalanced or a fanatic," Jon said. "They're the only reasons I can see for his doing such an about-face—from illustrious scientist to down-and-dirty terrorist."

Peter was gazing out at the land, his leathery face intense as he studied roads. "Going to have to pause our discussion a bit." They were approaching a small city built along a river. "That's Mâcon, right at the edge of Burgundy. River's called the Saône. Peaceful-looking little place, isn't it? Turns out, it is. Randi and I refueled here on our way to track you down, Jon. No problems, so I'm going to set us down here again. The gas tank's hungry. When was the last time you ate, Jon?"

"Damned if I remember."

"Then we'd best pick up more than petrol."

In the long, undulating shadows of late afternoon, Peter landed the OH-6 at the small airport.

Outside Bousmelet-sur-Seine, France

Émile Chambord leaned back in the desk chair and stretched. The stone walls, evil-looking medieval weapons, dusty suits of armor, and high vaulted ceiling of this windowless work area were cheerless, although a thick Berber rug covered the floor, and lamps cast warm pools of light. That he was working here in the armory where there were no windows was the way he wanted it. No windows, no distractions, and whenever worries about Thérèse entered his mind, he pushed them far away.

He gazed lovingly at his prototype on the long table. Although he enjoyed everything about it, he was particularly in awe of its speed and power. It tested each possible answer to any problem *simultaneously*, rather than sequentially, which was how the largest and fastest silicon-chip computers worked. In cyber terms, the world's fastest silicon super-computers took a long, long time. Still, they were faster than a human brain. But swiftest of all was his molecular machine, its velocity almost incomprehensible.

And the basis was in the gel packs, in the special DNA sequence he had created. The spiral string of DNA that curled inside every living cell—the natural chemistry underlying all living things—had been his artist's palette. And the result was that intractable problems such as those that cropped up in artificial intelligence systems, in fashioning complex computer networks like the information superhighway, and in conducting intricate games such as three-dimensional chess, which were impossible for the most powerful supercomputer, could easily be digested by his molecular marvel. After all, it was merely a matter of selecting the correct path through an enormous number of possible choices.

He was also fascinated by his brainchild's ability to continually alter its identity while using only one-hundredth of its power. It simply maintained a firewall that changed its access code faster than any conventional computer could crack it. In essence, his molecular machine "evolved" while being used, and the more it was used, the more it evolved. In the cold stone room, he smiled as he recalled the first image he had seen in his mind when he conceived this attribute. His prototype was like the Borg on the American television show *Star Trek*, which evolved instantly to find a fresh defense against any attack. Now he was using his constantly unfolding machine to counter the most insidious attack of all—on the soul of France.

For inspiration, he gazed again at the reproduction of the noble painting above his desk, and then with a determined heart, he resumed searching for clues to where Marty Zellerbach was hiding. He had easily entered Marty's computer system at his home in Washington and waltzed in seconds through the computer geek's specially designed software defenses. Unfortunately, Marty had not visited it since the night of the Pasteur attack, so Chambord found no clue to his whereabouts there. Disappointed, he left a little "gift" and moved on.

He knew the name of Marty's bank, so it was a simple matter to check his records. But again, there was no new activity. He thought for a moment and had another idea—Marty's credit card.

As a record of Marty's purchases appeared on the screen, Chambord's austere face smiled, and his intense eyes flashed. *Oui!* Yesterday, Marty had bought a laptop in Paris. He picked up the cellular telephone on the table beside him.

Vaduz, Liechtenstein

Carved out of the lush countryside between Switzerland and Austria, the small principality of Liechtenstein was often overlooked by ordinary tourists, while prized by foreigners who needed a safe place to transport or hide money. Liechtenstein was known for both its breathtaking scenery and absolute secrecy.

In the capital, Vaduz, twilight had cast dark shadows across the thoroughfare that edged the Rhine River. This suited Abu Auda. Still dressed in his Western clothes, he moved briskly along, avoiding eye contact, until he arrived at the door to the small, undistinguished private residence that had been described to him. He knocked three times, waited, and knocked four times.

He heard a bolt disengage inside, and the door cracked open.

In Arabic, Abu Auda spoke into the small space: *"Breet bate."* I want a room.

A man's voice answered, *"May-fah-hem-tiksh."* I don't understand.

Abu Auda repeated the code and added, "They have Mauritania."

The door swung open, and a small, dark man stared worriedly up. "Yes?"

Abu Auda pushed his way in. This was a major European stop for *hawalala,* an underground Arab railroad for moving, banking, laundering, and investing money. Unregulated and completely secret, with no real accounts that regulators could track, the network financed not only individuals but causes. This past year, nearly a billion U.S. dollars had moved through the European system alone.

"Where did Mauritania get his money?" Abu Auda continued in Arabic. "The source. From whose purse did the financing come?"

"You know I can't tell you that."

Abu Auda removed the pistol from the holster under his arm. He pointed it, and as the man stepped backward, Abu Auda followed. "Mauritania is being held by the people with the money. They are not of our Cause. I know the money was paid by a Captain Bonnard or a Dr. Chambord. But I do not believe they are alone in this. So now you *will* speak, and you will be thorough."

Aloft over France

A half hour after taking off again from Mâcon, Jon, Peter, and Randi finished the sandwiches they had bought at the small airport, and continued their analysis and discussion of the situation.

Peter said, "Whatever we decide to do to find Chambord and Bonnard, we'd best do it quickly. Time's not on our side. Whatever they're planning, they'll want to make it happen very, very soon."

Jon nodded. "Mauritania had planned to attack Israel this morning. Now that we know there's still a working molecular computer out there somewhere, and that Chambord and Bonnard are free and traveling, my guess is that we've bought ourselves some time, but not much."

Randi shivered. "Maybe not enough."

The sun had set, and darkness was creeping across the land. Ahead, an ocean of lights sparkled in the gray twilight. Paris. As they stared at the great city's sprawl, Jon's mind went back to the Pasteur Institute and the initial bombing that had brought him to Paris and Marty. It seemed a long time ago, although it was just last Monday that Fred Klein had appeared in Colorado to ask him to take on this assignment, which had led across two continents.

Now the focus was narrowed, and the price for failure was still unknown, except, they all agreed, it would be high. They must find Émile Chambord and his molecular computer. And when they found them, they were going to need a healthy and alert Marty.

Chapter
Thirty-four

Paris, France

Dr. Lochiel Cameron could see that Marty was irritated and frustrated. Marty was coming off his meds, pacing the room in his stiff, awkward gait as Dr. Cameron observed from a comfortable armchair, a bemused smile on his face. He was an upbeat, easygoing man who had seen enough war and devastation to find turning back the clock for aging beauties of both sexes in his exclusive plastic surgery clinic a not-unpleasant career.

"So you're worried about your friends," Dr. Cameron prompted.

Marty stopped and waved his chubby arms with aggravation. "What could they *possibly* be doing? While I decompose in this plush and I'm sure usuriously—if not criminally—overpriced butcher shop of yours, where *are* they? How long can it take to reach Grenoble and return? Is it located on Pluto? *I don't think so.*"

He resumed his rolling prowl across the room. The curtains were drawn against the night, and the place was cozy with nice furniture and warm lamplight—none of that overhead fluorescent glare that made most hospital rooms seem harsh. There was even the refreshing scent of a bouquet of newly cut peonies. But the comforting atmosphere was lost on Marty. He was thinking about only one thing: Where were Jon, Randi, and Peter? He was afraid that they had gone to Grenoble not to rescue Jon from possible death, but to all die together.

Dr. Cameron said mildly, "So you're upset."

Marty stopped in mid-step and turned to the doctor in horror. "Upset? *Upset!* Is that what you think I am? I am *distraught.* They are in trouble, I know it. *Injured.* Lying somewhere desolate *in their own blood!*" He clasped his hands together and shook them in front as his eyes gleamed with an idea. "I'll rescue them. *That's it.* I'll swoop down and pluck them from the talons of evil. But I must know exactly where they are. It's so *frustrating . . .*"

The door opened, and Marty turned, a sharp remark ready to be flung at whoever dared interrupt his misery.

But it was Jon standing there, tall, muscular, and imposing in his dark bomber jacket. Although his dusky face was battered, a grin as wide as the Atlantic Ocean was aimed at Marty. Crowded behind were Peter and Randi, also grinning. As he was growing up, Marty had not been good at reading people's emotions. Learning that the corners of an upturned mouth were a smile, which meant happiness, and that a frown could mean sadness, anger, or a range of other less joyful feelings had taken some time. But now Marty saw not only that his three friends were happy to be here, but they also had a sense of urgency about them, as if they had arrived only to leave again. Things were not good, but they were putting a brave face on the situation.

They strode into the room, Jon talking: "We're all right here, Mart. Great to see you. No need to worry about us."

Marty let out a whoop and then drew back and scowled. "Well, it's about time. I hope you three have been enjoying yourselves." He pulled himself up to his full height. "I, however, have been vegetating in this boring abattoir with no one but that . . . that"—he glared at Dr. Cameron in the armchair—"Scottish *barber.*"

Cameron chuckled. "As you can see, he's in fine shape. Tiptop and well on his way to complete recovery. Still, best keep him from any more injuries. And of course, if he gets nauseated or dizzy, he'll need to have his head examined."

Marty started to protest, but Jon laughed and threw an arm around Marty's shoulders. Marty grinned and looked Jon, Randi, and Peter up and down. "Well, at least you're back. You appear to be all in one piece."

"That we are, lad," Peter agreed.

Jon added, "Thanks to Randi and Peter."

"Fortunately, Jon was in a mood to be saved," Randi explained.

Jon started to release Marty's shoulder, but before he could, Marty turned quickly and hugged him. As he gave Jon one last little squeeze and moved away, Marty spoke in a low voice: "Gosh, Jon. You scared the *willies* out of me. I'm so glad you're safe. It just wasn't the same without you. For a long time, I really thought you were dead. Couldn't you start living a more sedentary life?"

"You mean like you?" Jon's navy-blue eyes twinkled. "You're the one who got the concussion from the bombing at the Pasteur Institute, not me."

Marty sighed. "I thought you might bring that up."

As Dr. Cameron said his good-byes and left, the disheveled and weary trio sank into chairs. Marty returned to his bed, punched and patted his pillows into a white mound, and settled back against them, a plump sultan on a cotton throne. "I sense urgency," he told them. "Does that mean it's not over? I'd hoped you'd tell me we could go home now."

"I wish," Randi said. She pulled off the band that held her ponytail and shook her hair free. She massaged her scalp with both hands. Blue half-circles of weariness showed under her black eyes. "We think they're going to try to strike again soon. I just hope there's time for us to stop them."

Marty asked, his eyebrows knit, "Where? When?"

To save time, Jon described only the high points of what had happened since his capture at the villa in Algeria, ending with their conclusion that Émile Chambord and Captain Bonnard had been using the Crescent Shield not only to do most of their dirty work, but to hide their complicity in a scheme to use the DNA prototype. Now the pair had disappeared with Thérèse Chambord.

"My thought is," Jon concluded, "that they've got to have a second prototype. Is that possible?"

Marty sat upright. "A *second* prototype? Of course! Émile had two so he could test various molecular sequences for efficiency, speed, and capacity at the same time. You see, molecular computers work by encoding the problem to be solved in the language of DNA—the base-four values are A, T, C, and G. Using them as a number system, the solution to any conceivable problem can be encoded along a DNA strand and—"

Jon interrupted. "Thanks, Marty. But finish what you were saying about Chambord's second prototype."

Marty blinked. He looked at the blank expressions on Peter's and Randi's faces and sighed dramatically. "Oh. Very well." Without missing a beat, he picked up where he had left off. "So, Émile's second setup vanished. Poof! Into thin air! Émile said he'd dismantled it because we were so close to the end that there was no need for another system. It didn't make a lot of sense to me, but it was his decision to make. All the bugs were ironed out, and it was only a matter of fine-tuning the prime system."

"When did the second one disappear?" Randi asked.

"Less than three days before the bombing, even though all the remaining big problems had been ironed out more than a week earlier."

"We've got to find the second one right away," Randi told him. "Was Chambord missing from the lab for any length of time? A weekend? A holiday?"

"Not that I remember. He often slept on a bed he had put into the lab."

"Think, lad," Peter pressed. "A few hours perhaps?"

Marty screwed up his face in concentration. "I usually went to my hotel room for a couple of hours' sleep every night, you see."

But he continued to think, summoning memory the way a computer does. From the hour the bomb had exploded at the Pasteur, his mind screened back minute by minute, day by day, his neural circuits connecting in a remarkably accurate reverse chronology until at last he nodded vigorously. He had it.

"Yes, twice! The night it disappeared he said we needed pizza, but Jean-Luc was off somewhere, I don't recall exactly where, so I went. I was gone perhaps fifteen minutes, and when I returned Émile wasn't there. He came back in another fifteen minutes or so, and we zapped the pizza in our microwave."

"So," Jon said, "he was gone at least a half hour?"

"Yes."

"And the second time?" Randi urged.

"The night *after* I noticed the second setup was gone, *he* was gone nearly six hours. He said he was so tired he was driving home to sleep in his own bed. It was true he was pooped. We both were."

Randi analyzed it. "So the night it disappeared, Chambord wasn't gone long. The next night, he was gone about six hours. It sounds to me as if the first night he probably just took it home. The second night, he drove it somewhere within three hours of the city, probably less."

"Why do you think he drove?" Peter asked. "Why not fly or go by rail?"

"The prototype's too big, too clumsy, with too many parts and pieces," Jon told him. "I've seen one, and it's definitely not portable."

"Jon's right," Marty agreed. "It would've required at least a van to transport, even dismantled. And Émile would've trusted no one but himself to move it." He sighed sadly. "This is all so incredible. Horribly incredible. Incredibly *horrible.*"

Peter was frowning. "He could've driven anywhere from Brussels to Brittany in three hours. But even if we're looking for a place less than two hours away, we're talking hundreds of square miles around Paris." He considered Marty. "Any way you could use that electronics wizardry of yours to solve our problem? Locate the bloody prototype for us?"

"Sorry, Peter." Marty shook his head. Then he picked up his new laptop from his bedside table and put it on his crossed legs. The modem was already connected to the phone line. "Even assuming Émile left the security software we designed for it in place, I wouldn't have the power to break through. Émile has had plenty of time to change everything, including the codes. Remember, we're up against the fastest, most powerful computer in the world. It *evolves* its codes to adapt to any attempt to locate it so swiftly that nothing we have today can track it."

Jon was watching. "So why have you turned your laptop on? Looks to me as if you're going online yourself."

"Clever of you, Jon," Marty said cheerfully. "Yes, indeedy. As we speak, I'm logging onto my supercomputer at home. I'll simply operate it from this laptop. With the use of my personally designed software, I hope to make a lie out of what I've just told you was impossible. Nothing to lose, and it'll be fun to try—" He stopped speaking abruptly, and his eyes grew large with astonishment. Then dismay. "Oh, *dear!* What a rotten *trick.* Darn you, Émile. You've taken advantage of my generous nature!"

"What is it?" Jon asked as he hurried to the bed to look at Marty's screen. There was a message in French on it.

"What's happened?" Randi asked worriedly.

Marty glared at the monitor, and his voice rose with indignant outrage. "How *dare* you enter the sanctity of my computer system. You . . . you *sinister* satrap! You'll pay for this, Émile. *You'll pay!*"

As Marty ranted, Jon read the message aloud to Peter and Randi in English:

Martin,

> *You must be more careful with your defensive software. It was masterful, but not against me or my machine. I've taken you offline, closed your back door, and blocked you out totally. You are helpless. The apprentice must yield to the master.*

> *Émile*

Marty raised his chin, defiant. "There's no way he can defeat me. I'm the Paladin, and the Paladin is on the side of truth and justice. I'll outwit him! I . . . I . . ."

As Jon moved away, Marty's fingers flew over the keyboard, and his gaze grew hard and focused as he tried to convince his home system to power itself back on. Glumly, Jon, Peter, and Randi watched. Time seemed to be passing much too swiftly. They needed to find Chambord and the prototype.

Marty's fingers slowed, and little spots of sweat appeared on his face. He looked up, miserable. "I'll get him yet. But not this way."

Outside Bousmelet-sur-Seine, France

In his quiet, windowless workroom, Émile Chambord inspected the message on his monitor. As he suspected he would, Zellerbach had contacted his home computer system in Washington, at which point he had received Chambord's message and the system had shut itself off. This made Chambord laugh out loud. He had outwitted the arrogant little American. And now that he had a trace on him, he would also be able to find him. He typed quickly, beginning the next stage of his search.

"Dr. Chambord."

The scientist looked up. "You have news?"

Brisk and compact, Captain Bonnard took the chair beside Chambord's desk. "I just received a report from Paris." His square face was unhappy. "Our people showed your photo of Dr. Zellerbach to the store clerk. He said Zellerbach wasn't with the man who used the credit card to buy the laptop. However, it did sound as if he could be one of Jon Smith's accomplices. But when my man checked the records for the sale, the address given was for Washington, D.C. There were no notations of any Paris address or phone number. Of course, since Zellerbach could merely have sent this man into the store, our people canvassed with the photo. Bad results again. No one recognized Zellerbach."

Chambord gave a small smile. "Don't give up, my friend. I've just learned a lesson—the power of the DNA computer is so limitless that one must readjust one's thinking of what's possible."

Bonnard crossed his legs, swinging one foot impatiently. "You have another way to locate him? We must, you know. He and the others understand too much. They won't be able to stop us now. But later . . . ah, yes. That could be catastrophic to our plans. We must eliminate them quickly."

Chambord hid his annoyance. He knew the stakes better than Bonnard. "Fortunately, Zellerbach visited his home system. I anticipate that he took precautions first, probably bouncing the signal around from country to country, from whatever phone number his modem is using. He may also have tried to further disguise his path by going through a large number of servers and an equal number of aliases."

"How can you trace through all that?" Bonnard asked. "That's standard to disguise an electronic trail. It's standard, because it works."

"Not against my molecular machine." With confidence, Dr. Chambord returned to his keypad. "In minutes, we'll have the phone number in Paris. And then it'll be a simple matter to discover the address that goes with it. After that, I have a little plan that'll put an end completely to *anyone's* pursuit."

Chapter Thirty-five

Paris, France

"So here's our situation," Jon was telling Randi, Peter, and Marty. "All of our agencies are working on this. Our governments are standing at highest alert. Our job is to do what they can't. From what Marty's told us about the second prototype, Chambord and Bonnard have to be somewhere two hours or so from Paris. Now, what else do we know, and what *don't* we know?"

"They're an ivory-tower scientist and a junior French officer," Randi said. "I wonder whether they did it all alone."

"Me, too." Jon leaned forward in his armchair, his face intense. "The whole operation smacks of someone else pulling the strings. We've got Captain Bonnard, who was operating around Paris with no apparent connection to the attack on the Pasteur, while the Pasteur was bombed and Dr. Chambord was 'kidnapped' by the Basques. The Basques spirit Chambord to Toledo, where they deliver him to the Crescent Shield. Then they turn right around and return to Paris, snatch Thérèse, and deliver her to Toledo, too. Meanwhile, Mauritania is sometimes in Paris, sometimes in Toledo, while Dr. Chambord and Captain Bonnard apparently don't contact one another until the villa in Algiers. Mauritania believes he's in equal partnership with Bonnard and Chambord until

Grenoble. So . . . who's watching over the whole thing, orchestrating, co-ordinating all the various people and aspects? It has to be someone close to both Frenchmen."

Peter added, "Someone with money. This is obviously an expensive operation. Who's paying for it?"

"Not Mauritania," Randi told them. "Langley says that ever since he left Bin Laden, Mauritania's resources have been sharply limited. Besides, if Chambord and Bonnard were using the Crescent Shield, they were certainly the initiators of the collaboration, so it's likely they were picking up the bills, too. I doubt that either an army captain or a pure scientist like Chambord would have that kind of money."

Marty came to life. "Certainly not Émile." He shook his round head. "Oh, dear, *no*. Émile's far from wealthy. You should see how modestly he lives. Besides, he has trouble keeping a desk drawer organized. I seriously doubt he could systematize that many people and activities."

"For a while, I thought it might be Captain Bonnard," Jon said. "After all, he came up through the ranks. That's both difficult and admirable. Still, he doesn't appear to be a true organizing leader, a mastermind. Certainly, he's no Napoleon, who also worked his way up the ranks. According to his file, Bonnard's current wife is from a prominent French family. There's wealth there, but not the kind we're looking for. So unless I've missed something, he strikes out on both counts, too."

As Jon, Randi, and Peter continued to talk, Marty crossed his arms and burrowed back into his pillows. Eyes closed, he allowed his mind to wing back over the past few weeks, flying high through a three-dimensional patchwork of sights, sounds, and odors. From the springboard of memory, he reexperienced the past, recalling with joyful clarity working with Émile, the excitement of one small success after another, the brainstorming sessions, the meals ordered in, the long days and longer nights, the odors of chemicals and equipment, the way the lab and office had grown on him, had felt more and more like home—

And he had it. Abruptly he uncrossed his arms, sat upright, and opened his eyes. He had remembered exactly what the lab and office looked like.

"That's it!" he announced loudly.

All three stared at him. "*What's* it?" Jon asked.

"Napoleon." Marty spread his arms grandly. "You mentioned Napoleon, Jon. That's what reminded me. What we're really looking for is an anomaly, something that doesn't fit. An oddity that points to what's missing in the equation. Surely you know that if you keep looking at the same information in the same way you'll keep coming up with the same answers. Utter waste of time."

"So what's missing, Mart?" Jon asked.

"*Why*," Marty said. "That's what's missing. *Why* is Émile doing this? Maybe the answer is Napoleon."

"He's doing it for Napoleon?" Peter said. "That's your priceless gem, lad?"

Marty threw a frown at Peter. "You could've remembered, too, Peter. I told you about it." As Peter tried to recall the mystery to which Marty referred, Marty shook his hands excitedly over his head. "The *print*. It didn't seem important at first, but now it looms large. It is, in fact, an *anomaly*."

"What print?" Jon asked.

"Émile had an excellent print of a painting hanging on his wall at the lab," Marty explained. "I think the original oil was by Jacques-Louis David, a famous French artist around the turn of the nineteenth century. The title was something like *Le Grande Armée's Return from Moscow*. I can't remember all the French. Well"—he moved the laptop onto the table and bounced to his feet, unable to sit still—"*this* one showed Napoleon in a big blue funk. I mean, who wouldn't be, after capturing Moscow, but then having to retreat because someone's burned down most of the city, there's nothing to eat, and winter's arrived? Napoleon started out with more than four hundred thousand troops, but by the time he got home to Paris, he had less than ten thousand left. So the painting shows Napoleon with his chin sunk down on his chest." Marty demonstrated. "He's riding his big white horse, and the gallant soldiers of his Old Guard are stumbling miserably through the snow behind like *total* ragamuffins. It's *so* sad."

"And that print was missing from Chambord's lab?" Jon said. "When?"

"It was gone the night of the bombing. When I arrived to pick up my paper, my first shock was the corpse. Then I noticed that the DNA prototype was gone. And finally I saw that the print was missing, too. At the time, the print's whereabouts seemed unimportant. Incidental, as you can imagine. Now, however, it seems glaringly strange. We *must* pay attention."

Randi puzzled, "Why would the Black Flame—Basques—steal a print about a French tragedy some two centuries ago?"

Marty rubbed his hands together excitedly. "Maybe they didn't." He paused for effect. "Maybe *Émile took it with him!*"

"But why?" Randi wondered. "It wasn't even the original painting."

Jon said quickly, "I think that Mart's saying the reason he took the print could tell us what was on Chambord's mind when he left with the terrorists, and maybe about why he's doing what he's doing."

Peter strode to the window. He peeled back the drape and studied the dark street below. "Never told you about another little problem MI6 dumped on me. We lost a bigwig general a few days ago—Sir Arnold Moore. Bomb in his Tornado, I'm afraid. The general was flying home to report information to the PM so hush-hush that he would only hint at it."

"What was the hint?" Jon said quickly.

"He said that what he knew might bear on you Americans' communications problems. The first attack, that is, that you Yanks told only us about." Peter let the drape fall back into place. He turned, his face grave. "I backtracked Moore through various contacts, you see. Their intel all toted up to a clandestine meeting of highly placed generals on the new Frenchie carrier, *Charles de Gaulle*. There was Moore, of course, representing Britain, plus generals from France, Italy, Spain, and Germany. I know the identity of the German—Otto Bittrich. So here's the knobby part: Seems the meeting was terribly sub rosa. Not unusual on the face of it. But then, come to find out, it was organized by the top French muckity muck at NATO himself, Jon's 'friend'—General Roland la Porte, and the order to sail that big, expensive warship apparently originated at NATO, but no one has been able to find the original signed order."

Jon said, "Roland la Porte is the deputy supreme commander of NATO."

"That he is," Peter said, his face both strained and solemn.

"And Captain Bonnard is his aide-de-camp."

"That, too."

Jon was silent, turning the new information over in his mind. "I wonder. I thought Captain Bonnard might be using La Porte, but what if it's the reverse? La Porte himself admitted the French high command, and presumably himself among them, had been keeping close tabs on Chambord's work. What if La Porte kept much closer tabs than anyone else, and then kept what he knew to himself? He did say he and Chambord were personal friends as well."

Marty stopped pacing. Slowly Peter nodded.

"Makes a terrible kind of sense," Randi said.

"Roland la Porte has *money*," Marty added. "I remember Émile talking about General La Porte. He admired him as a true patriot who loved France and saw its future. According to Émile, La Porte was mind-bogglingly rich."

"So rich he could've financed this operation?" Jon asked.

Everyone looked at Marty. "Sounded like it to me."

"I'll be a duck's uncle," Peter said. "The deputy supreme commander himself."

"Unbelievable," Randi said. "At NATO, he'd have access to all kinds of other resources, including a big warship like the *De Gaulle*."

Jon recalled the regal Frenchman, his pride and suspicion. "Dr. Chambord said La Porte was a 'true patriot who loved France and saw its future,' and Napoleon was, and still is, the peak of French greatness. And now it seems that the only thing other than the DNA prototype that Chambord took with him from his lab that night was a print of the beginning of the end for Napoleon. The beginning of the end for French 'greatness.' Are you all thinking what I'm thinking?"

"I expect we are," Peter said, his lean face solemn. "The glory of France."

"In which case, I may have an anomaly, too," Jon went on. "I noticed it in passing, but it never seemed significant. But now, I wonder."

"What is it?" Marty said.

"A castle," Jon told him. "It's a burnt-red color—probably constructed with some kind of red stone. I saw an oil painting of it when I was in General La Porte's Paris mansion. Then I saw a photograph of it, this time in his office at NATO. It's obviously important to him. So important he likes to keep a likeness nearby."

Marty hurried to his bed and grabbed his laptop. "Let's see if I can find it, and find if Émile was right about *le general's* financial health."

Randi looked at Peter. "What was the meeting aboard the *De Gaulle* about? That could also tell us a lot."

"Should find out, don't you think?" Peter said, heading to the door. "Would you be so kind, Randi, as to brace Langley for anything new? And, Jon, why don't you do likewise with your people?"

As Marty logged onto the Internet using the room's only line, the three rushed out to find telephones.

■

In Dr. Cameron's office, Jon dialed Fred Klein's secure scrambled line.

"You've found Émile Chambord and his damnable machine?" Klein asked without preamble.

"I wish. Tell me more about Captain Darius Bonnard and General La Porte. What exactly is the nature of their relationship?"

"It's long. Ongoing. Just as I described."

"Is there any indication that Captain Bonnard may have co-opted General La Porte? That Bonnard may be the power behind the general?"

Klein paused, thinking about the question. "The general saved Bonnard's life in Desert Storm when Bonnard was still whatever they call a top sergeant. Bonnard owes the general everything. I told you that before."

"What *haven't* you told me about them?"

There was a thoughtful pause, and Klein added details.

As Jon listened, the situation began to make more sense. Finally Klein finished.

"What's going on, Jon? Dammit, time's closing in on us. I can feel it like a noose. What's this sudden interest in Bonnard's connection to General La Porte? Have you found out something I don't know? Are you planning something? I hope to hell you are."

Smith told him about the second prototype.

"What! A *second* molecular computer?" Klein raged. "Why didn't you kill Chambord when you had the chance?"

The tension was getting to Jon, too. He snapped back, "Dammit, no one guessed about a second prototype. I figured I could save Chambord so he could go on working for the good of everyone. I made a judgment call, and with what we knew, I thought it was the right one. I had no idea it was all a charade to keep us from knowing Chambord was running the show, and neither did you."

Klein calmed down. "All right, what's done is done. Now we've got to get that second DNA machine. If you have an idea where it is and have a plan, I want to know."

"I don't have a plan, and I don't know where exactly the damn thing is except that it's in France somewhere. If there's a strike, it's going to be soon. Warn the president. Believe me, I'll be in touch the instant I have something concrete."

Jon broke the connection and sprinted back to Marty's room.

■

In the office of the hospital's accountant, Peter was exasperated as he tried to maintain his grip on his stilted German. "General Bittrich, you do not understand! This is—"

"I understand that MI6 wants information I don't have, Herr Howell."

"General, I know you were at the meeting on the *De Gaulle*. I also know that one of our generals who died a few days ago, Sir Arnold Moore, was with you. What you may not know is his death was no accident. Someone meant to kill him. And now I believe that the same person means to use a DNA computer to render the U.S. defenseless and then attack. It's urgent you tell me what General La Porte's secret meeting was about."

There was silence. "So Moore *was* murdered?"

"A bomb. He was on his way to fill in our PM about something vital he learned at the meeting. That's what we need to hear from you. What did General Moore learn? What was so devastating that his jet was bombed to stop him from relaying it?"

"You're certain of the bomb?"

"Yes. We have the jet's fuselage. It has been tested. There is no doubt."

There was a long, anxious pause.

At last, Otto Bittrich said, "Very well." He spoke carefully, making certain each word carried the proper weight. "The French general, La

Porte, wants a totally integrated European army independent of, and at least equal to, America's. NATO's inadequate for his purposes. So is the EU's small rapid deployment force. He envisions a truly United Europe—Europa. A continental world power to eventually surpass the United States. He's adamant that the United States's hegemony must be stopped. He argues that Europe is already positioned to become a contending super-power. If we don't take this place of prominence that's rightfully ours, he claims we'll end up as just another U.S. dependent—a large and favored colony at best, but ultimately still slaves to America's interests."

"Are you saying he wants to go to war against America?"

"He claims we're already at war with the United States in many, many ways."

"What do you say, General?"

Again Bittrich paused. "There's much I agree with in his ideas, Herr Howell."

Peter heard a faint hesitation. "I hear a *but*, sir. What did General Moore want to tell my prime minister?"

Bittrich was silent again. "I believe he suspected that General La Porte was planning to prove his point that we must not depend on America by showing the Americans unable to defend themselves."

"How?" Peter asked. He listened to the answer with growing alarm.

■

Downstairs in the same public phone booth she had used earlier, Randi slammed down the receiver. She was angry and worried. Langley had nothing new about General La Porte or Captain Bonnard. As she hurried through the lobby and back upstairs, she hoped the others had done better. When she reached Marty's room, Jon was standing sentry at the only window, watching the street, while Marty was still sitting on his bed, working at his laptop.

"*Nada*," she told them and closed the door behind her. "Langley was no damn help."

"I got something useful," Jon said from the window. "General La Porte saved Captain Bonnard's life in Desert Storm. As a result, Bonnard's utterly loyal and exhibits an exaggerated sense of the general's greatness." Again he gazed at the street. For a moment, he thought he saw a figure moving furtively a block away. "Bonnard will do anything—*anything*—the general asks, and then be panting for the next opportunity to please him." He looked into the distance for the figure. He—or she—had disappeared. He studied the traffic and few pedestrians closer to the private hospital.

"My, my. Such *largesse*." Marty looked up from his computer screen. "Okay, the answer is that General La Porte and his family are worth hundreds of millions, if you figure it in U.S. dollars. Altogether, approaching a half-billion dollars."

Jon exhaled. "A fellow could put together a nice little terrorist assault with that."

"Oh yes," Marty agreed. "General La Porte fits our profile perfectly, and the more I think about it, the more I remember how Émile had begun talking on and on about France. That it didn't get the respect it deserved. What a magnificent history it had, and its future could be even greater than the past if the proper people were put in charge. Every once in a while, he'd forget I'm American and say something particularly irritating about us. I remember once when he was talking about what a fine leader General La Porte was, really too big for his current position. He said it was disgusting that the great General La Porte had to work under an American."

"Yes," Jon told him. "That would be General Carlos Henze. He's NATO's Supreme Allied Commander."

"That sounds right. But it didn't matter that it was General Henze. The point was, he's American. See? My anomaly explains a lot. It's obvious now that Émile took the print of Napoleon with him because it's his inspiration—France will rise again."

"You found those financial details online?" Randi wondered.

"Easy as cracking an egg," Marty assured her. "It was a simple matter to determine his bank—French, of course. Then I tweaked some software programs I'm familiar with. With them souped up, I broke through the firewall and did a fast hit-and-run and escaped with quite a few records."

"What about the red castle?" Jon asked.

Marty was stricken. "Forgot. La Porte was so fascinating. I'll do it now."

Peter strode into the hospital room, almost running. His angular face was tight. "Just talked to General Bittrich. The meeting on the *De Gaulle* was called by La Porte himself to press his case for a completely integrated European military. Eventually, Bittrich thinks, a united Europe. One nation—Europa. Bittrich was damned cautious, but when I told him our General Moore had been murdered, he finally spilled it. What had alarmed Moore—and, it turns out, Bittrich, too—was that La Porte hammered at the electronic and communications failures the American military was having and strongly suggested there'd be more, proving that the American military could not defend even its own country."

Jon's eyebrows rose. "When they met on the *De Gaulle*, there was no way General La Porte could've heard about our utility grid and communications problems. Only our people and the top Brit leaders were in the loop."

"Exactly. The only way La Porte could've known was because he was behind the attacks. At the time, Bittrich dismissed his misgivings as an overreaction and also because he was concerned he was being influenced by the fact that he can't stand La Porte personally—a swaggering Frog, he called him." His gaze searched their faces. "In essence, Bittrich is saying he suspects La Porte is going to launch an attack on you Yanks, when all your defenses are down."

Jon asked, "When?"

"He suggested," Peter's voice became hard and bitter, "that 'if such an impossible thought could be in any way true, which, of course, I don't believe for a second,' it'd be what we feared—tonight."

"Why does he think that?" Randi asked.

"Because there's a crucial vote coming up in a special secret session of the Council of European Nations on Monday about whether to create a pan-European military. La Porte was instrumental in making this clandestine session happen so the issue could be voted on in secret."

The only sound was the ticking of the clock on Marty's bedside table.

Looking out the window to the street below, Jon noticed two men. It seemed to him he had seen them walk past the hospital twice.

Randi asked again, "But *when* tonight?"

"Aha!" Marty announced from the bed. "Château la Rouge. 'Red Castle.' Is this it?"

Jon strode from the window to check the monitor. "That's the castle in La Porte's painting and photo." He returned to the window and looked back at the others. "You want to know when? If I were La Porte, here's what I'd do. When it's six o'clock Saturday night in New York, it's three o'clock in the afternoon in California. Sports and on-the-town time on the East Coast, the same on the West, plus crowded beaches if the weather's good. The freeways are congested, too. But here in France, it's midnight. Quiet. Dark. The night hides a lot. To hurt the United States the most, and to conceal what I was doing, I'd launch the strike from France sometime around midnight."

Peter asked, "Where's this Château la Rouge, Marty?"

Marty was reading the screen. "It's old, medieval, made of . . . Normandy! It's located in Normandy."

"Two hours from Paris," Peter said. "Within range of where we decided the second computer would be."

Randi looked at the wall clock. "It's nearly nine o'clock. If Jon's right . . ."

"We'd best hurry," Peter said quietly.

"I said I'd call army intelligence." Jon started to turn from the window. He needed to alert Fred instantly, but he glanced down at the street just once more. He swore. "We've got visitors. They're armed. Two are walking in the hospital's front door."

Randi and Peter grabbed their weapons, and Randi sprinted to the door.

"Oh, my!" Marty said. His eyes grew large and frightened. "This is *terrible*. I've just lost the connection to the Internet. What's happened?"

Peter popped out the modem's hookup and tried the telephone. "It's dead!"

"They've cut the phone lines!" Marty's face paled.

Randi cracked open the door and listened.

Chapter
Thirty-six

Outside the door to Marty's room, the hallway was quiet. "Come on!" Randi whispered. "I saw another way out when I was looking for the phone booth downstairs."

Marty found his meds, while Jon snapped up the laptop. With Randi in the lead, they slipped quietly from the room and along the corridor past the closed doors of other hospital rooms. A nurse in a starched white uniform had just knocked at one. She paused, startled, her hand on the doorknob. They rushed past, unspeaking.

From the open stairwell, they heard Dr. Cameron's outraged voice float up in French: "*Halte!* Who are you? How *dare* you carry guns into my hospital!"

They increased their speed. Marty's face was bright red as he hurried to keep up. They passed a pair of elevators, and at the end of the hall Randi pushed her way through the fire-exit door just as footsteps pounded up the stairs behind them.

"Oh, oh! Wh-where to?" Marty tried.

Randi shushed him, and the four of them ran down the gray stairwell. At the bottom, Randi started to open the door, but Jon stopped her.

"What's on the other side?" he asked.

"We're below the first floor, so I assume it's some kind of basement." He nodded. "My turn."

She shrugged and stepped back. He handed the laptop to Marty and pulled out the curved knife he had taken from the Afghan. He opened the door a few inches, waiting for the hinges to creak. When they did not, he pressed it farther and saw a shadow move. He forced his breathing to calm. He looked back and touched his fingers to his lips. They nodded silently back.

He studied the shadow again, saw where the overhead light must be that had cast it, gauged the movement once more, and eased out.

There was a faint smell of gasoline. They were in a small underground garage packed with cars. The elevators were nearby, and a man with pale skin, dressed in ordinary clothes, was circling away from them, an Uzi in his hands.

Jon released the door, and as it swung back, he sprinted. The man turned around, blue eyes narrowed. It was too soon. Jon had hoped to slip up behind. His finger on the trigger, the man raised his weapon. No time. Jon threw the knife. It was not meant for throwing, not balanced properly, but he had nothing else. As it spun end over end, Jon lunged.

Just as the man compressed the trigger, the knife's handle hit his side, ruining his aim. Three bullets spit into the floor next to Jon's feet. Concrete chips sprayed the air. Jon slammed his shoulder into the gunman's chest, propelling him back into the side of a Volvo. Jon reared back and crashed a fist into his face. Blood spurted from the fellow's nose, but he merely grunted and swung the Uzi toward Jon's head. Jon ducked and dodged back, while behind him silenced gunfire spit.

As Jon looked up from his crouch, the man's chest erupted in blood and tissue. Jon spun around on his heels.

Peter stood off to the side, his 9mm Browning in his hands. "Sorry, Jon. No time for a fistfight. Must get the hell out of here. My rental car's outside. Used it to get Marty out of the Pompidou Hospital, so I doubt anyone's made it. Randi, grab everything in the poor bloke's pockets. Let's find out who the bloody hell he is. Jon, take the man's weapon. Let's *go*."

Outside Bousmelet-sur-Seine, France
There are moments that define a man, and General Roland la Porte knew deep within himself that this was one. A massive man of muscle and determination, he leaned on the balustrade of the highest tower in his

thirteenth-century castle and gazed out through the night, counting the stars, knowing the firmament was his. His castle was perched on a hill of red granite. Meticulously restored by his great-grandfather in the nineteenth century, the castle was illuminated tonight by the light of a three-quarter moon.

Nearby stood the crumbled, skeletal ruins of a ninth-century Carolingian castle, which had been built on the site of a Frankish fort, which in turn was on the remains of the fortified Roman camp that had preceded it. The history of this land, its structures, and his family were entwined. They were the history of France itself, including its rulers in the early days, and it never failed to fill him with pride—and a sense of responsibility.

As a child, he longed for his periodic visits to the castle. On nights like these, he would eagerly close his eyes in sleep, hoping to dream of the bearded Frankish warrior Dagovic, honored in family lore as the first of the unbroken line that eventually became the La Portes. By the age of ten, he was poring over the family's Carolingian, Capetian, and illuminated medieval manuscripts, although he had yet to master Latin and Old French. He would hold the manuscripts reverently on his lap as his grandfather related the inspiring tales that had been handed down. La Porte and France, France and La Porte . . . they had been the same, indistinguishable in his impressionable mind. As an adult, his belief had only strengthened.

"My General?" Darius Bonnard emerged through the tower door onto the high parapet. "Dr. Chambord says he will be ready in an hour. It's time for us to begin."

"Any news of Jon Smith and his associates?"

"No, sir." Bonnard's firm chin lifted, but his gaze was troubled. He was bareheaded, his short, clipped blond hair almost invisible in the moonlight. "Not since the clinic." He thought again of the murder of his man in the underground garage.

"Unfortunate that we lost one," La Porte said, as if reading his mind. But then, good commanders were all alike in that respect. Their men came second only to the mission itself. He made his voice kind, magnanimous, as he continued, "When this is over, I'll write the family personally to express my gratitude for their sacrifice."

"It's no sacrifice," Bonnard assured him. "The goal is noble. It's worth any price."

On the Highway to Bousmelet-sur-Seine

Once they were safely out of Paris and certain they were not being followed, Peter stopped the car at a large petrol station. In the bright fluorescent lights, Jon, Peter, and Randi ran to phone booths to report their suspicions about La Porte, Chambord, the castle, and the strike to their bosses. They had learned nothing from the pockets of the man whom Peter had shot. He had carried no identification, just cigarettes, money, and a package of M&M's. But on one of his fingers had been a telling detail—a ring with the insignia of the French Foreign Legion.

Jon arrived first and lifted the phone to his ear. There was no dial tone. He dropped in coins. No dial tone again. He tapped the tongue of the phone, but still the line gave no response, just as there had been no response from the phone in Marty's room. Puzzled, beginning to worry, he stepped away. Soon Peter and Randi joined him.

"Did you get a line out?" But even as he asked the question, Jon knew the answer from their concerned faces.

Randi shook her blond head. "My line was dead."

"Mine, too," Peter said. "Silent as a graveyard at four A.M. Don't like this one bit."

"Let's get daring." Randi took out her cell phone, turned it on, and entered a phone number. As she lifted it to listen, her face seemed to crumble. She shook her head angrily. "Nothing. What's going on!"

"Best if we could report in," Peter said. "A bit of help from our various agencies would be pleasant."

"Personally," Randi said, "I wouldn't object if someone high up sent an army battalion or three to meet us at La Porte's castle."

"Know what you mean." Jon trotted toward the station's shop. Through the plate-glass window he could see a clerk inside. Jon entered. Hanging from a wall was a television set. It was not turned on, but a radio was playing. As he approached the clerk, who was working behind the counter, the music stopped, and an announcer identified the local station.

Jon told the youth in French that he had tried to use the telephone outside. "It's not working."

The young man shrugged, unsurprised. "I know it. Lots of people have been complaining. They stop here from all over, and they don't have phone reception either. TV's off, too. I can get local stations on it and the radio, but nothing else. Cable's not working. Awful boring, you know."

"How long have you had the problem?"

"Oh, since about nine o'clock. Almost an hour now."

Jon's face showed no change in expression. Nine o'clock was when Marty's phone line in Paris had died. "Hope you get it fixed soon."

"Don't know how. Without the phones working, there's no way to report it."

Jon hurried back through to the car, where Randi had just finished pumping gas. Peter was opening the trunk, and Marty was standing beside him, looking a little giddy as he stared all around. He was staying off his meds, with the hope that they would find the molecular prototype and he would be in creative shape to stop whatever Chambord was setting in motion.

Jon told them what he had discovered.

"Émile!" Marty said instantly. "That *despicable* rat! Oh, dear. I didn't want to mention it, but I was very worried. This means it's finally happened. He's shut down *all* communications, wireless and regular."

"But won't that backfire on him?" Randi asked. "If we can't get online, how can he?"

"He has the DNA computer," Marty said simply. "He can talk to the satellites. Open a quick window to use them if he needs to."

"Must get a move on," Peter said. "Come here. Choose your poison."

Marty looked down into the trunk and jumped back with surprise. "Peter! It's an arsenal."

They gathered around. Inside was a polyglot cache of rifles, pistols, ammunition, and other supplies.

"Hell, Peter," Jon said. "You've got a whole armaments depot in here."

"Be prepared is my motto." Peter removed a pistol. "Old warhorse, you see. We learn a few things."

Jon already had the Uzi, so he chose a pistol, too.

Marty shook his head vehemently. "No."

Randi ignored him for now. "Do you have anything like a CIA climbing rig and air gun, Peter? That castle wall looked high."

"The very thing." Peter showed her a twin of the rig she had gotten from Barcelona CIA. "Borrowed it some time back, forgot to return it, tsk-tsk."

They climbed quickly back into the car, and Peter peeled it away, heading toward the highway again that would take them west toward the castle, where they fervently hoped they would find General La Porte and the DNA computer.

In the backseat, Marty was wringing his hands. "I assume this means we're on our own."

"We can't count on any help," Jon agreed.

"I'm very nervous about this, Jon," Marty said.

"Good that you are," Peter told him. "Keeps one alert. Buck up though. It could be worse. You could be sitting right smack in the middle of whatever unfortunate piece of *terra firma* those maniacs have targeted."

Outside Bousmelet-sur-Seine

Émile Chambord hesitated at the heavy, iron-studded door to the room where his daughter was confined. No matter how much he had tried to explain his views to Thérèse, she had refused to listen. This pained Chambord. He not only loved Thérèse, he respected her, admired her work and her struggle to excel at her art, without thought of financial reward. She had steadfastly resisted all invitations to go to Hollywood. She was a stage actress with a vision of truth that had nothing to do with popular success. He recalled an American editor saying, "A good writer is a rich writer, and a rich writer is a good writer." Substitute "actor" or "scientist" and one saw the shallow ethos of America, under which, until now, the world was doomed to live.

He sighed, took a deep breath, and unlocked the door. He stepped inside quietly, not bothering to lock it again.

Wrapped in a blanket, Thérèse was sitting at the narrow window across the small room in one of the high-backed baronial chairs that La

Porte favored. Because the general prized historical authenticity, the castle offered few amenities beyond thick rugs on the stone floors and tapestries hanging from the stone walls. A fire was alight in the big fireplace, but its warmth did little to offset the cold that seemed to radiate from every surface in the cavelike chamber. The air smelled dank and musty.

Thérèse did not even glance at him. She gazed steadily out the window at the stars. He joined her there, but he looked down. The ground was awash in the moon's snowy glow, showing the dark grass on the filled-in moat and, beyond that, the rolling Norman farms and woodlands that spread out and around. A shadowy orchard of old, gnarled apple trees hugged the castle.

He said, "It's nearly time, Thérèse. Almost midnight."

At last she looked up at him. "So midnight is when you do it. I'd hoped you'd come to your senses. That you were here to tell me you've refused to help those unconscionable men."

Chambord lost his temper. "Why can't you see that what we're doing will save us? We're offering a new dawn for Europe. The Americans are crushing us with their crass, cultural desert. They pollute our language, our ideas, our society. With them in charge, the world has no vision and little justice. They have only two values: How much can a man consume for the highest possible price, and how much can he produce for the least possible pay?" His upper lip curled in loathing.

Thérèse continued to stare at him as if he were an insect under one of his own microscopes. "Whatever their faults, they're not mass murderers."

"But they *are!* What about the effect of their policies in Africa, Asia, and Latin America?"

She paused, considering. Then she shook her head and laughed bitterly. "You don't care about any of that. You're not operating on altruism. You just want their power. You're just like General La Porte and Captain Bonnard."

"I want France to *rise*. Europe has the right to rule its own destiny!" He turned away so she would not see his pain. She was his daughter . . . how could she not understand?

Thérèse was silent. At last she took his hand, and her voice softened. "I want one world, too, but where people are simply people, and no one

has power over anyone else. 'France?' 'Europe?' 'The United States?' "
She shook her head sorrowfully. "The concepts are anachronisms. A
united world, that's what I want. A place where no one hates or murders
anyone in the name of God, country, culture, race, sexual orientation, or
anything else. Our differences are to be celebrated. They're strengths, not
weaknesses."

"You think the Americans want one world, Thérèse?"

"Do you and your general?"

"You will have a better chance of it with France and Europe than with
them."

"Do you remember after World War Two how the Americans helped
us rebuild? They helped us all, the Germans and the Japanese, too.
They've helped people all around the globe."

That far Chambord could not go. She refused to see the truth. "For
a price," he snapped. "In exchange for our individuality, our humanity,
our minds, our souls."

"And from what you tell me, your price tonight could be millions of
lives."

"You exaggerate, child. What we do will warn the world that America
cannot defend even itself, but the casualties will be relatively low. I insisted upon that. And we *are* at war with the Americans. Every minute,
every day, we have to fight, or they will overwhelm us. We are *not* like
them. We will be great again."

Thérèse released his hand and again stared out the window at the
stars. When she spoke, her voice was clear and sad. "I'll do everything I
can to save you, Papa. But I must also stop you."

Chambord remained motionless for another moment, but she did not
look at him again. He walked out of the room, locking the door behind
him.

Chapter Thirty-seven

They stopped again, this time at a small petrol station outside the village of Bousmelet-sur-Seine. The attendant nodded in answer to Jon's question: "*Oui, bien,* the count is at Château la Rouge. I filled the tank of his limousine earlier today. Everyone's glad. We don't see all that much of the great man since he took over NATO. Who could be better, I ask you?"

Jon smiled, noting that local pride had raised La Porte one more notch in the command structure at NATO.

"Is he alone?" Jon asked.

"Alas." The attendant removed his cap and crossed himself. "The countess passed away these many years." He glanced around at the night, even though there was no one else here. "There *was* a young lady at the castle for a while, but no one has seen her for more than a year. Some say that's good. That the count must set an example. But I say counts have been taking women not their wives up there for centuries, yes? And what of the peasant girls? It was a tanner's daughter who produced the great Duke William. Besides, I think the count's lonely, and he's still young. A great tragedy, yes?" And he roared with laughter.

Randi smiled and looked sympathetic. "Soldiers are often married to the army. I doubt Captain Bonnard brought his wife with him either."

"Ah, that one. He has no time for anyone but the count. Devoted to his lordship, he is. I'm surprised to know he's married at all."

As Jon took out euros to pay, the attendant studied them. "You needed little gas. What do you folks want with the count?"

"He invited us to drop in and tour the castle if we were ever in the area."

"Guess you got lucky. He's sure not here much. Funny, too. Had another guy asking about an hour ago. A big, black guy. Said he was in the Legion with the count and Captain Bonnard. Probably was. Wore the green beret, except he wore it sort of wrong, you know, more like the English wear berets. Kind of arrogant. Had funny greenish eyes. Never saw eyes like that on a black."

"What else was he wearing?" Jon asked.

"Like you, pants, jacket." The attendant eyed Randi. "Except his looked new."

"Thanks," Jon said, and he and Randi climbed back into the car. As Peter drove away, Jon asked him and Marty, "You heard?"

"We did," Peter said.

"Is the black man the one you called Abu Auda?" Marty asked.

"With those eyes, sounds like him," Randi said. "Which could mean the Crescent Shield also thinks Bonnard and Chambord are here. Maybe they're looking for Mauritania."

"Not to mention possibly getting their hands on the DNA computer if they can," Peter guessed, "and getting revenge on Chambord and Captain Bonnard."

"Having the Crescent Shield here is going to complicate matters," Jon said, "but they could turn out to be useful, too."

"How?" Randi said.

"Distraction. We don't know how many of his renegade Legionnaires La Porte has with him, but I bet it's a substantial number. It'll be good if they're worried by someone else."

They drove on in silence for another ten minutes through the moonlight, the road a pale pathway in the silent, rural night. There were no other cars on the road now. The lights of farmhouses and manor houses sparkled intermittently through the apple orchards and the outbuildings

and barns that probably housed equipment to make the cider and Cal-
vados for which the region was famous.

At last, Randi pointed ahead and upward. "There it is."

Marty, who had been mostly silent since they left the highway, suddenly said, "Medieval! A baronial bastion! You do not, I trust, expect me
to scramble up those ridiculous walls?" he worried. "I'm no mountain
goat."

The Château la Rouge was not the fine country estate the name would
have implied around Bordeaux or even in most of the Loire Valley. It
was a brooding medieval castle boasting battlements and two towers.
Moonlight had turned the granite an inky blood-red. Set high on a craggy
hill beside what looked like the jagged, gap-toothed ruins of a far older
castle, this was the Château la Rouge that Jon had seen in the painting
and photograph.

Peter studied the massive structure with a critical eye. "Send for the
siege train. It's a bloody old one, it is. Late twelfth or early thirteenth
century, I should say. Norman-English, from the look of it. The French
tended to like their fortresses a bit more elegant and stylish. Possibly as
old as Henry the Second, but I doubt it—"

"Forget the history, Peter," Randi interrupted. "What makes you think
we can climb up those walls without being spotted?"

"I don't climb," Marty announced.

"Shouldn't be difficult," Peter enthused. "Looks as if she's been up-
dated sometime in the last century or so. The moat's filled in, the portcullis
is gone, and the entryway is wide open. Of course, tonight they'll have that
entrance guarded. They've manicured the hill up to the walls, which is an
advantage for us. And my guess is we won't have to worry about boiling oil,
crossbows, and all that rigamarole from the battlements."

"Boiling oil." Marty shuddered. "Thanks, Peter. You've cheered me
enormously."

"My pleasure."

Peter turned off the headlights, and they cruised to the base of the
rocky hill where he paused the car. There in the moonlight they had a
clear view of a curved drive that led up to the front and in through the
tunnel-like entryway. As Peter had guessed, there was no gate or barrier,
and spring flowers grew in well-kept beds on either side. The nineteenth-

and twentieth-century La Portes had obviously been unworried about attack. But a pair of armed men in civilian clothes at the open front portal showed that the twenty-first-century La Porte was.

Peter eyed the two guards. "Soldiers. French. Probably the Legion."

"You can't possibly *know* that, Peter," Marty rebuked. "More of your superior man-of-action hyperbole again."

"*Au contraire, mon petit ami.* Every nation's military has its traditions, methods, and drill, which produce a different appearance and manner. A U.S. soldier shoulders arms on the right shoulder, the British on the left. Soldiers move, stand at attention, march, stop, salute, and generally hold themselves differently, according to the country. Any soldier can tell instantly who has trained the army of a Second- or Third-World nation by simply observing. Those guards are French soldiers, lad, and I'd bet the wine cellar on the Legion."

Exasperated, Marty said, "Poppycock! Even your French stinks!"

Peter laughed and rolled the car onward along the country road that curved out and around.

Jon spotted a helicopter. "Look! Up there!"

The chopper was perched on a squat barbican fifty feet up, its rotors protruding over the stone balustrade. "I'll bet that's how Chambord and Bonnard got in and out of Grenoble and flew here. Add in the military guards, La Porte's being here, and the Crescent Shield, and I'd say the DNA computer is here."

As Peter continued the car's circle of the castle, Randi said, "Swell. Now all we have to do is get *into* it."

Jon stared up the slope. "With our equipment, we'll be able to climb it. Pull off here, Peter."

Peter cut the motor and coasted the car off the road into a grove of old apple trees. The car bumped along until it stopped at a spot where the steep hillside met the wall at a higher point. Jon, Peter, and Randi got out. Peter pointed silently up to where the head and shoulders of a sentry moved along the parapet in the moonlit night.

They conversed in whispers. Sound carried far in the rural night.

"Anyone see any others?" Jon asked.

After studying the wall in both directions, they both shook their heads.

"Let's time that one," Peter said.

They clicked the timer function on their watches and waited. More than five minutes elapsed before they saw the head of the sentry return and disappear in the other direction. They waited again, and the man passed more quickly this time. Less than two minutes.

"Okay," Jon decided. "When he heads off to our right, we've got five minutes. That should be enough for at least two of us to make the top."

Peter nodded. "Should do."

"Unless," Randi said, "he hears us."

"We'll hope he doesn't," Jon said.

"Look!" Peter whispered, pointing to their left.

In the distance, hunched dark shapes were moving up the incline, heading to the castle's entry. The Crescent Shield.

■

Using arm and hand signals, Abu Auda urged his men through the old apple orchard and up the incline toward the wide gateway between two low towers. It had taken him most of the day since returning from Liechtenstein to assemble his reinforcements, many from other Islamic cells and even splinter groups. He had called ahead for help when he had discovered where this General La Porte and his lackey, the devious snake Bonnard, had taken the lying Dr. Chambord and his longtime comrade-in-arms, Mauritania.

Now his people numbered more than fifty rifles. He and his small cadre of veteran warriors herded the new men up toward the entrance. His scouts had counted the guards and sentries and reported only two were stationed at the gate, while fewer than five patrolled the entire rampart wall. What concerned him was his lack of information about how many French soldiers were hidden away inside the castle itself. In the end, he had decided it did not matter. His fifty fighters could defeat twice . . . three times their number, if need be.

But that was the lesser of Abu Auda's worries. If the battle went against them, these French renegades might murder Mauritania before he could be reached. Therefore, Abu Auda decided, it would be necessary to reach Mauritania first. For that, he would take a strong small party, scale the walls where the French sentries were thinnest, and rescue Mauritania as soon as the battle was well engaged by the bulk of his troops.

∎

"Let's go," Jon said as Peter opened his trunk again.

The three readied their equipment, while Marty remained rooted inside the car. Randi shoved the climbing rig and another H&K MP5K submachine gun into an SAS fanny pack, and Peter loaded a small cube of plastique explosive, some manual fuses, and a pair of grenades into another. He saw Jon watching him. "Handy for locked doors, thick walls, the like. Are we ready?"

Marty rolled down his window. "Have a pleasant climb. I'll guard the car."

"Out you come, Mart," Jon said. "You're our secret weapon."

Marty shook his head stubbornly. "I use doorways to enter structures, especially very high structures. In a dire emergency, I might consider a window. Ground floor, of course."

Randi said nothing. With her climbing equipment, she scrambled quietly up the steep grade. Jon exchanged a look with Peter and nodded to the other side of the car. Peter padded around to it.

"No time to play coy, Marty," Jon said cheerfully. "There's the wall. You're going up it one way or another." He opened the door and reached in to grab Marty.

Marty recoiled—directly into the bear hug of Peter, who dragged him protesting, but not too loudly, out of the car. Randi was already at the base of the castle, preparing her climbing rigs and the harness she would use to haul Marty to the top. Jon and Peter hustled the still reluctant and complaining Marty up the slope.

Randi checked to be sure they were coming, saw they were, and nodded acknowledgment. She stepped back, ready to shoot her grappling hook over the wall. But at the base of the castle, Marty stumbled over her gear, knocking her against the wall. The grappling hook clanged in the night. They all froze.

Above them sounded the unmistakable noise of running boots.

Peter whispered, "Everyone flatten to the wall!" He drew his SAS high-power Browning 9mm pistol. He screwed on the silencer.

Above them, a face appeared, trying to see who or what had disturbed the quiet night. But they were close to the wall, in a blind, shadowed area. The sentry leaned farther and farther over until he was half beyond the parapet. He saw them at the same instant Peter, taking careful aim with both hands, fired.

There was a soft *pop* from the silenced weapon, and then a faint, sharp grunt. The guard spilled noiselessly over the wall and landed with a thud almost at their feet. His pistol drawn, Jon bent over the fallen man.

He looked up. "Dead. French insignia on his ring."

"I'm going up," Randi told them, not looking at the dead soldier.

With careful aim, she shot the mini–grappling hook up. It made a small *clang* as its titanium points caught in the stone and held. She swarmed up on her automatic ratchet, and seconds later she leaned over and waved the all-clear.

The harness flew down. Peter and Jon quickly buckled it around a silent Marty, who had stopped protesting, his round face pale and serious as he stared at the body.

His voice shook a little, but he tried to smile as he said, "I'd really prefer an elevator. Perhaps a cable car?"

Seconds later, the first shots shattered the night at the entryway.

"Now!" Jon said. "Up you go!"

Chapter
Thirty-eight

Air Force One, **Heading West from Washington, D.C.**
The president's secretary, Mrs. Estelle Pike, poked her head into the airborne conference room, her frizzy hair wilder than usual. She arched an eyebrow and said, "Blue."

She lingered a second or two as the president swung around in his chair, away from the startled eyes of Charles Ouray, Emily Powell-Hill, the Joint Chiefs, and the DCI, who were sitting around the long conference table, to pick up the receiver of a blue radio phone that stood beside the ever-menacing red one.

"Yes?" He listened. "He's sure? Where *is* he? What!" Tension filled his voice. "The *whole* country? All right. Keep me posted."

President Castilla rotated back to face the eyes focused on him. They were the front line now, all of them aboard the flying White House. The Secret Service had insisted that going mobile in *Air Force One* was the prudent course, considering the volatile situation. The public was still in the dark. Everything possible was being done, but unless there was some kind of concrete way to warn and evacuate, the president had made the tough decision that the continuing communications problems be passed off to the media as a dangerous virus that was being corrected, and that the perpetrators would be found and the full force of the law brought down upon them.

Fully briefed and in constant touch by radio, the vice president and backups for everyone here were safely deep in bunkers in North Carolina, so that if the worst happened, the national government would go on. Spouses and children had also been evacuated to various secret underground sites. Although the president knew that there were no such provisions for the rest of the country, that it would be simply impossible, he agonized anyway. They must find a way to prevent what he feared.

He spoke calmly to his assembled advisers. "I'm informed the attack could be today or tonight. We have nothing more definite than that." He frowned and shook his head, sorrowful, frustrated. "And we don't know what or where."

The president saw a question behind all those eyes staring at him: What was his source of information? To whom had he been talking? And if *they* did not know, how reliable could this source or sources be? He had no intention of satisfying them: Covert-One and Fred Klein would remain utterly clandestine until he passed them on to his successor with the strong recommendation to maintain both the organization and the secrecy.

Finally, Emily Powell-Hill, his NSA, asked, "Is that a confirmed fact, Mr. President?"

"It's the most informed conclusion we have or are likely to have." Castilla studied their bleak faces, knowing they were going to hold up. Knowing he was. "But we're generally now aware where the DNA computer is, and that means there's a good chance we can still destroy it in time."

"*Where,* sir?" Admiral Stevens Brose asked.

"Somewhere in France. All communications in or out of the country have just been shut down there."

"Damnation!" White House chief of staff Ouray's voice shook. "*All* communication? *All* of France? Incredible!"

"If they've shut communications down," Powell-Hill said, "then they must be very close to doing it. It sure sounds to me as if it's got to be today, too."

The president's gaze swept the group. "We've had several days to prepare our best defenses. Even with all the cyber attacks, we should be ready. Are we?"

Admiral Stevens Brose cleared his throat, trying to keep an uncharacteristic note of dread from his voice. The admiral was as brave and resolute under fire as any other professional soldier, and a soldier could handle the uncertainty of when and where. Still, this blind dealing with an unstoppable computer against an unknown target was wearing on him, as it was on everyone else.

He said, "We're as ready as we can be, considering all our satellites and other communications are down, and our command codes compromised. We've been working around the clock, and ten hours more than that, to bring everything back online and change our codes." He hesitated. "But I'm not sure it'll really help. With what the DNA machine can do, even our latest encryptions will likely be broken, and we'll be out of commission again in minutes, perhaps seconds." He glanced at his fellow commanders. "Our one advantage is our new covert, experimental antimissile defense system. Since they don't know we have it, that may be enough." The admiral glanced at his fellow flag officers. "If the attack *is* going to be by missile."

The president nodded. "Based on what the DNA computer can do, and what little we know of the terrorists, it's most likely."

Air Force chief of staff Bruce Kelly's voice was decisive as he agreed, "No single ICBM from anywhere is going to get through the new antimissile system. I guarantee it."

"You're sure they don't know we have it?"

Around the packed room, the Joint Chiefs and the DCI nodded affirmative.

Admiral Brose answered for them all: "We're certain, Mr. President."

"Then we have nothing to worry about, do we?" the president said. He smiled around the silent room, but no one looked him in the eyes.

Château la Rouge, France
In the windowless armory at the top of the castle, where chain mail coats hung next to empty suits of armor, Dr. Émile Chambord raised his head and listened. There was gunfire outside. What was happening? Was someone shooting at the castle? The noise was muffled by the thick walls, but still, it was unmistakable.

Abruptly, the computer screen in front of him went blank.

Hurriedly he made adjustments and regained control. The prototype had never been easy to keep steady, and it had been drifting under his fingers. Twice he'd had a lock on the command codes of the old Soviet missile that General La Porte had selected, still in its silo thousands of miles away, and twice he had lost the codes as the temperamental apparatus of optical cables and gel packs destabilized. He needed every ounce of concentration and dexterity to do the job, and the nerve-racking gunfire did not help.

Was it growing louder? Coming closer? Who could it be? Maybe it was that Colonel Smith with American and English soldiers.

Worried, he glanced up at his favorite print, which he had hung above his desk. There was the beaten Napoleon and the remnants of the pride of France, marching back from Moscow only to be beaten again, this time by the English jackals who were lying in wait. He had bought the print as a young man and kept it with him, a reminder of how great his country had once been. For him, everything had changed with his wife's death. Everything but his devotion to France. Everything became the future of France.

He decided the gunfire might be coming from the Crescent Shield, here to rescue Mauritania. But maybe this time they would really steal the molecular computer and kidnap him as well.

He shrugged. It did not matter. They were all too late.

As he returned to his work, the door opened. Roland la Porte ducked his imposing body and entered. "Is the missile programmed?" he demanded. He straightened up, and his large size and personality seemed to fill the room. He was dressed casually in pleated trousers, a good Breton shirt, and a safari jacket. His black boots were polished to a high shine, and his dark, thick hair was smoothed back.

"Don't rush me," Chambord said, irritated. "That gunfire makes me nervous. Who is it?"

"Our old Islamic friends, the Crescent Shield. They're of no consequence. Bonnard and the Legionnaires will beat them off, and then we'll use the Islamics' dead bodies to help guarantee that it's they who're blamed and hunted. It's too bad you were interrupted before you could launch their strike against Israel. That would've provided additional cover for us."

Chambord said nothing. Both knew there had not been time to move their whole operation from Algeria, regroup, and send the missile against Jerusalem. Not when the attack against the United States was the primary goal. Everything must be wrapped up now, so La Porte could spend Sunday making phone calls to solidify support for the EU council vote on Monday.

Chambord was having problems. This was when he could have used Zellerbach's expertise. "The codes are more difficult to break into than the missile I reprogrammed for Mauritania," he complained. "This missile is as old, but its codes are new—"

General La Porte interrupted, "Put that aside for the moment. I have another assignment for you."

Chambord glanced at his watch. "We have only a half hour! I have to time the Russian satellite precisely to keep my window small. It's no easy matter to open communications to the satellite so I can do its work."

"Plenty of time for your miraculous machine, Doctor. I came to tell you that the Americans have a secret, experimental antimissile defense system. I didn't expect them to deploy it, but I've just learned they've brought it online. It hasn't been approved, but I know it's had success in tests. We can't risk the possibility it'll work, or that our project will fail. You must shut down this new antimissile system, as you have all their other defenses."

"How do you know so much?"

"We all spy on each other, even supposed allies," La Porte said with a shrug. "There are no friends among nations, only interests."

■

Up on the bare battlements, moonlight reflected off the walls of the castle proper and made the stone walkway along the top seem to flow with a river of blood. Through the mirage, Jon, Randi, and Peter scouted quickly. Marty went with Peter. There were two other sentries on top, and they were quickly dispatched, then the four rendezvoused.

Holding one of the FAMAS assault rifles he had picked up, Peter said simply, "Nothing."

Jon and Randi reported the same. "It's twenty-two minutes to midnight," Randi added. "So little time."

They sped to the long, dark curving stairwell that seemed to drop into dark infinity. Behind them, Marty hung back, a twin of Randi's H&K MP5K in both hands as if he were clinging to it for dear life. His gaze darted nervously.

"The Legionnaires are busy at the entrance," Jon told them. "That's why there aren't any more up here. We've got four stories and the towers to search. Let's split up. We can each take a floor. If anyone needs help, use the walkie-talkies."

"That's dangerous, Jon. Dividing our force," Randi objected.

"I know, but right now losing time is more dangerous. Mart?"

"I'll go with Peter."

Jon nodded. "Take the ground floor. I'll do the second, and Randi the third. We'll meet at the top. Let's go."

They ran down the spiral stone staircase, Peter and Marty leading. Randi peeled off, then Jon.

On the bottom floor, Peter slipped into the corridor first, Marty following. Dim electric lights were spaced widely apart and did little to dispel the dark. There were a few doors on both sides, all set into recesses in the thick walls. Marty opened each door carefully, while Peter waited, weapon up. They found no one. There was no furniture in the first rooms, an indication that at least part of the enormous historic castle was permanently unused.

"You have any idea how much it costs to heat one of these medieval monsters?" Peter whispered rhetorically.

Marty did not believe in rhetorical questions. "No, but if I had a computer, I'd calculate it in seconds." He freed one hand from his heavy rifle and snapped his fingers.

Peter snorted, and they continued their search. Occasionally, the noise of rapid bursts of gunfire penetrated the castle, and it seemed to them that another assault had occurred outside. Then there would be a period of silence, followed by more sporadic shots. In here, it was difficult to tell where the battle was and impossible to know whether there was an outcome, or what it was.

At last, having seen no signs of Dr. Chambord, his DNA machine, General La Porte, or Captain Bonnard, and ducking into rooms to avoid the few sentries patrolling the corridors, they ran back up to the top floor, where Jon and Randi joined them.

The quartet was moving down the hall, checking doors, when two soldiers rounded a corner and almost collided with them. The Frenchmen grabbed their assault rifles off their shoulders in seconds. While Marty stumbled back, his menacing submachine gun ready in case the soldiers broke loose, Randi and Jon swarmed the first one to the floor, and Peter was all over the second with his Fairbairn-Sykes stiletto. There was a sharp gasp, a silenced and muffled pistol report, and neither renegade French soldier moved again.

Marty swallowed hard, gulping air. He detested violence, but his round, gentle face was resolute as he guarded the corridor while the others dragged the corpses into an empty room. The door closed, and the foursome hurried on until Jon, who was in the lead now, stopped at a corner and raised a silencing hand.

He gestured to the others. They padded forward and stopped. Ahead a single sentry was posted outside the usual iron-reinforced wood door, lounging lazily against the stone wall, smoking a cigarette. His gaze was aimed away from them, focused on the door that it appeared he was guarding. Dressed in casual civilian clothes, he wore army boots and a dark green beret pulled down on the left side. His FAMAS assault rifle was slung over his shoulder. All of this indicated he was another French Legionnaire.

As the sentry smoked and yawned, Jon signaled the others again. They waited as he slid softly up behind the man and struck hard with the barrel of his Uzi. The guard dropped like a stone, unconscious. Peter and Jon dragged him into an empty room, gagged him, and tied him up with his own clothing and belt. But not before Randi thought to look and found an oversized iron key in his pocket. Jon appropriated the FAMAS assault rifle and extra ammunition, and they returned to the door that had been under guard.

Peter listened at it. "Someone's moving around inside," he whispered. He tried the door and shook his head. Locked. "They wouldn't guard Chambord."

"Unless it was for protection," Randi said.

"What would they protect him against?" Marty wondered.

"The Crescent Shield attack down below," Randi explained.

"Let's find out." Jon put the key into the lock. The lock had been freshly oiled and turned easily.

Randi pressed the door just wide enough and edged through. Peter slipped after her, while Jon and Marty stayed in the hall, guarding the rear.

Inside, the room was warmer than most, with a fire burning in a large fireplace. Furnished with an odd mixture of heavy medieval pieces and mundane modern, the small room appeared empty. Randi and Peter trained their weapons right and left, standing nearly back to back inside the doorway. Seeing no one, they advanced warily.

Thérèse Chambord arose like a white apparition from behind a long, massive chest of drawers, a heavy candlestick in her hand.

She said in surprised English, "Agent Russell?"

Randi demanded brusquely, "Where's your father? The DNA computer?"

"In the armory. I can take you." She put down the candlestick and hurried forward, tugging a blanket around her shoulders, still dressed stubbornly in her tattered white evening suit. Her bruised face was dirtier. "I heard gunfire. Was that you? Have you come to stop La Porte and my father?"

"Yes, but the gunfire isn't us. The Crescent Shield's outside."

"Oh, dear." Thérèse looked quickly around. "Jon? Is he—"

Jon stepped into the room. "What time's the attack planned for?"

"Midnight. We don't have much time."

"Eight minutes," Jon agreed grimly. "Tell us what you know."

"From what I've overheard, and what my father hinted, they're going to shoot a missile at the United States. I don't know the exact target."

"That'll do for now. Here, take this."

He handed her a FAMAS assault rifle, and they ran from the room.

Air Force One, **Aloft over Iowa**

Inside the conference room, President Castilla listened to the steady throb of the four powerful jet engines and checked the clock on the wall. Set to the Naval Observatory Master clock, which was based on fifty-eight atomic clocks, it was phenomenally accurate—to within ten nanoseconds. As the president stared at it, the numbers changed to 0552. When were the killers going to strike? The long day had worn them down, grinding nerves raw.

"So far, so good," he announced lightly to no one in particular, although the faces of his military and staff advisers were weary and anxious as they watched him.

"Yessir." Admiral Stevens Brose managed a wan smile. He cleared his throat as if he were finding it difficult to swallow. "We're prepared. STRATCOM is aloft, all our aircraft are on alert, and the new antimissile system's in place and ready to attack the instant there's a target. Everything's been done."

Samuel Castilla nodded. "Everything that *can* be done."

Through the hush that descended like a shroud over the long table, the National Security Adviser, Emily Powell-Hill, who carried the name of one of the greatest and most tragic Confederate generals of the Civil War, answered, "That's all anyone can do, Mr. President."

Chapter
Thirty-nine

Château la Rouge, France

In the old armory with its ancestral swords, maces, and battle axes, General La Porte stood beside Émile Chambord, his large hands grasped behind his jacket, as he stared at the computer screen where rows of numbers scrolled. La Porte's broad face was intense, his immobile gaze focused, although he understood nothing that Chambord was doing.

"Is the Americans' antimissile system down yet?" he asked impatiently.

"Another minute." Chambord touched more keys. "Yes . . . yes . . . there we are. Got it." He leaned back, flushed and exultant. "One very annoying antimissile system shut off and locked up tight."

La Porte's face radiated pleasure. He nodded. Still, his mouth was set in a hard, grim line, and his voice was harsh and demanding: "Finish programming the missile, Doctor. I want it activated and ready to launch."

Chambord glanced up at La Porte and resumed working, although he felt uneasy. He decided that the great general was not merely impatient, he was agitated. Chambord understood impatience and respected it. After all, it arose from eagerness. But agitation was another matter. Something about the general had changed, or perhaps it had been there all along, and now that they were so close to success, the general was revealing himself.

■

Jon and Randi raised their heads from the tower stairwell and studied the landing outside the armory. The air was less ventilated here, full of the dank odors of mold and old stone that seemed to permeate the castle. In the dim lighting, anyone watching would not see them unless their eyes were drawn by the faintest of movements among the shadows.

Jon checked his watch. Seven minutes until midnight. *Too little time.*

Impatiently he studied the door to the armory, which Thérèse Chambord had described. It was about twenty feet away. Two soldiers guarded there, but they were unlike the bored, careless sentry at Thérèse's door. Alert and ready, they stood with their feet spread and their weapons—two more stubby FAMAS assault rifles—conveniently in their hands as they watched all around and glanced periodically back at the door. They would be a lot harder to surprise, and there could be more soldiers inside the armory.

Jon and Randi lowered themselves and ran down the steps. Outside the stairwell on the floor below, the others were gathered, waiting anxiously.

Jon described the layout for them. "The stairs continue circling up into the tower. The landing outside the armory is deep, about twenty feet. It's lit by electric lights, but there aren't enough of them. There are a lot of shadows."

"Any way to flank them?" Peter asked.

Randi answered, "No way to get behind them."

Her words were almost obliterated by a violent escalation of the distant gunfire. It sounded closer, loud and echoing, as if the Crescent Shield had finally broken through some important defense. Perhaps they had finally fought their way into the castle itself.

Jon continued, "From the way the two guards kept looking at the door to the armory upstairs, my guess is that the general is in there with Chambord."

"I agree," Randi said.

"Might be just Captain Bonnard," Peter said. "Or both."

"Someone has to be leading the resistance against the Crescent Shield," Randi said. "Captain Bonnard's the logical one to do that."

"Right," Peter said. "My big worry is those two guards could retreat inside and hold it all night. After all, it's an armory. Armories always had the best defense in a castle. Let's reconnoiter. We've got to find some way to get into that room without alarming them."

"It's six minutes to midnight," Randi said worriedly.

"Oh, dear!" Marty whispered.

With nods all around, they dashed along the corridor toward the moonlight of the far window and a cross corridor. There was movement ahead where the corridors met. Jon saw it just in time to save them from being discovered.

His whisper was a bark, "Down!"

Ahead, figures began to move through the intersection, two and three at a time. Moonlight illuminated their faces as they crossed. One shone like ebony.

"Abu Auda," Randi said in a low voice. "It's a small group. They're being quiet, but I can hear doors opening and closing. They're looking for someone or something."

"Mauritania," Jon decided.

"Yes, Mauritania," Randi agreed. "They're a cutting-out party to free Mauritania."

"But first they've got to find him," Peter said. "That's why they're checking rooms."

Jon paused. "This can work to our advantage. If there were a firefight, it'd bring La Porte and maybe all his other men who aren't already battling the Crescent Shield."

"Once they're gone, getting into the armory will be a cinch," Randi said.

Peter nodded. "Let's give the buggers a firefight."

With Marty following gamely, they ran on toward the intersection. Jon peered around the corner. Far down the hall, just before it turned, Abu Auda worked with what looked like picklocks to open a door, while his men guarded the corridor.

Jon whispered a description of what he saw. Then: "Abu Auda's pushing in the door. They're all busy with what's inside the room. Now's our chance." He gave them quick instructions, and they ran from their hiding places and into the shadowy passageway.

He and Randi knelt, while Peter, Marty, and Thérèse stood behind. They opened fire at the Crescent Shield terrorists.

The volley whined and slammed against the walls and ceiling. One terrorist fell with a scream. Abu Auda and the rest whirled, dropped flat across the corridor, and returned fire. Mauritania crawled from the room and into the hall. He grabbed the fallen man's weapon and joined in. The din reverberated and magnified along the stone passage.

▪

As strings of apparently unintelligible numbers, symbols, and letters filled his screen, Dr. Chambord battled to reprogram the old Soviet missile in the far-away Arctic taiga. He did not understand why he was having so much trouble, why the codes were new.

"We should've stayed with the first missile you chose, General," he said over his shoulder to La Porte, who sat behind him against the far wall. Two soldiers stood guard on either side of the general. "That missile was as simple to break into as the one the Shield wanted to send against Jerusalem. But this one's codes are different, more difficult. Actually, cutting edge."

"You must find a way, Doctor," the general insisted. "Immediately."

Dr. Chambord did not bother to nod. His fingers continued to pound the keyboard. At last, he stopped and worriedly studied the screen. With relief, he announced, "All right. There. It's done. One reprogrammed ICBM. Aimed, ready, and timed to launch automatically at midnight."

He had started to turn toward La Porte, but he stopped as if suddenly paralyzed. He frowned, and, almost in slow motion, his gaze returned to his monitor again. Tormented by fear, he touched a few keys and watched the answer to his question appear on the screen. *He was right.*

His hands jerked off the keyboard as if he had received an electric shock. He spun his chair around. His voice rose: "There's a nuclear warhead on that missile you had me program! It's *not* decommissioned. It's *fully* armed and operational! That's why there are new codes on it. My God! How could you make such a *mistake?* It's nuclear, General. *Nuclear!* This is no simple missile strike to make a point!" He whirled back to his keyboard. His breath came in gasps of fear and outrage. He muttered, "There's still time. I must shut it down . . . there's still time—"

A bullet screamed past Chambord's ear and chipped stone into his face. "What!" He jumped, turned, and saw the pistol in the general's hand.

La Porte's voice was calm, calculating. "Move away from the keyboard, Doctor."

Dr. Chambord inhaled sharply, afraid. He was angry, but he was also beginning to understand that his own life was in danger. "Tell me you didn't intend this diabolical act, General. A *nuclear* attack. Unbelievable!"

From his high-backed, antique chair, La Porte lowered his pistol, allowing it to dangle casually in his big hand. His booming voice said confidentially, "There's been no mistake, Doctor. A conventional warhead wouldn't have provided the concussive shock Europe and France needed. This way, there can be no hesitation. They'll see we must make a new beginning. After this, they'll vote on Monday the way I wish."

Dr. Chambord frowned again. "But you said . . . you told me—"

La Porte sighed, bored. "I simply affirmed what your bourgeois conscience wanted to hear. You still have that silly peasant fear to dare the ultimate. Take my advice, Doctor. *Always* dare. Who dares, wins, my poor Chambord. Even the English and the unfathomable Americans sometimes see the truth in that."

Dr. Chambord was an introverted man, unaccustomed to expressing emotion. In fact, he was uncomfortable with both tears and laughter, a characteristic of narrow feelings that his wife had occasionally complained about. He missed her now especially. But then, he had missed her every day since her death. He had always told her that the mind was an infinitely complex system, and even if he did not express his emotions, he felt them as deeply as she.

As these thoughts occurred to him, he found himself calming. It became clear what he must do.

He knit his fingers together in front of him and said earnestly, "You'll murder outright at least a half million with the ICBM. The radiation will kill untold additional millions. It will lay waste to . . ." He stopped and stared.

The general's pistol had risen again, and now it pointed at Chambord's heart. The general had a haughty expression on his face, and Chambord had a sudden impression that the tall chair on which he sat was no chair. It was a throne.

Outraged, Dr. Chambord cursed. "That's *it!* You intended this all along. *That's* why you picked Omaha. It's not just because it's the headquarters of the U.S. Strategic Command and a more important military target than even the Pentagon. Or because it's a hub of information services and telecommunications industries. It's because it's the Heartland, as they call it, where people think of themselves as safe because they're buried in the middle of the continent. The whole United States thinks of the Midwest as safe. With one blow, you show that the safest people in the safest place are unsafe by turning their 'heartland' into a wasteland, while you cripple America's military. So many deaths just to make a point. You're a monster, La Porte! A *monster*."

General La Porte shrugged. "It's necessary."

"Armageddon." Chambord could barely breathe.

"From the ashes, the phoenix of France—of Europe—will rise again."

"You're mad, La Porte."

La Porte stood, his size and personality again dominating the armory. "Possibly mad, Doctor. But unfortunately for you, I'm not crazy. When the authorities arrive, they'll find the bodies of Mauritania, of Captain Bonnard, and of you."

"You'll be gone." Chambord's voice sounded dead even to himself. "It'll be as if you were never here. They won't know you're behind all this."

"Naturally. I couldn't hope to explain the use of my castle in your horrible plot, should you and Captain Bonnard survive. I appreciate all your help."

"Our dream was a lie."

"No lie. Just not as small as you thought." The general's two pistol shots exploded in the vaulted room. "Good-bye, Chambord. You've served France well."

Eyes open, the scientist fell from his chair like a deflated toy.

At the same moment, a violent fusillade of gunfire seemed to come from everywhere. La Porte stiffened. The Crescent Shield had been at the other end of the castle. How could they be so close now?

He thundered toward the door, gesturing to the two Legionnaires inside the armory to follow. In the corridor, he paused to bark orders to the two waiting sentries, and all five bolted down the stairs.

■

"Back!" Jon warned over the din and flying bullets.

Noise no longer mattered, so they raced back along the corridor toward the spiral stairway that led up into the east tower. In the confined space of the stone walls, the firing behind them sounded as if it came from an army.

Above them, the door to the armory slammed open, followed by a shout in rapid French. Meanwhile, from below, there were new noises. Booted feet were pounding upward. The Legionnaires to the rescue.

Jon, Randi, Peter, Marty, and Thérèse dove into two empty rooms on either side of the hall.

Breathing hard, Jon cracked open his door and saw Peter inch his open, too. They watched La Porte, out of uniform, and four Legionnaires burst past, heading toward where the Crescent Shield's cutting-out party was still firing, attacked by Legionnaires, Jon guessed. General La Porte bellowed an order that was lost in a thunderous fusillade.

Jon and Peter slid out into the passage, followed by the others. They tore onward to the tower stairs while in the distance behind them the Legionnaires and the Crescent Shield continued to battle.

Jon in the lead, the four others following, they climbed swiftly. At the top, they paused and looked carefully all around. The door to the armory stood wide open, and there were no sounds from inside. The shadowy landing with its weak electric lights and narrow windows built for the use of archers was abandoned.

"What does it mean?" Marty wanted to know.

Jon motioned for silence. With hand signals, he sent Peter and Randi into the armory. "Marty, Thérèse, and I'll cover the stairs," he whispered.

Almost instantly, Randi was back out. "Everybody, come in here." She beckoned them inside. "Hurry."

Marty dashed in after her, looking for the prototype, with Thérèse right behind. Jon brought up the rear, watching for danger. They stopped together, stunned by the sight of Émile Chambord on the carpet beside his desk. He was pitched over onto his face, as if he had fallen forward from his chair.

Thérèse covered her cheeks with her hands. "Papa! Oh no!" She ran to him.

"Oh, dear. Oh, dear." Marty followed and patted her shoulder.

Thérèse sobbed, dropped to her knees, and rolled her father over. There were two bullet holes in his chest. Blood matted his shirt.

"Is he alive, Jon? Tell me whether he's alive!"

As Jon crouched beside her, he looked at his watch. "Mart! The computer. It's less than two minutes to midnight!"

Marty shook his round head as if to clear it. "Okay, Jon." He fell into Émile Chambord's chair and went to work on the keyboard.

Peter ran toward the door. "Let's go, Randi. Somebody has to watch their backs."

Nodding agreement, she tore after him. Their dark clothes faded into the landing's long shadows.

Jon checked Dr. Chambord. "Looks as if both of the bullets entered your father's heart. I'm sorry, Thérèse. He died instantly."

She nodded and wept.

Shaking his head, Jon stood up and hurried around to where he could stand behind Marty and be available if needed. At the same time, he surveyed the old armory, with its medieval armaments, shields, and armor hanging from the stone walls and leaning in corners. The room was vast, with quite a bit of furniture, all of it old, heavy wood. The ceiling was high, and the electric lights inadequate to thoroughly illuminate it. In fact, it appeared to him that fully three-quarters of the big room was without light. The fixtures were only in this section near the door. Still, Jon could see far enough back to make out stacks of wood crates, which he assumed held ammunition.

"Faster, you monster," Marty exhorted the silent apparatus. "Resist the master, will you? You cannot defeat the Paladin. There, that's better. *Zounds*, you slippery beast. Aha! You can squirm, and you can flee all you want, but you can't hide from—" He jerked and was silent.

"What is it, Marty?" Jon asked quickly. "What do you see?" He stared at the numbers, symbols, and letters as they scaled the screen, line after line. Although he could do rudimentary programming, he had no idea what any of them meant.

Marty bounced in the chair as if it were a hot seat. "Snake! Dragon! You cannot defeat the hero, the knight, the warrior. Calm . . . calm . . . there now . . . there . . . ah! I have you, you filthy jabberwock, you . . . Oh God!"

"Something's happened, Marty. Tell me what it is!"

He looked up at Jon, his sturdy face pale. "Émile picked an operational Russian ICBM. It's armed. *Nuclear* armed. And now it's . . . it's . . . launched!" He gasped as he returned to translate the information on the screen. "The missile's in the air. It's *gone!*"

Jon's chest tightened. His mouth went dry. "Where's it going, Mart? What's the target?"

Marty blinked. "Omaha." He stared at the monitor and then back up at Jon, his face a mask of misery and alarm. "We're too late."

Chapter Forty

Air Force One, Landing in Omaha

Alone in his private quarters, the powerful throb of the four jet engines in his ears, President Castilla stared at his reflection in the window as *Air Force One*'s wheels touched the runway in a solid landing. Soon he and his people would be safe in the heavily fortified underground bunkers of the U.S. Strategic Command—or STRATCOM as everyone called it— here at Offutt Air Force Base. STRATCOM was the beating heart of the country's defense, charged with the planning, targeting, and wartime deployment of strategic forces. While NORAD monitored the skies, STRATCOM coordinated any retaliatory strikes.

He adjusted his gaze and looked out the window: Yes, an *Air Force One*–style jet was speeding down another runway, about to lift off. One of the fleet was always stationed at STRATCOM for emergencies. Now it would be a diversion, attracting the attention of any enemy searching for him.

The president heaved a deep sigh, feeling guilty for the lives that were put in peril to protect him and his office. He turned from the window. As the big jet slowed and began to taxi, he picked up the microphone of a large short-wave radio.

"How are you holding up, Brandon?"

From his bunker in North Carolina, Vice President Brandon Erikson said, "Good, Sam, good. You?"

"Tolerable. Starting to sweat though. Could use a shower."

"I know."

"Ready to take over, Brandon?"

"There won't be any need for that."

The president gave a mirthless chuckle. "Always liked your confidence. I'll be in touch." He clicked off. As he adjusted his weight uneasily in the chair, a sharp knocking hammered his door. "Come!"

Chuck Ouray entered. His face was a gray mask, and his legs appeared wobbly. "It's STRATCOM command center, sir. The experimental missile defense has crashed. There's nothing left for us to do. We're totally helpless. The chiefs are talking to the scientists, trying to get everything back up, but they're not optimistic."

"On my way."

Château la Rouge

Tension filled the dank old armory. Jon peered anxiously over Marty's shoulder at the computer screen. The room was cold and quiet. The only sounds were of muted gunfire and the clicking of the keyboard as Marty frantically worked.

Jon did not want to interrupt Marty. Still: "Can you abort the missile?"

"I'm trying." Marty's voice was hoarse, as if he had forgotten how to talk. He glanced up. "Darn it, I did too good a job teaching Émile. He's done a lot of damage . . . and I'm to blame!" His gaze returned to the monitor, and he pounded the keyboard, searching for a way to stop the missile. "Émile learned fast . . . I've found it. Oh *no!* The missile's at its apogee—halfway across the Atlantic!"

Jon felt himself tremble. His nerves were as taut as a violin string. He took a breath to relax and clamped a reassuring hand on Marty's shoulder. "You've got to find some way . . . *any* way . . . to stop that nuclear warhead, Mart."

■

Captain Darius Bonnard leaned against the stone wall, his bloody left arm dangling useless, a wadded shirt pressed against his bleeding side, as he struggled to maintain consciousness. Most of the men were behind a barricade of heavy medieval furniture around the corner. He could hear the general calling orders and encouraging them. Bonnard listened with a small smile on his face. He had expected to die in some glorious Legion battle against a powerful enemy of France, but this apparently small contest might be even more worthy, and the enemy the most crucial of all. After all, this was a clear-cut struggle for the future.

As he comforted himself with those thoughts, he saw a sweaty soldier of the Second Legion Regiment rushing toward him, heading for the barricade.

Bonnard held up his hand. "Stop. Report."

"We found Maurice, tied and gagged. He was guarding the Chambord woman. He says his attackers were three men and an armed woman. The Islamics wouldn't have a female soldier."

Bonnard staggered upright. It had to be that CIA witch, which meant Jon Smith and his people were here. Leaning on the Legionnaire's shoulder, he stumbled around the corner, fell behind the barricade, and crawled to where La Porte was crouched and firing at the wall of furniture at the distant end of the passage.

Bonnard panted. "Colonel Smith's here, General. In the castle. He's got three people with him."

La Porte frowned and checked his watch. It was seconds before midnight. He gave a brief, satisfied smile. "Do not concern yourself, Darius. They're too late—" He paused, realizing the number was significant. *Four.* There should be only *three*—Smith, the Englishman Howell, and the CIA woman. "Zellerbach! They must have brought *Zellerbach*, too. If anyone can interfere with the attack, it's him." He bawled orders. Then: "Retreat! To the armory. *Go!*"

As the men raced away, La Porte gazed at his longtime aide, who looked badly wounded. With luck, he would die. Still, it was a risk to wait. He checked to make certain the Legionnaires' backs were turned.

"What is it, *mon Général?*" Bonnard was watching him weakly, puzzled.

La Porte felt a moment of sentiment. "Thank you for all your good services." Then he shrugged and whispered, *"Bon voyage, Darius."* He shot him in the head, jumped to his feet, and trotted after his soldiers.

Omaha, Nebraska

The president and his entourage were packed into three heavily armored SUVs, speeding across Offutt's tarmac. Inside his SUV, the president's radio crackled. He picked it up and listened as a disembodied voice from the command center reported, "We're not making any headway, Mr. President." The man's tones hinted at barely controlled panic. "The codes keep readjusting. We can't imagine how they did this. It's impossible for a computer to react so fast . . ."

"Not impossible for *this* computer," Chief of Staff Ouray muttered.

The president and Emily Powell-Hill ignored him as the radio voice crackled on, ". . . it's got to be reacting automatically to a random pattern like a boxer in a ring. Wait . . . dammit, no . . ."

Abruptly a new radio-transmitted voice interrupted. A woman. "We've got a bogie on the radar, sir. It's a missile. Incoming. Russian ICBM. *Nuclear.* My God. It's . . . what? Say that again? You're sure?" Her tone changed, grew authoritative and calm, strong and responsible. "Mr. President. It's aimed at Omaha, sir. I don't think we're going to be able to stop it. It's too late. Get down below, or leave the air space immediately."

The first voice, rising now, returned: ". . . I can't get a lock. I can't . . ."

Château la Rouge

Abu Auda cocked his head, listening. The electric wall lamps had been shot out, and the corridor was in smoky twilight. Slowly he arose behind the barricade, and his desert-trained eyes studied the opposing wall of furniture.

"They're gone, Khalid," he told Mauritania. *"Inshallah!"* he celebrated.

The men of the Crescent Shield, weary and wounded, shouted a cheer and clambered over the barricade.

Mauritania raised a hand for silence. "Do you hear it?"

They listened. For the moment, there was no gunfire anywhere in the castle. But there was the noise of running feet. Boots. It had to be the Legionnaires of the French general, running not toward them, but the other way—toward the keep.

Mauritania's cold blue eyes flashed. "Come, Abu Auda, we must collect the rest of our men."

"Good. We'll leave this accursed castle to fight another day against the enemies of Islam."

Mauritania, still wearing the tattered bedouin robes he'd had on since Algeria, shook his head. "No, my warrior friend. We don't leave this castle without what you came for."

"We came for *you*, Mauritania."

"Then you're a fool. For our cause, we need Chambord and his miraculous machine. I won't go without it. We'll find the rest of our men, and then the French general. The pig, La Porte. Where he is, the computer will be."

■

In the dimly lit armory with its musty weapons and chilly air, Marty let out another raging monologue as he struggled to abort the nuclear missile as it closed in on its target.

On the carpet near his feet, Thérèse Chambord stirred. Ever since Jon had pronounced her father dead, she had sat motionless beside him, weeping quietly, holding his hand, almost in a trance.

Now as Marty suddenly resumed ranting, she lifted her head, listening. . . .

". . . You cannot win, you unenlightened beast! I don't care how difficult that diabolical Émile's codes are. I will flay you alive and hang your scaly skin on my walls with all the other fire-breathing dragons I've bested in mortal combat. There, you feeble creature, take *that*! Yes, there goes another defense . . . take *this* . . . Aha!"

Meanwhile, outside on the tower landing, Peter and Randi crouched in long shadows, guarding the armory. The air smelled of dust and cordite floating up from below, stinging their noses.

"Hear that, Peter?" Randi asked in her low, throaty voice.

Her weapon was trained on the enclosed stairwell, which descended from here all the way to the castle's first level as well as rising into the east tower above them. There was an opening the size of a large door at each level.

"Indeed I do hear it. Buggers just won't quit. Annoying." Peter's gun was trained on the opening to the stairwell, too.

They listened to boots climbing up toward them, trying to be quiet on the stone steps. As soon as the first of the Legionnaires appeared, Randi and Peter fired. There was a spray of blood as a bullet shattered the fellow's temple. He fell back. There was a sudden scramble as the rest of the Legionnaires retreated.

Peter turned and called an urgent warning into the armory: "Heads up. La Porte's men have arrived!"

"Hurry it up in there!" Randi shouted. "It sounds as if there are a lot more than we expected!"

Thérèse, still seated on the floor beside her father's corpse, seemed to rally. "I'll help." She squeezed her father's hand and rested it on his chest. She laid his other hand on top of the first. She sighed, picked up the FAMAS rifle Jon had given her, and stood. She looked frail and distraught in the armory's musky light.

Jon said, "Are you all right?"

"No. But I will be." It was almost as if a wave of energy coursed through her, and she seemed to gather herself. She gazed down at her father, a sad smile on her face. "He lived a good life and did important work. At the end, he was betrayed by a delusion. I'll always remember him as a great man."

"I understand. Be careful out there."

She nodded. With her free hand, she collected the ammunition Jon had given her and moved off toward the landing. She broke into a trot as she disappeared out the door.

Almost immediately Jon heard her FAMAS open fire to help repel another attack up the stairs. The responding fire was blistering. La Porte's renegade soldiers were fighting back this time. The noise echoed through the armory, sending chills up Jon's spine. He wanted to be out there, helping them.

Jon said, "Mart? How are you doing? Are you making any progress? Is there anything I can do to help?" If they had little time to escape, America had less.

Marty was leaning intently over his keyboard. There was an air of expectation about him, perhaps even hope. His portly body was almost doubled over, coiled tight as a spring. "Die! Die! *Die!* You monstrous monster of . . ." He sprang up.

"What is it?" Jon asked. "What's happened!"

Marty pirouetted, raised his arms above his head, and pumped his fists up and down with excitement.

"Dammit, Marty. Tell me what's happened!"

"Look! Look!" Marty pointed at the monitor.

As the gunfire lessened again out on the landing, Jon stared. Instead of the monotonous lines of numbers and letters, the black monitor sparkled with silver-white stars, a rendition of the night sky. On the right side was an outline of the French coast, while on the left were landmarks indicating the United States as far west as Omaha, Nebraska. A dotted red line was moving in an arced path toward Omaha. At the end of the line, seemingly pulling it along, was a tiny red arrow.

"Does this show the progress of the missile Chambord launched?" Jon asked. "The one with the nuclear warhead?"

"Yes. Keep your eyes on the screen." Marty looked at his watch and counted, "Five . . . four . . . three . . . two . . . *one!*"

The red arrow exploded in a small white burst, like a puff of whipped cream.

Jon stared, hoping he understood correctly. "Is that the missile?"

"*Was* the missile!" Marty did a wobbly dance on the stone floor. "*It's gone!*"

"That's *it?* You're sure, Mart?" Jon stared, allowing himself the first tendrils of excitement. "*Absolutely sure?*"

"I made it blow itself up! While it was still over the ocean. It never even reached our coast!" He twirled and listed over to kiss the monitor, nearly losing his balance. "Wonderful machine! I love you, machine!" A tear appeared at the corner of his eye. "America's safe, Jon."

Chapter
Forty-one

In the old armory, Marty skipped in a circle, celebrating his triumphant destruction of the nuclear missile that would have killed millions of Americans. Jon watched his joy for a few seconds, still absorbing the great news himself, while outside on the landing, occasional bursts of gunfire told him that Peter, Randi, and Thérèse were holding on, defending the tower from being overrun by the Legionnaires.

But they could not stop them forever. They were badly outnumbered. Now that the missile threat was over, they needed to escape.

Marty stopped to face Jon. His voice was breathy and filled with relief, as if he could hardly believe it himself. "America's safe, Jon. America's safe!"

"But we're not, Marty." Jon ran to the door to check on the activity on the landing. "Can you restore all the satellite communications?"

"Of course."

"Do it."

Marty swung back to the computer and resumed work.

Jon leaned out to where Peter, Randi, and Thérèse guarded the stairs. They were kneeling and lying flat, finding cover where they could in the large, shadowy space.

"Can you hold them a few more minutes?" he asked.

"Make it damned few," Randi warned, her face worried.

He nodded and rushed back to Marty. "How much longer?"

"Wait . . . wait . . . there!" Marty grinned up at him. "Compared to stopping the missile, this was a stroll on the beach. The communications are clear."

"Good. Send this." Jon rattled off a series of numbers, a code that guaranteed his message would reach Fred Klein. "Then add: *La Porte, Normandy, Château la Rouge, now.*"

Marty's fingers flew. He was bouncing in his chair, still excited, radiating optimism. "Done. What next?"

"Next we run."

Marty looked shocked. He frowned and shook his head. "No, Jon. We can't just leave the computer. We'll dismantle it. That way we can take it with us."

"Wrong," Jon snapped. He had tried that already, and the firing outside the armory was growing louder. "We don't have time."

Marty wailed, "But, Jon, we *have* to take the prototype. What if General La Porte's people recapture it?"

"They won't." Jon grabbed the protesting genius and dragged him toward the door.

"Let go, Jon," Marty said huffily. "I can walk by myself."

"*Run.*"

On the landing, Peter, Randi, and Thérèse had beaten the renegade Legionnaires back down the steps once more. Thérèse had ripped up her last remaining sleeve and used it to bind a bloody flesh wound on Peter's thigh. Randi had been hit in the upper arm, the bullet going clean through without any major damage. A tight bandage stemmed the bleeding.

"What happened?" Randi asked. "Did you stop the strike?"

"You bet," Jon assured them. "Marty did it again."

"Took you bloody long enough," Peter grumbled, but his leathery face was spread in a large smile as he continued to watch the stairwell.

Jon crouched beside Peter. "Give me a grenade."

Peter, old soldier that he was, asked no questions. He removed a hand grenade from his backpack and passed it over to Jon without a word.

"I'll be right back."

Jon ran back into the armory, laid the grenade on top of the tray of gel packs, and pulled the pin. He hurtled away as if all the hounds of Hades were on his heels.

As he burst back out onto the landing, he shouted, "Everyone down!"

They fell flat onto the stone floor. The grenade exploded behind them, sending steel fragments and wood splinters flying past in a deadly hail. At the top of the stairs, a Legionnaire cried out, blood spurting from his face where shards cut him. He fell back down out of sight.

"What in hell did you do that for, Jon?" Randi demanded.

"The gel packs," Jon explained. "They're the key to the molecular computer. They contain the DNA sequence that Chambord created. Any scientist near his level of expertise could've used just one of them to reproduce Chambord's work."

Marty nodded, his expression miserable. "They wouldn't have needed even a full gel pack. All anyone had to do was scrape up some residue to get a sample."

Jon said, "The gel packs had to be completely destroyed in case they fell into the wrong hands."

They stopped talking as the sound of booted feet making another charge up the stairs echoed toward them. Peter, Randi, and Jon ran to the stairwell and fired down. No Legionnaires were in sight. The bullets ricocheted below, and they heard angry curses and the noises of a retreating scramble.

Marty had been looking around the tower landing, beginning to grasp the desperate struggle out here, while he had been at work inside the armory on the DNA computer. He gazed at them and swallowed hard. He tried to make his voice cheerful.

"Is . . . is this a 'grand' battle, Peter?"

"Grand," Peter said, "but probably short. Those stairs down, I fear, are the only way out of the tower. And the Legionnaires don't seem willing to give us safe passage."

"We're trapped?" Marty's face stretched in terror.

"Unless we figure something else out," Randi agreed.

As if to echo the dire pronouncements, General La Porte's booming voice shouted up in French, "You must surrender, Colonel Smith! We outnumber you three to one, and more of my men arrive every minute. You can't escape past us."

Randi said, "The general isn't going to be in a forgiving mood when he learns we blew his scheme."

"Not to mention that he can't leave any of us alive if he plans to get away clean," Peter pointed out.

Randi said, "That's probably why he shot Dr. Chambord, and I don't hear Captain Bonnard's voice down there. Do any of you?"

Heavy gunfire interrupted her. It sounded as if it were coming from the floor below. They readied themselves, but this time there was no charge up the stairwell. Instead, the firing moved farther away, growing louder and more intense. They heard shouts in Arabic, Pashto, and other languages.

"The Crescent Shield's very near," Thérèse realized.

"They're attacking La Porte's group from the rear," Peter decided. "And while dying for one's country may have its points, let's hope our Islamic friends have made that option less necessary for us."

Marty had been watching Jon, who had been studying the stairwell, his weapon grasped at the ready. "You have a plan, Jon, I hope?"

"No reason to go down," he decided. "We'll go up into the tower. With Randy's climbing gear, Peter's plastique, and a few more grenades, it's our best chance."

"And there's that pleasant little chopper sitting out there on the barbican we spotted when we arrived," Peter reminded them.

"Stupendous!" Marty started up the stairs in his awkward gait. "The race is to the swift, o paladins. Let us be *very* swift."

As the others raced after Marty, Peter and Jon sent a final long volley down the stairs.

"Two stories, I should think," Peter said as he turned and ran upward.

But a sudden draft of heat made Jon stop. He stepped back onto the landing. Smoke rolled out from the armory door, and then flames. All that old, oversized wood furniture that La Porte favored must have caught fire from the grenade explosion.

He hurried up the stone stairs, remembering the crates of ammo he had also seen in the armory, stacked in the back. The boots of La Porte's men hammered behind him, closing in. Jon caught up with the others, and he and Peter grabbed the wobbling Marty by each arm and propelled him along between them.

Thérèse had pulled out ahead, running like a gazelle, while Randi dropped back to cover the rear. She turned frequently to slow the pursuit with bursts of her MP5K.

"Across the tower!" Thérèse was breathing hard, a white streak in the darkness.

"Randi and I'll hold off the Legionnaires here," Jon told them. "Thérèse, you take Marty and run ahead and pick a window. Not one of the archers' windows. Get something we can crawl through, as close to the barbican as you can get. Peter, fuse some plastique and plant it ten yards or so away."

Peter nodded, while Jon and Randi dropped to the stone floor to open fire on the lead pursuers. Their bullets felled the first two quickly, while the third plunged back down the circular stairs. The injured two did not move. For a moment, there was no pursuit, while the gunfire grew heavier from what was now far below. Apparently La Porte and his men were being kept so busy by the Crescent Shield that they could spare only a few for this pursuit, but that could change quickly.

The faint sound of voices drifted up the stairs, followed by footsteps trying not to be heard. There was also the vague odor of smoke from a wood fire, not only the gun smoke one would expect. Jon debated whether to tell the others about the flames and the boxes of ammo in the armory.

In the end, he decided against it. There was nothing they could do about it now, except accelerate every action. Escape as quickly as possible. Which was what they were doing already.

"Done," Peter called out softly.

Jon and Randi fired another volley at the first Legionnaire who came into sight, sending him scurrying back.

Then they ran after Peter. The three had reached a cross corridor at the far side of the tower when Peter's plastique exploded in a shattering blast that flung them forward hard, onto their faces. Behind them, the corridor collapsed in a tangle of stone and smoke. Ahead, Thérèse stood in the doorway to one of the tower's rooms, gesturing them to come ahead.

Coughing, Peter picked a grenade from his web belt and crouched where he could watch the smoking stone rubble.

Again, Randi and Jon ran. The room had three narrow windows as well as a good-sized one, which was where Thérèse and Marty were waiting anxiously.

"We can see the helicopter from here," Marty told Randi. Then he worried: "It looks very small."

"It'll do, if we can get to it." Randi hooked her mini–grappling hook into a crevice on the tower wall outside the window, threw the coiled nylon-covered wire down to the ramparts seven levels below, slid into the harness, and dropped.

As soon as she had landed, Jon said, "You next, Marty."

"Oh, very well." Marty sat on the windowsill and shut his eyes. "I'm inured to danger."

The harness was back almost instantly, and Thérèse and Jon strapped him into it and lowered him over the side. Marty landed, the harness sped back up, and Thérèse followed him down just as a grenade exploded out in the passageway.

Screams and yells followed as Peter sprinted into the room. His face was looking particularly grim. "I'm here, Jon. Let's bunk."

Jon motioned to the window. "You first, Peter. Age before beauty."

"For that remark, my boy, you can stay." Peter tossed the last grenade to Jon and glided over the edge just as the harness returned.

As Peter buckled himself in and disappeared, Jon waited, his gaze on the door. His heart was pounding.

When the harness reappeared, he snared it and quickly crawled inside. Just then, two Legionnaires stormed into the room. As he dangled high above the parapet, Jon pulled the pin, lobbed the grenade, and released the lock so he could drop down the castle's wall.

As he sped downward, the detonation made the wire swing violently, and he felt the hook slip. He inhaled and increased his speed dangerously, hoping he had time to reach the bottom before the hook broke free. His rib cage tightened as he realized how much gray smoke was drifting out of some of the tower's windows.

At last, just as his feet touched the rampart, the hook burst out and fell, nearly hitting him. With relief, he saw that Peter, Marty, and Thérèse were already running off toward the barbican where the little scout helicopter was parked.

Shouts erupted not from above, but from along the rampart wall.

"It's the Crescent Shield this time!" Randi shouted. "Faster!"

Jon and Randi tore after their friends. Peter was already behind the controls of the shuddering helicopter, its rotors spinning, and Thérèse and Marty were strapped into passenger seats. Jon and Randi leaped in, too.

Peter lifted off, banking the chopper violently away from the castle as the first Crescent Shield soldiers came into view, firing as they ran.

Bullets pierced the walls and pinged off the landing struts. Everyone was breathing hard. They looked at one another silently, unable to speak, as Peter pushed the chopper farther and farther away from La Porte's red-stone castle. The stars were a glittery display in the smooth night sky, untouched as if nothing unusual had just happened. Jon thought about General La Porte, about the Crescent Shield, about all the havoc and terror of the last few days, and wondered again at how so much evil could be done in the name of good.

Nearly a mile from the castle, they were just beginning to relax when they heard a volcanic roar. It shook the air around them, and the helicopter shuddered.

They whipped around in their seats just in time to see the east tower of Château la Rouge disappear in a violent outburst of fire and stone. Smoke billowed. Red and gold flames shot up against the night sky. Debris shimmered as it flew through the air.

"Good God, Jon," Peter said. "I'm impressed. What happened?" He turned the helicopter around so it faced back at the castle. He hovered there so they could watch.

"Yes. Well, I meant to mention that," Jon said.

"Mention what?" Randi asked instantly. "What've you been holding back?"

Jon shrugged. "Ammunition. Crates of ammo stored at the back of the armory."

Peter's voice rose. "You exploded a grenade in a room where there were ammo supplies? And you didn't warn us?"

"Hey, so you didn't notice the crates," Jon said huffily. "Do I have to point everything out to you? Besides, the ammo was pretty far away."

"Don't feel bad, Peter," Marty said helpfully. "I didn't see the ammunition either."

Thérèse's face had blanched white. "Neither did I, for which I'm now very grateful."

"The whole point of this long, dangerous exercise was to stop the threat of the DNA computer." Randi was staring at Jon, fighting a smile at the guilty look on his handsome face. "You succeeded, Jon. You blew it up with the grenade."

"We succeeded," Jon agreed, "despite everything."

Peter nodded gruffly. Then he smiled. "Are we ready to go home now?"

For another minute, they continued to study the display as the fire spread through the great old castle in the distance. Then Peter banked the chopper in a long slow circle, preparing to resume their flight southeast toward Paris. Jon and Randi pulled out their cell phones to make full reports to their bosses. Thérèse leaned back in her seat and sighed wearily.

"See those little bright specks in the sky?" Marty asked no one in particular, peering east. "They look like lightning bugs. Can anyone tell me what they really are?"

Everyone stared as the points of light grew larger.

"NATO helicopters," Jon said at last. "I count twenty of them."

"They're heading for the castle," Randi decided.

"Guess your message got through, Jon." Marty described how Jon had given him a code to alert his superiors to the castle at Château la Rouge. "I sent it just before Jon destroyed the prototype."

Suddenly the dark night air seemed full of the aircraft—large, troop-carrying helicopters that dwarfed their little Bell scout. The newcomers were flying in a pack, passing to the north in perfect formation. Moonlight made them glow like otherworldly beasts, and their rotors looked like spinning silver swords.

The accumulation of so many was breathtaking. The big choppers landed across the moonlit Norman farmland, still in formation. NATO soldiers jumped out, spread out, and moved at a fast trot toward the burning castle, where the flames licked higher and had spread into what appeared to be half the castle. There was a precision and decisiveness about the troops that was reassuring.

"Pleasant to see NATO in action," Jon said in vast understatement.

Marty nodded and sighed. "Peter, we've seen enough. Take us back to Paris. I want to go home."

"Right you are," Peter said, and they resumed the journey.

Epilogue

A Month Later
Fort Collins, Colorado
It was one of those sunny June days for which Colorado was famous. Blue skies, balmy air, and the aromatic scent of pine drifting on a light breeze. Jon walked into the utilitarian building that housed the secret CDC-USAMRIID laboratories where he and other scientists were laboring to create the world's "first" DNA computer.

He nodded and greeted the lab assistants, secretaries, and clerks by name, and they said hello back. This was the first time some had seen him since he left, and they stopped to say it was great that he was able to return. How was his grandmother?

"Gave us all quite a scare," he said over and over. "Almost died. She's on the mend now."

When he had arrived two days ago at this rustic Colorado State University campus, all of the events in France, Spain, and Algeria were still fresh, although the stress was beginning to fade. Memory could be a blessing that way. Hold on to the good; let go of the bad. He had spent ten days with Fred Klein, going over everything in detail. Covert-One's files were growing, and each new piece of information, name, location, and comprehension of those who would harm others on scales large and small was grist for future grinding. At the top of the list was the terrorist leader, the pseudonymous M. Mauritania, who had somehow escaped the devastation at the castle. He had disappeared, as vaporous as the billowing white robes he favored.

From what Jon could figure out, a few others of the Crescent Shield must have managed to get out with him. There were not as many dead terrorists as Jon, Randi, and Peter had speculated in their various reports. The corpse of Abu Auda, however, had been found with several shots to the back. No one knew who had fired those bullets, of course, since no one alive—renegade Legionnaires or terrorists—was captured in the burning hulk of the castle.

Even the French general who had been ultimately behind it all, Roland la Porte, was dead. He had taken a bullet to his head that blasted off half his skull. Somehow he'd had time to dress in his uniform, his chest full of medals and ribbons, before he shot himself. The pistol was in his hand, and his impeccably pressed tunic was blood-soaked.

It was a sad ending in some ways, Jon reflected as he climbed the stairs to the meeting room. So much potential perverted. But that was what it was all about, why Covert-One existed. Fred Klein had sent a watered-down version of Jon's report over to army intelligence, as a cover for his supposed employment there. That way, if General Carlos Henze or Randi Russell or even Thérèse Chambord went looking, they would find that he had been legitimately hired as a freelancer.

No one liked to believe life was as fragile as it really was. So the various intelligence agencies had circled their media wagons, and the CIA, the Department of Defense, and the Oval Office had stuck to their stories about wizard hackers and brand-new viruses and the solid strength of the U.S. military and all its communications. With time, the ruckus would die completely. People moved on. Other crises happened. Already it was off the front page and soon it would be firmly, irrevocably old news.

Jon pushed his way into the conference room and took up a post in the back as his fellow researchers filed in. It was the weekly meeting for them to discuss new experimental avenues that looked promising in their quest for a molecular computer. They were a motley crew, jovial, highly intelligent, and pretty much uncontrollable. Talk about mavericks. The best scientists always had a rogue streak. Otherwise, they would not be intrigued by the unexplored. Someone was brewing coffee. The smell drifted into the room. A couple of the scientists ran out to grab cups.

By the time everyone had settled in, there were some thirty men and women packed on folding metal chairs. After business was conducted, the team's lead scientist turned the meeting over to Jon.

He went to the front of the room. Behind him, windows looked out onto the green Colorado campus. "You've all probably been wondering where the hell I've been the last few weeks," Jon began, his face serious. "Well . . ."

From the left, Larry Schulenberg called out, "Were you gone, Jon? I had no idea."

Amid the general laughter, others took up the cry . . . "Never noticed." . . . "Are you sure, Jon? I wasn't just daydreaming?" . . . "Were you? Really?"

"All right," Jon said, laughing, too. "I guess I deserved that. Let me rephrase. In case anyone happened to notice, I've been away." His expression turned serious again. "One of the things I've been doing is thinking about our work. I may have come up with some ideas. For instance, it occurred to me that we've been neglecting the possibility of using light-emitting molecules for our switches. With them, we could do more than have an on-off switch, we could have one with gradations, like a dimmer switch."

Larry Schulenberg said, "You're talking about using molecules not only to compute, but also to *detect* the computations."

"That," someone else said, excited, "would be a hell of a feat."

"You could then pick up the light by conventional means and translate it," a third speculated. "Maybe the light energy could be absorbed in some kind of coated metal plate that could then emit energy."

Jon nodded as they continued to talk animatedly to one another.

At last he interrupted, "Another problem we've been having is with reversing the flow of information as freely as a silicon-based computer can. Maybe one solution would be to use a second interface between our DNA molecules and the switch. You know, we've been limiting our ideas to solid-phase constructions—there's no real reason we have to have the DNA attached to chips. Why not use solution chemistry? We'd have a lot more flexibility."

"He's right!" someone shouted. "Why not go with biomolecular gels? Roslyn, didn't you do your Ph.D. research on biopolymers? Could we adapt that new gel pack technology?"

Dr. Roslyn James took over the discussion for a few minutes, drawing on the well-used white board and bringing the group up to speed on the latest advances in biogel research.

The meeting quickly took on a life of its own. Some were already making notes. Others tossed out opinions and more ideas. One thing led to another, and soon the whole room was talking. Jon stayed with them, and they brainstormed through the morning. Maybe nothing would come of it. After all, there had to be more than one way to create a molecular machine, and Jon did not have enough of the details of Émile Chambord's masterpiece to be able to give them the answers that would lead to easy reproduction. But what he was able to offer was a good jumping-off point.

They broke for lunch. Some would continue the discussions during and after eating, while others would head straight for their labs, intent on their own lines of research.

Jon strolled down the hall, intending to go to the cafeteria. Then it would be right back to the lab for him. He was eager to return to his work. He was thinking about polymers when his cell phone rang.

Jon answered it.

"Hello, Colonel. This is Fred Klein." His voice was cheerful, a far different tone from just a few weeks ago.

Jon chuckled to himself. "As if I wouldn't recognize you."

Someone grabbed Jon's arm. He flinched. And caught himself. If the interruption had been a car's backfire, he knew he would have dove for cover. It was going to take a while to get used to the safety of ordinary life, but he was ready. His mind and body were almost healed, but still . . . he was weary.

"Are you going to join us, Jon?" Larry Schulenberg asked, glancing at the cell phone in Jon's hand.

"Yeah. In a few minutes. Save me some meat loaf. Got a call to take first."

Schulenberg grinned, and the overhead light caught the diamond in his ear and reflected it with a flash of silver-blue that reminded Jon of Chambord's gel packs.

"Girlfriend?" Schulenberg inquired politely.

"Not yet." Jon promised, "You'll be the first to know."

"Right." Schulenberg laughed heartily and went into the elevator.

"Hold on, Fred," Jon said into the phone. "I'm going outside where we can talk."

The noontime sun was hot, the rays through the clear mountain air like lasers as he strolled out the door and down the steps. Being in the mountains reminded him of Peter. The last time they had talked, Peter was back in his lair in the Sierras, hiding out from Whitehall. They had some new project for him, and he was reluctant. Of course, he would not reveal to Jon what it was.

Jon put on his sunglasses and said into the phone, "You have my full attention."

"Talked to Randi lately?" Fred asked conversationally.

"Of course not. She's off somewhere on assignment. But Marty e-mailed me this morning. He's settled in and swears he'll never leave home again."

"We've heard that before."

Jon smiled. "You're checking up on me."

"Am I? Well, I suppose I am. You had a rough time over there."

"We all did. You, too. It's tough to be the one behind the scenes, waiting, not knowing." There was a loose thread that worried Jon: "What about Mauritania? Is there any information about him?"

"As a matter of fact, he was my excuse to phone. You just didn't let me get to him fast enough. I've got good news. He's been sighted in Iraq. An MI6 asset reported a man who fits his description and then other eye-witnesses came forward who make it a sure fit. We'll get Mauritania now."

Jon's mind swept back through the events in his chase of Chambord and the molecular computer, to Mauritania's cold-blooded willingness to trade others' deaths for his dreams. "Good. Let me know when you find him. Meanwhile, I'm back in harness here. We've got a DNA computer to build."